Louise Voss has been in the music ███████ ███ ears, working for Virgin Record███████ ███████ uct manager for an independ███████ ███████ ast two years she has been D███████ ██████ y in London. She lives i███████ ██████ her husband and three-year-ol███████

To find out more about this book see the author's website www.tobesomeone.com

Acclaim for *TO BE SOMEONE*

'Louise Voss's punchy début novel offers an insider's view of the music business, telling the story of a pop star turned DJ whose life comes tumbling down after a disfiguring accident'
Independent on Sunday

'As a music promoter of ten years' standing, first-time novelist Louise Voss is ideally placed to write this touching tribute to the power that pop songs have to soundtrack every pivotal moment of our lives ... Voss creates a bittersweet world in which few endings are particularly happy, apart from the ones that you create of your own free will ... Give it a spin'
Heat

'A beautifully written début novel'
OK Magazine

'It's just brilliant ... Funny, smart, believable, honest, moving ... a lovely book'
Phil Jupitus

'Louise Voss' novel is warm and funny with touches of sadness. It has been likened to a cross between Nick Hornby's *High Fidelity* and Kevin Sampson's rock 'n' roll tale, *Powder*'
NME

'A curl-up comfort read'
Glamour

'It's storytelling at its best'
Now Magazine

'Début novelist and music business veteran, Louise Voss has created a warm, witty, affectionate book, which moves easily from Helena's present-day situation to reliving past experiences and memories. At times tender and deeply moving, it can also be both light-hearted and funny. Highly recommended. . .
What's On In London

'This heartwarming and witty novel by first-time author Louise Voss is guaranteed to make you laugh and cry . . . A perfect summer read, but remember to keep a box of tissues nearby'
Kingston Informer

'This is a very moving and touching story that almost everyone will be able to relate to. It gets you thinking about your own life and what songs you would use to pinpoint important events . . . This is a truly mesmerising story'
What's Happening South

'*To Be Someone* is not all sad. It is funny and lively and provides a fascinating view of the music business'
Salisbury Journal

TO BE SOMEONE

Louise Voss

BLACK SWAN

TO BE SOMEONE
A BLACK SWAN BOOK : 0 552 99902 4

Originally published in Great Britain by Bantam Press,
a division of Transworld Publishers

PRINTING HISTORY
Bantam Press edition published 2001
Black Swan edition published 2002

1 3 5 7 9 10 8 6 4 2

Set in 11/12pt Melior by
Falcon Oast Graphic Art Ltd.

Black Swan Books are published by Transworld Publishers,
61–63 Uxbridge Road, London W5 5SA,
a division of The Random House Group Ltd,
in Australia by Random House Australia (Pty) Ltd,
20 Alfred Street, Milsons Point, Sydney, NSW 2061, Australia,
in New Zealand by Random House New Zealand Ltd,
18 Poland Road, Glenfield, Auckland 10, New Zealand
and in South Africa by Random House (Pty) Ltd,
Endulini, 5a Jubilee Road, Parktown 2193, South Africa.

Printed and bound in Great Britain by
Clays Ltd, St Ives plc.

Dedicated, with much love, to Jackie Graham (1966–1995), who inspired not only this book, but everyone who was fortunate enough to be close to her.

TO BE SOMEONE

Prologue

Helena Nicholls
c/o Ron Pickett
Pickett Management Services
14a Gloucester Place
London W1

6 August 1998

Geoff Hadleigh
Programme Director
New World FM Radio
59 New Cavendish Street
London W1

Dear Geoff,

Thanks for visiting me in hospital back in May. Sorry it's
taken me so long to reply to your kind offer of a night-time
show for New World. I've been thinking things over and
the answer's yes, I'll take the job, if it's still open. I'm
better now, thank God. After a few months of having the
Sword of Damocles hanging over me – well, the Penknife
of Damocles, at least – I've finally been given the all-clear
and both ears are once more fully functional. I could start

work in a few weeks. I understand that we're talking about the 2 a.m.–4 a.m. show.

My only condition is no advance publicity. It's humiliating enough for the breakfast show DJ to get demoted to the graveyard shift, without having to go through that how-the-mighty-fall thing from the tabloids again. I'm sure you recall what it was like after my accident.

Since it obviously won't be practical for me to play requests – not at 2 a.m. – please find enclosed the proposed playlist for my first show back on air. I know it's a little unusual, not to mention overzealous, to submit a playlist ahead of time like this, but I wanted you to know that I've put a lot of thought into each record. Believe me, this show will be GREAT for New World FM, you wait and see.

All the best, and thanks for the lilies,

Helena Nicholls

Playlist

'The Ballad Of Tom Jones'	Space with Cerys of Catatonia
'I Get The Sweetest Feeling'	Jackie Wilson
'(Get Your Kicks On) Route 66'	Sandie Shaw
'Wichita Lineman'	Glen Campbell
'Sunday Girl'	Blondie
'Sitting In Limbo'	Jimmy Cliff
'N.I.T.A.'	Young Marble Giants
'Oliver's Army'	Elvis Costello and The Attractions
'There There My Dear'	Dexys Midnight Runners
'Ghosts'	Japan
'To Be Someone'	The Jam
'Shipbuilding'	Robert Wyatt
'Deep Blue Dream'	The Big Blue OST
'Lovesong'	The Cure
'Kinky Afro'	Happy Mondays
'I'll Be Home'	Randy Newman
'Safe From Harm'	Massive Attack
'Don't Wanna Know Bout Evil'	Spill
'I Can't Stand The Rain'	Ann Peebles
'This Is A Low'	Blur

Waking Up In Hospital

There was a story about a drunken seventeenth-century shepherd I discovered in a book at school once, when Sam and I were doing a history project about Salisbury Cathedral.

When I awoke in hospital a day after the accident, I was oblivious to the operations that had removed my damaged eyeball, reconstructed my nose, wired my jaw and stitched my cheek, and I didn't realize that I was deaf in one ear, but I clearly remembered that legless peasant.

It was the annual Whit-week fayre in the Cathedral Close, with cattle and sheep for sale in rickety wattle pens; urchins peddling ribbons and knick-knacks; a well-patronized ale and cider tent; merchants, farmers, and the usual cast of cut-purses and tricksters milling around. Anyway, a local shepherd patronized the ale tent so thoroughly that he convinced himself and his friends that he'd suddenly learned to fly. Before anyone could stop him, he bolted into the cathedral and up the little staircase hewn from the thickness of the nave walls, right to the top of the tower. At the point where the tower meets the spire, there is a room with doors, which opens out onto all four vistas of the surrounding valley. He climbed onto the ledge through the door overlooking the festivities beneath, spread his arms wide and leaped into the void, planning to sail

13

away over the cattle pens and maypole dancers. Predictably enough, he couldn't fly. But the memorable part of the story was that, because he was so drunk, he staggered away completely unhurt. A little dazed and confused, probably, but then he was in that state *before* he jumped 300 feet to the ground.

Though I couldn't remember at first what had happened to me, I knew that I'd had some kind of fall, because all I could think about was that peasant plummeting to earth, head first. In the past I'd always imagined him sort of floating down to the soft green grass of the Cathedral Close, a soporific smile on his pissed face, falling in slow motion, like a Disney character drifting off to sleep on a pile of feathers. Now, however, he fell through my mind like a boulder, gathering speed, leaving a crater in the lawn outside the North Front.

I envied him the miracle of his intact skull. I didn't know what state my own was in, but I had an unbelievable headache, and my whole face hurt like hell. Hazily I remembered something else I'd learned at school: that if you dropped an egg off the top of the cathedral it wouldn't necessarily smash, not if it landed the right way up. I began to envy the egg.

In my morphine-sodden mind I saw an image of my nose breaking on a dark floor, like a wrong-way-up egg; and then, like a flour-bomb, a great cloud of cocaine spilling out on impact. This was more information than I felt able to handle, so I went back to sleep again.

The next time I opened my one remaining eye there was a familiar face peering anxiously at me, wavering in and out of focus.

'Another flagon of ale, wench,' I mumbled, but all I heard was, 'Mmmh mmmh mmmh.' It seemed that someone had their hand over my mouth. Not funny, I thought, trying to shake it off. The movement set every nerve in every cranny of my skull jangling and pulsing with yet more pain. Christ, have I ever got a hangover.

Or did I fall off a roof? My brain couldn't fully articulate the scenario, but I had an embryonic vision of myself having performed some vastly heroic action, saving someone from a fire or something. Goody, I thought vaguely, that'll do my public profile good.

I reached a hand up towards my face to try and wrest away the joker who was preventing my speech, but someone restrained me gently.

It was my mother, her face looming into mine, lips moving but no sound. She looked awful, red-eyed, with her normally immaculately coiffed hair all whooshed messily up and to the side, like she'd just spent an hour with her head stuck out of the window of a moving car.

It wasn't until she shifted position so her mouth was near my right ear that I could actually hear what she was saying. 'Don't try to talk, darling, your jaw is all wired up because you broke it in the fall.'

Oh, a broken jaw. Well, that would soon mend, I thought. But it must be serious if Mum had flown over from New Jersey; she'd hardly been back at all since we emigrated there in 1980. Besides, judging by the throbbing I thought it must have been my nose that was broken.

I gave a pathetic whine and pointed towards it. Mum stroked the back of my hand with her finger as if I were a newborn kitten. Her voice was strained and distorted, like she was speaking to me from the bottom of a fish tank.

'You broke your nose as well, sweetheart.'

This was getting worse. I tried to glance across the bed, to see if Dad was there, too, but there was something heavy resting on my left eye, and I couldn't turn my head far enough to see out of my right. Oh no. Not my eye, too.

Mum read my mind. 'I'm so sorry, Helena darling. You got some glass in your eye, and the doctors had to operate. Don't worry about it now, though. Just try and get some more sleep.'

15

My free eyebrow crumpled up in consternation. Even through all the painkillers I could tell she was keeping something from me; but I didn't feel ready to find out what. This all felt like a weird, horrible dream. Perhaps the cocaine had been laced with PCP or something and I was hallucinating.

Oh God, the coke.

Oh God, the nightclub.

Oh *God*, the see-sawing with Justin.

Shit. What had I done?

A big nurse with hoofy shoes came in and stuck a needle in my arm without asking permission. I wondered if this was how it had been for Sam at the end, this awful swirly painful feeling, as much emotional as physical, knowing and yet not knowing what was going on. Seeing details but not the big picture. I'd never been in hospital before, other than to visit Sam. It was a disturbing shift of perspective, for me to be the one lying propped up in Sam's place. She'd lain there for so many weeks, white on white, a tube in her throat to breathe through. As I floated back off to sleep, I imagined that I had become Sam – a comforting feeling because it meant that she was still alive. Or maybe I was dead.

The doctor officially broke the news about my eye very gravely and slightly patronizingly, as if I were a small child whose hamster had died. I half expected him to say, 'Your eye has gone up to live with Jesus,' but instead he began to talk about 'options': prosthetics, breakthroughs in medical science, blah, blah, until I cut him off. I'd always been really squeamish about eyes in general, to the point where I'd nearly passed out when Sam once explained to me how the doctors had operated on her cataracts, so the thought that my eyeball had actually been *removed* was too much to bear. Denial was clearly the only sensible option.

After a week in hospital, once I was vaguely *compos mentis* again, I made them move me to the second floor. My original ground-floor room came complete with paparazzi jostling about on stepladders outside, and I couldn't bear having the blinds pulled down day and night. It was bad enough only having one eye and one working ear, let alone dwelling permanently in artificial light.

Apparently the police came regularly and moved them on, but they were constantly hassling the receptionists and nurses, claiming to be relatives, friends, therapists. One even tried to convince the staff nurse that he was my personal tarot-card reader. I hadn't had so much press attention since Blue Idea broke up, and I'd almost forgotten how hideous it was.

I couldn't understand why the press were so interested in my accident. Yes, I was still pretty well-known in London since I'd had the New World breakfast show; but I tried to keep a low profile and I didn't really go out to the groovy places any more. I was certainly no Zoë Ball or Lisa I'Anson; more like a Whispering Bob Harris – long in the tooth.

Then I found out. One of the hospital cleaners slunk into my room about a week after I arrived, clutching a blurry tabloid, all soft and greying from too much handling.

'Didn't want to bother you before, Miss Nicholls, what with you being so bashed up an' stuff, but wouldya autograph this for me sister? She loved Blue Idea; cried for days when you all split up. A nasty business, weren't it?'

I couldn't believe my eye when I saw the headline and accompanying picture. SEEMED LIKE A BLUE IDEA AT THE TIME! it pulsated at me. And the picture – oh, Jesus, the shame. Me on Justin's back, legs kicked in the air, stockings and a flash of knicker showing, eyes closed and a goofy expression. To think I'd believed we looked cool.

'A few too many at the UKMAs, chaps? Shortly after this picture was taken at Britain's top music-industry award show, these high-jinx ended in near tragedy for

17

Helena Nicholls of former chart-topping band Blue Idea. Nicholls (31), now a DJ at top London station New World, is in intensive care with extensive facial injuries, including the loss of her left eye. Her fellow band member and now successful solo artist Justin Becker (33) escaped unharmed . . .'

The piece rambled on about Justin for a couple more paragraphs, and then concluded with a first-hand account of how we were both 'off our trollies on drugs'. I was outraged, until I remembered that it was true.

I screwed up the paper in fury, trying to scream as loudly as I could through my wired-up jaw at the hapless cleaner to get out, leave me alone, fuck off. But the only sound I managed to produce was a high-pitched groan, like a rutting dolphin or a ferret in a trap. Thankfully it was enough to summon a passing nurse, who realized what was going on, ejected the cleaner, removed the tabloid and administered a sedative.

So it was no great surprise when I received a visitor a couple of days later. It was Geoff Hadleigh, the boss of New World. He brought me an enormous bunch of white lilies, and I didn't have the energy to tell him I couldn't stand them; their sickly perfume and funereal smell, and their nasty, staining orange pollen.

Thankfully my jaw had been unwired the day before and I could talk again, after a fashion, although it was really embarrassing. One of my front teeth had broken in half horizontally, and the other one had split vertically, resulting in a ludicrously thick, spluttering lisp as my tongue couldn't decide where to put itself – I didn't even want to think about the aesthetic effect, it all just added to the humiliation.

Geoff was a weaselly, gummy sort of man, skinny and loose in his jeans in a manner indicating under-endowment. We'd never really got on; his deputy programme director, Gus, had originally hired me for an evening shift, so I wasn't one of Geoff's 'people'.

Plus, Geoff had obviously never thought that in just a few months I'd build up such a big following. Eventually, when the slot had come free, he'd been pressured by Gus, the other board members, listeners and production staff to promote me to the coveted breakfast show, where I'd worked to prove myself day and night, researching, broadcasting, writing and taking hardly any time off.

My trademark as a DJ was to take requests on air from the public, but I would only ever play their selected record if they could give me a valid reason *why* it was so important to them. What they were doing when they heard it, what they felt, wore, ate, touched, said, and why this was memorable.

I was tough, too. My listeners knew it wasn't enough to ring up and say, 'Please play "The Power Of Love" because my girlfriend and I were dancing to it when I proposed'. Oh no. I wanted to know what her exact response was, what kind of party they were at, what sort of shoes she was wearing, what brand of perfume.

People confessed secrets, scandals and tragedies to me. Sometimes they cried, or said how much better they felt for getting it off their chest. The press had in the past compared me to a disc-spinning Frasier Crane, or 'Claire Rayner in a DJ booth'.

Damn, I was good at it. 'God is in the details,' I always said, and, 'It's not just about the music.' It was so important to set the scene, get people to dredge their minds for even the tiniest little piece of extra information. It made the record even more precious to them, while giving them a few minutes of fame and a Londonwide audience.

At first I worried that people would find it all too self-indulgent, and get bored listening to strangers' stories of woe, but I was wrong, the format was a runaway success. Listeners really did want to know why 'Only You' by Yazoo reminded Sharon from Herne Hill of how she once hid behind a crumbling car-park wall in school uniform. When they found out it was because she was two-timing her boyfriend with an amber-eyed sixth former, and that the amber-eyed sixth former was killed in a car crash six weeks later, there were tears all round the M25.

Eat your heart out, Simon Bates.

But it was another reason why Geoff Hadleigh wasn't my biggest fan. Commercial stations had strict quotas of records to stick to, playlists A, B and C. He thought I'd never be able to fit requests in around the morning rituals of news, travel bulletins and ad breaks. But I had. We'd struck a deal whereby I could get away with 60 per cent playlisted tracks, and 40 per cent requests – unheard of on a breakfast show. It hadn't made me popular with the other DJs, but I didn't care. I knew I was a good DJ.

It felt so different to being in Blue Idea, where, even though I'd written the songs, I'd never felt it was truly my achievement because it was a group effort. New World was a whole new and revelatory ball game, where I'd succeeded because people liked my personality. Plus I didn't have to go on tour for months at a time. It had come to mean everything to me. And my hard work had paid off: I'd doubled the station's breakfast-show listenership in less than a year.

'Hello, Helena. You look . . . um . . . well, you *have* been in the wars, haven't you?'

'I thuppothe you're here to fire me, aren't you, Geoff,' I said, as if my mouth were full of peanuts.

He sat down on a chair next to the bed, pulled a capacious handkerchief from his jeans pocket and blew his nose with a squeaky sound like a balloon deflating. I wondered if I was supposed to think he was crying.

'Of course not, Helena; we at New World would hate to lose you!'

'But?'

'But . . . you're going to be recovering from this . . . accident for quite some time, aren't you? You must realize that we can't just get a temp to cover for you.

Our listeners need continuity in their DJ, especially in the morning drive time. By the time you're well enough to come back – if ever – they will have got used to—'

I cut him off. 'What do you mean, *if ever*?'

'Well, um, I understand that your hearing is damaged, as well as you being, erm, physically impaired. If that didn't return to normal then, to put it bluntly, there's no such thing as a deaf DJ. I'm afraid you couldn't possibly drive your own desk any more.'

For someone so nervous he went straight for the jugular. Bastard. It was hard to disguise the loss of my eye, but I hadn't wanted anyone to know about my deafness. Obviously there was no such thing as patient confidentiality, no matter how costly the hospital bills were.

'Whoth doing my thow at the moment?' I asked jealously.

Geoff picked up and replaced several of my get-well-soon cards without looking at the messages. 'Ralph Porter,' he said, almost defensively.

I exhaled with disgust. Ralph Porter couldn't DJ his way out of a wet paper bag. I was about to inform Geoff of this, but he ploughed on, 'So I've come here with a proposal for you, Helena. You take as much time as you need to get better, and then, when you are, there'll still be a job waiting for you at New World. I can't let you go back to the breakfast show, but I'll give you a regular night slot.'

Oh no, not the graveyard shift after all my hard work. No.

'But if my hearing returnth to normal, then thurely . . . ?'

I tried hard not to plead, but failed. How could I do a request show at 2 a.m.? The big audience was what made it work so well – telling your stories to the whole of London. I even had bumper stickers saying, 'Helena Let Me Tell London My Song'. Who would care, in the middle of the night, when the only listeners were

21

nightwatchmen and drug-addled losers? It just wouldn't work.

But Geoff was getting into his stride, possibly becoming used to the dreadful sight of my scarred and bruised face.

'I'm sorry, Helena, but it's not as simple as your health. You wouldn't believe the amount of flak I've had from the press and the watchdogs about allegations that you and Justin were on cocaine at the UKMAs. Frankly, you're lucky I'm not firing you.'

'You can't prove anything,' I muttered sulkily.

'Let's hope not, for all our sakes. Personally, I don't need proof. I was on the same table as you that night, remember. I saw what you were like.'

He got up, still holding the flowers he'd brought with him. They dripped a spiteful puddle of water onto the floor.

'I'm sorry, Helena. I know how hard you've worked. I'll give these to the nurse to put in a vase on my way out, shall I? Let me know if you want to take the job. Whenever you're ready.'

A Beach At Low Tide

Today I looked in a mirror for the first time. Intentionally, I mean, not just the accidental glance in the reflection of the window at night, or like when the towel covering the mirror in the bathroom slipped as I was washing my hands — I'd made Nurse Grace rig it up as soon as I was well enough to get myself in and out of the en suite. I'd turned away instantly, without letting myself get a proper look, but even that split second had been enough to inform me that, yes, I was in fact a dead ringer for the Elephant Man.

But that morning Grace had said, 'Ooh, Helena, you look so much better. The swelling's really gone down. Once the stitches are out you'll almost be back to normal.'

I had more movement in my jaw every day, and the dressings on my face had been reduced to one big one where my eye used to be. Physically, I was on the mend.

The better I got, the more my vanity began to return. I made the nurses wash my hair — even though it hurt like mad to lean my head back — instead of tying a scarf over it, because it had got greasy enough to fry eggs on. I also became aware that my breath smelled foul. I hadn't been able to clean my remaining teeth — ugh! — since the accident. Mouthwash alone didn't quite seem to hit the spot. I didn't think anyone except me would care – Mum used to wipe my ass, so I was sure a spot of halitosis didn't bother her. The nurses, ditto – but that wasn't the point. Thankfully an orthodontist was booked to come in and cap my stumpy teeth at the end of the week, which meant I'd be able to talk normally again.

This sudden resurgence of interest in my appearance made everyone very pleased with me, including the psychotherapist, who Mum summoned to my bedside twice a week to tell me that a spot of depression was 'normal' and 'to be expected'. They all thought it meant my gloom was subsiding, and I was returning to my old self. But I was depressed *before* the accident, I felt like shouting.

Once or twice, though, I did allow a minnow of optimism to flash in my chest. Perhaps it would be OK, perhaps I could be normal again. But the minnow always swam off again instantly. I'd be half blind and scarred for the rest of my life, my deafness still hadn't healed and Sam would always be dead. Sorry folks, I thought. It's only vanity.

I'd been afraid to look at myself before, but now I felt that I had to know how bad it really was. On some people scars could look quite distinguished. Suitably psyched up, I shuffled into the bathroom and closed the door. Pulling the cord to switch on the light, I held my breath and moved towards the towel that veiled the mirror. I remembered my old face with affection and regret, like a lost love. How my only gripes about it had been the beginnings of those lines that Homer Simpson has, the ones that run down from nostril to mouth on each side, and the faint wrinkles on my forehead, even when I wasn't frowning, like a beach at low tide.

Feeling like Dorian Gray, I closed my eyes and twitched the towel down.

Oh – my – God. If that was an improvement, I must have been unrecognizable before. Tears flowed down my bumpy, discoloured face as I stared at it, bristling with stitches and striped with skin grafts. My formerly wonderful nose looked like the model for a Cubist painting. One of my eyebrows had all but disappeared, and I didn't even dare examine my ridiculous teeth; the ulcers peppering my tongue told me how jagged they were.

The whole effect was as if someone had removed all the bits of my face and then reassembled them without following the instructions properly. My forehead was more wrinkly than ever. Basically, I was pig ugly.

I didn't stop crying until just before my doctor's visit two hours later. When he came in to check my progress I made a last-ditch attempt at optimism.

'So once all this heals up, I will look *kind* of how I looked before, won't I?'

The doctor gave me one of those rueful upside-down smiles, and took my wrist between his fingers to monitor my pulse.

'Well, yes, of course,' he said doubtfully. '*Kind* of.'

The Plan

I'd been lying in bed, listening one-eared to Ralph Porter's breakfast show through my Walkman headphones, but after only five minutes I couldn't stand it any more. The show was testosterone-soaked rubbish, and hearing it in mono was making my head ache. I clicked off the radio and instead stared one-eyed at the dust motes sailing around in the morning sunlight, wondering how old flecks of carpet, dandruff and navel fluff managed to look so sparkly and beautiful. I wished I could shrink down to that size, pure, uncomplicated, free; I couldn't think of anything better.

Then the dust motes reminded me of my favourite movie soundtrack, *The Big Blue*, which had been my touring album in 1988, at the height of Blue Idea's success. It was such a wonderfully mellow record; I'd played it through headphones in tour buses and private jets across the world, whenever I wanted to transform from a world-weary lump of exhaustion to a tiny, light atom, floating blissfully about in space.

I imagined myself phoning up my own breakfast show and requesting 'Deep Blue Dream' from *The Big Blue*. Would I play it for me? Yes, I thought, if I described to London exactly how I'd felt back then, reclining in all those luxuriantly upholstered velour seats, being waited on hand and foot, in the days when I was unscarred and in demand. I should have been

26

revelling in the attention, but Sam had been lying ill in hospital at that time, hovering, wraith-like, between dreaming and death, and there'd been nothing I could do but worry.

In the remembering I tasted the bubbles of British Airways Buck's Fizz on my tongue, felt the slippery texture of the linen napkins at the Four Seasons in Tokyo, saw the sun rise and set through so many airplane windows. I heard the screams of fans in fifty different countries, how they made my name sound new in each different language. And I remembered how nothing had mattered to me except Sam's recovery. Behind it all, the tape of 'Deep Blue Dream' spooled softly, nostalgically, in my head.

The pain of my losses stabbed me suddenly. My eye, my job, my looks, my Sam – all gone. It surprised me how much it hurt to lose my job. Only Sam's death had hurt more. I didn't want to do a 2-a.m. show. I didn't want to do a show that wasn't about people's memories, their music.

But I couldn't just slink away in disgrace. I don't *do* disgrace, I thought. There had to be some other option. I thought about what I really wanted out of life, what exactly it was that I'd been working towards all these years.

Eventually, what I came up with was me, Helena Nicholls, being somebody. Not as a songwriter or band member or even as a DJ, not as a friend or girlfriend or daughter, however important all those things were, but as me. I wanted people to remember my name with admiration, not scorn. Not, 'Oh, her, she was that DJ who got high and smashed up her face. And didn't she used to be in some Eighties band?'

And right now I was in serious danger of meeting that didn't-she-used-to-be fate. Helena Nicholls, made a prat of herself and was never seen again.

The situation required drastic measures.

A plan started to form in my mind, gathering its genesis around itself like a snail shell's twirl, tighter and tighter, until all my ducks lined up, quack, quack, quack, in an orderly fashion, and I thought, Yes, now I know exactly what I'm going to do.

I'll tell Geoff Hadleigh I accept his offer of a job, I decided, and I'll tell him that my hearing has recovered, whether it has or not. Starting from now, I'll make a list of all the records that have played behind my life, *my* requests, and write down, in detail, exactly why I've picked them. A life's soundtrack would take more than just a five-minute explanation. If I talked about it on air, I'd never have time to play the songs themselves, hence the accompanying manuscript.

When I come to broadcast all the songs, even though it will be 2 a.m. and the show's ratings will be minuscule, it will make radio history. Once everybody realizes what I've done.

What I'm going to do immediately after the show.

It will make me a legend. Bigger than I ever was in Blue Idea, or as a hip breakfast DJ, and certainly bigger than the silly tart who broke her face on a dance floor. Justin's career will rocket. All our old records will be re-released. It'll make all the papers. Hopefully I'll get a posthumous publishing deal for the book, and the New World show could be released on a compilation CD. Perhaps even a Hollywood movie . . .

I got out a pen and a pad of lined A4, which Mum had brought me, hoping in vain that I might cheer up enough to write some song lyrics, and prepared to take the plunge. I can do this, I told myself. I can write. I'd won awards for my songs; I'd written hundreds of letters to Sam, and kept a diary for a little while. In fact, I'd already been published, if you counted the abysmally puerile *Bluezine*, a fanzine the record company made me churn out when we were on the road.

Hell, I'd been meaning to write my autobiography for years. This would just be a different way of doing it. Using the songs would help focus me – I didn't want to do one of those all-encompassing tomes which subscribed to the more-is-more philosophy – and besides, I'd never be able to remember it all without thinking of the records that went along with it.

It felt so weird, not having to think in rhymes and verses, with no breaks for middle eights or guitar solos. This was my life; it needed to be fluent, complete, yet selective. No choruses or intros, no neat bite-sized chunks.

I was going to begin at the beginning, me and Sam, but then I thought, No. Start with the accident, then you'll get it out of the way and not have to think about it again. It had its own record, very definitely: Space, with Cerys from Catatonia, 'The Ballad Of Tom Jones'. It was a pity, really. I'd always loved that song, the humour and harmonies, and sexy Cerys to boot. Now I loathed it. For days after I regained consciousness it kept going through my battered head. It was such a bizarrely chirpy song to induce such terrible memories.

'The Ballad Of Tom Jones'
Space, with Cerys of Catatonia

It happened on the night of the UK Music Awards, the biggest of the annual music business back-slapping events. I'd been to the UKMAs six times altogether, and Sam had come with me as my guest on three occasions.

This time it was all different. I wasn't on the Ringside Records table any more, I was no longer in one of the planet's bestselling bands and nor did I have a solo career, like Justin. Worst of all, Sam wasn't sitting beside me, starry-eyed, because she was dead.

I suppose I should have been thankful that at least I still had a career. I was with a new set of colleagues — my fellow DJs and other assorted top brass from New World FM. The DJs mostly cold-shouldered me, but I was used to it; they were just jealous.

I was determined to have a good time regardless, thinking that a night out might cheer me up a bit and take my mind off Sam. But, of course, that was stupid. I wanted her there so badly I felt sick.

To my joy and relief at seeing a friendly face, I bumped into Justin later. It was the first time I'd seen him for over two years. He had a mad glitter in his eyes, and his shirt was rumpled, torn out of his trousers by the teenagers who'd waited hours for him outside on an unseasonably chilly Spring night. When I'd arrived they were all there, pressed up against the barriers lining the red carpet, not even noticing the cold night air that turned their star-studded breath cloudy. Not that they'd paid much attention to me, though.

Justin looked gorgeous, of course. It was funny how I'd never seriously fancied him, apart from a two-minute crush when we'd first met. I was possibly the only straight woman on earth who didn't. I think it must have had something to do with rank socks, transit vans, audible bodily functions and other such traumatic memories from the band's early days.

He told me I looked beautiful, too, and I really knew it. It took a tiny edge off the fist of grief in my chest, to see myself as everyone else was seeing me. I was wearing my backless velvet dress; its soft folds of burned orange caressing my breasts, tight across my belly and hips, and swirling erotically around my legs. The chill of air-conditioned air which occasionally skittered up and down my bare spine turned me on like a lover's fingers.

I remembered how Sam had once said that even the air-conditioning was making her feel sexy. Sam *adored* the UKMAs, for the sense of spectacle of the whole event. She used to bang on about it being 'an awesome collision of the huge and the tiny', pointing everything out to me as if I couldn't see it myself: the enormous venue; the tiny sparkling lights, winking and blinking across the ceiling like stars; the massive banks of speakers; the small performers on stage, blown up huge by video screens; little reedy voices making industry small talk around big tables; glitter everywhere, on the women's cleavages and cheekbones, and in the men's eyes as they sized up the talent. Sam didn't miss a thing. And when Blue Idea won Best International Group – we were an American band; I was the only Brit – two years in a row, she was embarrassingly pleased for me. Even on the years we didn't win, she wouldn't shut up about how proud of me she was. 'It's because I can see the respect in everyone's eyes when they look at you,' she'd said. 'And these aren't your fans; they're your peers. That makes it even better.'

Justin knew Sam, I thought, a long time ago. I'd better tell him.

'Justin,' I said. 'I've got some bad news, I'm afraid.'

Justin looked anxiously down at himself to make sure his flies weren't undone, and then wiped under his nose in case the news was that something horrible had crawled out of his nostril to alight on his upper lip.

'No, not about *you*,' I said crossly. Honestly, he was so vain.

'My friend Sam died a couple of months ago.'

Justin arranged his face in an expression of vague condolence, without a flicker of recognition.

'Sam. You know, my English friend who used to visit me the whole time. You shagged her. Gorgeous, tall, grey eyes, long legs.'

My voice quivered with the pain of describing someone I'd never see again.

Light still didn't dawn in Justin's eyes, but he made a good pretence of remembering. 'Ohhhh, right! Now I know who you mean. Oh Jesus, H, that's terrible. You poor baby! Such a cute girl, too. What a bummer. Come here.'

He tried to envelop me in a bear hug, but I pushed him away. I didn't want to start crying amongst all the sparkly people.

'OK then, Ms Nicholls, only one thing for it, and it's in a small packet in my top pocket. Come on, a flat surface and a credit card awaits us.'

I tutted irritably. 'You know I don't like cocaine,' I said.

'Wrong,' replied Justin, frogmarching me towards the backstage loos. 'I know that you actually *love* cocaine, and that's why you never do it. You're afraid of getting hooked. Well, I think that's totally sensible and mature of you, but give yourself a break, just this once. It'll make you feel much better.'

He was partly right about the fear bit, but it wasn't the only reason I abstained. I'd spent years enduring the company of bug-eyed, bollock-talking, coked-up prats the world over, and I had no desire whatsoever to join their chopped-out ranks. Plus Sam hadn't approved.

But Sam wasn't there.

We ended up in a cubicle in the Ladies', with Justin sculpting two huge chrysalises with his credit card on the toilet lid. I wondered how many lines he'd already ingested, since he'd suddenly become totally paranoid, grumbling *sotto voce* throughout the entire operation.

'What if someone sees us?' he asked.

'So what? Everyone else is doing the same thing. Listen.'

I angled my ear towards the thin partition of the cubicle next to ours, and pointed down towards the heel of a man's boot, which could be seen underneath the wall. The sound of sniffs and gruff mutters was clearly audible.

'Not *everyone*. I have to be so careful, Helena. People might not recognize you any more, but I could end up with my face splashed all over the papers. It could ruin my career!'

'What do you mean? You're the one with the gram in your breast pocket, so it can't bother you too much. And besides, you aren't the only one with a career; I've got a face to get splashed across the tabloids and a career to be ruined, too, you know.'

How prophetic. The papers weren't all my face ended up splashed over. But all I was concerned with at that moment was the fat, tapered line of cocaine camouflaged before me on the white porcelain altar. I knelt in worship, not even caring that my beautiful dress was trailing on the sticky tiled floor.

The UKMAs eventually wore down to a tired crawl. People were beginning to huddle around their tables in a jumble of black ties and diamanté, like affluent refugees waiting to be rehoused. The mini-fairground rides no longer had to be queued for, and there were puddles of vomit in discreet corners of the arena.

At 2 a.m. Justin and I decided it was time to move on, and so we managed to fight our way through the hordes of drunk and fractious A&R men milling around outside, to claim Justin's pre-booked limo. We headed back into Soho, to a club where his promotions company were holding a private party. We were both wired, and we knew this was the place to be seen. I wanted so badly to be seen. I was suddenly fed up with the more low-key fame of being a DJ, hungry for the old thrill of adoration I needed to justify my existence.

The air in the club was muggy with cigarette smoke and overly subtle lighting, claustrophobic after the vast hangar of the Docklands Arena. It was a tableau of studied, strained chic, with everyone dressed up to the nines, but well the worse for wear, trying to hold it all together.

Jus had a crowd of acolytes constantly hanging around him, and I felt put out. Although he'd always been the focal point of the band, as the token female, and songwriter, I'd usually received more than my fair share of adulation, too. But it had been a while.

It was a boring party, dull music, drunk people. I was considering going home, but then it all changed. After a lot of worthier-than-thou trip hop, 'The Ballad Of Tom Jones' suddenly came blasting over the PA, perking me up more successfully than all the lines of coke I'd had.

'Let's dance,' I said, dragging Jus away from his sycophants towards a raised part of the dance floor, which was empty except for the swirling lights swooping and glancing over its blackness, giving it the appearance of a deep, murky pool.

'To this? You never dance! And besides, no-one can dance to this,' he protested, trying to shake off my hand as we climbed up the three steps at the side of the stage.

Justin was right. It must have been the coke talking, since I'd never been much of a dancer, other than a bit of jigging around on stage with my bass, and the song was about as impossible to dance to as 'Come On Eileen'. It was my one big chance to show off – a whole 400 square feet of media possibilities all to ourselves, like in the old days of the band; no competition, but in this case no inspiration, either. There was no way I was going to shuffle around half-heartedly and then skulk sheepishly off again in defeat.

A memory came back to me of an old playground game Sam and I used to play; the junior-school equivalent of drugs, I supposed. A head rush of shifting gravity and stretched boundaries, the scary exhilaration of having no choice but to trust your partner implicitly, blood pounding in your ears and rushing scarlet around behind your eyeballs.

'*I* know,' I said, like the ten-year-old me. 'Turn around, put your back against mine. Now link arms with me from behind.'

Jus obliged, puzzled. We were still alone on the stage, and already people were shooting glances at us from the bar area, wondering why we were standing back to back. I noticed, and the buzz in my head intensified. I began to bend forwards, trying to pull him up onto my back. He twigged what I was proposing and twisted away from me.

'Stop it, Helena! You're crazy; you can't seesaw me in the middle of a stage. Besides, I'm way heavier than you.'

I was mortified. To stop now would make me look ridiculous, just when I was beginning to attract some attention, too.

'It's cool.' I grabbed his arms behind his back and relocked them in mine. 'Please, let's have a go. It'll be a laugh. What happened to the old daredevil Justin that we all knew and loved? You'd have done this five years ago; people will think you've lost your nerve!'

I knew all the right buttons to push, and it worked a treat.

'Go ahead, then, Wonder Woman,' he said. 'Jeez, talk about putting me in some embarrassing situations. I'll never live this down.'

I could feel the warmth of his sticky skin through his thin silk shirt, and the way his shoulder blades nudged me just below my own. It felt nice, safe and familiar on my bare back. We were actually around the same height, but that night, in my three-inch wedge heels, I was taller. The hairs on his forearms tickled mine as we wriggled around a bit to get comfortable.

'Ready?' I asked over one shoulder. 'I'll go first.'

So right there, in front of a half-amused, half-aghast crowd of minor media personalities, we began see-sawing each other up and down, my legs flying in the air as I balanced on his back, then my own creaking spine taking the weight of the somewhat heavier Justin. He held back at first, worried I wouldn't be able to support him, but soon we got into a groove. Up and down, blood rushing to my head as I leaned forward to swing him up, and then my own cocaine-enhanced flight into the disco night, serenaded by Cerys. Then he began to relax and enjoy it, too, and we were laughing, harder and harder. I saw a blur of grinning faces below me and I thought they were laughing with us.

But then the laughter and the exertion and the drugs started to take their toll on my body, and my knees gave a tiny little tremble as I hoisted Jus horizontal for the last time. The tremble ran down my right leg and into my ankle, which twisted slightly. It was enough to make me lose my balance, and I began to lurch heavily to the right, towards the edge of the stage. Jus was in full flight, and the second before I stumbled he gave a joyful whoop and kicked his legs as high as he could, his full weight pressed along my back.

I fell. But I didn't *just* fall, the way you do when you

trip on an uneven paving slab or down a step. My arms, you recall, were tightly pinioned to my sides, and worse, at that particular moment they were pulled even further away from the ground by Justin's joyous ascent.

I slipped off the stage and fell three feet, literally flat on my face. Look no hands, nose impacting first. All eleven stone of Jus landed on top of me, mashing my head still further into the dance floor.

But it got worse. In the six or so inches of sprung wooden floor with which my head collided, some other careless reveller had recently dropped their champagne glass. It had broken, of course, and yes, it was still lying there in wait for my tender face.

Over the ringing in my ears I was aware of a distant crunching sound. Immediately before passing out, I noticed several jagged pieces of ivory swim sedately past me in a bubbling puddle of blood. Goodbye, expensive teenage dental-correction work.

The last thing I remember was little Tommy Scott of Space singing about not coming from Wales, and thinking, Sam, oh Sam, please help me.

Intrusion

'Daddy! DADD-DEEE! MUMMY!'

I'd been lost in writing about my first meeting with Sam, and the cry nearly made me jump out of my patchwork skin. All my misaligned facial bones rubbed painfully together, and I stopped scribbling, irritated. The voice came from my left, near the door. I couldn't see anybody, although if I turned my head as far as possible I could tell the door was ajar.

A storm of histrionic childish sobbing ensued. By rolling onto my left side I could see a bundle of purple and pink fun-fur crumpled pitifully on the floor by my bed.

'Er, *hello*?' I said, trying to make my voice as laden with sarcasm as possible, despite being aware that this probably wasn't the most effective method of dealing with a stray, distraught toddler.

The crying intensified and my head started to throb. Honestly, couldn't I even plan my own suicide in peace? So much for my privacy and protection; if theatrical two-year-olds could wander in and out at will, then what was to stop a *Sun* photographer or a deranged stalker? I began to feel very put out.

Gingerly, I slid out of bed and to my knees on the floor, where I stretched out my hand and poked the little girl's furry shoulder.

'Where'th your mummy?'

38

She looked up at me then, and the sight of my stitched and bruised face caused her to leap to her feet in one move, like a vertical take-off. Recoiling with horror, she ran and hid behind my visitor's armchair. At least she was shocked into silence, though.

'I like your coat,' I mumbled encouragingly. It was true, I did. I contemplated asking her where she'd got it from, on the off-chance they did it in grown-up sizes.

'Pink flowerth,' came a hesitant reply. I saw a small finger stroke one of the said pink flowers.

'Very nith,' I said. 'Will you come and talk to me now?'

'NO! You got panda-bear face like my mummy! I want my mummy!'

I tried hard not to be hurt or angry, deciding that a frosty 'Do you know who I *am*?' might not do the trick here.

'Where ith your mummy?' I asked again.

'No more nap, Mummy! Wake up now!' The finger wagged accusingly, and the tone became quite stern.

'Would you like a thweetie?' I ventured.

Pathetically, I was by now quite enjoying the distraction from my project. It was much harder work than I'd imagined, writing with only one eye to mediate between brain and paper. In slow motion, I reached for the tin of travel sweets my mother had left behind on her last visit – very insensitive of her, too, I thought. My jaw was still very tender, and I was enduring meals whose consistency my current visitor had probably outgrown at five months of age.

Mutely, the hand stretched out.

'Well, come on then, I won't bite. Although the chanth would be a fine thing.'

She sidled out, eyes downcast. Apart from the chubby red face clashing with her pink and purple coat, she was pretty cute. Skinny little curls sprouted vertically from her head, and her teary eyes held worldly-wise blue depths. I handed her a wrapped sweet.

'Tankoo,' she said politely.

'You're welcome.'

She had just crinkled off the paper and popped it into her mouth when my least-favourite nurse, Catriona, knocked and stuck her head round the door.

'Oh, thank heavens, there she is!' she said crossly. 'Ruby, your daddy's been looking everywhere for you!'

Catriona retreated and returned almost immediately with a blond, curly-haired man, grey around the eyes with exhaustion and what looked like abject misery. They marched into the room, ignoring me completely.

'What am I, chopped liver?' I said to no-one in particular. I was still kneeling on the floor in my nightie, feeling suddenly vulnerable.

'Ruby Middleton, what have I told you about wandering off?' said the man, half-heartedly.

'Daddy! My daddy!' came the ecstatic reply, as Ruby hurled herself at her father's kneecaps. Suddenly we all heard a very strange noise emanating from the depths of the fur coat, a kind of gurgling, hawking sound. Alarmed, the man prised her away from his knees and peered into her puce face.

'Oh my God, she's choking!' he yelled. 'Nurse!'

Catriona, who had just left the room, hurried back in and grabbed Ruby. Inverting her briskly, she slapped her lengthily and enthusiastically between the shoulder blades.

A small green boiled sweet dislodged itself from Ruby's windpipe and flew across the room, bouncing against the far wall and finally coming to rest under my bed. Ruby, howling, was turned back up the right way, and clung to her father. We all looked silently in the direction of the offending travel sweet, until Catriona spoke.

'Well, for heaven's sake! Who on earth was daft enough to give a boiled sweet to a toddler! Some people have absolutely no sense. I mean, really!'

At that moment she and Ruby's dad simultaneously spotted the tin of sweets on my nightstand.

'Thorry,' I muttered, climbing back into bed, furious with myself for feeling so guilty.

Catriona sniffed and left the room, and I was alone with the man and Ruby. I waited for him to give me a piece of his mind, and was preparing to tell him to sling his hook and leave me in peace when he suddenly grinned at me. I was totally disarmed.

'I really am thorry,' I said again, more genuinely this time. I felt confused. What was the correct etiquette for receiving unintentionally visiting strangers in hospital?

The man looked as though the same thought had just passed through his own head.

'No, *I'm* sorry,' he said, 'on behalf of Trouble here. It's terrible of us to barge in when you're trying to recover in peace and quiet. We'll get out of your hair now.'

All of a sudden I didn't want them to leave. Apart from Mum arriving from the US, hideous Geoff Hadleigh and a quick, embarrassed fly-past from my production team at New World, I hadn't had any visitors. Justin had sent flowers, but hadn't shown his (unblemished) face, which had really upset me, and the other band members were all in the States. I was devastated to realize how few friends I really had now that Sam was gone.

'Would Ruby like a drink?' I heard myself ask.

The man hesitated.

'Oringe, pleathe!' said Ruby enthusiastically.

At that moment, Rosemary the tea lady hove serendipitously into sight with her trolley.

'You could have thome tea with me, too, if you like,' I said, cringing at how needy I sounded. Billy No-Mates, indeed.

'Well, that would be nice,' the man said, un-certainly. 'I'm Toby, by the way. And you've met Ruby, obviously.'

He stretched out his arm and we shook hands tentatively.

'Helena,' I replied, relieved and embarrassed that he

was staying. Strangely, once I looked properly at him he seemed slightly familiar.

Rosemary poured us both a cup of tea, handing Toby his with a faintly censorious, 'There you go, Mr Middleton. White no sugar.'

'Thanks, Rosemary,' he replied.

The thick plottens, I thought. Does he work here, or something?

'There'th thome cartonth of Ribena in that cupboard there. Would you like to give Ruby one?'

I pointed to my locker, and Toby obligingly extracted the drink, unwrapping the straw and piercing the carton's foil hole with a pop.

Ruby sidled over and took the drink silently, obviously cowed by her recent near-death experience. With her free hand she spent the next five minutes opening and closing the locker door to hear the magnetic click of its catch. It was irritating, but better than listening to her howling.

'Pleathe, thit down,' I said to Toby, pointing to the shiny armchair. The whole situation felt horribly awkward.

'So, what are you in here for, then?' asked Toby politely, looking away from my technicoloured puffy, stitched face.

'Oh, my varicothe veinth are playing me up again,' I managed, as airily as I could. He smiled, and again I thought I recognized him.

'Actually, I, er, had a fall,' I said, feeling like an old lady who'd fallen off a kerb. 'Onto thome broken glath. My teef were knocked out, too, which ith why I thound like thith.'

Toby winced sympathetically. 'Ouch,' he said.

'Ouch,' echoed Ruby. 'Me kith it better.'

'I with you could,' I said, with feeling. 'Thankth for the offer.'

'I kith Mummy better, but she still seeps,' Ruby added conversationally. We were definitely speaking the same language.

Toby's face scrunched up with pain. 'My wife's in intensive care. She was in a car accident,' he said, looking at the floor. 'She's fractured her skull and is still unconscious.'

'I'm tho thorry,' I said again. My lisp was irritating the hell out of me. It made everything sound so trite. There was a short silence. I stared at the wall, noticing the silhouette of a small long-legged insect that had been carelessly painted into the emulsion. It made me even more depressed. When I looked back at Toby, he had the same empty expression of desperation on his face that I recognized from my own when Sam had been so ill.

Eventually Toby spoke. 'Rubes just can't understand why she won't wake up. It's terrible. She gets so frustrated. I wonder if I'm doing the right thing, bringing her here at all, especially since Kate's face is still so swollen, but I'm sure it helps her to hear Ruby's voice . . .'

'My friend jutht died, a few month' ago,' I blurted out shamelessly, unable to help myself. Suddenly it felt as if both our sorrows had sparked and ignited into one great big furnace of hot grief. When I looked up we were both in tears, embarrassed and overcome.

'Don't cry, Daddy,' said Ruby, her tone suggesting that this wasn't a one-off. 'Don't cry, lady,' she added, slurping her drink noisily through the straw. She climbed onto Toby's knee and threaded an arm around his neck. He hugged her back. I had never felt so alone.

'It'th all tho unfair!' I bawled, not really knowing whether I was crying for Sam, for Toby's wife, for Toby, or for myself.

Toby wiped his eyes and moved over to hand me a box of tissues, Ruby still clinging round his neck. I couldn't blow my nose on account of it being broken, so I dabbed delicately above my top lip instead.

'I'm sorry about your friend. Had you known each other a long time?'

We managed watery grins at one another in

43

acknowledgement of the bizarreness of the situation.

'Yeah, thince we were about five. Tham wath my betht friend in the world. I don't know what to do with mythelf without her.'

My watery grin drizzled away. Toby's head suddenly shot up.

'Oh no! Sam died? Jesus, that's terrible!'

I stared at him, and gulped with shock. All my old steel shutters clanged down around me. Bang, bang.

'How do you know Tham?' I hissed.

Ruby's eyes grew like saucers as she followed the exchange. Toby groaned. A blush crawled up his neck, into his cheeks and over his ears.

'I knew I should have admitted it straight away, but I thought you wouldn't want to be recognized. I don't – didn't – know Sam, but I do know you. We met, years ago, when Blue Idea were on tour in London. I interviewed you for *Melody Maker*, and you told me all about Sam, and the charity record, and how she had recovered from the leukaemia. You were so happy she was better.'

I thought I was about to explode.

'I don't believe it! You're a *journalitht*! You complete thcumbag. How could you do thith to me? Did you thend her in firtht, to get into my room?'

I pointed at Ruby, who shrank back, terrified.

'Wath thith whole thing planned? Ith there a photographer out there? Who'th the piece for? Or are you auctioning it to the highetht bidder? Get the fuck out of here, now, before I call the polithe!'

Toby stood up, clutching Ruby, panic and grief printed across both their faces.

'No, Helena, please, you've got it all wrong. I didn't even know you'd had an accident. Honest. I swear it's not a set-up. I didn't even recognize you at first, until you said your name. Please, I—'

'Jutht get out!' I yelled feebly, completely unable to think straight.

They shot through the door in a blur of fake fur and

curls, Ruby gripping her juice carton so hard that Ribena sprayed up through the straw and across the carpet in their wake.

I cried and cried, even though it made my face throb with pain. I didn't care; I wanted it to hurt. All I could think was how soon could I make this stop? How soon could I do the show?

And the answer was . . . as soon as I got it all written down.

'I Get The Sweetest Feeling'

Jackie Wilson

Sam Grant was five when we first met, and I had recently turned six. I was in the backyard playing on my swing – a dangerous-looking contraption, with frayed green nylon ropes and a plank for a seat, which my father had rigged up for me from a sturdy low branch of the big chestnut tree. The tree itself was in our garden, but the branch holding the swing wandered out and stuck over the fence into a separate paved area where my family's garage was.

I was swinging mightily back and forth, sitting with my back to the garage. Humming tunelessly and kicking my legs to make myself go higher, I was enjoying the sensation of the wind flapping my skirt up and catching underneath my hair. I was at the apex of the swing's trajectory, eyeing the bloomers hanging on next door's washing line, when a massive, metallic BOOM rang out in front of me and almost caused me to plummet from my seat. I managed to hang on, but listed heavily towards the left-hand rope, which made the swing twirl around, out of control. I hadn't noticed the two figures standing near by until I rotated limply to a halt. Then I heard the sound of scornful laughter.

'Not very good, are you? Let's have a go,' said a voice.

I turned to see a boy and a girl in the yard. The boy

was holding a football, and had a mean expression on his less-than-clean face. He looked to be a couple of years older than me. The girl was smaller, and thin. She had her fingers in her mouth, and was lagging behind the boy, looking anxious. She was jiggling her legs, perhaps from nerves, although it looked to me more like the sort of fidgeting brought on by having wet one's knickers. Her red woollen tights sagged in wrinkles around her skinny ankles, and I could see their low crotch showing underneath the hem of her short purple-and-red checked pinafore dress. Then I looked back at the boy, and realized what had startled me on the swing.

'Did you just kick that into the door?' I asked, pointing indignantly at the football.

As if to demonstrate, the boy drop-kicked the ball again, sending it crashing into the pale-green, metallic up-and-over garage door. I was outraged. 'I'm telling my dad on you. Buzz off! You nearly made me fall off of my swing!'

The boy swaggered towards me threateningly. I felt a little nervous.

He moved closer and retrieved his ball. 'Give us a go on your stupid swing, then.'

'No! Buzz off!' I'd heard some bigger boys say this in the playground the week before, and had been saving it up for a suitable occasion. This most definitely was a situation that called for strong language. The girl still lurked behind her brother, not meeting my eyes. I glared at both of them, hating the intrusion, when a woman's voice yelled from the end of the street: 'Dylan! Sa-am! Where are you? Tea's ready! I'm not telling you again!'

To my relief the boy started to turn away. 'You'd better let me play on it next time, fatso,' he said menacingly, and ran out of the yard. His sister stayed in her spot, fidgeting even more. We stared at each other. Eventually she took her fingers out of her mouth and said, 'That's my brother Dylan.

47

He's often a bully. Can I come and call for you later?'

I was taken aback, but disarmed. In retrospect, I don't know what endeared me to her; I must have been a fairly intimidating sight, standing there guarding my territory with an aggressive scowl on my face and hands firmly planted on hefty little hips. Possibly it was the lure of the forbidden swing. Anyhow, I graciously conceded that she could, if only to spite her awful brother.

It transpired that the Grants had just moved to Salisbury to run the pub on the corner, the Prince of Wales. By happy coincidence, Sam also ended up in my form at school, although there was almost a year between us; I was the oldest in the class, and she the youngest.

This put the final seal on our friendship. For the duration of our primary school years we pretty much lived in each other's pockets: we played at the pub, in my bedroom, or raced unsteadily through the terraced streets around our houses on our baby bicycles, first with stabilizers, and later without.

Mostly we tried to avoid Dylan, who by the age of nine had acquired a worrying head for business. He used to round up a few of his friends on a regular basis and charge them 5p each to see Sam and me reluctantly show them our underwear. This weekly ritual was known locally as 'Bum Time', and I believe that for double the admission fee we'd actually pull down our knickers for a quick flash to the more affluent members of the group. I don't recall what Sam and I got out of this arrangement – none of the takings, that was for sure; more like a deep and permanent feeling of mortification that lasted into adulthood. Dylan threatened to give us Chinese burns if we refused to oblige.

The fact that Sam's parents ran a pub made her something of an icon at school: everyone thought it was the coolest thing parents could do. In the early Seventies the Prince of Wales was a standard locals' pub, open at lunchtimes and in the evenings only, in accordance with the restricted licensing laws of the time. Sam and I were allowed to sit downstairs in the bar after school, before the evening session began. It was the biggest thrill, sliding around on the leatherette benches, learning how to flip beer mats from the edges of the pockmarked tables, revolving the wheel on the jukebox to make the selections clunk laboriously round. Sometimes Mr Grant gave me 10p to put a record on, and I always chose 'I Get The Sweetest Feeling' by Jackie Wilson, because it's just such a happy song. I loved the 'plink, plink, plink, plink . . . hmmmm' of the introduction, and the fat, deeply satisfying brassy noises going on in the background. To this day, it's one of my favourite records.

The jukebox was only one of the gadgets which made the Prince of Wales an Aladdin's Cave of technological wizardry. We didn't even have a black-and-white television at home until I was eight; the Grants had two colour sets, one in the bar, stuck high up on the wall with a bracket, and one upstairs in their sitting room. They had the first microwave oven I'd ever seen, as well as pinball and fruit machines, which we weren't allowed to touch. Sam even had one of those kiddie synthesizers with the coloured piano keys, as well as a record player *and* a radio. I was so envious.

During business hours we were not allowed to set foot in the bar, and so we played upstairs in the residential part. The Prince of Wales was a very old building, a public house since its inception in the eighteenth century, and was full of appealing little features. As a child I failed to appreciate them, but in retrospect I remember the sloping floors and ceilings, wood-panelled walls, odd cupboards everywhere and narrow hallways, interspersed every few yards with two or three crooked steps up to another level and around a new corner.

These passageways were the venue for one of our

favourite games: The Great Continental Quilt Bobsleigh Race. Continental quilts, as they were called in those days, were a total novelty in themselves. I had never seen one before, and begged and begged my mother to buy me one, explaining at great length how labour-saving they were – no more constant bed-making or sheet-ironing. Unfortunately she regarded anything continental as being French, and therefore somehow sweaty and unhygienic, and it was a few more years before she capitulated and bought duvets for *toute la famille*. My fascination was such that I would drag Sam's quilt off her bed and into the sitting room, initially, I suppose, so we could both lie on it and watch TV. Then one day it became a method of transport.

'I know,' I said. 'I'm Cinderella going to the ball in my carriage. You be my horse and pull me.' I plumped down in the middle and gathered up the edges around me, leaving the two front corners for Sam to pick up. She neighed obligingly, bared her teeth, shook her mane and hauled me, with difficulty, out of the sitting room and down the long hall back to the bedroom doorway. I remember catching sight of myself in a hall mirror, and noticing with pleasure the regal air about my demeanour, the queenly tilt to my chin and my gentle poise as Sam bumped me slowly forward to meet my prince. I was visualizing the adoration of all the lords and ladies at the ball, not just the prince, but everyone. That was the first time I was aware of craving the spotlight.

Sam dragged me back again, faster this time, so I could drop my glass slipper on the way home. That, however, was done less gracefully. I fiddled with the strap of my scuffed blue T-bar Clark's sandal, pulling it off with a jerk, which made me lose my balance and lurch over backwards. I then lobbed the shoe over my shoulder, where it hit the wall with a jingle of its buckle, leaving a dirty mark.

'If that was real glass you'd have broken it,' Sam told

me disapprovingly. I did a quick role switch from princess to prince, retracing my steps down the corridor to tenderly retrieve the bulky soled sandal, holding it to my chest and then my lips, looking wistfully back towards the bedroom door for my princess. The drama was lost on Sam; she was too busy trying to rub the scuff mark off the wallpaper by spitting on her doll's dress and wiping it on the wall. The doll was wearing the dress at the time, and the friction from Sam's rubbing only caused its porcelain fingernails to add little scritchy marks next to the original scuff.

We kept refining the quilt scenarios, and over time they evolved into more of a sport than a charade, which we practised zealously when Dylan wasn't around to laugh at us. One of us would sit on the quilt, wrapping its back and sides around us for padding, and the other would pick up the front and drag it, plus passenger, down the hallway from the starting line of the sitting room. Because the hall was so narrow and sloped gently down, with the little sets of stairs and turns breaking up its length, it made quite a respectable bobsleigh run. We managed to get quite a speed up. The idea was to get to the finish line – the kitchen doorway – without the passenger falling off or the puller falling over.

The only problem was that our weights weren't well balanced enough to get the maximum momentum. When I was the puller, I'd gallop full tilt for the first flight of steps, charge down them, hurtle round the first bend, and more often than not be left holding an empty quilt, Sam having been catapulted, screaming, into a cupboard door, or picking splinters from her palms further back up the course. And when she pulled me, she would puff and pant, heaving with all her strength to drag me to the top of the three little stairs, where gravity would kick in and I would invariably cascade down faster than her, catching her in the back of the knees on the way. We once heard her mother commenting in puzzled tones to her father about how quickly their new hall carpet had developed a nasty shiny streak down its centre.

Daisies and the Guinea Pig

It was a slightly better week. I had my teeth capped, which was a huge relief, and I received two new cards. The first was from Toby and Ruby, a simple get-well-soon card with their names inside. The card had a big white daisy on the front, and was followed into my room, within minutes, by a delivery of an enormous bunch of Michaelmas daisies, my favourite flower. I was finding it increasingly tough to feel hard-done-by and cheated by that sunny couple with their curly hair and serious eyes. But I kept trying to dismiss the memory of their visit. Toby obviously had a guilty conscience, I told myself, otherwise why hadn't he brought me the flowers in person?

The second card was from Cynthia Grant, Sam's mother. She'd sent it to my home address, and Mum, who was staying at my house, had brought it into the hospital with her.

I recognized Cynthia's writing on the envelope, and immediately got a tense, choked-up feeling in my throat. It was so nice of her to think of me, but I almost resented hearing from her simply because she wasn't Sam. We'd kept in touch since Sam died, but had only seen each other once. I'd called in on her and we had sat in her homely front room, knowing that underneath our feet was Sam's abandoned basement flat, both of us wishing we could be down there having tea with Sam instead. And the worst thing of all was that Sam's name never once came into the conversation. We both knew she was the reason we were sitting there together over syrupy flapjacks and Earl Grey, and I'm sure we were both aching to talk about her, to get into one of those 'Do you remember when Sam . . . ?' conversations, but we didn't. I assumed we were both afraid of upsetting the other, and we avoided the subject of our loss studiously, as if the very mention of her name would have incurred some embarrassing forfeit.

'Who's it from?' asked Mum.

'Cynthia,' I replied dully. 'She says she might come and visit.'

'Oh well, if she's not too busy, I guess that would be nice for you,' Mum ventured, looking disapprovingly at a postcard David and Joe from the band had sent me. It was a cartoon depicting two doctors examining a man with a camera jammed up his bottom, and had the caption, 'Yes, doctor, it's one of the worst cases of media intrusion I've ever seen.' On the back they'd written: 'Get well soon, little sis. Wish we could be there for you, but we're just about to start a Bowie tour. Well, it pays the bills. Can we come stay with you next time we're in the UK? Love you lots, D&J.'

Mum propped the cards back up on the window ledge with the dozens of others, moving the offensive camera-up-bottom one to the back. There was so little space left up there that she had to slot Toby's card inside another one, which irritated me. What was the point of bothering to put it on display if no-one could see it? All those supposed well-wishers clogging up my window sill with cheap sentiment because they couldn't be bothered to actually visit me in person. Well, except for my production team, but I didn't think that them shuffling in for ten minutes really counted.

I made her move the daisy card back into my line of vision.

'No, it won't be nice,' I said. 'She'll just sit here and

torture me by looking and sounding exactly like Sam, and we won't even be able to talk about her. I hope she doesn't come. In fact, I'm glad I'm not getting any visitors. I look like a freak. My life is over. I wish everybody would just go away.'

Mum took my hand, but I shook it off and looked away. I didn't want her sympathy.

'I heard the nurse mention that Toby was asking after you again,' she said, casually. 'Is that the Toby who sent that card?'

I ignored her and opened my notebook. I'd started writing about my blissful childhood, when Sam and I were first friends, and it had become almost an obsession. It was the one thing that kept me sane, and kept the black dog of my depression in his kennel.

'Who's Toby, Helena dear?' Mum's hopeful tone made my skin crawl with irritation.

'Nobody, Mum. He's just a journalist trying to get a story on me. He says his wife's in intensive care but . . .'

But what? Of course I knew deep down that Toby's wife really was in a coma somewhere down the corridor. Nobody could be calculating and callous enough to invent a story like that. Not to mention the child. 'Me kith Mummy better,' echoed in my head, and I suddenly felt a deep and long-overdue wash of shame. Did I really think he'd put Ruby up to that? I remembered Toby quite clearly now, from our one meeting all those years ago. The thing that had most impressed me about him, apart from his disarming smile, had been his obvious openness and honesty. I'd really fancied him.

'Well, the flowers he sent you are pretty. And why would he be bothering to write a story on you if his wife is that sick, for pity's sake? I think you're being rather overdramatic and unfair on the poor man. He's got enough on his plate without you slandering him.'

Mum sounded quite cross. I realized she'd probably already gleaned the sad tale of my meeting with Toby from Catriona the nurse, and was just fishing to get my point of view. For once I didn't jump down her throat and defend myself. I just nodded miserably.

'Have you even thanked him for the flowers?'

'No,' I whispered, feeling about six years old and in disgrace.

Mum tutted and rose to leave, tucking the stiff tortoiseshell handles of her handbag firmly over her forearm. She was clearly enjoying exercising a different emotion with me; not one pulled from the tired old selection grab bag of Pity, Sympathy, Patience and Understanding, all much overused since my accident. No, today we had Displeasure, and boy, it was a refreshing change for her.

'Well, honey, I'll leave you to your . . . *memoirs*,' she said disapprovingly. 'I need to get back and ring your father. Heaven knows how he's coping over there on his own. I expect the house has gone to rack and ruin. He told me last week that he put dishwasher salt in the salt cellar; and he expected me to be pleased with him for using his initiative! Honestly, he is the limit.'

She kissed the top of my head, and tried to get a sneaky peek at the writing on my pad. Pre-empting her, I turned it upside down on my lap so the words weren't visible. Mum was torn between being pleased that I was doing something creative to keep me occupied, and being absolutely paranoid that she'd been cast in my memoirs as New Jersey's answer to Hyacinth Bucket. We didn't exactly have a close mother–daughter relationship; not that it was bad, just very distant, in all senses of the word.

After Mum finally left, I tried to get down to work. But being in hospital was not dissimilar to being on a promo tour – waiting ages for room service while an endless succession of people *wanted* things from you – and I found myself constantly interrupted. There was an orderly asking me to tick what I wanted for dinner from the menu list – why bother, I thought. It all tastes the same when it's pureed; a nurse wanting to change my dressings; the doctor checking on my skin graft; Rosemary the tea lady; and finally, when my patience was about to snap, my mobile phone rang.

Sighing, I put down the note pad and wriggled laboriously across the mattress towards my locker to reach the illicitly switched-on phone. Wriggling gradually was less painful than directly leaning over.

'Yes?' I snapped, holding the phone, out of habit, to my damaged left ear and wondering why I couldn't hear anything. 'Who is it?' Through my right ear and over the top of my head I could hear a faint guinea-pig squeak from the receiver, which alerted me to the problem. I transferred the phone to the other side, and the guinea pig turned itself into Justin.

'Oh, it's you,' I said unenthusiastically. I was still deeply hurt that he hadn't called or visited.

'H, Jesus. I'm so, so sorry. I can't believe what's happened to you. I came in the ambulance with you, you know. It was a nightmare; paps everywhere, people screaming. I'll never forget the sight of you lying there on the floor with blood coming out of—'

'IF you don't mind, Jus, I'd rather not know, thanks,' I interrupted stiffly. It was too humiliating even to contemplate.

'Listen, baby, I'm totally cut up that I haven't been able to visit you since, you know, but I've been doing PAs and a couple of TVs in South America. I told you I was flying out the day after the UKMAs, didn't I?'

First I'd heard of it. But I gave him the benefit of the doubt. After all, my memory of that night was probably not all that it should have been.

'So why didn't you call me, then?'

There was a brief pause. 'Man, H, I didn't think you'd wanna hear from me. It was all my fault. You wouldn't believe how shit I feel about it.'

He really did sound sincere, and I felt for him.

'Oh Justin, please. Of course it wasn't your fault; it was my idea, wasn't it? *I* talked *you* into it. Don't give yourself a hard time. To be honest, I'm more gutted that you haven't been in touch.'

57

'Do you mean that?' I could hear the relief in his voice.

'Of course, you moron.'

'So how are you now, then?'

'Still in hospital, but better now I've had my teeth capped, thanks. I broke both the front ones in different directions and it made me sound like Daffy Duck. And I expect you heard I lost my eye. I'm still deaf in one ear, I've got a skin graft on my face, a ton of stitches and a broken nose. Oh, and concussion, obviously.' I couldn't face the prospect of more ham-fisted commiserations, so I ploughed on. 'But that's almost better, and hopefully I'll be going home next week. So when are you next in London?'

'Not for a while now. I'll be doing a bunch of promo in the US for the next two months, and then I'm out on tour. Why don't you fly over for a visit soon?'

'I don't think I'm up to flying. Besides, I've got . . . stuff to do here.'

'Oh right, of course. I forgot, you're the top DJ now. Well, duty calls. I'm sure London's hepcats can't stand to have their morning coffee and muffins without your sexy voice telling them what's what.'

I didn't have the stomach to tell him I'd lost my job. 'We don't eat muffins for breakfast here.'

'Eggs and bacon, then. Whatever. Listen, babes, I have to run. I've got a photoshoot for some Brazilian mag in twenty minutes. Did you get my flowers?'

'Yeah. Thanks, Jus. They were lovely. Take care, OK? And don't feel guilty about anything.'

'OK. Love you, honey. Get well soon,' said Justin, hanging up happily. I knew that I'd be forgotten again in an instant; being Justin Becker was a full-time job, one which didn't leave room for unproductive emotions like guilt and remorse. But that said, he was, like all three of my former band members, a good mate and a warm-hearted person – once you scratched beneath the vinyl of the pop star. I was glad we'd at least talked before I got to implement The Plan.

Funny how *his* career hadn't been harmed by allegations of drugs, though.

Justin's suggestion of a visit to the States gave me an idea. I dialled my agent Ron's number, and listened to a lengthy answering machine inform me that the offices of Pickett Management Services were currently closed, and if I left a message they'd get back to me pronto.

'Ron, it's Helena. Thanks for the card. I'm still in hospital, but I'm on the mend. I just wanted to tell you that I'm going to go and stay with my folks in New Jersey for a few months, until all the fuss dies down. Geoff Hadleigh's fired me, but I feel like a break from work anyhow. So please could you keep all my mail and any messages for me until I get back? I don't know exactly when that'll be, but I'll call you. The main thing is to please not tell anyone where I am. Just say that I'm away. Thanks. Bye.'

That should keep the press off my back, I thought.

'(Get Your Kicks On) Route 66'

Sandie Shaw

A few months after Sam and I first met, I saw my first snowstorm. I'd woken up and opened my bedroom curtains to be startled by huge, fat whirling flakes bouncing off the glass and bumbling silently down to land on the place where the garden path used to be. And it wasn't just the garden path, everything had been swallowed up: houses, trees, our street, and even, oh no, the spire of Salisbury Cathedral! I ran along the landing in a panic to tell my parents, but as was often the case, their bedroom door was forbiddingly closed.

'Mummy, Daddy, it's snowing and the spire's gone. Let me in.'

There was a long pause. I rattled the door handle and it opened a fraction and then stopped, which meant they had flicked across the catch. I caught a glimpse of its skinny upside-down waggling finger on the other side of the door. A finger whose sole job was to tell me to go away.

'Pleeease can I come in? I'm scared.'

Then the sound of my mother's voice, blanket-heavy and slow, like the snow. The voice she used before she put her make-up on.

'Don't be silly, Helena, the spire hasn't gone. You just can't see it because of the snow. Be a good girl and get yourself some cereal, would you? Put it in your

Peter Rabbit bowl, and mind you don't spill the milk. We'll be down soon.'

'But why can't I come in?'

This time Dad spoke. 'Your mother's terribly tired, Helena. Please just do as she asks and go and have breakfast.'

I leaned my head on the door in frustration.

'I *hate* it when you lock the door,' I said, and stomped down the stairs, slapping each banister as I went.

After breakfast, once I'd had a bit of time to get used to the dizzying blur outside the window, I went to stand in the living room to get a better view. I traced the flakes' descent down the window pane with my fingertips, until they became numb with cold. I could see my breath and it made me shiver.

I had dressed myself in my favourite cardigan of fuzzy yellow wool. It made me feel like an Easter chick. But even this didn't keep out the cold from the window. The fur of my sleeves stood upright, like hairs on goose-flesh, and I felt like the cardy was colder than I was. So I took two steps back into the warmer centre of the room to warm us both up.

Eventually the snow-intensified silence became too oppressive, so I gave in to the forbidden game of switching on the big wooden radiogram on the low shelf. One of my favourite things to do was to twiddle the radio's tuning knob and see the green fluorescent needle rush from left to right across the dial, past all the numbers and dots and markings. The language I could make it speak was fascinating; I imagined a country where everyone talked in those strange, jumpy fragments of sentences, interspersed with blasts of jazz trumpet, organ or soprano, and the scratchy hiss and fuzz of static fading in and out, linking words. Perhaps I was even tuning in to God's language.

That day, however, I got a song straight away, a song I recognized because my dad had bought the LP just a few months before. It was Shelley Beach, my favourite singer. It was a bouncy, jolly sort of song about . . . well, actually I wasn't quite sure what it was about. Getting your kicks on Root 66. I remembered last year's church fête, and the table with the prize-winning marrows and things, which all had numbers on them. Perhaps it was like one of those sideshows where you queued up to throw wet sponges at people who couldn't move, only this was queuing up to kick large vegetables, which seemed a strange choice of subject for a song. They were usually about kissing and stuff.

I liked Shelley a lot. I imagined she was right there in the room with me, ready to come outside and help me and Sam build a snowman, although she'd need to wrap up a bit warmer. On Dad's record, I remembered her wearing little more than a gold bikini and a crown.

'That was a smashing number for you: the very lovely Sandie Shaw singing "(Get Your Kicks On) Route 66", a song from her last record, *The Sandie Shaw Supplement*,' said a man when the song finished.

Through the floor of the bedroom above my head I heard the muffled thump of a parent getting out of bed, and I hastily turned off the radio. Sandie Shaw? I thought. No, he must have got it wrong. That's Shelley Beach.

Dad used to listen to that record all the time; although, come to think of it, I hadn't heard it recently. Not since the night Mum went a bit wiry-lipped and accused Dad of fancying Shelley Beach. I had a quick flick through the records in the LP box, a thick square green box with a flip-up top which smelled of dusty paper and sweet vinyl and, sure enough, *The Sandie Shaw Supplement* was missing.

So was her name really Sandie Shaw? I preferred Shelley Beach; I thought it suited her image better. The picture had shown her lolling on a chilly-looking beach. Maybe that was why I'd misremembered her name.

All was quiet, above and below. The snow against

the window seemed to press the silence further into the house. The only sound in the room was a clock, ticking robustly on the mantelpiece above the square brick fireplace. Even though I couldn't tell the time properly, I liked to watch the gleaming hands trace their slow path.

I soon got bored. There were none of my toys in there, it was too cold to be by the window, and no fun to watch the snow if you couldn't feel its chill. I wondered if it was worth the risk of getting shouted at by going upstairs again. Really, even by their standards my parents had been up there for ages.

I decided to give it a few more minutes. I noticed that yellow fluff had got onto my tartan kilt, and I tried to pick it off, frowning with concentration as my small hands grappled with the microscopic fibres. There was too much, so I gave up and stared at my shoes. They felt like part of my body, as if I had shoes instead of feet. Actually, they looked similar to my legs – sturdy, scratched and reddish-brown with mottled white patches. Like my cardigan and myself, my shoes were also cold.

Finally, eventually, I heard my mother tread heavily downstairs in her fluffy mules.

'Mummy!' I cried, running out to meet her and trying to leap into her arms as she stepped off the bottom stair. But her arms stayed by her sides and she didn't even try to catch me. She was wearing her quilted nylon dressing gown, a garment so shiny that I slipped right down her, landing painfully hard on her foot.

'Ow! Goodness, Helena, must you be so boisterous? You're far too big and heavy for me to carry you these days. Have you had breakfast?'

She opened the front door to take the milk bottles off the step, and a flurry of snow whirled into the hallway, making everything even colder, as if the Ice Queen herself had driven the milk float that morning.

I squeaked and ran into the kitchen. 'Don't let it in! Don't let it in!'

Mum followed me, limping slightly, and put the milk bottles on the kitchen counter.

'I asked you a question, dear. Have you had breakfast or not?'

I nodded, still dancing round her, as if my surfeit of energy could help boost her lack of it.

'And look, Mummy, I got dressed all by myself, too, shoes and everything.'

'So I noticed,' she said, rubbing her toe. 'You're a good girl, really. I'm sorry Mummy's so tired this morning.'

I watched as she stuck the spout of the kettle under the cold tap, filled it up, plonked it on the cooker, struck a match and lit the gas ring. She shivered as the blue flames licked around the kettle's sides, and when she turned around to get a bowl out of the cupboard, her face looked like another square of her dressing gown, taut, shiny and puffy.

Fattypuff, I thought, making a mental note to ask Sam if she agreed with my diagnosis. We had discussed the strange fluctuations in my mother's girth, and referred to the two extremes as either Fattypuff or Thinifer. I liked Mummy best when she was neither, when she was just in the middle. Then she let me pretend she was my pony, or made biscuits with me, or showed me how to glue strips of paper together into multicoloured chains. Her make-up stayed on all day, and she was happy.

'Will you help me make a snowman later, Mummy?'

We weren't into an advanced Fattypuff condition yet, so I was reasonably hopeful of an affirmative answer. But it was not to be.

'Why don't you wait till Sam comes over? I'm sure she'd like to build a snowman with you.'

'What about Dad? Will he help us?'

Mum pressed in the silver-foil top of one of the milk bottles with her thumb, and tried to pour the milk into the flowery milk jug. Nothing happened.

'Oh, for heaven's sake!' Mum said, much more

crossly than I thought necessary. 'The wretched milk's frozen.'

I heard the sound of the front door opening and then closing again before I had time to run into the hall.

'Where's Daddy gone?' I asked, trying not to think of my father being swallowed up by the snow.

Mum sighed and sat down, as if the milk and I were in some kind of conspiracy against her. 'Nowhere, dear. He's just popping down to the shops to pick something up for me from the chemist, that's all. So, about this snowman. I'll get you a carrot for his nose if you go and fetch two pieces of coal from the coal scuttle for his eyes. How about that?'

It would have to do. I hoped Sam knew how to construct men out of snow, because I hadn't the first idea. On cue, there was a scuffling outside the back door and a timid knock.

I brightened. Mum unbolted the door and admitted a chilly Sam, making her stand on the mat and stamp the snow off her little blue wellies before allowing her in properly.

Sam looked like a stuffed toy animal, with numerous layers of coats and woollies, scarves, mitts, elasticated waists, cuffs and neck bands. Her outer coat was so thick that her arms were forced unnaturally away from her sides at a 45-degree angle to her body. A red face peered out at me through swathes of nylon parka fur.

'Coming out to play? It's nearly stopped snowing,' she chirped.

I looked at Mum, and she nodded, as happy to see Sam as I was.

I submitted to the swaddling routine and trotted nervously out into the back garden with Sam, leaving Mum slumped on a stool at the breakfast bar with a steaming cup of black tea.

It was a bit like seeing the ocean for the first time: scary to begin with, and then completely exhilarating when you got used to it. I noticed with surprise that despite the chilly flakes on my face, I felt much warmer outside than I had earlier in the sitting room.

I looked at the orange nose and black eyes in my hands. 'Do you know how to do snowmen?'

Sam shook her head. 'Like sandcastles?'

I shrugged. 'Maybe. But we haven't got a spade.'

'And it's a bit cold, isn't it, snow?'

Sam pointed at the frost sparkling on a tree branch above our heads.

'Let's do dancing instead, like at a ball. We can pretend the tree is the chand-*liere*. You know, those big lampshade things they have, with candles and stuff.'

I had no idea what she was talking about, but obligingly dropped my carrot and coal, reached one gloved hand around her waist and pressed the other woolly mitt against hers. We waltzed clumsily around the garden, trying to step in a fresh patch of snow at every twirl.

'I think Mummy's going Fattypuff again,' I said.

Sam nodded knowingly but changed the subject. 'Oh dear. Who are you going to be today? I'm going to be Valerie Singleton.'

I considered for a minute as we trod the light fantastic. The garden seemed much bigger when it was all white, with no edges.

'Sandie Shaw, but I call her Shelley Beach. She's a singer, you know. I really like that song she does about church fêtes.'

Sam nodded again, equally knowingly. 'Yes. That's my favourite, too.'

We did a few more circuits of the lawn, dancing further and further out, until we were almost at next door's fence and our footprints had claimed every bit of pure snow.

Mum opened the back door and stuck her head out. 'Keep off my flowerbeds, you girls, or you'll squash my crocuses!'

Making Amends

There was a tap at the door. Grace, the nicest nurse, stuck her head in. 'Are you up for a visitor, Helena?'

'Who is it?'

'It's Toby Middleton. He's asking to see you.'

I hesitated. Time to mend a few bridges. 'OK.'

I reached for my dark glasses and hastily smeared a slick of Burt's Bees lipgloss over my chapped and bumpy lips. Funny how there was once a time when I wouldn't let anyone see me without extensive make-up. That all seemed kind of pointless now.

Toby sidled into the room, alone. 'Hello,' he said, nervously.

'Hi,' I replied. 'Please sit down.'

'Thanks. Oh, hey, you aren't lisping! And your teeth look great.'

'Thanks.'

He sat and waited for the apology we both knew he was due. Inwardly, I commended his courage; a lesser man wouldn't have risked another earbashing. But I suppose if your wife is in a coma, you don't really care about getting abused by a battered old harridan like me.

'Listen, I'm really, really sorry about what I said before. You're not a scumbag or anything, of course you aren't, and thank you so much for the card and the daisies. You really shouldn't have after I behaved so appallingly. I feel like a total shit, with your wife so ill and stuff. How is she?'

'Still the same, but thanks for asking. I wanted to apologize to you, too. I think we both felt a bit vulnerable that day. I should have been honest with you from the start.'

Toby took off his glasses and polished them on his shirt. I noticed his thick textured wedding ring. Rugged and solid, like him.

I nodded. 'It all just got too much for me. I've been so paranoid about the press after that hideous picture of me they took right before the accident. And then, when I started to cry like that, I suppose I assumed the worst: that you were going to expose me again.'

'What do you mean again? That piece I did on you was very complimentary! BLUE IDEA'S GREEN-EYED DEAR — terrible headline, I know, but it wasn't exactly an exposé.'

Toby sounded quite hurt, but when I looked at him, the corners of his mouth were twitching upwards.

'No, not that *you'd* expose me again. Actually, I quite liked your article, even though my eyes aren't green at all, more swamp-coloured really. I meant that *I'd* get exposed again. It's all been so humiliating, and I've lost my job, and . . . oh God, I'm doing it again. Going on about me when you've got such awful problems.'

Toby grinned properly. 'Well, as Bette Midler said, "That's enough about me; what do *you* think of me?" Actually, it's quite refreshing to hear someone else's woes. I get sick of talking about mine. Have you really lost your job? What do you do these days? I'm sure I'd know about it if you were in another band.'

Somewhat huffy that he wasn't aware of my DJ incarnation, I told him about the New World breakfast show.

'Cool. A DJ! Yes, that figures. I bet you make a brilliant DJ. I don't live in London any more. We moved to the country so Kate could have a bigger studio – she's a potter – and we don't get New World out in Hampshire. Otherwise I'd definitely have tuned in to your show.'

'But I'm not a DJ any more. At least . . . oh, well, it's a long story. So why is Kate in hospital here if you live in Hampshire?'

Toby took a deep breath, and I winced at the thought that I was being insensitive.

'Sorry. Listen, you don't have to talk about it if you don't want to . . .'

'It's fine. It's really quite nice talking to someone who isn't upset about her, too. She had the accident one night here in London. I didn't even know she was in town. She'd told me she was going to see someone about a commission in Portsmouth, but I suppose the meeting must have been moved up here. So when they phoned to say there'd been a crash, I didn't believe it could be her.

'Anyway, this was the hospital they brought her to because it has an ICU and plastic surgery. When she's better she's going to need some work on her face; she's got a major facial fracture, running from her eyebrow down to her jaw. They'll have to put in a titanium staple. It seemed silly to move her again when this hospital's so good, so Ruby and I have been staying with my sister Lulu in Fulham. That's where Ruby is today.'

I nodded sympathetically, my face aching at the memory of my own recent plastic surgery. My injuries suddenly felt trivial in comparison – a few dozen stitches, a couple of strips of skin relocated from thigh to face. At least I'd had no truck with titanium staples, whatever the hell they might be.

'So are you still a journalist?' I tried not to spit when I said the word.

Toby noticed and took me to task. 'Hey, there's a bit of a difference between a *Melody Maker* journalist and a tabloid hack, you know. Don't tar us all with the same brush. Anyway, no, I'm not. I never made very

69

much money from my writing, so I jacked it in and set up my own Internet music company. It means I can work from home and be close to Ruby and Kate . . . Well, Ruby, anyhow. Kate hasn't been around much recently. She's taken on quite a few big commissions, and organizing those seems to take more time than actually making the pots. God knows what's going to happen with them now.'

He stood up abruptly. 'I really should go and see Kate. I just wanted to check that you're OK and feeling better.' He rammed his hands into his jeans pockets as if he thought I might grab them and beg him to stay.

'Thanks,' I said. I'd been wondering if I dared ask him to come again, but his gesture decided me against it. Besides, he had enough on his plate.

Toby opened the door and looked back towards my bed. All of a sudden he seemed fascinated by the jug of water on top of my locker.

'Um, would it be OK if I popped back again tomorrow? It's, you know, really nice to have a conversation with someone when I come and visit Kate. It gets quite hard to, er, just sit and talk to a person who doesn't reply. Would you mind?'

'No,' I said. 'I wouldn't mind.'

'Wichita Lineman'
Glen Campbell

THE HEL-SAM BOX OF IMPORTANT STUFF!
KEEP OUT! UNLESS YOU ARE HELENA JANE
NICHOLLS OR SAMANTHA GRANT!

In the event of the untiemally death of either of
us, this box is to go immidiatally to the other
one's house and stay there. No-one else is ever,
ever, allowed to look inside. It's all completely
Top Secret.

I sat back on my heels and admired my handiwork, purple felt-pen blotches all over my hands. Sam was lying on her stomach next to me, laboriously gluing shiny paper flowers onto an old hat box, her tongue sticking out of the side of her mouth.

'What do you think?' I waved the piece of card at her.

'Needs some glitter,' Sam replied.

'Give us the glue, then.' I grabbed it and squeezed twirls of Bostick around the edges of my cardboard notice. I shook generous quantities of silver glitter over an area approximately sixteen foot square, some of which managed to land on the intended target.

'Watch it!' said Sam crossly as I frosted her flowers, the whole hat box, our hands and faces and the carpet. 'Your mum will kill us if she sees the mess in here.'

We were illicitly camped out in my parents' bedroom because, later that day, a new extra-specially comfortable bed was going to be delivered to help Mum sleep better. It was to be a surprise for her from Dad, who had dismantled the old one and gone to take it to the dump. Its departure had left a brighter, lusher, thicker square of blue carpet, protected from years of harsh sunlight by the darkness of the bed's cool underbelly. It was, of course, impossible for us not to play on it.

'This is our magic carpet to fly us away,' I'd said as we crept into the room.

We had adopted Ali Baba positions, kneeling up, arms folded across horizontally, imagining the square slowly lifting up and out the window, carrying us to a place where Dylan's Chinese burns and homework didn't exist.

However, the carpet's stubborn refusal to levitate eventually became a little disappointing, so we transformed it into a stage instead, and choreographed a *Guys and Dolls* dance routine to show my mother on her return from the doctor's, a sort of welcome-new-bed ceremony.

We were all set, hair blow-dried into monster flicks and as many plastic necklaces as we could find in Mum's jewellery box. I was a Guy, sporting Dad's bright-green best shirt, its flared collar flapping around my neck like Dumbo's ears. Sam was wearing a matching – or as close as we could get – chartreuse towel round her waist as a skirt. She always got to be the Doll because she was more petite. Actually, I wasn't much of a fan of *Guys and Dolls*, but I went along with it because Sam would have to do the Carl Douglas 'Kung Fu Fighting' routine with me later.

Ages had passed, and still we hadn't heard the sound of Mum's key in the lock. So to while away the time, we decided to decorate the hat box, which had been designated the Hel-Sam Box of Important Stuff.

72

'Can I keep it at my house?' Sam asked when I had finally succeeded in sticking the decorated label on its lid.

'OK. For a while.' I was frantically trying to brush glue and glitter off the sleeve of Dad's shirt. By this stage I was quite keen to be rid of the evidence. 'I'd better sweep this carpet. Stay there, I'll be back in a minute.'

I was just galloping down the stairs to retrieve the carpet-sweeper when the front door began to open. I could tell immediately, before Mum had even entered the house, how uptight she was. It was a Thinifer period, and I had developed a kind of sixth sense about the state of her moods.

'Hello, Mummy. Come and see, me and Sam have got a dance for you,' I said nervously, helping her out of her swing coat.

'Sam and *I*,' Mum corrected automatically. Several beads of sweat had managed to struggle through the thick blanket of face-powder covering her forehead, and she stopped in front of the hall mirror to pat them away with a tissue.

'And we've decorated the hat box you gave us. It's going to be the Hel-Sam Box of Important Stuff. We're not watching telly, like you said. We're amusing ourselves.'

I took my mother's hand and tried to drag her upstairs, and for the first time she noticed my appearance.

'Helena, what on earth are you wearing? And what's that all over the sleeves? Felt pen? And glue? You're covered in glitter! How could you be so naughty and thoughtless to do gluing in Daddy's best shirt!'

My head drooped. 'But I had to wear it; it's part of your surprise,' I said in a small voice. 'Come and see.'

I was miserably aware that Mum was working herself up into a full Thinifer rage. Her eyes were bugging out, and a drop of the escaping sweat on her forehead was making a bid for freedom down the side of her cheek.

'For heaven's sake, Helena!' she snapped. 'I told you and Sam to play quietly until I came back. I did not tell you to rootle through your father's wardrobe and then get his best shirt all mucky. And if there's that much glitter on you, what sort of state is your bedroom floor in, might I ask?'

'It's perfectly clean,' I said, truthfully, my heart sinking further. Mum bustled past me and up the stairs.

'Good. I'm sorry, Helena, but I'm too tired to watch you do anything at the moment. I'm going for a lie down in my . . . *Oh!'*

I raced up after her to find Sam standing in the middle of my parents' bedless room, clad in necklaces and a green towel, hair in a flick that could put your eye out, but thankfully with no incriminating signs of the box, glue, felt-tip pens or coloured paper. Even more fortunately, the sun had gone behind a cloud, making the glitter in the carpet invisible.

'What have you done with the *bed*?' screeched my mother, as if Sam and I had personally carried it, iron bedstead, mattress and all, down the stairs and into the coal shed.

'Nothing,' we chorused.

I didn't want to let out the secret, but some explanation was obviously required.

'You're getting a new bed. It's a surprise from Daddy,' I admitted reluctantly.

'It certainly *is*,' said Mum, tight-lipped. 'Now just go away, you two, out from under my feet. Put that towel back in the airing cupboard, and that shirt'll have to be washed. If the glue doesn't come off it you'll be buying Daddy a new one from your pocket money. And who gave you permission to put on my necklaces and use my curling tongs? GO!'

Sam shot out of the room, but I lingered for a moment. 'But why can't we do our dance for you, Mummy?'

She flopped down on the vanity stool in front of her dressing table and fanned herself with a copy of the previous week's *Radio Times*, which she'd picked out of the waste-paper basket for that purpose.

'I'm sorry, love,' she said, making an effort. My mother always seemed to be apologizing to me. 'Maybe later, eh?'

I lost my temper. Hot tears of frustration burst out of my eyes and I stamped my foot on the magic carpet. 'You're always sorry, and you're always telling me to go away! Well one of these days I'll go and I won't come back! In fact, I'm going to go and live at the Grants. Mrs Grant never tells me to go away. In fact, I wish Mrs Grant was my mother instead of you. So there!'

I ripped off the necklaces and the gluey green shirt, just catching Mum's stricken, defeated look as I flounced out of the room.

Sam was waiting for me at the bottom of the stairs. 'Come on, Augenbrau, let's go to my place,' she said sympathetically, putting an arm around my neck as we went through the back gate towards the Prince of Wales.

Augenbrau was one of our many code names for one another. It was usually accompanied by sweeping a forefinger slowly across one's eyebrow while looking shiftily from right to left, and could be used in any language, although it sounded best in German. We already knew the word for 'eyebrow' in about six different languages.

Raking a glittery hand across my eyes and sniffing unattractively, I said in a tremulous voice, 'Where's the Hel-Sam Box? And how did you hide all the bits of felt and glue and stuff?'

'It's all in your room. I swept up most of the glitter with your mum's hairbrush,' Sam said sheepishly. 'As long as she doesn't want to do her hair until you've had a chance to clean the brush a bit, we should be all right.'

I smiled at her, ruefully giving the sign of the eyebrow to show my gratitude. 'Thanks. You're one hell of an eyebrow, girl.'

Arriving at the pub, we cut through the bar. Mr Grant looked up from wiping beer mugs to give us a cheery wave as we headed up the stairs. Dylan was sitting at the kitchen table when we arrived, leafing through the pages of *Shoot!* magazine and picking his nose. 'What's the matter with you then, fatso?' he said to me without looking up.

'Get lost, moron,' I retorted as we passed through the kitchen in search of Mrs Grant. She was in the living room, ironing shirts and dancing around to the Jacksons singing 'Never Can Say Goodbye' on the tinny transistor which dangled by its plastic handle from the doorknob. Fascinated, we watched her fluorescent polyester-clad hips shimmying to and fro, until she spotted us in the doorway and wiggled to a halt.

'Oh, hello girls! What are you up to?' she asked in a cheerful voice. Unlike my own mother, Mrs Grant always seemed to be in a good mood.

'Helena's had an argument with her mum because her dad's taken the bed and she wouldn't let us do our dance for her and she's all cross and Thinifer,' gabbled Sam.

'I can't do anything right. I don't think Mummy loves me,' I said dramatically, making my eyes tear up again with self pity.

Mrs Grant smiled faintly and propped the iron up on its base. She leaned across the ironing board to talk to me, the contours of her breasts puffing out sympathetically across its scorched surface. 'Listen, sweetheart. Your mummy loves you *very* much. I think she just gets tired a lot of the time, doesn't she?'

'But why?' I asked. '*You* don't.'

She laughed. 'Oh, I do. It goes with the territory. Maybe not quite as tired as your mummy, though. Just try and be a good girl for her. I think that's all you can do, really. She often doesn't feel well, and it's very hard to be jolly when you're poorly, isn't it?'

'But, Mum,' Sam joined in. 'Mrs Nicholls is really

scary when she's cross! Even more scary than the witch in *HR Pufnstuf*.'

Mrs Grant gave her a look, and picked up the iron again to attack a recalcitrant crease in one of Mr Grant's sleeves. 'Don't worry about it, Helena love. Why not do something extra nice for her later? Make her one of your super cards or something.'

'All right,' I said, feeling fobbed off. 'Thank you, Mrs Grant.'

'Oh, good gracious! How many times have I told you to call me Cynthia?'

Many times, it was true, but I just couldn't bring myself to call a parent by their Christian name. Somehow it didn't seem right. I loved that she always asked me to, though. It made me feel very grown up.

Just then a different song came on the radio. Mrs Grant immediately turned up the volume. 'Listen, girls, it's the "Wichita Lineman",' she said. 'I *love* Glen Campbell.'

Sam rolled her eyes and looked bored, but I began to listen. It was a bit confusing – Glen needed me more than wanted me, wanted me for all time, but what did that have to do with tennis?

'Um, Mrs Gra— erm, Cyth-nia, is Wichita like Wimbledon? You know, where they have the tennis tournaments?'

I pictured Glen as a lanky thirteen-year-old dressed in a purple shirt and green shorts, crouched at the side of a tennis court, poised to run out after stray balls. Perhaps he was in love with Billie Jean King, and that was who he was singing about, although he did sound a bit old to be a linesman.

Mrs Grant looked askance at me. 'I don't think so, poppet. It's just a place in the middle of America.'

It was no clearer to me than Root 66 had been three years earlier, but the tender sentiment of the song sent a sudden wave of emotion funnelling up inside me, and I began to cry again, for real this time.

Mrs Grant seemed concerned. 'Aaah. Come here, duckling, and give me a hug.'

She came out from behind the ironing board and gathered me into her arms, bracelets jingling. She smelled of Chanel No. 5. I knew this because Sam and I had often sneaked into her bedroom for an illicit squirt while she was working in the bar downstairs.

I buried my face in her generous bosom and wept. Right then, I really did wish she was my mother.

Ruby's Toes

'Toby,' I said next time he came in. 'Do you feel sorry for me?'

Toby looked surprised. 'Of course,' he replied.

'Well, I don't want your damn pity.' I looked away from him. I had the distinct feeling that he was rolling his eyes. At least he had two to roll.

'*You* feel sorry for yourself, don't you?' he said. 'I don't see why everyone else shouldn't, too. If you don't want me to visit you any more, just say so.'

We sat in huffy silence for a minute. Then he spoke again. 'Ruby said goodbye to all her toes this morning, individually, before they went into her socks.'

I was determined not to smile. What difference was that going to make to me? Perhaps it would be better for him not to come again. I had masses of work to do on my manuscript, and Mum's visits were more than enough distraction.

'Listen, Helena, I know what you mean. I get that, too, you know; that look in people's eyes when they talk to me: Oh, that poor poor man, wife in a coma and a toddler to look after. It's the same sort of thing, and it's a nightmare. But you've got to keep remembering that they do care, most of them, and are genuinely horrified that you're having to face some-thing so awful.'

My lip trembled. 'But what happens when I leave

here and go home? Then it's just going to be weeks of photographers trying to stick lenses in my face, jumping out at me from behind bushes, that kind of thing. The whole country is going to pity me. I don't think I can stand that.'

Toby reached over and picked up my hand. 'You're strong, Helena. You've got through so much. You can get over this, too. "Over This", right?'

I groaned. 'Over This' was the title of the song I'd written for Sam when she was first ill with leukaemia. It later became a huge hit for Blue Idea.

'You asked me about that song in your interview, didn't you?'

Toby laughed. 'Yeah. I was terrified you were going to break down and cry, or punch me or something, but you were strong then as well. I was really pleased it went so well. Best interview I ever did, actually.'

'Really?' I realized that he was stroking my hand in a, well, a *caressing* sort of way. The more I concentrated, the more sexual it felt, as he rubbed tiny circles and sweeping streaks up the inside of my thumb, and began to feel the little web of skin between each of my fingers. To my amazement I felt like I was getting pink in all kinds of places.

The door swung open and my mother appeared, hidden behind a large box and a bulging bag of fruit from Waitrose.

'I've brought in your juicer, Helena. Vitamin C is terribly good for the healing process, you know, and you don't get enough. That tiddly little glass of orange they give you at breakfast is just . . . oh!'

She nearly dropped the juicer when she saw Toby and me. I snatched my hand away immediately, but it was too late.

'*Hello*,' said Mum in a very Leslie Phillips voice, delight written all over her face. She strode purposefully towards Toby, in a manner not unlike a charging rhinoceros, and he shrank back slightly.

'Eve Nicholls, Helena's mother. And you are?'

Toby stood up manfully and shook her outstretched hand. 'Pleased to meet you, Mrs Nicholls, I'm Toby Middleton.'

'Well, I must say, Helena's kept you very quiet. Have you only just heard about her accident? Not that it matters now anyway, does it? The main thing is that you're here. So when did you two meet?'

I moaned. This day was getting worse by the minute. 'Mum, Toby's not my boyfriend. We met here, the other week, although we knew each other a bit from ages ago. His wife's in intensive care in a coma.'

Mum opted to cover up her embarrassment with censure. 'Oh, my Lord! So you're the guy whose poor, poor wife is unconscious. How dreadful for her. Well, we mustn't keep you, I'm sure she'll be wondering where you are. They do say that people in comas understand a lot more than we give them credit for, don't they?'

Toby looked at his watch. 'Actually, I came a little early to have a chat with Helena, so Kate won't be missing me yet, but I suppose I'd better be getting on. Very nice to meet you, Mrs Nicholls. I hope we meet again. Bye, Helena. See you tomorrow.'

I waved feebly, wondering how soon I could get Mum booked on a flight back to America. Really, enough was enough. Even though her visits were now down to an hour or two each day, her presence seemed to hover around me constantly, like a sort of knitting ectoplasm. It had been quite nice having her there at the beginning, but now she was bored rigid and worried about Dad at home on his own, and I just wanted to get on with my manuscript. We had spent more time together since the accident than in the whole of the last fifteen years, and the strain was beginning to tell on us both.

Mum began to unpack the juice extractor. 'It's too bad,' she said thoughtfully. 'He seemed so nice, but there he was, taking advantage of you in your vulnerable state and practically cheating on his poor comatose wife. Men! You watch yourself with that one, Helena.'

'Sunday Girl'
Blondie

My father was 'something important in computers', according to my mother, although she, like most other people in 1980, had only the haziest notion of what computers actually did. The company he worked for in Salisbury was owned by a giant American corporation, the top dogs of which had decided to reward him with a huge promotion and a sub-company of his own to run in Freehold, New Jersey. In the States.

'I'll have to talk it over with the family,' he'd said when he got the news. 'It's a very big step.'

He broke it to my mother at dinner that night as she was ladling out the macaroni cheese.

'No,' Mum said, 'absolutely not.' She slammed the plate down in front of him, and a yellow curl of macaroni detached itself and slid onto his lap.

I looked up, surprised. I hadn't even been listening to what he'd said, since I was planning in my head what to wear to Melanie Welling's fourteenth birthday party the following night. Melanie was a friend of ours from school, and her uncle was, allegedly, a member of Madness. Even more thrillingly, the word on the lacrosse field was that said uncle would be at the party.

'What?' I said, wondering if Mum would let me wear her Marks & Spencer pale-blue eye shadow. It had this really nice iridescence to it.

Dad repeated his news while scraping the macaroni off his trouser leg with his knife.

'NO!' I screamed, all thoughts of make-up and pop stars instantly flying out the window.

'You don't know what this means to me,' he pleaded.

Mum sat down very suddenly. 'Well, I know what it means to *me*, George. It means goodbye to all my friends, goodbye to my nice house, goodbye to Salisbury.'

I couldn't say anything further, terror had seized my throat and was holding it closed. I stared hard at the steaming bowl of peas in the centre of the table. Macaroni cheese and peas was my favourite meal, but I wasn't hungry any more.

'Eve, Helena, listen. We'll have an even nicer house, and you'll make new friends. And we'll have so much more money, I'm sure we'll be able to afford regular visits back here.'

'Forget it, I like this house and these friends. I'm sorry, George.'

And so the debate continued, pleas and retorts, back and forth to one another. I followed them with my eyes, rooting silently and fearfully for my mother, as if they were playing a tennis match on whose outcome my life depended. The steam from the untouched peas gradually dwindled to nothing, and they took on a dull, glazed appearance. They looked as shocked as I felt.

Eventually my mother's defences began to crumble. 'I do know how hard you've worked for this, George, really I do. How long did you say it would be for?'

With absolute horror I watched her edge towards capitulation.

'Five years firm, then contract renewable by mutual agreement.'

'Well, I suppose now is as good a time as any, before Helena starts her O levels. And it would be lovely to have a big comfortable house. How much more money did you say you'd get?'

I could almost see the dollar signs in my mother's eyes. It was as good as over. I pushed away my chair and stormed out of the room.

Two weeks later our house was on the market, I was enrolled by telephone in a totally foreign 'high' school – whatever that meant – and our airline tickets were booked. We were leaving in three weeks' time. Sam and I had not been out of each other's sight for more than a couple of hours since the bombshell dropped. We hated the world.

There were three removal men, all dressed in identical royal-blue boiler suits with their company logo on the breast pocket – 'Shipleys Ships Safely'. Huge sheets of off-white paper lay everywhere, and the sound of scrunching and heavy breathing hung in the air as the men wrapped, packed, lifted and carried.

Sam and I drifted despondently from room to room; as soon as the men had cleared enough space, we sat down back-to-back in the middle of the carpet, and remained there until that room had been emptied around us. And so on to the next room. I had to do this, otherwise I wouldn't have believed we were actually leaving. Up to this point I had not. It had been like a bad dream and I had closed my ears to all talk of real estate, junior and senior high schools, social security numbers and work visas. This was what made it real, seeing our possessions wrapped up and carried away, and much as I hated it, part of me realized it was important to accept it.

At first the removal men took our presence as a sign that we were interested in them and tried to engage us in friendly banter. When they were met with stony silence or abrupt monosyllables, they soon began to mutter about us being in the way. There was a young, jovial Irish man with huge ears, who glanced surreptitiously at Sam's legs more often than he probably should have done; a balding middle-aged barrel-chested man who sighed deeply every time he lifted up a box; and an officious grey-haired man with a clip-board, who was obviously the boss.

When they went outside for a tea break with their thermos flasks and Dunhill Extras, Sam picked up the clipboard and inspected the list attached to it, an inventory of the Nicholls family:

56 – Coffee Table (SITTING ROOM)
57 – Box assorted ornaments and vase (S. ROOM)
58 – Sofa (DITTO)
59 – Radio (DITTO)

Peering at this over her shoulder, I lifted the chewed stub of pencil dangling from the board by a grubby piece of frayed string, and with a couple of deft pencil strokes I changed the 57 to a 52, the 59 to a 69, and inserted an H between the S and I of 'SITTING ROOM'. Before the men returned, we hastily returned the clipboard to its resting place on top of a crate, sniggering guiltily.

I had been more rebellious of late, with Sam my willing partner, although we hadn't got into any serious trouble. My parents were not behaving ration-ally by taking me away from my home, this place I'd lived my whole life, so why should I?

But even though she seemed to be veering towards a Fattypuff period of lethargy and depression, my mother had been remarkably understanding about our little protestations. She didn't even say 'serves you right' when we stole Dad's razor from the bathroom, and I shaved off the bit of hair in front of my left ear – it grew back as a frighteningly bristly sideburn and I was deeply traumatized. All the same, I felt grateful that she'd never discovered us behind the garage, spluttering and coughing over a bent and creased-up Marlboro cigarette, which we'd finagled from the floor of the Prince of Wales one afternoon.

On moving day, however, Mum gave up trying to get us out from under the men's feet. She was too distracted, stage-managing Dad in getting everything finalized: the gas turned off, the fridge defrosted, the curtains unhooked.

Sam and I sat and watched more boxes go, stayed in the empty space for a while, moved to the next room, sat again. It was so strange seeing all the rooms with no furniture or pictures, like catching a shameful glimpse of somebody's father naked. Walls loomed down on us, blank and shabby-looking, with darker squares where paintings had hung.

Once all the rooms were empty, we sat side by side on the stairs.

'Are you sure you don't want to go round to Melanie's house for a bit?' Sam said. 'Bridget and Jo were going over this afternoon to look at the programme from The Specials concert Mel went to with her brother.'

'No thanks,' I said crossly. 'I've already said goodbye to them. This is hard enough as it is.'

'Funny how Melanie's uncle turned out not to be in Madness at all, wasn't it?' said Sam.

'Mmm. Not much of a surprise, though. She's such a fibber. Good fun, but . . .'

I paused, thinking of my other schoolfriends, the ones who Sam would now inevitably get much closer to. I found I didn't wish to talk about them any more.

'Don't forget about me, will you?' I said abruptly.

My father came down the hallway, carrying golf clubs. 'Not getting in the way I hope, are you girls? Helena, don't you have things to do?'

'No. My case is all packed. We're not in the way.'

'Jolly good, jolly good. Almost time for lunch,' he muttered absently. 'Now, where did I put my nine iron?'

Sam patted my shoulder, waiting till Dad had gone before answering me. 'Don't be daft. How could I possibly forget my best friend?'

We sat in silence again, both of us choked.

'Are you still all right about me keeping the Hel-Sam box?' Sam asked eventually.

'S'pose so. It's a good thing there isn't much in there yet. You'll need the space to keep all my letters.'

'But where are you going to put *my* letters to *you*?' Sam wailed and suddenly burst into tears. I couldn't comfort her.

Mum called us down for lunch: cheese and pickle sandwiches, Marks & Spencer's pork pies, a six-pack of crisps and orange squash. We had to eat in the garden off paper plates because everything had gone from the kitchen and dining room. Sam and I lolled on a hairy tartan travel rug, sniffling and flicking ants off each other's thighs, while my parents sat on sherbet-striped picnic chairs.

Mum and Dad had linked fingers with each other across the red plastic arms of their chairs and were eating with their free outside hands. Emotions were beginning to run high all round.

'Oh, George,' said my mother, surveying her rose bushes, 'I'll miss this garden so much.' There was a quiver in her voice, so she took a hasty slurp of squash out of a plastic cup to hide it.

'Our new house will have a lovely garden, too, you'll see. We might even be able to afford someone to come in and mow the lawn,' said Dad soothingly, squeezing her hand.

'They don't call them gardens in America. They call them yards,' Sam mused, thickly.

I was irritated. 'Well, that's ridiculous! How can a yard have grass and flowers and stuff? A yard is concrete!'

'Don't yell at me. It's not my fault. I'm just telling you,' Sam snapped back.

'I wasn't yelling. I just don't think it makes sense.'

'Girls! Simmer down.' My mother had recovered her composure. 'If you've finished your lunch, throw your plates and cups in the outside bin.'

'Can I go over and say goodbye to the Grants please?'

'Yes, dear, if you've packed. We have to leave in about an hour, so don't be long.'

An hour! I couldn't bear it. I trailed miserably down the garden path behind Sam, who was neatly rolling up her paper plate and stuffing it into her cup. I looked around the garden, at the wiry grass creeping up between the paving stones, the apple tree, the little pond. I knew I'd miss it as much as my mother would. A sparrow hopped across the lawn in front of me. Did they have sparrows in America? I wondered, already nostalgic.

Sam turned round when she reached the gate. 'Come on, hurry up, Augenbrau,' she said. 'I've got a present for you.'

'Here,' she said, once we were in her bedroom at the pub. She thrust an album at me: Blondie's *Parallel Lines*.

I took it, speechless for a moment. 'Sam, not your Blondie record! That's your favourite.'

'I want you to have it,' she said bravely. 'I want you to have something of mine that I really, really like, because that makes it a better present.'

'Thanks,' I said, thinking fast. 'I've got something for you, too.'

I undid the seed-pearl necklace Mum and Dad had given me for my twelfth birthday and put it round Sam's neck.

'This is for you, because it looks like the one Debbie Harry's wearing on the record sleeve. If you put it on with your mum's white petticoat, those high-heeled slippers of hers and a little bandage tied round the middle of your arm, you'll look the spit of her. Well, at least you would if you had blond hair.'

Sam was touched and awestruck, by both the gift and the comparison. We were both desperate to have eyes as incredible and cheekbones as pointy as Debbie's.

'Really? Your necklace? Didn't your parents give you that?'

'Yes,' I said nobly. 'But, like you said, it's the more personal things that make the best presents. Just don't wear it when you come and stay with me in America. Have we got time to listen to the record once more?'

I went over to the stereo and plopped the album onto the turntable. Sam's record player was the coolest I'd ever seen; it played both sides of an LP without you having to get up and turn it over manually. Its needle was on an arm which, when the A side finished, skimmed across the surface of the vinyl, turned a laborious and creaky 180-degree angle and played the B side upside down.

So we closed an era with *Parallel Lines*, summoning up the emotional reserves to dance around Sam's bedroom for one last time in a new-wave, imaginary-microphone rite of passage. But we were just going through the motions; it wasn't any fun.

'Do you really think I look like Blondie?' asked Sam, as we pouted half-heartedly in front of the mirror to 'Sunday Girl'.

'I've told you before, Sam, Blondie's the band, not the singer. And yes, you could pass as her little sister.'

I sighed. Much as I too wanted to look like Debbie, I knew that in reality I bore a closer resemblance to Ermintrude from *The Magic Roundabout*. I wasn't at all sure if I even possessed cheekbones.

Sam picked up on my train of thought. 'You know what? If your hair was a bit longer, I think you'd look quite a lot like Kate Bush,' she remarked kindly.

Cynthia knocked on the bedroom door. 'Helena, your mother just telephoned. She asked me to tell you to come home straight away. The taxi's on its way.'

Sam turned off the record in the middle of 'Sunday Girl', and I felt as if all the music in the world had stopped for ever. I had a sudden childish desire to run into Sam's wardrobe and hide there amongst all her clothes, clothes which weren't being ripped off their hangers and crushed into packing cases to be carried halfway round the world. All the blouses I'd

90

borrowed; all the jeans I couldn't fit into. Her Olivia Newton-John nightie, which was so staticky that it could power a small generator; the shirt she'd worn when Martin Trubshaw tried to kiss her; the school skirt with the wonky hem, which we'd taken up ourselves; the thick bottle-green gym knickers she'd still have to endure and I wouldn't. I thought I'd even miss those hideous knickers. I felt myself crumple up from the inside.

Mrs Grant hugged me, stroking my hair and pinching my cheek gently, as if I were six years old. 'Oh, Helena love! What are we going to do without you? Sam is going to be a right old misery guts, I bet. Sam, please tell me you won't start moping around here, sulking all day, like that brother of yours.'

Sam managed a wavery smile and made a face.

'Don't worry, girls, a little ocean between you won't ruin your friendship. It would take a lot more than that. I wouldn't mind betting you'll be back before you know it, Helena. You'll keep in touch, and time will fly by, you'll see.'

'Thank you, erm, C-C-C-Cynthia.' As usual, her name wouldn't come out without a struggle, and I felt foolish and emotional.

Sam took my hand and we all walked back downstairs in silence.

Mrs Grant gave me a final hug and kiss at the door. 'Well, I'd better get back to the bottling up. Mind how you go, sweetheart, and we'll see you *soon*, OK.'

Mr Grant flapped his tea towel at me and said, 'Look after yourself, love. Keep in touch,' to which I responded with a tiny smile and a sad little wave. I couldn't remember ever feeling this bad in my life.

Back at the house everything was gone. Only our bulging suitcases sat in the hallway, lined up like fat policemen on parade. My mother was leaning exhaustedly against the kitchen counter, peering into an open compact, primping up her hair and powdering her nose.

'Oh good, there you are, Helena. I think we're almost ready, so you and Sam should say your farewells. The taxi's here now, so make it as quick as you can, dear. Heavens, look at me. I'm worn out! This moving business certainly is tiring.' She snapped the compact shut and put it back into her cavernous patent-leather handbag.

Sam and I went upstairs, to the room that had been my bedroom since I'd been a baby, and which would probably be some other girl's bedroom within the next couple of months. We sat down cross-legged in the middle of the floor, and I stared at the faint blu-tack marks on the wall where my John Travolta posters had been stuck.

The wallpaper in my room was comprised of thousands of tiny air-filled pockets, as though the walls were papered with yellow-painted bubblewrap. I used to deflate the pockets by pressing them with my fingertips; the wall all around where my pillow had been, in the radius of a child's arm's length, was an inverted sweep of pressed-in paper bubbles, like grass that's been flattened after being picnicked on. I had a sudden urge to pop a few last ones for old times' sake.

Neither of us could speak for a while. 'Don't forget me, either, will you,' Sam said eventually.

The hinges of my jaw were aching so painfully from the effort of not crying that I could hardly reply. 'Now you're being daft.' I had a sudden thought. 'Do you think we're too old to cut our thumbs and mingle our blood in a friendship pact or something?'

'Yeah,' said Sam, wrinkling up her nose. 'Definitely too old. Besides, it would *hurt*.'

I was relieved. I hadn't much liked the idea, either, but it seemed appropriate. 'OK. Well, I'll write to you all the time, and we'll see each other for holidays, and . . .'

My voice cracked and I couldn't hold back the sobs any longer. This set Sam off again, too, and we wrapped our arms around each other, rocking back and forth in our misery. We were interrupted by my mother's heavy tread on the stairs.

'Oh, you poor dears,' she said when she saw us. 'I'm sorry. We really have to go now.' She came over and knelt down beside us, putting an arm around each of our shoulders. I breathed in her distinctive smell: lipstick and wool. Sam rested her head against Mum and cried even harder. She let us stay like that for another minute or so, then pulled a pack of paper tissues from her pocket, giving us one each.

'Come on now, have a good blow. This isn't easy for any of us,' she said, standing up and pulling us gently to our feet. We blew our noses, wiped the tears off our faces and traipsed reluctantly out of the house.

Dad was in the front garden, smoking a pipe, having finished loading the cases into the boot of the taxi. He came over and gave Sam a hug when we appeared at the door, which prompted fresh floods. The taxi driver, elbow out of the window, drummed his fingers impatiently on the roof of his car as Mum fussed around with keys and passports and plane tickets.

Finally we were all set, and Mum and I climbed into the back seat of the car, Dad in the front. Sam was standing on the bottom bar of the iron front gate, swinging backwards and forwards, crying.

As the taxi pulled away, I twisted round to look at her out of the window. She raised a forefinger to her face and traced her eyebrow with it. 'You're one helluvan eyebrow, girl!' she yelled suddenly.

The car turned the corner at the end of our street and she disappeared from view.

My mother looked at me, a puzzled expression on her face. 'One hell of a *what*, did she say?'

I wept ceaselessly all the way up the M3, all the way through dinner that night in a hotel near Heathrow Airport and halfway across the Atlantic the next day.

Friends

Toby came to see me again the next day, carrying two styrofoam cups of tea.

'I checked the coast was clear. Want to come and sit in the garden?' He offered me his forearm.

I was relieved to see him. 'God, I thought you might not dare to come back after meeting my mother. I'm really sorry about that, by the way.'

'Oh, don't worry, your mother's fine. It's you I'm scared of. Are you coming then, or what?'

I laughed, and then stopped, not entirely sure that he was joking. 'OK. Let me just get my disguise on first.'

I donned my dark glasses and a long blond wig, which I'd made Mum bring in from home. It was an Abba wig from a fancy-dress party Sam and I had gone to years ago; she'd worn the matching brunette wig. I wondered what had happened to it.

Toby chuckled when he saw me.

'Wow! "Voulez-Vous"?'

Yes, please, I thought. 'How did you know it's from an Abba costume?' I said instead.

'Come on, all straight blond wigs are Abba wigs, aren't they?'

We walked slowly along the corridor and took the lift up to the hospital's little roof garden. It was lovely to see nothing but shrubs and sky, and to feel warm air on my stitches.

'Is your mum always that . . . erm . . . keen to meet your friends?' Toby asked as we sat down on a wooden bench.

'Basically, yes; the male ones, anyway. She's just desperate to get me hitched. She's already hopeful that I'll get something together with the physio, the shrink or the surgeon. It's so embarrassing.'

'Don't worry,' Toby said. 'Mothers will be mothers. So haven't you ever been married?'

I took a slurp of tea. 'No. I almost came close to it, quite recently, actually, but thank God I saw the light. Vinnie was a serial-philandering, commitment-phobic, dishonest asshole.'

Toby laughed. 'So you're obviously still fond of him, then.'

I managed a smile, a rare reaction to the mention of Vinnie's name, but I didn't want Toby to think I was a freak for never having been married. 'I know, mad, isn't it. I picked a right dud. Of course I had loads of, like, casual boyfriends and stuff, when I was in the band – no shortage of offers – but we were on the road for so long it seemed a bit pointless having long-distance relationships. We just had no time to ourselves. And men did sometimes try to take advantage. I suppose I never really wised up to their little tricks.'

I trailed off awkwardly, but Toby didn't seem to mind me slagging off his gender. I changed the subject. 'How long have you been married, then?'

'Five years,' Toby replied. 'We were together for four years before that, too.'

'So Kate wasn't the girl you were with when we met before, after that interview?' I asked cautiously, remembering the silly slapper who'd been all over Justin.

Toby laughed hollowly. 'Thank God, no. That was Lorraine. My first nightmare relationship.'

'What happened?' I wondered if 'first nightmare relationship' meant 'first of many nightmares' or 'first relationship, which just happened to be a nightmare'.

'I bought a flat so we could live together. It was a lot more than I could afford, but she insisted we got it and said she'd pay a third of the mortgage. To cut a long story short, I ended up paying for everything because she said she was skint. Next thing, she announced she'd saved up two thousand pounds and was off to New York on holiday without me.'

I was appalled. 'That's outrageous!'

'Yeah, I suppose it was,' said Toby glumly. 'Plus it turned out she was having an affair, although by the time I finally kicked her out, I didn't even care. I just wanted rid of her. But it was fine in the end, because I met Kate quite soon afterwards.'

I felt a pang in my chest at the mention of his wife. Suddenly I didn't want to hear any more about Toby's love life.

'Toby?'

'Yeah?'

'Do you have many, you know, friends?'

Toby considered the question. A sparrow hopped onto a nearby tub of crocuses and watched us suspiciously.

'Well, not really. It sounds weird, but Ruby's my best friend, and she's two. And Kate, of course. The pair of them were enough for me, in the friends department. I have a good mate called Bill, who was my best man, and a couple of university friends I see occasionally, and that's about it. Kate's much more sociable than me. That's why I'm here now, actually; there are two of her art-school buddies in with her and it was getting a bit crowded.'

Nice, I thought. Glad that I could provide a bit of back-up entertainment to pass the time. I'd been sort of hoping that he might include me in his list of friends.

'What about you?' Toby asked. 'You've got tons of cards in your room, I bet you're really popular.'

I snorted. 'Oh yeah, and my room's overflowing with

visitors – *not*. Apart from my mother, who doesn't count. What does that tell you?'

Toby looked me in the eye. 'It tells me that you and Sam were so close, and you were so tied up with the band from such a young age, that you might not have had the time or the inclination to make any other friends, and now maybe you're regretting it.'

I stood up, suddenly annoyed. Bloody Toby and his bloody perfect life – well, I never said I was rational. 'I don't need the amateur psychology, thanks. I get enough of that from the psychotherapist, and he's a waste of space. Anyway, I'm a bit tired now, so I think I'll get back to my room. Maybe see you around, if you've got the time.'

'Ruby'll be here tomorrow, too. I'd like to bring her in, if you don't mind.'

I shrugged and walked away, back into the hospital building. As I pressed the button to summon the lift, a blurry reflection in the metal doors loomed up behind me. Toby had followed me. He dropped our two unfinished cups of tea into a nearby bin with a soft slosh, reached out his hand and gently squeezed my fingers.

'See you tomorrow, then,' he said, leaning forward and kissing me very tenderly on the lips. I was ashamed at his proximity to my mangled features, but the sweetness of his kiss was too tempting, and like a reflex I put my hand up behind his head, pulling him closer. Everything about him was so inviting, as he roped me in, first with the coil of his curls and then with the warmth of his tongue gently touching mine, coaxing my poor traumatized nerve endings out of retirement. I felt like the stillborn puppy in *101 Dalmatians* being rubbed back to life, poking his tiny nose out of a towel, blinking sleepily at the world.

The kiss went on for a long time, our bodies being pressed closer and closer together, until Toby affectionately and absently rubbed his nose against my broken one.

'YEOUCH!' I screeched, leaping away from him,

clutching my nose in both hands. My wig got knocked over one ear and my glasses went flying, exposing the dressing on my left eye socket.

Toby jumped with fright and backed up against the lift doors, palms flat behind him, as if I'd pulled a knife on him. Then he recovered himself and rushed over to me, picking up my shades and straightening my wig.

'Helena, God, I'm so sorry! I got so carried away I totally forgot about your poor nose. Are you OK?'

I nodded mutely, doubled over, my remaining eye watering with pain. It was true to say that the moment was lost.

The lift eventually rattled up to the top floor, the doors wheezed open and I staggered in, reeling. Toby followed, white with remorse, incapable of doing anything except pat my shoulder manfully, as if we were business colleagues at a golfing lunch.

We descended in silence to the second floor, where I got out. 'Off you go to see your wife, then,' was my mumbled parting shot. But once my nose had stopped hurting, I relived that kiss over and over again, so much so that I clean forgot to do any writing that day.

'Sitting In Limbo'
Jimmy Cliff

We moved into our new American house. It was made
of wooden planks, with screen doors, a huge verandah
with a swinging love seat and a mind-boggling
selection of numbers in its address. We had a free-
standing mailbox instead of a slot in the front door. We
had a dishwasher, garbage disposal, a barbecue, a
coffee machine and a video recorder with a remote
control on the end of a long cable. I had never seen any
of these things before, not even at the Grants, but I still
preferred our old brick terraced house in Salisbury
with its yellow front door.

Mum got her huge 'yard', complete with an even
bigger set of rosebushes. She quickly introduced herself to everybody on our block, and before long she
was hosting canasta parties and doing charitable
works, when her health permitted it. Dad, well, I
wasn't exactly sure what he did, but he seemed quite
happy doing it every weekday and then coming home
for a large Gordon's and tonic.

I went to school, and instead of being in the third
year at grammar school, I became a grown-up tenth-
grader, going in a year ahead of my age because of
when my birthday fell and my good reports from the
UK. I did well at school – I had no other distractions,
and anyway, everything was so different that I had to
give it my full attention. I'd never heard of trick or

99

treating or show and tell, and I had no idea why you shouldn't wear white trousers after Labor Day, who 98 per cent of the American presidents had been, what a soda fountain was, or where the Adirondacks were. In my adolescent *Weltschmerz* I decided that I didn't really get the point of America.

17 September 1980

Dear Mas Tnarg (Pig Dealer and Donkey Buyer),

Going to school here is still very weird. Everyone has lockers and there are no pegs. We don't play lacrosse or netball; it's all stuff like 'track' – running – and tennis and basketball, which is sort of like netball, except you can run with the ball.

I don't understand what the girls in my class are talking about most of the time; they're always huddled in corners, whispering about boys I don't know, bands I haven't heard of and TV stars I don't recognize. So mostly I just keep my head down and concentrate on the lessons, which are easy. I'm getting more As here than I ever did at South Wilts!

So no, I haven't really made any friends yet. It's too hard. I don't have anything in common with any of them, and I think they think I'm a snob because I don't talk to them. They think I'm weird, too, because of my accent and clothes, and because I didn't know what Reeses Pieces are – turns out they're revolting little chocolate things with peanut butter inside. Puke.

I miss you so much. I miss your mum and dad, and the pub, and Melanie and Bridge and Jo. I even miss Dylan sometimes . . . but not very often! I bet I'll never get a boyfriend. The boys here all seem to like girls who are cheerleaders. I'm not sure what cheerleaders do, except that there's a lot of ra-ra-ra-ing and shaking big pom-poms and wearing very short skirts.

I want to come home for Christmas, but I don't think Mum and Dad will let me. Mum's gone full-on Fattypuff and hasn't been out for ages. She keeps on at me to 'join a club' or 'do some sports' – me!? – but there's no way. I spend enough time at that stupid school every day, why would I want to spend more?

Dad bought a new car. It's called a Lincoln Towncar, but I keep calling it a Lincoln Townhouse, and it gets on his nerves.

Here's another quote for you. Send more back, although I don't understand what 'Don't say mattress to Mr Lambert' means. Is it from Monty Python? This is my new favourite: 'She came home and sewed on the verandah.' I did try to draw you a picture of it, you know, but when I'd finished it looked more like a picture of a woman with a horse trough stuck to her leg, so I decided not to send it.

Anyway, I'm writing this in a 'math' class, so I'd better go. Please say thanks to Melanie for her postcard. I'll write back soon. Don't tell her I was taking the mickey, but this is what her card said, 'Hiya, Helena, How be you these days. OK yah, I hope. Well, life is extremely boring isn't it, *nein*? Anyway, I can't even think of anything to say, so until another day, bye for now, Melanie'!

Lots of love,
Helena xxx

PS. The best thing about living here is yard sales. They're like jumble sales but in people's front gardens. Yes, you were right, they are called yards. I bought a brilliant record last month; it's reggae and it's called *The Harder They Come*, by lots of different bands. I didn't know what it was when I bought it, I just liked the cover, but it's fab. I'll tape it for you. The best track is called 'Sitting In Limbo'. xx

I knew I should have made more of an effort to fit in at school, but I felt so resentful. I'd had a social life in Salisbury. Sam and I had other friends; we were just beginning to get invited to the right parties and be noticed by the right people. But now, for me, that was all gone. It gave me a depressing, guilty satisfaction to see my mother's face as I slouched in after school every day, grabbed a drink and headed straight up to my bedroom to write to Sam and listen to records.

101

Life seemed grey, endless, boring. Most of the time I felt like a supermarket trolley lying in a ditch, one wheel spinning uselessly round and round. The movie soundtrack *The Harder They Come* was beginning to become an obsession, though. I felt it kept me sane. I played it over and over again, endlessly, particularly the mellow Jimmy Cliff track 'Sitting In Limbo', which was the least reggae-ish of the tracks, but the loveliest. It had this gorgeous trickling keyboard sound, which was like water running over stones, I thought perhaps in the River of Babylon.

After listening to that Jimmy Cliff track about 400 times the words had imprinted themselves onto my soul, and they bothered me.

'And I know that my faith will lead me on'. I, too, was sitting in limbo, but I didn't have anything to lead me on. I began to spend more and more time wondering what it was to have faith, until one day something happened, and I found out.

Sam and I continued to send each other long, heart-rending letters about how we hated our lives apart, and how we were saving up to move to London together and become famous actresses. One school lunch hour, as I was composing one of these missives in the library, a tubby eleventh-grader with frizzy brown hair and hippy sandals came up to me.

'You're Helena, aren't you?' she said.

I nodded, taking in both her cool batik shoulder bag and her rather horrible nylon flared skirt.

'I'm Margie. I live on the next block from you. Your mom talked to mine at the grocery store the other day and told her how lonely you are here.'

I blushed and looked at the floor, making a mental note to kill my mother.

'Well listen, if you'd like to meet some cool kids, some friends and I have a kind of study group every Wednesday. We hang out at my place and listen to Carole King and chat. Why don't you come along next time? Six o'clock at 1114 Connecticut

Street. It would be, like, totally rad if you could make it!'

It took me so long to get round the 'totally rad' bit that I didn't properly take in the fact that I'd been invited somewhere. Then I was delighted and terrified in equal measures.

That Wednesday, after school, I spent ages putting on black eyeliner and backcombing my hair into a fashionable bird's nest. I carefully put on my smart black pinstriped jacket – half of a man's suit which I'd found in a thrift shop – and black tube skirt, with a turquoise shirt and a long string of white plastic beads knotted around my neck to complete the ensemble. As I dressed, constantly and critically looking at my reflection in the mirror on the back of my bedroom door, I worried nervously about whether there would be either alcohol or boys at this soirée.

At six ten – fashionably late – I rang the door chimes of 1114, wishing Sam was with me. I could already hear strains of 'It's Too Late' wafting out into the hallway and under the front door, and I took this to be a good sign.

Margie let me in. She took a brief startled look at my panda eyes. 'Oh, wow, you look . . . great! Come on in and meet the gang.'

I followed her through to the living room, where seven or eight older kids from school were sitting on the shiny three-piece suite or the violent orange hairball-swirled carpet. Although I'd never spoken to any of them before, I knew immediately, and with a sinking heart, that most of them were very definitely what Sam and I would call prats.

'Hey, everybody, this is Helena. She just moved here from Great Britain! Helena, this is Simon, Randy, Bethany, Mary-Ellen, Rich, Sue and Susie.'

'Hello,' I said unhappily. I observed them all looking nonplussed at my party clothes.

'Have a seat, Helena. We won't bug you with questions about who Prince Charles is dating until later. We're about to start.'

103

I sat down on the edge of a small flip-up chair with a feeling of dread. My fears were confirmed when suddenly lots of pale-green hardback books appeared and Carole King was turned down to an inaudible hum.

'Bethany, why don't you start today?' said Margie.

Bethany flipped open her Bible, for, of course, that was what it was, and announced dramatically, 'Psalm 121!'

I was frozen to my chair with horror and embarrassment, feeling as if the black kohl circles around my eyes were spreading across my face until I was sure I looked like a coal miner in drag. Resentful thoughts spun round in my head as Bethany's strong voice rang on for what seemed like hours. I had changed my mind; Jimmy Cliff could *keep* his faith, although I bet he'd never had to sit around with nerds like this lot. It seemed to me that a much nicer way to Find God would be by hanging out with Jimmy, Toots and the Maytals and Desmond Dekker. Was Jah the same as Jesus, anyway?

Then Mary-Ellen took over. The lilt and cadences of her voice were softer than Bethany's, and her emotive intonation of the ancient verses somehow made it easier for me to listen. After a while I began to feel drawn in by it. The words were soothing, justly measured and poured as though from a jug of something thick and comforting. I had a sudden image of my mother stroking the damp hair back from my flushed forehead once when I'd had flu.

The other kids still seemed dweeby to me, but by the end of that oddly peaceful evening, I felt as if I'd 'got it', and that particular 'it' was something I might need. After some earnest discussion of the psalms' meanings and merits, in which I declined to participate, a glass of lemonade and the B side of 'Tapestry', I left, agreeing to come to their church that Sunday, and thinking I would rather die than admit to anyone what I'd just done.

I certainly couldn't bring myself to tell my parents. On Sunday morning I just slipped out of the house, knowing that they probably wouldn't even realize I'd gone. I'd passed the church many times before without really noticing it; it was one of those modern, bland-looking red-brick buildings with an abstract swirl of stained glass above the front doors and a handkerchief of grass on either side of the path from the sidewalk.

I skulked around outside for a few minutes, my qualms getting worse. Two chirpy ladies in loud hats clutching, respectively, a sheaf of service sheets and a stack of hymn books spotted me and pounced enthusiastically.

'Come in, come in! Welcome to our church. We haven't seen you before, have we? Well, I'm sure you'll enjoy our lovely service. My name is Thelma and this is Veronica. What's your name? Please don't forget to fill out a visitor's slip, which you'll find at the end of your pew, and here, let me pin this nice pink ribbon on your lapel so we all know you're a newcomer!'

I thought I might throw up. There may as well have been a large neon arrow pointing at my head, flashing the words 'HEATHEN FOREIGN STRANGER'. I wanted to go home, but the ribbon on my jacket bound me to the place like a prisoner's ID number tattooed on his arm. It would have seemed churlish to undo the pin, throw down the ribbon and just leave. I stood in the entry porch and dithered, arms full of a church-goer's paraphernalia, unable either to walk out or go inside.

At that moment, Mary-Ellen and Randy arrived and rescued me. 'Helena, hi! Glad you could make it. Come sit with us.'

I smiled, semi-gratefully, and allowed myself to be swept inside and up the aisle to a pew, worryingly close to the front of the church. It was nice not to be the lone outsider any more, but I would still rather have lurked in a distant corner at the back by the doors for easy escape.

I stared at my selection of hymn books, prayer books and pamphlets. Mary-Ellen and Randy were on their knees next to me, and as I couldn't quite make myself join them, I acted busy by looking up all the hymns advertised for the service. They were posted on the wall, magnetic numbers stuck onto a nasty white board. This didn't take very long, so I watched a jolly girl guitarist strumming gently at the front of the congregation. She wasn't playing 'Kumbaya', but she might as well have been.

After a few more minutes the choir – mostly women, large and red-cassocked – and priest wandered in, and the service opened with a lusty rendition of 'Amazing Grace'. So far so good, although it was strange to me that the choir just sat on chairs in front of the congregation, instead of being tucked away in choir stalls out of sight. There was no organ, just a tinny upright piano and a couple of guitars. I didn't like the modernity of the whole set-up. It seemed to me that a church wasn't a proper church unless it was ancient and had a high altar, a corrugation of stout organ pipes running up the wall, tombstones under the floor and a lot of processing around with banners and so on. Where I came from the hymns were posted on an old wooden tablet, probably similar in shape to the one Moses had brought down the mountain, with big wooden squares with numbers on them slotted into grooves in the tablet. None of this white plastic and Velcro. In combination with the pine pews and wooden floors, the ambience seemed too lightweight for any serious spiritual conviction.

The service proceeded not too scarily, the usual prayers and announcements and exhortations. There seemed to be a constant stream of people trailing up the aisle to read biblical chunks from the podium at the front. As their heights were invariably different, each one had to readjust the microphone before they spoke, and every time, the readings would be preceded by squawks of feedback, and often a thud or two as the reader's chin or forehead connected heavily with the unwieldy mic stand as they wrestled with it.

The minister himself was mild, unassuming and youngish; a stigmata of acne scars on his cheeks undermining his dubious authority. I thought he looked more like an accountant or a science teacher than a man of the cloth. He was skinny and appeared rather nervous as he guided his flock through the service.

I was getting slightly bored. We were half an hour in and I didn't feel at all spiritual. I looked around some more, at the high exposed brick walls with their trendy woven wall hangings spaced evenly every fifteen feet or so. Actually, these were very pretty, imaginatively designed depictions of harvest festivals, loaves and fishes, Noah's Ark, the Garden of Eden, or embroidered announcements like 'Jesus Saves!' and 'The Light of the World'. The colours were bold and unfaded, and the pictures abstract and artistic enough to be interesting as well as aesthetically appealing. I was sure I'd seen the same tapestries in other churches.

I wondered idly if there was a book of *Church Wall Hanging Patterns for Beginners* in existence, over which the ladies of the Women's Institute worldwide pored painstakingly. Or maybe you could just buy the finished product by mail order, or perhaps by phone: 'Hmm, I'll take one "St Paul on the Road to Damascus" in plum and gold, and' – flipping through the pages – 'a "Jesus Walking on the Water" – the turquoise and aquamarine, not the silver. One hundred and fifty dollars plus postage and packing? OK, here's my American Express number . . .'

A ripple of excitement passed through the congregation and brought my wandering mind back to the service. The minister was introducing today's guest preacher, who was striding up to the podium as he spoke. I didn't catch his name as I was too busy studying his wide snappy suit, ruddy face, the oversized

Bible he was holding like a shield in front of him and his thick, plastered-down hair, the exact same pale grey-blond as Kim Novak's eyebrows in *Vertigo*, which I'd seen on television the night before. He fitted much better the picture I had in my mind of an American preacher. He thanked the junior accountant and launched into his sermon in the big, booming voice I would have expected, which had no need of the troublesome microphone.

Something strange happened to me during his sermon. It was as though he was a wizard who'd cast a spell on me, and I was enthralled and awe-struck. He launched into a story about a young boy with church-going friends, who scoffed at religion and laughed at their devotion. 'I don't have time for this stuff now,' the boy had said. 'There's far too much to do. I have to ride my bike and watch TV and build model airplanes; I don't want to be stuck in some boring old church. No, there'll be plenty of time for that later, when I'm grown up. God can wait.' But, the very next day the boy was run over and killed by a truck when he was out riding his bicycle.

'*The–Very–Next–Day*,' said the preacher, loudly and ominously, staring ferociously at each member of the congregation in turn. He stared at me for so long I nearly fainted. A mulberry blush enveloped me, not just sweeping to the roots of my hair, but crawling inside my nostrils and eardrums, too.

'That boy did not have plenty of time. He found out to his cost that you cannot ignore Jesus, you CANNOT turn your back on Him. He loves you, like no human ever could or will. You must not snub Him. God alone knows when your time will come to face Him and repent, but you do not. So you must not be like this foolish boy, you must repent now!'

I was literally on the edge of my seat, freaked out and sweating, but absolutely hooked. Randy and Mary-Ellen next to me seemed riveted, too, but less anxiously so. I supposed they didn't have anything to worry about. They were well in there already. A combination of fear and exhilaration sent adrenalin coursing through my body. I had never felt like this before. How could I have been so lax, so dumb as to ignore the one who cared so deeply about me, who loved me unconditionally for who I was? I had only one chance to prove myself worthy of His love, and this was it. The preacher's voice got louder and his face redder.

'Jesus WANTS you!' he yelled, pounding the podium with his fist. I imagined myself with a glow surrounding me, holding Jesus's hand and looking into His eyes; Jesus smiles at me sadly but with ineffable love. Suddenly everything else in my little world seemed unimportant – the pain of separation from Sam, what people thought of me, how I hated my body – none of it mattered in the slightest any more.

'Who has the courage to take this first step? Who will hand their life over to Jesus before it's too late? Who will admit they were wrong? Who among you will change your path to the path leading to Heaven? Right here, right now. Remember, you don't have the time you thought you did! *This is the most important thing you will ever do . . .*'

To my amazement my hand shot up into the air, uncontrolled, like a hiccup. I couldn't stop myself; I didn't want to stop. I stood up, glancing briefly back at the sea of faces behind me, but not taking them in. I was crying and shaking, but proud of myself. Someone appeared from nowhere and guided me out of my pew and up the aisle to the front. The preacher put his hand heavily on the top of my head and said, 'Bless you, child,' and I felt the tiny click of his chunky signet ring against my scalp, like the first tap of a teaspoon on the shell of a boiled egg.

Then I was led away to a quiet room off to the side. I was dimly aware of others following me, each with their own guide. There was a middle-aged man in a golf sweater, another girl of about my age who was also crying and a sheepish-looking teenage boy. We all knelt and prayed together for forgiveness and redemption. I felt like the miserable sinner that I was, but I knew I had been saved. It felt like a very lucky escape. I promised then and there to be a virgin until I got married, that God would be my only love until that time.

The preacher came in and prayed with us. He was sweating heavily and his pale helmet of hair seemed as if it had been injected with air; it now looked bouffant and alive from his evangelical exertions. He blessed us each again and gave us a tiny metallic cross pin, which I pinned next to my visitor's pink ribbon. Then we were led back to our seats, accompanied by strains of the guitarist, who had struck up again. It felt like the part in a wedding where the bride and groom and their family went off somewhere to sign the bridal register, and the rest of the congregation sat and whispered to each other while a jowly soprano quavered out a tune to keep everyone from getting bored.

I didn't know what had hit me. I felt overwhelmed, as if there was a new and worthy person inside my body. Mary-Ellen squeezed my arm when I returned. 'Welcome, Helena. Congratulations,' she said, and Randy whispered 'Praise the Lord' into my other ear. We all stood up to sing the final hymn, a modern happy-clappy number. I wasn't even embarrassed when everybody put their hands in the air and a few people called out, 'Thank yew, Jeesus!'

The service was over. I shakily filled out the visitor's form at the end of the pew, and walked back down the aisle with Randy and Mary-Ellen. Strangers congratulated me all the way, smiling and clapping me on the shoulder. I felt proud and self-righteous, and only a tiny bit foolish.

I Hear Thunder

Where was all that joy now, I thought, dropping my open notebook onto my lap, and flopping against the back of my visitor's armchair with exhaustion. My wrist ached and my fingers were cramped into a writer's claw from the effort of so much longhand. I wondered how different my life would have been if I'd remained a Christian. I wouldn't be in this mess, that was for sure. But then I'd have had no money or success, either, ergo no fame. I'd never have survived in the band if I'd kept the Church as my priority. I imagined myself instead as a leading light in the Freehold NJ Baptist Church, organizing Youth Groups and Pot Luck Suppers, married to an earnest young minister with bum-fluff and stiffly creased pants. Three kids, stretch marks and *tons* of wrinkles from taking on the cares of the entire parish. No, on reflection, fame had to have been better, even if the fate of my eternal soul was in question.

'Is this a bad time?' Toby and Ruby hovered in the doorway. I was both embarrassed and delighted to see them, although Ruby looked anxious that I might start shouting again, and Toby had an unreadable, closed expression on his face.

'No, no, come in. I'd just finished the bit I was on. Sorry I was so grumpy yesterday, Toby. It was a bit of a bad day. Well, apart from about three minutes of it.'

I blushed at my flirtatious remark, but Toby didn't acknowledge it, nor did he ask how my nose was feeling. All the warmth in his face seemed to have been wiped away, like an erased Etch-a-Sketch. Suddenly I felt foolish and ugly, as if he was only visiting me because he'd said he would. He was obviously mortified at what had happened the day before outside the lift.

Ruby sidled into the room and insisted that Toby lifted her up onto my bed, out of reach of me and my scary face. She was wearing baby Nikes, black sweat pants and a black sleeveless zip-up jacket.

I decided to act as if nothing had happened. 'Wow, Ruby, you look really cool. You have some lovely clothes, you know.'

'Tankoo, that's kind,' Ruby said condescendingly, sticking her finger into her mouth and smiling graciously. She seemed to have concluded that perhaps I wasn't so bad after all.

Toby sat down next to her on the bed. 'Don't worry about yesterday. It's forgotten. So what are you working on?'

He had a bright, false tone, which I assumed was his *pas-devant-les-enfants* voice, or maybe his let's-pretend-we-never-kissed-at-all voice. Then I realized he'd asked me a question. I looked down at the pages of scribble resting open on my knee and hastily closed the notebook. I hadn't yet told him about the manuscript, in case he somehow guessed about The Plan.

'I'm, erm, writing a book about my life.'

Toby acted impressed. 'How incredible! And what a fantastically positive thing to do; I bet that's really helping you emotionally, too.'

'Mm,' I said. 'It's certainly – er – focusing my mind. How's Kate?'

Toby's face twisted into another strange expression: half sheepish, half pleased.

'Good news,' he said. 'We've just been with her for an hour, and guess what? Ruby sang her favourite song

112

to her, and she moved her finger! Twice! The doctor says that's a sign that she might finally be coming out of it.'

He hugged Ruby and ruffled her curls. 'You're such a great girl, aren't you, my angel.'

Ruby beamed and nodded.

I felt a sudden flash of envy for Kate, despite her awful accident. She would wake up and recover with the support and love of these two wonderful people, and doubtless her life would be further enriched by her dice with death, and she and Toby would be more deeply in love than ever. Toby had, of course, already realized what a hideous mistake he'd made by kissing me, and how much he really adored Kate. Well, bully for them.

I was horrified by my churlish reaction. 'God, Toby, that's great. I'm so pleased for you. Honestly. You must be over the moon. And, Ruby, aren't you clever, making your mummy better. What did you sing to her?'

Ruby considered for a minute. 'I . . . funder.'

'Sorry?'

'I . . . *funder.*'

I looked towards Toby for assistance.

'I hear thunder,' he translated.

'Oh, right. I don't think I know that one. How does it go?'

'It's the pre-school version of "Frère Jacques". Will you sing it for Helena, Rubes? It'll help her get all better, too.'

Ruby sat up to attention and began to sing tune-lessly, with Toby mouthing the words beside her:

> 'I . . . funder, I . . . funder,
> 'Ark doan you? 'Ark doan you?
> pipper papper waindops
> pipper papper waindops,
> I wet froo
> THO-ARE-YOU!'

113

The song was accompanied by gestures – clapping for the thunder, cupping a hand around her ear for the 'hark don't you,' finger-twitching for the pitter-patter, plucking at her jacket, indicating that she was wet through, and a final crescendo of pointing. It was really sweet, and if I hadn't been so pissed off with Toby I could quite easily have welled up with soppy tears.

'Aw, Ruby, that was brilliant. No wonder your mummy is getting all better now. She probably wants to hear it over and over.'

Needing no more encouragement, Ruby began again. Toby hastily tried a distraction technique. 'Hey, Ruby, remember Nurse Grace said she'd found a box of toys for you? Shall we go and see if you can play with them for a bit?'

'Oooh, toys,' said Ruby gleefully. 'Bye, lady, thee you later.'

'It's *Helena*, Ruby. Say goodbye to Helena.'

'Bye, Ellna.'

'Bye, Ruby.'

'Helena, I'll just go and get her sorted. Grace said she'd take her off my hands for ten minutes, then we can have a proper chat, OK?'

He gave me a meaningful, although still stern look, and I thought, Right, earwig. It's going to be the now-my-wife's-on-the-mend-I'll-see-you-around chat.

Nonetheless, once they'd disappeared I slipped on my silk Liberty dressing gown and quickly ran a comb through my hair. I wanted to be dumped with dignity.

But perhaps I was wrong. Perhaps he was just being standoffish so Ruby didn't suspect anything. Perhaps he was coming back for a repeat of yesterday's tryst. I hopped into the bathroom for another swig of mouthwash and to dab some perfume on my neck. I realized I didn't want to be dumped at all.

The guilt that had been absent yesterday now pricked at my skin, as abrasive and intrusive as the deodorant I'd just sprayed under my arms. Where was my membership of the sisterhood? Here I was, hoping to seduce an unconscious woman's husband. I felt ashamed of myself. But not ashamed enough to hope it didn't happen again.

Ten minutes went by and Toby didn't come back. I sat for a further ten minutes, posed in my armchair watching *Time Team* on TV, haughty and abandoned, like Miss Havisham. Then I began to get worried, and fed up with watching a lot of loosely woven people getting excited about pot shards. I went out into the corridor and looked up and down. No sign of either of them.

Eventually Catriona appeared. 'Oh, sorry, Helena, I forgot to tell you. Toby asked me to send his apologies, but we had to get him back to his wife pronto. They seem to think she's coming round.'

'Great,' I said. 'That's really great.'

'N.I.T.A.'

Young Marble Giants

The next year was much happier than I'd imagined it would be, despite missing Sam terribly.

'Jesus has buttered your paws,' said Margie wisely, a couple of months after I'd joined the Church.

'I beg your pardon?' I said – I'd also discovered that the more English I sounded, the more popular I became.

'You're like a kitty with a new owner. The Lord has taken you from the pet store of your old existence, brought you to a new home and buttered your paws. That's what you do with cats to help them settle into a new place. Licking off all the butter helps them relax, so by the time they're done they feel like they belong there.'

'Oh, er, right,' I'd said.

But in a way it was true. The Church had given me a sense of belonging. Although I didn't exactly gel with most of the other God-struck teenagers, having a routine of my own did help ease the sting of reading Sam's letters about boyfriends and parties and rumours of Melanie Welling's famous friends.

I went to church every Sunday and to Bible class each Wednesday. Within weeks I'd joined the choir, so choir practice on Thursdays occupied another of my previously empty evenings.

I *loved* being in the choir. I had a deepish, clear

voice, and could easily pick up harmonies on the hymns and spirituals, even without the music in front of me. I also loved being in front of the congregation, dressed in an all-encompassing red cassock. It was my first experience of public performance, and I was hooked. It wasn't just the cassock which surrounded me, either. My new faith swirled and eddied about me constantly, like an aura; I felt protected by it, elevated and really, really loved.

At first my fourteen-year-old self wanted to keep it private for fear of ridicule, but as time went by my confidence grew, and I was no longer ashamed of doing lunchtime Bible study with my church cronies. I sometimes felt as though I could swing from the rafters proclaiming that Jesus was Lord.

My parents were greatly relieved at the change in me. Their previously homesick and withdrawn daughter had transformed into something approximating a ray of sunshine. In fact, had I not been so happy, I think they would have found it rather disturbing.

One Sunday I dragged them along to church with me, but they didn't enjoy it. When we got home again, I overheard Mum mutter to Dad, 'Rather vulgar, don't you think, George?'

I was furious. I burst into the living room, making my mother spill her sherry on the leatherette pouffe. 'You're such hypocrites!' I yelled. 'You say you believe in God, you dragged me to Sunday school all those years, and now, when I finally have a faith of my own, you sneer at it. How dare you!'

My father pulled out his handkerchief and tried to mop up the spilt sherry, looking anxious. 'Now calm down, Helena. Nobody's sneering. Don't shout at your mother.'

Mum had the grace to look ashamed. She put her hand on my arm. 'Oh, Helena, I'm sorry. I wasn't sneering at you or your faith, really. We're both so pleased that you're so much happier and settled.

117

We've been so worried about you. It's just, well, you know, your father and I aren't used to people being so . . . vocal in their beliefs. It certainly wasn't like that at St Thomas's.'

I couldn't help grinning. It was true; they had both looked mortified when the congregation's hands had started waving in the air during the first hymn. My father hadn't known where to put himself. And in truth I was rather relieved they hadn't taken to my church. If there was such a thing as a spiritual style, I felt my parents would definitely have cramped mine.

'OK, Mum. Sorry I shouted at you.'

Dad, looking relieved that the crisis was over, went out into the garden to practise his golf swing, Mum poured herself another sherry and put her feet up to read a gardening magazine and I went upstairs to listen to my new favourite record, *Colossal Youth* by Young Marble Giants, and to try and write to Sam. Normality had resumed.

Although we still corresponded regularly, I'd recently been having trouble finding things to write about. After I first got converted, I wrote her screeds and screeds of babble about how wonderful my life was now, and how she MUST try Jesus, as though He were a new and desirable brand of lipstick. My enthusiasm for my new religion was so overwhelming that I was genuinely surprised when Sam didn't immediately follow suit and get converted, too.

Even from across the Atlantic, I thought I could suffuse her with the same joy as it gave me. I really wanted her to be as happy as I was. Her replies ignored my pleas entirely, which just made me more insistent, until one day I got a brief note from her that was unlike her usual chatty missives.

Dear Helena,

Thanks for your letter. I'm writing this in Home Economics before Miss Parry notices. My cheese and onion pie is in the oven and I'm supposed to be clearing up. Sorry if this letter's got flour all over it. Have you heard of Hazel O'Connor? She's had a couple of hits here, including a fantastic song called 'Will You?', and we went to see her at the City Hall. Can you believe it, a proper pop concert in Salisbury? It was absolutely brilliant. Melanie said she read in *Smash Hits* that the saxophone player was blind, but he was wearing a wristwatch on stage, so now we aren't sure.

Uh-oh, Miss P's on the warpath . . .

(Later. Breaktime.)
It was really funny in PE today, we were playing netball and Marie-Thérèse Higgins got a teeny fly or something on her arm. She flicked it off and said, 'Get off me, you nasty little orgasm!' – she meant 'organism'. Melanie, Bridget and I all cracked up laughing.

Anyway, this was only meant to be a quick note. Write soon and tell me what you're up to at school. Any nice boys yet? I don't mean to be nasty or anything, but please stop going on about God; it's driving me mad. I'm really happy for you, honest, but horses for courses. I just can't see me getting into all that church stuff.

Lots of love and sloppy kisses,
Sam xxx

After receiving that note I didn't go to church for two weeks. I was overcome with a huge, bitter, impotent rage that, because my stupid parents made me move to this stupid country, I now had to derive any enjoyment from life out of a bunch of geeky, earnest people, whose idea of a good time was going for a cookout on the New Jersey shores and singing hymns lustily round a campfire.

Why couldn't I be normal, like Sam, and go to pop concerts, read *Smash Hits* and discuss orgasms with Melanie Welling? I didn't even know what an orgasm was. I enquired that night at Bible study, only *nobody else knew either*, and some of them were at least

119

sixteen! It wasn't until I asked Mum later, and she went red and told me off, that I realized it was something rude.

But my period of doubting didn't last long. I decided that it was a test from God, and that I should just ignore Sam's reluctance to think about her soul until such time as I could personally convince her, face to face. I certainly didn't want it to spoil our friendship.

So I continued to write to Sam, without the proselytizing, but it wasn't easy. One day, after listening to the whole of side one of *Colossal Youth*, I sat chewing my pen in the post-LP silence, trying to think of something interesting and non-church related to put in a letter. The remnants of the track 'N.I.T.A.' chased themselves around my head, and I thought how simple the band made it sound, just a few notes on a synthesizer, some choppy background guitar and a clear voice. I could do that, I thought.

Magically, the Young Marble Giants melody faded out and a line from an unwritten song popped into my mind instead. This was followed by another one, so I put the letter aside and wrote them down before I forgot them.

'Jesus, you talk to me every day;
Jesus, you hear what I have to say.'

I contemplated the crucifix on my desk for a few minutes, Jesus's furled fingers and skewered brass feet.

'Thank you, Jesus, for being there for me,
Thank you, Jesus, for setting me free.'

I thought this was marvellous. I had an instant fantasy of débuting the finished song, solo, in front of an adoring and appreciative congregation, who rose to their feet, cheering when it was over. But I wasn't *quite* happy with the tune; there seemed to be something missing. I could hear in my head how I wanted it to sound, but singing it wasn't good enough. I decided that it needed accompaniment – guitar, or a good, solid synth – to do it more justice.

I didn't have a guitar, but there was an alternative solution to the synthesizer. I crept downstairs, past my mother, who had nodded off over her magazine, reading glasses askew at the tip of her nose, and into the dining room where our old piano lived. Closing the door behind me, I slid onto the piano's tapestry stool and lifted up the heavy wooden lid. The old familiar smell of musty ivory and furniture polish filled my nostrils, reminding me of my brief spell as a childhood piano prodigy. I'd lasted less than a year before getting bored at having to do scales all the time.

None of us ever played this piano any more. I didn't know why my parents had bothered to bring it all the way across the Atlantic. There were faded circles on the little wood squares at either end of the keyboard, where drunken party guests had left their icy glasses of whisky while hammering out painfully inaccurate renditions of the 'Maple Leaf Rag'; battle scars which couldn't be polished off with Pledge.

I played a soft, experimental scale. The F key stuck, rendering only a dull 'thunk' when pressed. I remembered being responsible for that – actually that was the day I stopped playing the piano. I was about seven years old, and I'd got so frustrated with my pudgy fingers tripping over the notes that I'd banged my finger down hard on each one, as if I was trying to drum the sequence into the piano's stupid brain. It had beaten me at my own game, stubbornly and permanently sticking down a vital note. So as to avoid being held responsible for my vandalism, I insisted to my parents that I didn't wish to continue with piano lessons, in the hope that they might not notice the damage. And indeed it was probably several years before they did, by which time I was well off the hook.

Using a higher octave to avoid the errant key, I plinked out my tune again, making a few subtle alterations as I went along. Bingo! All the notes fell perfectly into place, and I'd created a catchy and sweet backing track to the melody. I played it over and over again, to make sure I didn't forget it, and then went back up to my bedroom to write the rest of the verses. I was thrilled at what I believed to be my creative genius.

That night, as I was saying my prayers, I concluded that my song really did need a guitar; some cool Young Marble Giantesque strumming over the vocals. Besides, guitars were much more where it was at than boring old synths. I wanted to be a new-wave Christian.

The more I thought about it, the more fixated I became. I had to have a guitar. But how? It was early summer, ages before my birthday. I turned it over to the Lord, trying not to plead too much, but unable to resist bargaining with Him.

'If I had a guitar I would be able to praise Thy glory much better. Not in a hippy drippy "Kumbaya" sort of way, but a proper, modern way. The Eighties way.' I stopped and then added, 'Only if it is Thy will.'

I went to sleep, content that if it was meant to be, it would be. After all, I could see no reason why I should be denied an instrument of praise. I saw myself bringing the entire youth population of Freehold to Jesus's arms by way of my radical and totally cool approach to worship.

The following weekend I went over to Mary-Ellen's house to help her with some schoolwork. She and I had become quite friendly of late. She was a genuine person, not a borderline religious nut, as I couldn't help considering the likes of Margie and some of her friends to be. Mary-Ellen was doing a geography project on Scotland, and had asked for my assistance, not that I'd ever been there, or knew anything about it, but I thought that at least I could tell her how to pronounce Edinburgh and Glasgow correctly.

She lived a few blocks away from me, and as I turned the corner into her tree-lined road, I noticed a large yard sale on the other side of the street. I still couldn't resist yard sales – they were the closest thing Freehold had to a good old church-hall jumble sale – and I went over to have a poke around. The house itself was shabby and unkempt, by far the least affluent-looking on the block. Most of the stuff was laid out on the front porch and, surprisingly, the pickings were very rich: cool books, records, some decent-looking grandad shirts and posters. Usually I had to sort through a multitude of used Tupperware and broken kitchen utensils to find anything worth taking home.

A sullen girl of about eighteen sat on the stoop, presumably in charge. I couldn't help noticing what massive feet she had, encased in cheap plastic sandals. She was talking to an older man, who was, I presumed, either a neighbour or another customer.

'Yeah, Scott run away and joined the Marines without tellin' no-one. Mama's so mad at him she's sellin' all his gear. She says she don't never wanna see him again.'

Wow, I thought, that's harsh. Selling all his things! Poor Scott. Nevertheless, I picked up a battered copy of *Catcher in the Rye* and a stripy shirt.

'How much are these?' I asked.

'Book's five cents, shirt's a quarter,' she replied, chewing the ends of her hair. I fumbled in my pocket for the change, paid her, and turned to walk away with my purchases under my arm. Just then the screen door slammed and someone came out onto the porch. I heard a screechy Southern voice: 'Janeane, I'm gettin' rid of this, too. It'll only clutter up the place. Don't see no point in keepin' it.'

The daughter sounded shocked. 'Mama, you're never sellin' Scotty's *guitar*.'

I wheeled around and stared. Sure enough, the sour-faced owner of the voice had propped a hard black guitar travelling case against the side of the porch. My heart sang.

'Thank you, Jesus. Thank you, thank you,' I whispered under my breath. I approached the woman, who glared at me. 'Er, how much do you want for the guitar?'

'Fifteen bucks,' she snapped. Her eyes were small and mean. I was starting to understand why Scott had left home.

Janeane looked even more horrified. 'Fifteen bucks? Mama, let me take it downtown to Merchants. They buy used guitars; it's worth more than that.'

'No Janeane, I jus' want it out my sight. I doan care about the money.'

'I'll take it!' I interrupted. 'Please could you hold it for me while I go over to my friend's house and borrow some money? I'll be right back. Mary-Ellen Randall, your neighbour, that's my friend; she lives across the street.'

The woman nodded, tight-lipped, at me, and I felt her eyes boring into my back as I hurried across the road to Mary-Ellen's house.

I rang her doorbell, and pounded on the door so hard that Mary-Ellen stuck her head out of the window.

'Helena, what's the matter?'

'Oh, oh, Mary-Ellen, please come quick; there's this guitar, but I don't have enough money. I wonder, I mean, please could you . . . ?'

'I'll be right down,' she said.

A moment later her blond head loomed behind the frosted glass of the front door, and she opened it, beckoning me inside. I dumped the book and shirt on the Randalls' hall table as Mary-Ellen looked on, mystified.

'OK, what guitar? Where?'

I took a deep breath. 'It's across the road, at a yard sale. It's only fifteen dollars, but I only have five on me. Do you think you could possibly lend me the other ten until tomorrow? It's just that I've been praying all week for a guitar, and now here it is. I'm sure it's meant to be!'

Mary-Ellen nodded sagely. 'Sounds like it is. Hold on, I'll get my purse.' I could have hugged her.

We walked back across the street. Mary-Ellen shuddered slightly when she saw which house.

'That's the Applebaums' place; they moved up from Tennessee a while back. They're a little . . . *unusual*.'

I had the feeling that if she weren't so Christian she would have elaborated, and normally I would have asked her to, but at that moment I couldn't have cared less if they'd all had two heads. We approached the porch. The guitar case was still there.

'What kind of condition is it in?' Mary-Ellen enquired.

'Erm, actually, I haven't looked at it yet,' I admitted, feeling a bit foolish.

'Well, you'd better before you give them any money,' she hissed in my ear. Mrs Applebaum was standing belligerently in front of the door, her hands on her hips.

'Mrs Applebaum. Hi, it's me again, about the guitar. Could I have a look at it, please?' I asked. She nodded once, and I walked over to the case. Laying it flat on the grass, I popped the stiff metal catches open and pulled the lid up.

'It's HUGE,' said Mary-Ellen in awed tones. 'Why does it only have four strings?'

Damn! I thought. It's a bass. Now what? This was an unexpected turn of events. I stared at it. It was in fairly good condition; black, with a lovely pearl-effect white scratch plate. I plucked each of the heavy strings with a forefinger, and they all made unpleasant and unmelodic muffled twanging sounds. How on earth did you get it to play? I wondered. Suddenly I felt terribly disappointed, and I nearly closed the case and walked away. But then I thought about my prayers, and how much more than coincidence it had felt when

Mrs Applebaum had brought the guitar outside at the precise moment I was there. No, I had prayed for a guitar and God had sent me a guitar. Everything else I would figure out.

'I'll take it,' I said, standing up. Mary-Ellen and I pooled our resources, and I paid Janeane. Mrs Applebaum had vanished into the house, but she reappeared at that point, lugging a small black-box thing, trailing cables.

'Here,' she said, thrusting it at me. 'I sure don't know what this is, but it goes with the guitar. Take the darn thing.'

A practice amp! I offered up another silent prayer. I wouldn't have had the first idea how to go about buying one of those. I collected the stray wires together in a coil and looped them over my forearm.

'Thank you *very* much, Mrs Applebaum,' I said sincerely, toying with the idea of adding that I hoped Scotty came back soon, but wisely thinking better of it.

'Bye, Mrs Applebaum,' added Mary-Ellen, closing the guitar case for me and picking it up. We processed back across the road with my strange electrical acquisitions; the start of my future as a bassist.

☆

My Messed-Up Head

Toby's visits to my room dramatically decreased in length and frequency as Kate began to recover. He did still pop in occasionally, but nothing was said about our kiss, and he avoided the subject of Kate's progress or any reference to the future. I felt glad in one way and gutted in another.

It would be no good at all for me to go forging complicated relationships with married men at this point in my life, not when I was planning such a huge . . . *thing*. All my energies had to go into The Plan, and some days I even enjoyed it: I had a secret that no-one else knew about. But on other days I was really sad that I couldn't share it with Toby, and that I could never be part of his future.

One morning, before visiting time, I got dressed. I left my room quite often for little walks, but this was the first time I'd worn proper clothes instead of just pyjamas and a dressing gown. It felt like a big deal.

Mum had brought me in a couple of outfits the day before, since I obviously couldn't wear the dress I'd had on at the UKMAs. I didn't know what had happened to that dress – incinerated, I hoped. I shuddered at the thought of the beautiful orange velvet all sticky and matted with blood.

My freshly laundered jeans felt cool and stiff on my

still-shaky legs, and the buttons did up with far more ease than before – newly ironed jeans usually required a lying-down hip raiser to make ends meet. Wow – if I kept going at this rate I'd be able to die skinny! Just what I'd always wanted.

I put on a big cardigan and a baseball cap, and walked slowly out into the corridor. Catriona was writing up some notes at the nurses' station at the end.

'Where's Kate Middleton's room?' I asked.

Catriona looked up, surprised.

'You're up and out early, Helena. And dressed, too. Good for you. It's a bit early for visiting, though. Kate's still in quite a bad way. She gets tired very easily.'

'I don't want to visit her,' I said, a bit too sharply. 'I mean, not now. I just thought I'd find out where she is, in case I decide to go later, after my walk. You won't tell her that I might visit, will you?'

Catriona looked at me as if I had a screw loose. 'Turn right, through the double doors, room seventeen. She's still in intensive care, but we'll be moving her downstairs to a non-ICU room tomorrow, all being well.'

I thanked her and shuffled off. I still had this weird, floaty feeling whenever I walked anywhere, so I hung on to the wall to prevent me from weaving about like a drunkard.

The blinds were down on room 17, to my annoyance. I'd just wanted a peek at Kate, to see what she looked like. It was a totally unfair thing to do, since I would have so loathed anyone trying that with me, but my curiosity was overpowering. I was sure I'd dislike her – talented, arty, loads of friends, gorgeous husband and daughter. Beautiful, too. Toby had said that her scars wouldn't show, the lucky bitch. Really, Helena, I thought. You're often not a very nice person, are you?

I loitered casually around in the corridor for a bit, then gave up, intending to go back to my own room to carry on with my writing. I reckoned I was about a quarter of the way through the manuscript, which meant D-day minus three-quarters.

One corridor further down, I heard Nurse Grace's voice floating through an open door: 'Oh, Ruby love, I haven't got any sweeties. Bad for your teeth anyway, makes them all mossy and soft. Yeuch! How about making a nice house out of some of this Lego?'

I couldn't resist walking along and peeking into the room. 'Hi, Grace. Hi, Ruby.'

Grace looked up, relief at seeing me potato-printed all over her face. She was half sitting, half lying on the purple carpet-tiled floor of the relatives' waiting room, with Ruby straddling her, both of them looking squashed in between too many armchairs and coffee tables. They were surrounded by a plastic picnic of bits of Lego, unfeasibly simplistic dump trucks and locomotives, and a scattering of chunky animal play- ing cards.

Ruby was in the process of frisking Grace, briskly and efficiently, keeping up a low growling chant of ''Weeties, 'weeties, 'weeties.' When she spotted me, she released Grace and ran up to me, smiling winsomely.

'You got 'weeties, Ellna!' she announced hopefully.

I laughed. 'My disguise obviously isn't as foolproof as I'd thought,' I said to Grace, crouching down so I was at eye-level with Ruby. 'You're a sucker for punishment, Ruby,' I told her. 'Don't you remember what happened last time I gave you a sweet?'

Ruby considered. 'Oh yeth,' she said, cowed. 'I done coughing.'

She backed away momentarily, worried perhaps that I might jam a gobstopper down her oesophagus. Then she brightened again. 'How 'bout play Animal Nap, yeah?' She took my hand and dragged me to the pile of toys on the floor.

'Animal Snap,' explained Grace helpfully. 'Oh, Helena, you wouldn't do me a huge favour and play with her for a bit, would you? I won't be far away, just outside in the store cupboard. I'm supposed to be doing a stock-take, but I wanted to give Kate and Toby a bit of time on their own.'

I began to sweat at the thought that Toby might have caught me hanging around outside Kate's room.

'He's in there now, is he?' I asked as casually as I could manage.

Grace stood up, brushing a little piece of red Lego off the knee of her tights and smoothing down her uniform. 'Well, he was on his way to her room. He said he had something to do first.'

My heart leaped. Perhaps he'd been planning to sneak in to see me first. Damn, damn, I wasn't there. My own fault for—

Just then Ruby piped up. 'Daddy went to do poo. In *toilet*,' she explained carefully. 'Then he go thee my mummy.'

I was deflated. So much for the romantic notions. But if I hung out with Ruby for a while, then at least I'd probably get to see Toby when he returned, post-dump and post-visit.

'Will you show me how to play Animal Snap, Ruby?' I asked.

'I get cardth,' she said enthusiastically.

Grace laughed again. 'Thanks, Helena. I'm just next door if you need me. I warn you, though. This may not be the tension-filled fast-moving game you remember from your childhood, OK?'

She swished out, waving gratefully at me as she went.

'Right,' said Ruby bossily. 'Eye down.'

It took me a few seconds to realize that she wasn't referring to my injured face, but was ordering me to join her where she lay on her tummy on the floor. I thought about the logistics of this; it was a small room, and I'd have had to lie with my legs wedged underneath an armchair, thus risking looking a total prat when Toby came back.

'Tell you what, Ruby. You lie there and I'll sit next to you. Here, shall I deal?' I sat cross-legged on the dusty carpet, split the pack of animal cards approximately in half, and gave Ruby one of the piles.

'I go firtht.' Very slowly, she selected two cards and put them face down on the carpet. 'Your turn,' she said.

Discreetly, I turned one of Ruby's cards over – a giraffe – before adding a zebra of my own.

Ruby put down a horse, face up this time. 'Horthey.'

I turned over a tiger. 'Tiger.'

The game continued with a tortuous lack of speed, until I placed a pig on the pile, to which Ruby added an identical pig. There was a long pause.

I pointed meaningfully at the twin pigs. 'Two pigs, Ruby.'

Ruby gazed blankly at them.

I tried again. 'Look, Ruby, what do you say when you've got two cards the same?'

Another blank look, then, 'Pigth?' she suggested.

'No. How about: Sn . . .' I began, waiting for her to catch on.

Nothing.

'Snaaaa . . . ?'

Light finally dawned. 'NAAAAP!' she yelled, as if coming out of delayed shock, and grabbed all the cards. 'New game now. Deal prop'ly, Ellna.'

I shuffled the pack and did as I was told. Ruby wiggled around on her stomach until she was lying next to me.

'Deal cardth on my botham,' she commanded, sticking her backside in the air and looking back at me over her shoulder in a very sex-kittenish fashion.

I giggled. 'On your *bottom*?'

'Yeth, on my botham.'

Feeling perhaps that this was not entirely appropriate behaviour from either of us, but not wanting to risk her wrath, I obliged, dealing Ruby's hand onto the seat of her stripy velour leggings.

Ruby roared with appreciative laughter and rolled around, scattering the cards around her. 'More!' she shouted, and I began to laugh, too, flipping the cards one by one onto the moving target of her little butt. I felt an unfamiliar stiffness in my chest, and worried for a second that I'd strained something, until I realized that it was just the exertion of laughing out loud after such a long time.

Ruby, encouraged by my response, was becoming more and more overexcited, squirming like an eel in a fishing net and squealing with joy. I was just beginning to wonder how to go about calming her down a bit when she flipped over onto her back, spread her legs wide, grabbed her crotch and yelled, 'DEAL THEM ON MY DINKY!'

Of course that had to be the moment that Toby appeared in the doorway. Ruby looked up at him. 'Nice poo, Daddy?'

For a second he and I gazed at each other, and then at Ruby, spreadeagled on the floor, surrounded by animal playing cards.

Toby's face was inscrutable. 'Yes thanks, Rubes.'

She beamed up at him. 'Oh, good *boy*, Daddy!'

That was it. I exploded, belly-laughing until I was worried I'd pop open my skin grafts. To my relief, Toby joined in, and the three of us were united in a magic circle of cartoon zebras and lions and warm, briefly uncomplicated pleasure. Ruby ran over to Toby and he scooped her up into an enormous hug, which somehow seemed to include me, too.

'Grandma's here, darling,' he said to her. 'She's with Mummy. Let's go and see them.'

I began to collect the scattered cards, my spirits already beginning to plummet again.

'Stay there, Helena, would you? I'll just drop Ruby off and nip back, OK?'

'Bye, Ellna, nithe to meet you,' said Ruby solemnly, puckering her lips into a fish's mouth and pressing the tenderest little kiss onto my scarred cheek. Those

Middletons and their casual kisses, I thought, trying not to seem too absurdly pleased.

Once they were gone, I spent a few minutes slowly tidying up all the toys, and then sat down and flipped through the very poor selection of tatty women's magazines. I was just gazing at a recipe for a radio-active-looking zabaglione and wondering if Toby was actually going to come back at all this time, when I glanced up to find him framed in the doorway, looking at me. I jumped, in my skin and in my heart.

'Didn't see you there.'

'Sorry. I did knock.'

I pointed at my ear, as if there might be a small out-of-order sign swinging from it, like a novelty earring. 'Not loudly enough, obviously.' I worried that he'd think I was annoyed, so I continued, 'But it doesn't matter. It's good to see you. How's Kate?'

Toby came in and sat next to me, dragging his chair closer so our arms were almost touching. 'She's OK. How are you?'

'OK. You?'

We laughed at the small talk.

'I've missed you,' I said without thinking.

'I know what you mean,' he replied, tucking a strand of my hair back underneath my cap. 'I'm so sorry, Helena, about the way I've been so . . . stand-offish with you. I want to see you so badly, but when I do, I feel so guilty about Kate. And, of course, I can't let Ruby see the way I feel about you. She picks up on everything.'

He was looking so tenderly into my face that I didn't even mind when he gently traced the scars on my cheek and eyebrow with his finger.

'Augenbrau,' I whispered, thinking of Sam, and how much she would have liked Toby.

'What?'

'Nothing,' I said hastily, feeling silly. 'God, Toby, what are we doing here? I don't even know if there's something between us or nothing at all. You say you

133

feel guilty about Kate. Were things bad between you before?'

Toby leaned his head back in his chair in a gesture of desperation. 'You have no idea what a complete and utter lowlife I feel when I think about Kate, but I can't change the fact that I fell in love with you the first time we met. It makes me sick to think that I didn't do something about it then, or in the months or even years since then, but you were away on the road, and by the time you came back to the UK I'd met Kate. I was afraid to organize another interview, or a back-stage pass to see you, because I knew it would compromise my relationship with her. As it's doing now.

'I do love Kate; she's my wife and the mother of my child. But you . . .' He looked at me with such passion in his eyes that I almost forgave him for having a wife.

'I want to feel every bit of you next to me,' he whispered. 'Please.'

'Except my nose, if you don't mind,' I said, grinning.

I stood up and straddled him in his chair, pressing myself against him until as much of our bodies as possible were connected. My stomach felt his stomach, my breasts touched his chest, my arms wrapped themselves around his back. Our lips met, and then our tongues, and finally, with a shiver of electricity we could both feel, there was a clash of hard and soft at the heart of us.

That kiss went on even longer than the elevator kiss. It was the strangest and most wonderful thing that had ever happened to me – in a hospital, surrounded by death and pain, me and a married man nearly ripping each other's clothes off. It was utterly surreal. But after crying together and laughing together, it seemed natural that Toby and I were practically making love right there in that chair, surrounded by watchful furniture and out-of-date women's magazines. Perhaps it was the air of heightened emotion which exists in hospitals, the sense that nothing was as it should be, neither perspective, time or even conscience.

I had no idea how much time elapsed. Just as I thought I was going to explode with lust, there was a sharp, accusatory knock at the door. I leaped off Toby as quickly as I could and rolled back into my own chair, puce in the face and aching with passion and exertion. Toby adjusted his trousers and sat up straight, running a hand swiftly through his curly hair, as if that would erase all the obvious signs of infidelity.

The door opened after a pause which seemed, even to us, discreetly lengthy. Grace came in and gave us both a Paddington stare.

'Kate's mother was just wondering where you'd got to,' she said to Toby, disapprovingly. 'She wants you to nip out and get some toiletries for Kate.'

Toby didn't dare stand up. He cleared his throat noisily. 'Right, thanks. I'll be there in a second.'

Grace retreated without another word, and Toby and I looked at each other mutely.

'Well, at least it wasn't the mother-in-law,' he said with a straight face. I leaned over to kiss him again, but he groaned and pushed me away.

'No, please don't, Helena, or else I'll never be able to . . . to get myself together,' he said, gesturing crotchwards.

'Do you think Grace will say anything?' I asked.

Toby shook his head. 'It's none of her business. Anyway, I'm sure she wouldn't. She didn't even see anything, so it would only be speculation. For all she knows we might just have been playing an extra-exciting game of Animal Snap.'

'That's *Strip* Animal Snap,' I said, and we laughed at the idea.

Eventually Toby was able to stand up unencumbered. He touched my hand lightly. 'See you later, then.'

'Will I?'

'I hope so.'

The door closed quietly behind him, and I was left

once more thinking how incongruous it was to feel lustful in a hospital. All my other emotions, however, fitted in quite well with the surroundings: confusion, guilt, longing. Grief.

'Oliver's Army'
Elvis Costello and The Attractions

I quickly worked out how to plug the bass into the amp, and what all the knobs and dials did. I also bought a book called *Bass Guitar for Beginners*, but I didn't pay it much attention because of its marked predilection for the dreaded scales. Instead I figured out my own method of playing, using a lot of chords, as if it were a regular six-string guitar, my original choice of instrument. I loved the deep, almost sinister sound the strings made in harmony. Physically, it wasn't easy to learn, and for weeks I played wincing with pain as the hard strings cut into my tender fingers. I dipped my fingertips in vinegar every night to try and toughen them up, and thereafter always associated that sharp smell with my early attempts to get to grips with the unwieldy guitar.

The theory, however, came easily to me, and I learned quickly which notes sounded good together. Even though I didn't do formal scales, I could soon perform rhythmical runs up and down the strings. I started playing along to the LPs in my collection, as well as composing more and more religious songs. I was in my element.

Finally, a few months after I started playing, I was allowed to teach the choir one of my songs at our Thursday evening practice – a better number than my first creation; my songwriting had mercifully matured as rapidly as my guitar skills. We sang it in church that Sunday, with me accompanying on the bass. I didn't get the standing ovation I'd envisioned, but I got a healthy round of applause and a warm glow of pride inside my chest. It was the best moment of my life.

I began taking my bass on the bus to school with me on certain days, so I could practise in one of the three music rooms in the basement. They had quite good equipment down there – bigger amps and even some effects pedals. I had told the music teacher, Mr Penfold, that I was learning to play, and he encouraged me to get involved with the school orchestra. I told him that I wasn't quite ready for that yet, so he offered to give me a spot of coaching when he had a free lunchtime. It was very kind of him, and his occasional input did help me with the more technical and theoretical aspects of playing, but the additional lunchtime practices helped the most.

I became even more of an anomaly at school. Prior to my conversion I had overheard a boy refer to me as 'that kinda cool fat English chick'. I was aloof and withdrawn, but wasn't really given a hard time, even about my chubbiness, because of the inherent cool factor of my accent and charity-shop chic. At the age of fifteen, when the other girls were wearing bright-pink blouses, ra-ra skirts and stilettos, I dressed almost exclusively in black or in men's second-hand clothes. A few of the football-jock types threw the odd comment in my direction, but I never rose to the bait. I just thought they were all stupid. After I started going to church, and was seen at school associating with the 'God-botherers', people decided that I was even weirder, and much less cool than they'd thought. I knew this, but couldn't have cared less now that I was bolstered by the protective cushion of my beliefs. But when word got around that I played bass, the curve on the graph of my acceptability began to climb again.

One day I was sitting on the school bus, my guitar case propped up against the seat next to me, reading an old copy of *Melody Maker* that Sam had sent me a while back, when the boy behind me leaned over my shoulder. 'Wow! *Melody Maker*. Awesome.'

I twisted my head back to look at him. He was cute, with big brown eyes, floppy blond hair and not too many active zits, just the purple shadows of past ones scattering his jaw line.

'Yes, my friend in England mails them over to me.'

We got into a conversation about the English music scene, and ended up talking all the way to school. The boy said he was heavily into Elvis Costello and Ian Dury and the Blockheads. He told me that his name was Justin Becker, he was in the year above me, and he had a band. He didn't usually get the bus to school, but his bike was in the shop. He asked me lots of questions: my name, how long I'd been there, if I'd been to any gigs – I hadn't – and how long I'd been playing bass for. I answered him methodically, trying to keep cool, but feeling, for the first time ever, the rush of adrenalin derived from fancying someone. Not very optimistically, I wondered if he was a Christian.

When the bus dropped us off outside the school gate, Justin said, 'Well, nice to meet you, Helena. See you around, I guess. Good luck with the bass.'

He was gone before I could reply. I felt a bit let down that he hadn't even invited me to see his band play. I thought about him all day, and at recess I asked Mary-Ellen what she knew about him.

'Justin Becker? Oh, he's totally the heart-throb of the twelfth grade. He always has a bunch of girls running after him. I didn't know he had a band. Still, it figures, I guess. I hear he's very arrogant.'

I was delighted to have been chatted up by a heart-throb but despondent that he had so many suitors already. I decided not to tell Mary-Ellen that I fancied him. In any case, I didn't think she'd understand.

Except for distant glimpses in the hallway, I didn't see Justin again for a couple of weeks. After a few days I put him out of my mind, remembering my vow of chastity and my commitment to the Church. One lunchtime, however, I was down in the practice room, plugging away on the bass, when I felt someone's presence. I turned around and saw Justin lolling in the door frame, watching me, chewing on a toothpick and running his fingers affectedly through his thick blond hair.

'Oh, hello,' I squeaked, embarrassed. I'd been in a hurry that morning, and hadn't realized until I got to school that I'd only applied mascara and eye-liner to one eye. I kept the naked side of my face turned stiffly away from him in the hope he wouldn't notice.

'Hi. Hey, you're not bad, you know. What was your name again?'

I was crushed that he'd forgotten. 'Helena Nicholls,' I said a little crossly.

'Want to be in my band? My bass player just left.'

I couldn't believe what I was hearing. A real live band! Now that was something I could write and tell Sam about.

'What sort of band is it?' I asked, playing it cool and trying not to appear as though my neck was in a brace.

'Well, you know, it's like, I'm the singer, right? And, well, actually, that's it right now. The guy who played bass left because Coach was gonna kick him off the football team unless he went to more practices. And we nearly got a drummer but, like, his parents wouldn't let him get any drums. But it's gonna be awesome! There's this other guy, Joe, who might join also, and he plays keyboards. So, whaddaya think?'

Sounds pretty lame to me, was what I thought. 'What kind of music?' I said instead.

'Well, sorta like Blondie, although with no girl singer, of course, or The Stranglers. We don't have too many songs at the moment, mostly cover versions really. You write?'

I nodded, hoping he wouldn't ask me what sort of songs I wrote. I wasn't sure about the whole thing. Half-assed were the words which sprang to mind. However, the idea of being in a band, particularly one that was just Justin and me, was undeniably appealing. I would get to go to his house and everything.

'We could have a rehearsal and see how it goes,' I said tentatively.

He smiled and the blood rushed into my cheeks, making me feel dizzy.

'Great. How about tomorrow night?'

Luckily that wasn't Bible study or choir practice night. 'Fine. Where?'

'Seven twelve Indiana. Say, six o'clock?'

'OK.'

'OK, see you then.' He slouched back round the door frame out of sight, and I heard his rubber-soled sneakers squelch away on the parquet floor. I took a deep breath, inhaling the strong school smell of adolescents and antiseptic, and swallowed down my excitement. I'd just give it a go. Maybe I could even adapt a couple of my songs so they weren't about God? It would be easy enough to do, and I loved the idea of hearing them performed by a real band. I felt faintly traitorous at this thought, but quelled it by reasoning that it was all additional practice for me, practice that would better serve my mission of praising the Lord through my gift of music.

The rehearsal was not a huge success. It was just the two of us in the Beckers' basement games room, and at first I was so nervous being in Justin's presence that I couldn't seem to play anything properly. We had a stab at 'Oliver's Army', reading the lyrics out of Justin's Elvis Costello and The Attractions songbook, but Justin wasn't very good at playing his guitar – he couldn't get the chords right, the song sounded truly awful without drums and his mum kept coming down to complain about the noise.

Justin was a total poser, and sang as if performing in

141

front of thousands, instead of a quivering cat and his harassed-looking mother. He did have a wonderful voice, though. After a while he abandoned the guitar, and we sang the song in harmony, with just my bass to keep time. It didn't sound too bad, and I was a little more cheered. We decided that, if we could find a drummer and a keyboard player, we might have something. I told him that the following week I'd bring in a couple of my songs for us to try. At that point Mrs Becker reappeared to say that my father had arrived to collect me, so we called it a day. As I packed up my bass and amp, I asked Justin if the band had a name yet.

'Blue Idea,' he said firmly, smiling his gorgeous smile at me. 'We're gonna be huge. You wait.'

I wondered if that 'we' included me, but I didn't have the nerve to ask. Instead I said goodbye to Justin and his mother, and, much to Dad's irritation, sang the harmony line to 'Oliver's Army' loudly all the way home in the car, my brain filling in the crashing jubilant staccato of the piano chords and Elvis's mellow but nasal tenor: 'And I would rather be anywhere else, tha-an here to-daaay. Woah, oh, oh, ohhh-oh. Woah oh-oh-oh-ohhhhh.'

The following week I went back to Justin's house. When I arrived, there were two other boys in the basement, drinking Dr Pepper and horsing around with Justin. I instantly felt even more shy and out of place, especially since Justin showed no sign of introducing me. I got on with tuning up my bass until finally the shorter of the two, a nerdy-looking character with thick black-rimmed glasses and tufty black hair, came over. 'Hi, Helena, I'm David,' he said. 'That's Joe over there, in case you didn't know.'

I waved hesitantly across the room to Joe, who was trying to slam-dunk a foam basketball into a wall-mounted hoop. He was incredibly tall and lanky, with a neck and wrists that seemed to go on for ever, and he had heavy metal braces all over his teeth. He waved back at me in a friendly fashion. I vaguely recognized both him and David from school.

After a while I got fed up with waiting for something to happen, and just started to play a bass riff over and over again. Eventually David sat down on a stool behind a shabby-looking three-piece drum kit and picked up the beat; Joe wandered over and started playing some melancholic accompanying chords on a little Casio keyboard he'd brought with him, and Justin managed to add a reggae-style guitar skank over the top of it all. It didn't sound half bad. We bashed away for almost ten minutes until the tune died a natural death and we all petered out, ending it with a cacophony of crashing drums and writhing, frantic guitar chords – luckily Mrs Becker was out that day. Justin was windmilling his right arm round and round, as though he were Pete Townshend on stage at the Rainbow, until I was afraid he might try and smash up his guitar on the three-quarter-sized pool table.

In the ear-ringing silence that followed, we all looked at one another, grinning and flushed with the success of our first ever jam session. Justin and Joe exchanged triumphant high-fives and all three boys whooped and yelled with excitement.

After that we started to play together regularly, quickly learning to belt out versions of our favourite pop and new-wave songs with great conviction. I also taught them the melodies of several songs I'd written, substituting the words 'my Lord' with 'my love' where appropriate. I don't think anyone guessed that they'd ever been anything but simple rock songs about being in love, or finding one's way home. I'd deleted the line that originally explained that 'home' was, in fact, 'Heaven'. It worked a treat.

1 May 1982

Dear Tan Smarg (Squirrel Comber and Hedgehog Brusher),

Get this, I'm in a band! We're called Blue Idea, and it's me and three boys from school, Justin Becker, David Somerstein and Joe Jennings. They're all seniors (like 6th formers). Justin is really, really gorgeous. It's his band – I can't believe he's letting me be in it, too. And I've started writing pop songs, so we might even do them as part of our set!

Oh, guess what, I nearly made such a fool of myself – what's new, I hear you cry. You know when, ages ago, you used to really like that awful group Guys and Dolls? Well, I'd kind of got them mixed up in my mind with an American band called The New York Dolls, who are punks. We were round at Justin's rehearsing, and The New York Dolls came on TV, all leather jackets and outrageous make-up and long hair. I said to Joe, 'Boy, they really had a change of image, didn't they.' It wasn't till later that I realized my mistake! Luckily Joe had no idea what I was on about.

I'm so excited about being in a real band. I wish you were here, so you could sing backing vocals or something. Wouldn't that be a laugh? You never know, maybe Blue Idea will come and play Salisbury City Hall some time. I'll give you a backstage pass and Melanie will be totally jealous!

Lots of love,
Helena xx

Soon band practice took over from choir practice as the high point of my week. I was still going to church every Sunday without fail, and to Margie's Bible study class most Wednesdays. But I wasn't that keen on Margie anyway, and it was not difficult to start skipping a few of those here and there. Besides, the band missed few opportunities to make jibes at me for being a Bible-thumping dweeb. At first I rose above it, but as they began to take up more and more of my time, it was hard not to be influenced by them.

We made our triumphantly awful début in the living room at one of Justin's mates' parties on a Saturday night, a few months after we'd first practised. We performed all cover versions, as we weren't yet confident enough to do any of my songs, and we wanted to make sure our first audience got the crowd-pleasing numbers they obviously wanted. It was terrible, but no-one at the party seemed to mind. They danced and cheered, and someone spilt a plastic cup of beer over me and my bass – a good time was had by all. I didn't get home until 1.30 a.m., sneaking up the stairs on tiptoe so my parents wouldn't hear me. They hadn't waited up, so I thought I'd got away with it, but the next day I received the first of a series of lectures involving the phrases 'concentrating on your school work', 'not getting in with the wrong crowd' and 'what's wrong with just being in the choir?' It was all water off a duck's back to me.

That morning, in church, I was so tired that I dropped off during the sermon – not an ideal thing to do in my very noticeable spot in the choir, out in front of the congregation. My neighbour had to nudge me awake, and I could see Margie shooting daggers at me from her front-row pew. Since I'd joined the band she had become almost openly antagonistic towards me, in a very *Christian* way, of course. I had no idea why, and nor did I care.

In fact, I was very happy. I'd gradually become one of the boys, and after a while, even Justin's smouldering grins ceased to move me. I liked him, but he could be an arrogant little creep. Instead of blushing and simpering in his presence, I started to bully and push him to be more reliable, practise his feeble guitar playing and cut down on smoking so as to preserve his voice. Eventually, as we learned more and more of my songs, I emerged as the natural leader of the band, and I revelled in the responsibility.

I was so relieved not to fancy Justin any more that I thought for a while I was well and truly back on my spiritual path. But it turned out to be something more insidiously compelling than hormones which ultimately made me stray: the new and heady sensation of raw ambition.

☆

Home Sweet Home

It was another two days before I saw Toby again. All the hospital emotions stirred up by the last kiss had been quietly simmering together, and were just coming to a boil of resentment. Why were we doing this? I knew enough about men to be completely sure that whatever happened he'd never leave his wife.

I was scribbling away at my manuscript like a mad woman when, out of the blue, he appeared at my door.

'Hello, stranger,' I said. 'Come in.'

'It's only been two days,' he replied defensively, but he came in anyway. He did kiss me, but only a peck, and I could tell immediately from the way his eyes slid away from my face that we weren't about to carry on where we'd left off in the visitors' room.

'How's the book going?'

'Good, I think. I'm getting there, slowly.'

'So what happens when you finish? Are you trying to find a publisher?'

'Not at the moment, no. I'm sure it won't be a problem, though.'

Toby laughed. 'No, you're a celebrity. Of course it won't be. Publishers welcome people like you with open arms, don't they?'

'That wasn't what I meant.'

'What did you mean, then?'

I sighed and put the notebook back under my pillow. 'Nothing.'

Toby looked at my legs. 'I like your jeans. I thought so the other day, only I didn't get a chance to mention it. I mean, it's good to see you in real clothes. Surely you'll be going home soon, won't you? You seem so much better.'

I stood up and walked over to the window, peering out between the slats of the blind at the huge Edwardian guest houses and hotels across the road.

'The doctor's going to let me know when he comes in today. He doesn't want to talk about fitting me with a fake eye until I decide whether or not I really want one. I'm not sure. And I think everything else is OK now, except my ear and a bit of leftover concussion. I still wobble a bit when I walk, so it depends on that.'

'So, tell me more about your book. Is it about Blue Idea?'

I felt a bit uneasy talking about it, but he seemed genuinely interested, and genuinely *not* interested in a repeat of what had happened after the Animal Snap game.

'It's about everything. Childhood, Sam, moving to America, being a teenager. The band. I'm just getting to that bit now. I've got some letters somewhere that I'll probably add in later, too, and they'll help me cross-check dates and stuff.'

'How do you remember everything without them?'

I felt prickles on my neck. I mustn't give too much away, I thought. 'I, um, think of what records I was listening to at the time, and then I think back to how I felt.'

'Oh yeah, that's how you DJ, isn't it? I've been doing my homework. So you're taking your own requests now, are you? Cool. That would make a great show!'

'Yeah, I suppose it might.' I had to bite my lip to prevent myself from blurting out The Plan. Suddenly it was no longer any fun at all, keeping it to myself. With effort I changed the subject. 'Do you have a

148

favourite record, Toby? I'm not putting you on the spot. You don't even have to say why it's your favourite, I'm just curious.'

'Phew! Bit of an impossible question, that one. There are so many I absolutely adore that I'm not sure if I could narrow it down to one. Lou Reed's 'Perfect Day', perhaps. Bowie's 'Life On Mars' or 'Another Girl Another Planet', just as an example of a perfect pop song. I'd need to think about it more before giving you a definite answer, though.'

'Fair enough. I notice you haven't mentioned any of Blue Idea's records?'

Toby went red. He was so easy to tease.

'God, Toby, I don't know how you ever managed to be a journalist. You blush far too easily. I'm joking!'

He stuck his finger up at me flirtatiously, and all of a sudden he looked so cute that I had a small, ballooning urge to leap on top of him again.

Then he became serious again. 'So what will you do with yourself once you get home and your mother's gone back to the States?'

'I don't know. Celebrate, probably. No, I'll finish the book and then . . . Well, that's it, really.' Toby was obviously remembering me saying I didn't have many friends.

'There'll be someone to look after you, though, won't there?'

I scowled at him. 'I won't need looking after. I'm going home because I'm better, aren't I?'

'But I mean, what are your long-term plans?'

He knew I'd lost my job, but I hadn't told him about Geoff's offer of the night-time show.

'I haven't got any long-term plans, just one short-term one.'

As soon as I said it, I thought, What a giveaway. A huge cliff edge of bitterness had crept into my voice, and I honestly didn't know if I'd manufactured it for Toby's benefit or if it was genuine. The only thing I did know for sure was that one more kiss like the last one and I might not be able to go through with The Plan.

'You will be all right, won't you?' Toby persisted. 'I mean, I know you've been a bit depressed and everything. I'm worried about you, that's all.'

My indecision and his reversion to guilt mode were beginning to annoy me. 'Oh, no need to worry. I *am* going to top myself, but not right now, OK? I would hate to give you something else to feel guilty about.'

Toby looked at me with what was probably the look he gave Ruby when she drew on the sofa with Magic Marker: cross and disappointed. All of a sudden I made up my mind. I was going to push him further, goad him into leaving, and then I could just get on with The Plan. He'd had enough traumas lately, and I was sick of him blowing hot and cold with me.

I took a deep breath. 'You really think that's what I'm going to do, don't you? You think I'm actually writing a book about my life so that I'll be remembered after I'm dead? Well, if you think you've got it all sussed, then fine. Perhaps you *want* me to do it, so you'll be able to tell everyone that you knew me, that you kissed me a couple of times. Would that give you a thrill? Or maybe you'd like to write my obituary for me? Go ahead, the job's vacant.'

Emotions flitted across Toby's face: astonishment, hurt and fury. He moved across the room to where I stood by the window and grabbed me by the shoulders, almost shaking me.

'You listen to me, Helena. I'm sorry if I've got it all wrong – I hope to God I *have* got it all wrong – but you're bang out of order. Don't you even say that as a joke, or even THINK it, you understand? And how could you say I'd actually want you to do something as sick as that? What's the matter with you anyway? I've told you how I feel, and how hard this all is for me. Can't you cut me some slack, for God's sake?'

I felt dangerously out of control. 'I'll think and do whatever I bloody well want to. Get off me. How dare you tell me what to do after you've messed me around the way you have. You come on to me and kiss me, then your wife wakes up and you ignore me. We have another kiss, and now you act like nothing's happened. You've treated me like shit, and I want you to get lost and leave me alone – for good. I won't be second best.'

I wrenched his hands from my shoulders.

Toby's arms flopped down to his sides, and he turned his back on me. 'It's not like that,' he said in a voice I'd never heard him use before. 'I never meant to mess you around, and I'm sorry. But you know what else I'm sorry about? I'm sorry that you obviously think so little of me. So I'll do what you want and get lost now. OK?'

He started to walk out of the room, slowly, as if he was waiting for me to stop him. Every stitch of me wanted him to stay, but I didn't move or speak. After the fattest of pregnant pauses he finally picked up the pace and left.

Operation Send Toby Away had worked a treat, much better than I could have hoped for.

The doctor came round later and told me yes, I could go home. Mum booked us a taxi, and I packed up my notebooks and pens, washbag and nightclothes, said goodbye to the nurses and put on my Abba disguise.

Toby didn't come back, and I didn't leave my number or address for him. It would be best that way, I told myself bitterly.

Being in my own house again was so blissful that I temporarily forgot about the row with Toby. I cried like a virgin bride being lifted across the threshold as I came through the front door – the joy of being reunited with my bed, my coffee mugs, my refrigerator. I was convinced that even my toilet seat was more comfortable than the hospital one.

With Mum staying there in my absence everything was spookily perfect-looking; the house plants were all green and perky, drunk on Baby Bio, there was no dust on the TV screen, the kitchen surfaces were as swabbed and sterile as an operating theatre. The stag beetle in the outside drain and the small spider who'd been living in the fireplace had upped sticks and moved on, obviously in search of a quiet life.

'You put your feet up, honey, and I'll make us a nice cup of tea,' she trilled when I came downstairs after a whirlwind tour to reacquaint myself with my home. Then she stopped and clapped her hand over her mouth. 'No, wait,' she said. 'I nearly forgot, there's a very exciting message on the answerphone for you.'

My heart leaped as I approached the flashing red light on the machine. Toby? Maybe he'd tracked down my number after he'd realized I'd been discharged.

I pressed Play, but the voice I heard was that of a whiny American woman. 'Oh, hi there, Helena, here's a blast from the past! It's your old buddy Margie, here in England. I called your mom a few weeks ago and she told me you'd be happy to have me to stay when I was over. I'm here in Man-chester for a conference, which finishes on Wednesday. So if that's still OK with you, I'll see you then, around six, yeah? I'm like, *so* looking forward to catching up with your totally exciting life!'

I flopped into an armchair, unable to stand under the dual weight of disappointment and fury. 'Totally fuckin' rad,' I muttered under my breath.

Mum appeared in the doorway and took in my livid face. 'Isn't that marvellous, honey?' she said nervously. 'Your old friend Margie coming to stay! Won't it be a tonic for you to have some girly chats with someone other than your old mum?'

I felt too exhausted and miserable to shout at her. 'No, Mum, it is not marvellous. I haven't spoken to her for about seventeen years. She's a preachy little cow who practically told me I'd rot in hell when Blue Idea got signed. I'm obviously the only wealthy person she knows in London, and she's after some free accommodation. You had no right at all to give out my phone number. And she's coming tonight, my first day home.'

'But I thought you liked Margie.' She was pleating the freshly ironed tea towel in her hands.

I sighed. 'I never bloody liked Margie. It was Mary-Ellen who was the sweet one out of that church lot. *She* was quite nice, but the others were a bunch of nuts, and Margie was the worst. What am I going to do?'

Mum came over and knelt by my armchair. She put down her tea towel and stroked the hair away from my scarred forehead, apparently summoning up more reserves of mummyhood than she knew she possessed.

'OK, here's the deal,' she said. 'Let her stay tonight, because she'll have a problem finding anywhere else now. I'll make sure she leaves again tomorrow. She doesn't know that you've had an accident – I guess the press coverage didn't reach America – so it's quite reasonable to ask her to go. And if you don't want to talk to her this evening, just say you're tired and I'll tell you to go to bed. How's that?'

'All right then,' I said, managing a smile. It was so nice to be taken care of. I had a sudden bottomless pang of remorse at what I was going to have to put her through in a matter of weeks after I'd waved her off at the airport.

'Thanks, Mum.'

'There There My Dear'
Dexys Midnight Runners

By the time Blue Idea finally got to do business with a real record company, I'd already played out the scene in my head a thousand times. As I sat with the rest of the band in a brand-new restaurant in Greenwich Village, near the offices of Ringside Records, I went over it one more time: 'Let's talk money, yes. Now how does half a million sound to you?' or maybe, 'You'll have that platinum record before you know it, you mark my words.'

Ringside's director of A&R, Mr Wallberger, was late, so we sat nervously, saying little and feeling very out of place. The waiting staff hovered around in packs, looking down their noses at us. Eventually, a put-out-looking boy detached himself reluctantly from the other waiters and came to plonk menus and iced water in front of us.

We had come a very long way since the night of our first show, almost a year before. I could barely even remember it now, although I still had a faint stain on one of my white shirts from the beer someone had spilt down me. Since then we had practised and practised, and I'd written more songs and we had played in public at every possible opportunity. We'd rocked out to impress our classmates at school dances, got dressed up formally to perform at Justin's cousin's wedding reception, done David's brother's bar mitzvah, and played dozens of dark and sweaty all-ages rock nights at the local bar.

I sipped my iced water, trying to still my over-optimistic imagination by attempting to recall our first five gigs, in order. I failed miserably, but at that precise moment I was so nervous I was hard pushed to remember my own address.

Finally the door opened and Mr Wallberger walked in, accompanied by his A&R manager, a skinny, hippy English guy called Willy Watts-Davis. Willy had been our introduction to Ringside Records. He had, by chance, heard a set we'd played in Asbury Park. He had driven down to see another Freehold band called Saul, who were headlining at the same venue that night, but he was so excited with us that he spent the duration of Saul's set chatting to us out in the parking lot. Justin assured him they were terrible anyway and that he wasn't missing a thing. Willy had then arranged an opening slot for us at that sleazy Manhattan mecca of punk rock, CBGB's, the following week so Mr Wallberger could come and check us out. It was an outstanding stroke of luck. We had previously made a cheap demo tape and sent it to various record companies, but we'd had no response – unsurprisingly, since it sounded absolutely awful.

We'd seen them standing by the bar at the CB's show; they were easy to spot, there only being about eight people in the place. Neither of them were a bit how I'd imagined record company people to look; I was convinced they all wore sharp Armani suits with just a T-shirt underneath, chunky gold necklaces, loafers and no socks, sported ludicrously skinny plaits to compensate for their bald spots, sniffed continuously and constantly rushed off to the toilet to do more drugs.

But no, Mr Wallberger was large and clumsy-looking, thirty-fiveish, with a mop of curly brown hair, too-tight corduroys and a scruffy button-down shirt. He looked as if he didn't have a penny to his name.

155

Willy had been hovering nervously around behind his boss, patchwork flares flapping around his skeletal ankles. I couldn't see if he had his fingers crossed or not, but I wouldn't have minded taking a bet that he had.

We'd played our hearts out, knowing that this kind of a chance was so slim as to be practically unheard of. When Mr Wallberger came up to us after the set and invited us to lunch the next day to 'talk some business', we were beside ourselves with excitement.

Ringside Records – a real record label! I was sure that Dexys Midnight Runners' first album had been released on Ringside UK, and they were a fantastic band. A few months earlier I'd got Sam to send us a tape of *Searching For The Young Soul Rebels*, and when it arrived in the post we almost wore it out, committing every single note to memory, and as many of the words as we could pick out. Justin decided to make Kevin Rowland his role model, and started sporting woolly hats and quoting from *Taxi Driver*. He wanted us to learn 'There There My Dear', thinking that Blue Idea's lack of a horn section would enable us to totally reinterpret the song; but our attempts at a rendition just sounded ridiculous, completely pointless and bald, like a newly shorn sheep. Finally, when Justin tried to get us all to go out for runs together, because he'd read in *NME* that Kevin did the same, we rebelled and chucked out the tape. Consequently, it was months before we finally discovered that in fact the record had come out on EMI, not Ringside.

Anyway, the night before our meeting we all stayed in Brooklyn, with Joe's Aunt Sandi. The boys slept on her living-room floor, and I got the guest bedroom, but I hadn't been able to sleep for more than a couple of hours with the anticipation. For most of the night I'd lain awake whispering, 'Please God, let us get a deal. Please God, let him want to sign us. Please God, we're not in it for the money or the fame' – something of a lie.

I wasn't awfully optimistic, though. I saw no particular reason for God to shower his largesse upon me at this particular juncture, even if he did overlook the fib. I hadn't been to church for over six weeks, and I'd left the choir a long time before that. I viewed this lapse as merely a temporary suspension of progress along my spiritual path whilst sorting out my career, and I fervently asked God to understand my position. But somehow I kept forgetting to say my prayers at night. I *must* go to church this Sunday, I thought, deal or no deal.

So there we all were, hellos and apologies for lateness proffered and accepted. The multitudinous waiting staff cheered up slightly when the big guns arrived; they seemed to be able to detect the presence of a platinum Amex, despite the smokescreen of our collective scruffy appearances.

'Hello Mr Wallberger,' I said, and shook his hand.

'No, please, no-one calls me that. Call me Rob.'

I knew immediately that this would be impossible, far worse than having to call Sam's mum Cynthia. It was months before I realized that the music industry really was a first-name-only business.

We all ordered Cokes and designer-type sandwiches, which were just becoming popular in New York – radicchio and brie, ham with red onion compote, that sort of thing. I could barely swallow with nerves, and when asked a question I choked on a mouthful of Coke, which spurted fizzily and painfully out of my nose. Justin sniggered and I wanted to cry with embarrassment, but the Ringside Brothers kindly affected not to notice. The bass line to 'There There My Dear' thudded persistently and annoyingly through my head, a sort of defence mechanism.

They chatted to us about nothing much for what seemed like far too long: the excessive number of waiters in the place – approximately three per customer – the annoyingly slow service and the bad attitude of said waiters.

157

'People are much nicer to you in England,' Willy sighed wistfully, and I could tell how homesick he was.

I was plucking up courage to ask him how long he'd lived in New York, and to explain my own British roots, when Mr Wallberger put down his glass.

'So, like I said, I enjoyed the show,' he began casually. 'I think there's definitely something there. You're all very green, of course, and the band still lacks cohesion, but once you've done a few weeks on the road I'm sure that would sharpen up. Your music isn't what's hip at the moment, you're not exactly new wave, or post-punk, either, but I'm willing to take a chance with you and put out your first record. I think it's time for something new, and I think you have the talent. Like I said, I'm willing to take a punt on you guys and see how it goes.'

This was not quite the ecstatic welcome I'd expected.

'How much will you give us?' said Justin, to the point as usual. I blushed at his directness and folded my napkin up into tiny, panicked sections underneath the table. Our naivety seemed to hover over the table, choking me like a cloud of exhaust fumes. I wished we had a manager. But a week ago we hadn't needed a manager.

'You'd get an advance to record the album and get you out on the road – all recoupable, of course – we'll have to decide what the amount would be. Enough to cover your expenses, anyway.'

'What does "recoupable" mean?' asked David innocently.

I cringed even more, although I didn't know, either. To his credit, Mr Wallberger didn't laugh or even smirk at us. I think that was what convinced me this would be a good deal to do.

'Recoupable means that we give you money up front – that's the advance – and then once your record starts selling we take a percentage of the money from each record sold and use it to pay back the advance. It's like a loan.'

David and Justin were horrified. 'So how do we make any money then?' Justin demanded.

'Well, the idea is that we've signed you because you'll sell a helluva lot more records than it takes to recoup the advance, then we all start making a profit. Sometimes that happens with the first record, sometimes not until the second or third, sometimes never. It's a chance we have to take.'

Joe asked, 'So what if we don't sell any records, does that mean we owe you all that money?'

This time Mr Wallberger did laugh, but not in a condescending way. 'Oh no, it's our loss. You see, once you've made a record that we believe will sell, it's our job to sell it. That's why we have marketing and promotions people. Someone to take it to radio, someone to get press about the band and the record, someone to make sure it's in the stores, and so on.'

I had a mental image of an army of uniformed workers knocking on radio station doors all over the country with big baskets full of our records, saying, 'Here, have one of these,' but I didn't really see what good that would do. I couldn't associate the person in the radio station *having* the record with people going out and actually *buying* it. It was too big a leap of the imagination to picture the record being played on the radio at all. We had a couple of decent stations near us in Freehold, but the reception from our house was terrible, so I rarely listened at home. I had no concept of college radio charts or specialty shows playing new bands. It was all a mystery to me, and from the expressions on the others' faces I knew it was the same for them.

'But you don't have to worry about all that stuff just yet; it's early days. Let us take care of that. All you need to do is think about it for a while. We'll send you a draft contract, you can talk it over with each other and your folks, and then call me. Here's my card. No obligations. Once we've started the ball rolling, come by the offices and meet the team.'

'Yeah, and call me, like, any time if you have any questions,' chimed in Willy, who had been nodding in earnest assent during the last twenty minutes until I was worried his head might drop off. With every nod a little waft of patchouli drifted across to my side of the table.

I dropped my balled-up napkin surreptitiously onto the floor. A contract! Maybe this thing really was going to happen. I felt excitement rising in my throat like a blush, and 'There There My Dear' exploded into a crescendo in my mind.

Willy opened his mouth to say something else, but Justin sneezed suddenly and drowned him out. Willy tried again; Justin sneezed again. And again. And again. Every time Willy tried to speak, Jus sneezed, until Willy lapsed into embarrassed silence. David and Joe smirked, and I alternately examined my fingernails and my surroundings until normal service could be resumed.

'Normal service', it seemed, did not apply to the restaurant. Mr Wallberger was waving his Amex card indiscreetly in the air, trying to attract a waiter's attention, but they all seemed to have been struck blind. Meanwhile, Justin sneezed on and on, pausing only to wipe his streaming eyes with his napkin. Eventually one of the young men sauntered over with our bill, and held it out to Mr Wallberger, who threw his credit card onto the saucer without looking at the amount owed. I tried to imagine my parents doing that, and almost laughed out loud at the thought. I wondered if I would ever be rich enough to not care how much lunch cost.

We said elated goodbyes, left the restaurant and walked along to West 4th Street to get the subway back to Brooklyn. Justin finally stopped sneezing, and we sang the Dexys tunes full blast all the way back to Aunt Sandi's place, substituting the words we weren't sure of with choruses of la-la-las. There was a sense of unreality about the whole thing, emphasized by each of us calling out a different song title from *Searching For The Young Soul Rebels* to sing. We couldn't quite believe we had our *own* songs to sing from now on, and that people might actually want to hear them.

A draft contract was duly dispatched to us. Aunt Sandi had a boyfriend who was an attorney, and he looked it over for us, also showing it to a friend of his who was in entertainment law. It was deemed to be not a bad deal for a new, unknown band. We would have to sign options for five records with Ringside, which meant that after each record we made, they could decide if they wanted us to make another one. If not, they could drop us, but we couldn't voluntarily leave Ringside without breaking the contract until the five records were made. It seemed to be a very big commitment on our part and not very much on Ringside's, but apparently this was standard.

I started to worry that I wouldn't be able to write enough good songs fast enough, but Jus pointed out that if the songs weren't any good we'd get dropped anyway, in which case I wouldn't have to worry.

'Oh great, thanks. Pressure me, why don't you?' I told him.

Then Aunt Sandi's boyfriend commented that, as the songwriter, I would get more money than the others because I'd get publishing royalties as well as the artist royalties, which cheered me up no end. Justin looked sulky. After all, I thought, I already have over fifty songs written, and I've only been at it for a year and a half. Many of them were religious, and I didn't think that Ringside or the band would appreciate them, but that was beside the point.

We would get $20,000 up front for the first record, out of which we would be required to pay for our studio time and expenses, a producer, equipment purchase or rental and a van.

'That's a *lot* of money,' said Joe.

161

'Will there be any left over for me to buy a new car with?' David wanted to know.

'It's not our money,' I reminded him. 'Remember what Mr Wallberger said, it's an advance. We have to pay it back again later.'

'How will we keep track of everything?' I added as an afterthought.

'You need a manager,' said Aunt Sandi's boyfriend firmly. 'I'll ask my colleague if he knows anyone good.'

That was how Mickey the Manager came into our lives. Mickey looked like he should have been a lifeguard on an LA beach. He was very tanned, with a rugged face and a moustache modelled on Magnum PI. He had a couple of other bands on his roster, one of whom had recently become quite successful, and he was fond of spewing out clichés like 'stick with me, kids, I'm going places.' Boys apparently joined bands so they could meet girls – well, that was certainly the reason Joe had joined Blue Idea – and I was sure Mickey had started a management company for the same reason, because he couldn't actually play an instrument or sing. He always had some ditzy little dolly on his arm, picked up from a show the night before. But his womanizing notwithstanding, we all quite liked him. He had a warm heart under his sharkish exterior, and he did seem to work very hard for us and his other bands. We gave him a lot of healthy shit about how many polyester open-to-the-waist shirts he possessed, and the revolving door through which his girlfriends appeared to pass, but he took it all with good humour.

'Hey, I'm young' – he wasn't – 'I'm a mover and a shaker, and I'm gorgeous' – also debatable – 'why would I want to be tied down with a wife and kids?' Justin had finally met someone who could outdo him in the arrogance stakes.

Within three months of our lunch meeting with Mr Wallberger and Willy the contract was signed, we had a lawyer, a manager, some studio time booked for

162

demoing and a lot of money in a new bank account, which Mickey set up for us and which was overseen by an accountant, also found by Mickey.

We felt like a real band at last. I graduated from high school – the last of the four of us to do so – and told my parents that I was going to defer college for a year to see if my musical career would take off.

Everyone in Freehold knew about our deal; the local paper did a small feature about us when we got signed. All our old school friends were beside themselves with envy. The lead singer of Saul punched Justin in the face in the supermarket parking lot, and Margie hissed, 'Hell is a very *hot* place, you know,' at me from her front porch when I passed her house one day.

My parents professed to being proud of my new enterprise, but couldn't contain their horror that I wasn't pursuing further education, at least for the foreseeable future. I thought they were secretly convinced that I would transform overnight into a heroin-shooting, Mohican-sporting, foul-mouthed menace to society, who would embarrass them in front of their country club friends. This was, in a nutshell, how they viewed the protagonists of popular music, even though I told them punk was dead.

I phoned Sam to tell her we'd been signed, and she was hysterical with delight and pride. 'Well,' she said when she'd calmed down. 'My news is that I've got a Saturday job at Price Rite, I haven't had my O-level results yet, but I think I did all right – they want me to enrol for four A levels and an S level; and that swine Mark Symonds dumped me. So I think you win first prize for interesting news!'

I commiserated with her about Mark, although I'd never liked him. He had acne and was not, in my opinion, good enough for Sam. When I'd been over to stay with the Grants in Salisbury the previous Christmas, he and I had fought, subtly but constantly and viciously, for Sam's attention.

If the truth be known, however, I was also quite

jealous that Sam had a boyfriend and I didn't. I was sixteen and had never even been on a date. I was absolutely humbled by my pathetic track record. Sam was the only one I confided in about it, and she was very nice to me.

'Don't worry, Helena, you'll meet someone. Now you've been signed I bet you get loads of blokes after you. You're far too good for those meat-head high-school boys, anyway.' That was all very well for *her* to say, with her long slim legs and huge grey eyes.

I still had a massive crush on the doorman of the local club we'd played at countless times in the past year. He was at least twenty-one, and enormous, with monstrous biceps bulging out of a lurid Misfits T-shirt. He always smiled at me, and sometimes commented, 'Yeah, cool set, guys,' to us afterwards. I felt sure he said this specifically in my direction, and I fantasized that it was only a matter of days before he asked me out.

Every time we played the club I spent hours getting ready, trying to look as Gothic as I could, until the night we got on stage and I saw the door open and a beautiful punk girl walk in. She was tiny and elfin, with pink hair, black lace gloves and purple laddered tights. My doorman immediately locked her in the most passionate embrace I had ever seen. They were like two snails stuck together, and they didn't come up for air once throughout our whole opening number. When the song finished, I intentionally sent as much feedback as I could through the speaker, sending the snogging couple, not to mention the rest of the audience, leaping vertically into the air like electrocuted cats.

Oh well, perhaps Sam was right, maybe I *would* get a boyfriend now we were signed. He would be a musician, too, not just some scummy old bouncer.

I was, however, very impressed by the news of Sam's academic aspirations. '*Four* A levels and an S level? Cor, Sam, you'll be busy,' I'd said to her.

For a second I stopped thinking about the patent lack of romance in my life, and wondered instead if a patent lack of qualifications would be detrimental to my future ambitions, especially if I planned to move back to England. Sam would end up with examination certificates coming out of her ears, while I wouldn't have an O level to my name.

But no, I decided, I'm going to be famous. I'll concentrate on that, and worry about everything else later.

☆

You Look So Different

Mum was in the downstairs loo when the doorbell rang at seven o'clock that night.

'Sorry Helena, you'll have to get that. It's probably Margie,' she called through the door. I could hear the embarrassment in her voice at having to be so vulgar as to speak and pee simultaneously.

I plodded up the hall, feeling like the butler from Trumpton, or was it Chigley, and reluctantly opened the front door.

A hugely fat woman surrounded by an extended family of suitcases stood in the front porch. Only the man-made fibres of her clothes and the wedge of frizzy hair identified her as the Margie I remembered.

Margie, however, had even less clues to go on. 'Hi!' she said brightly and politely. 'Is this the Nicholls residence?'

'It certainly is!' I confirmed, equally brightly, adjusting my eye patch.

'Is Helena home? I'm an old school friend, Margie Westerburg. I believe I'm expected.'

I feigned shock and joyful surprise. 'Margie! Oh, I'm so sorry, I didn't recognize you. Well, it has been such a long time. Do come in.'

Margie looked at me, confused. Even though I was enjoying winding her up, I felt sick with hurt that I was so unrecognizable.

'Helena?' she asked, in a small, shocked voice.

'As I live and breathe,' I said heartily. 'Excuse me if I don't help you with your herd of bags, I just came out of hospital today.'

To my horror, Margie burst into loud, snotty tears. 'Oh my Lord, what *happened* to you? Your poor face! And what's the matter with your eye? You look so different, I . . . Oh, sweet Jesus, bless you!'

I turned away from her abruptly and stomped back down the tiled hallway, just as Mum flushed the toilet and emerged, adjusting her skirt.

I left her to greet Margie and fill her in on all the gory details, and went out into the back garden, where I stared at the birds commuting home across the apricot-streaked sky.

I felt utterly heartbroken. It wasn't just Margie's shock at my appearance, although that was bad enough. It was the comment, 'You look so different.'

The last time anyone had said that to me was years ago, and it had been Sam. I'd brought her to see Blue Idea headline Wembley Stadium, at an all-day concert with lots of bands. It was the first time she'd ever seen me perform to a huge crowd like that – her illness had meant she'd missed both our previous big UK tours.

It was a sweltering day, and Sam was tired, so while I got ready she had taken a little nap on the dusty old sofa in my dressing room. She'd woken up just as the make-up lady had finished working miracles on me, and I was in all my stage finery.

'Oh, Helena,' Sam had said, staring at me like I'd been beamed down from another planet. There was real awe in her voice. 'You look so different.'

'Kinky Afro', I thought now, was the song for that day. Because of my memory of Sam's sheer bliss as we danced around to it, hidden at the side of the stage, during the Happy Mondays set. I'd never seen her so happy. It was wonderful.

'Are you all right, darling?' asked Mum, who

appeared next to me, red in the face from the exertion of shepherding Margie's cases in. 'Why don't you come in and fix us all a drink?'

I nodded and came back inside, the whiny guitar intro of 'Kinky Afro' coiling up in my head.

'Drink, Margie?' I enquired, opening the sideboard to reveal my standing-room-only collection of the hard stuff. 'I've got gin, vodka, scotch, wine and beer in the fridge.'

'Oh, just a soda, please,' Margie interrupted hastily. 'I don't touch a drop of alcohol. Never have done.'

Her eyes roved around the room, obviously trying to take in anything other than my offensive face. 'You have a lovely home. Have you lived here long?'

'About five years, now. Glad you like it.'

I poured Margie a tepid Diet Coke and handed it to her, spitefully omitting to add ice. This crime was enough to cause the average American to rush to the airport and jump on the first available plane home, but sadly Margie was made of sterner stuff.

'You Brits sure do like your drinks warm, don't you? I'm kinda used to it now, though.'

'Mum? G&T?'

'Yes please, dear,' said my mother. 'I'll get the ice.' She marched pointedly into the kitchen to find the ice bucket. Traitor, I thought.

Drinks dispensed and chilled, we all sat awkwardly in the living room. Mum and I sat together on one sofa, because Margie's bulk seemed to spread across most of the other one.

'Say, Helena, you *have* lost weight,' Margie began. She'd been looking at my thighs, perhaps because it was easier than looking into my eye.

You haven't, you fat cow, I thought, berating myself for being such a bitch.

'Oh, that fell off years ago,' I managed airily. 'Being on tour was pretty physical work, even though people think you're just sitting around in tour buses all day.'

Margie nodded knowingly, as if she went on tour the

whole time. 'It sure was incredible, wasn't it, how you guys got to be so huge?'

I resisted the temptation to say the same went for her. 'Yeah, I suppose it was. It was a pretty interesting few years.'

I had no desire to dredge up my life history for Margie. I was saving it for the manuscript. 'So, what do you do with yourself these days? You mentioned you were over here for a conference?'

Margie's face lit up. 'Oh, yes, it was real fascinating. I'm a rep for a firm which sells evangelical products, and we had our annual sales conference in Man-chester for the first time. It's such a thrill to be in the UK. I've never been here before. And it was wonderful to meet all the other reps. Such a sense of community.'

'Sorry to be ignorant, but what are evangelical products?' I asked earnestly.

Mum grinned into her G&T, making ice bounce off her teeth as she swallowed.

Margie didn't notice. 'Gosh, all sorts of things, really. You know, hymn books and chalices and kneelers.'

I had a sudden thought. 'Hey, you don't sell those big wall-hanging things, do you, like the ones we had in church?'

Margie nodded ecstatically. 'Yes, yes, that's right. You remember those? Well, I'm not surprised. They are so beautiful.'

I actually managed a smile. 'Yeah, they were. You know, I always wondered how churches got hold of them. Who'd have thought you'd end up selling them?' Me, for one. It seemed perfectly fitting.

Mum got up from the sofa and began to head for the kitchen. 'Are you hungry, Margie? I was going to make a little supper for us all, if you'd like some?'

Margie nodded enthusiastically. 'Yes, thank you, Mrs Nicholls, that would be wonderful.'

'Oh, for heaven's sake, Margie, please call me Eve. We're all grown-ups now.'

169

I thought of Cynthia Grant and how she'd wanted me to call her Cynthia long before Sam and I were grown-ups. I must get in touch with her before The Plan, see her one last time.

Mum vanished off to rustle up a meal, and I realized Margie had asked me something. 'Excuse me, Margie, what? I'm still a little deaf in one ear.'

'I SAID, ARE YOU IN TOUCH WITH ANYONE ELSE FROM FREEHOLD?'

I rolled my eye. 'It's OK, I'm not that deaf; there's no need to shout. No, I'm not in touch with anyone, actually, apart from the Blue Idea boys. Mum keeps me up to date with the news, although she hadn't heard anything from you until your call a few weeks ago. You still live there, then? Are you married?'

Margie puffed her chubby cheeks up into two rueful cushions. 'Yes, I still live in Freehold. Guess I'll never leave the old place. And no, I'm not married. I was engaged, actually, until last year. But my fiancé left me for someone else.'

'I'm sorry to hear that,' I said. 'That must have been terrible.'

'Well, Jesus got me through it. He always does. I hope He's been helping you in your time of trial, too, Helena.'

'Yeah,' I replied hastily, trying not to add 'whatever'. 'So, do you know if Mary-Ellen Randall still lives locally?'

Margie nodded enthusiastically. 'Oh, yes. I see her at church every week. She was so excited when I told her I was coming to visit you. "Do send Helena my fondest love," she said. "I wish I could see her, too. She was such a lovely girl."'

I was touched. 'That's nice. I always liked Mary-Ellen. Send her my love, too, won't you? Is she happy?'

Margie looked at me as if I were mad. 'She sure is. She has the Lord in her heart and a wonderful family – two children and a cute husband. Great job, too; she co-ordinates missionary placements in the Third World. Of course she's happy.'

Instead of feeling my usual envy, I was pleased that Mary-Ellen was happy. She deserved it. For a second, though, I wished I'd kept up my faith. It must be wonderful to be content that whatever life threw at you you'd be OK, as long as you had God and a supportive community of like-minded people around you.

The telephone rang, and then stopped again. After a couple of minutes, Mum appeared back in the living room, cordless phone in one hand, potato peeler in the other. 'It's for you,' she said.

'Who is it?' I hissed at her, annoyed that she had answered it in the first place. Missing a heartbeat, I wondered if she was going to say Toby.

'Cynthia Grant,' she replied in a slightly strained voice.

I stood up and took the receiver, waiting for Mum to get back to spud-bashing; but she continued to loom in front of me, clutching the peeler in a rather defensive manner.

'Hi, Cynthia, it's me,' I said into the phone. 'I was just thinking about you.'

'Helena, love,' said Cynthia's voice warmly. 'How are you feeling? I'm so happy for you that you're out of hospital, but I feel so guilty for not visiting. Were you thinking that you're going to hate me for ever now?'

I laughed. 'Of course not. It would be impossible for anyone to hate you, least of all me.'

'Well, I rang the hospital. I was going to pop in and see you tomorrow, because I'm coming up to London to meet some girlfriends for lunch. But now you're home, I don't think I'm going to have time to come all the way over to Twickenham. I'm so sorry. I wanted to ring anyway, though, to say welcome back.'

'Oh, don't worry. It was really sweet of you to think of me. And thanks for the card, too. To be honest, I'm feeling pretty wiped out. *I'm not really up for too many visitors.*'

171

I raised my voice a tone for the last sentence, but Margie appeared to be comfortably engrossed in a *Marie Claire* she'd found in the magazine rack. Mum, however, was still looming strangely. I made a face at her and she turned abruptly and left the room.

Something occurred to me. 'Cynthia, there is one thing. You remember when I came down to Salisbury last time, you asked if I wanted to take that hat box, you know, our, er, Hel-Sam box, and I said no, I couldn't face it yet? Well, I wondered if I could get it picked up by courier. I've started to write a book, and it would really help to have a rummage through it.'

'Oh, Helena, of course you can, love. I've been keeping it here for you. What a wonderful idea. You always were a clever girl. Make sure you autograph me a copy, won't you?'

I felt a moment's sadness, for both of us, that I wouldn't be around to do any book signings when the book saw the light of day. 'Sure.'

'I'll get the box wrapped up and addressed, ready for collection. Mind, it's quite heavy. It'll be ever so expensive to have it couriered. Are you sure you don't want to wait until I can drive up with it? It would have to be next week, though, I—'

I cut her off. 'No, no, really, you don't need to do that. I can afford it. And, Cynthia?'

'Yes, love?'

'You won't look inside it, will you?'

Old habits died hard.

Cynthia laughed. 'Well, I've managed to contain my curiosity for about twenty years, so I think I can probably resist for another few days!'

I laughed, sheepishly. 'Sorry, I can't believe I said that! There's nothing very exciting in there anyway, as far as I can remember. It's just stuff like our old baby teeth, my second-favourite gonk and Sam's four-leaf clover. You know, things we thought were a big deal at the time.'

'Sam certainly thought that clover was a big deal,'

Cynthia said, a wistfulness creeping into her voice.

She'd brought up Sam's name. Much as I longed to talk about her, I wasn't sure I was up to it, I still felt too delicate. And besides, I certainly couldn't cope with doing it within earshot of Margie, marooned on the sofa, and Mum sulking in the kitchen. Briskly, I headed the encroaching emotional tenor of the conversation off at the pass. 'Yes, well, it's mainly the letters I'm interested in. Thanks for doing that for me. I really appreciate it. I have to go now, though. I have a friend from Freehold here, and we're about to have supper.'

We said our goodbyes fondly, promising to keep in touch. I replaced the phone, got myself a second gin and tonic, and poured Margie another Diet Coke, with ice. When I handed it to her, she put down the *Marie Claire* and, for the first time, looked straight at me.

'You know, Helena, I owe you an apology.'

I was taken aback. 'You do? What for?'

Margie looked sheepish. 'I prayed so hard about this at the time, and since, but I know I didn't behave in a very Christian way towards you when we were at school.'

'But you were the one who first introduced me to the Church.'

'No, not that. It's just . . . when you joined Blue Idea and started to go out and play all your rock concerts, I was, well, jealous.'

I was flabbergasted. 'Really? Why?'

'I'm not sure. I think it was because you could sing and play guitar so well. I always wanted to be in the choir, but I'm like, totally tone deaf, and there you were, up doing solos in weeks. And then you got in with the band, stopped coming to church, and got real successful and all. I pretended to myself that I disapproved because you'd turned your back on Jesus. I guess that was part of it, but who was I to judge you? Besides, I can't deny that I just felt so envious of you,

173

getting all rich and famous like that. So I'm sorry. I hope you forgive me.'

I grinned. What a turn-up. 'Of course I forgive you, Margie. You weren't all that horrible to me, anyhow. No worse than a lot of others in Freehold.'

Margie smiled back. She seemed genuinely relieved, and I felt a sudden wash of affection for her. It made me remember the kindness and humility of the Freehold Christians that had so touched me as a teenager. They were really nice people, underneath all the dogma and proselytizing.

In the end, Margie's company at dinner turned out to be tolerably pleasant; we sat around my vast kitchen table, reminiscing about the few subjects we could claim to have in common. Mum, however, was uncharacteristically quiet throughout the meal. I put it down to her not really knowing the people Margie and I were discussing, but when Margie eventually lumbered off to the spare room to bed, I realized there was more to it.

'I'll clear up, dear,' Mum said, tight-lipped, as I attempted to carry some bowls over to the dishwasher.

'Thanks, Mum. And thanks for cooking, too. It was lovely. Well, for someone who claims to be allergic to dairy, Margie sure managed to put away the ice cream, don't you think?'

Mum didn't answer me. She seemed to have taken it upon herself to rearrange the contents of my freezer.

'Mum? Are you all right?' With horror, I noticed that her shoulders were quaking. 'What's the matter? Are you sick?'

Mum shut the freezer door with a controlled *thunk* and, ripping off a piece of kitchen towel from a roll impaled on a wooden holder, she blew her nose and dabbed at the corners of her eyes. Then she picked up the entire kitchen-roll holder and brandished it at me. For a minute I thought she was going to throw it, but instead she pointed at its heavy rounded base.

'Are you aware that this isn't an ordinary kitchen-roll holder?' she said in a high-pitched, verging-on-the-hysterical voice I hadn't heard since the Thinifer days of yore.

I waited for her to say, 'In fact, this kitchen-roll holder has special powers! It's Wonder Woman's own kitchen-roll holder, and it doubles as a laser gun!' My mother, I thought, has finally flipped.

'No,' she continued. 'It's also a device for squeezing the water out of cooked cabbage: it's a *cabbage press*.'

'No kidding. Who knew?' I said weakly. 'Mum, sit down. What's wrong? Talk to me, please.'

Mum replaced the kitchen-roll holder/cabbage press and sat down opposite me. 'Helena,' she began, 'I want you to know that your father and I . . . Well, we've always tried to do our best for you.'

'I know,' I said. 'What's brought this on?'

Her eyes filled up again. My mother hardly ever cried. 'Do you still . . . Do you still . . . wish that Cynthia was your mother instead of me?' She looked at me, vulnerability naked in her eyes.

I remembered instantly the occasion to which she was referring. 'Mum! Of course not! That was one comment, made in a temper, when I was *nine years old*! Every kid says that kind of stuff to their mother at some stage. Surely you haven't been dwelling on it ever since?'

'Oh, Helena,' she sobbed. 'I'm so glad to know that. It was just hearing you on the phone to her tonight. You sounded so close, and she cares about you very much. But please know that I do, too. I feel so guilty for the way I neglected you – emotionally, I mean – when you were little. I always felt so unwell, you see, and Daddy spent all his time taking care of me. It worked out for us, that you and Sam were such close friends, and that you were happy to be at the Grants so much, but I look back and think, What have I done? Especially now, seeing you like this, after what's happened . . . the drugs and so on. I always worried that something like this would happen, but once the band split up I thought, No, she'll be OK now. But you aren't.'

I put my hand on top of hers on the table. I didn't really know what to say at first. 'It's not your fault, Mum. And, apart from that night, I don't do drugs. I never have done. That was a one-off because I was upset about Sam.'

It seemed incredible that in all these years we'd never had a heart-to-heart before. 'Why *were* you so sick when I was a kid? You had all those fluctuations and mood swings and stuff. I never knew where I was with you.'

'I'm so sorry. I'm really, really, sorry. But surely you knew that I had a thyroid problem?'

I gaped at her. 'A *thyroid* problem?'

Mum dried her eyes again. 'I can't believe you didn't know that, Helena. I thought I told you years ago. I contracted it after you were born: post-natal thyroiditis. In most women it goes away on its own, only mine never did. I kept swinging from hypo to hyper – underactive and overactive. The doctors couldn't keep up with it. They'd give me drugs to boost it when I was underactive, only usually by that time I was heading the other way, which made it twice as bad. It was only when we moved to the States that I finally got the right medication and it settled down. It was dreadful. I just felt permanently dreadful. That's why you're an only child. Neither Daddy or I could face the risk of it getting worse with another pregnancy.'

'Oh,' I said. 'I had no idea.'

'Well, really, Helena. You must have noticed that something was wrong.' Mum felt sufficiently unburdened to continue clearing the table.

'Of course I did. But I didn't know what to think. When I was a bit older I wondered about all kinds of things. You know, an eating disorder; clinical depression, maybe; even a drink problem, except that I know you get a headache after two G & Ts. Anyway, that was why I never asked. I thought it was

176

something ... sensitive that you wouldn't want to discuss.'

I was too ashamed to admit that actually, once I joined the band, it wasn't an issue to which I ever gave much thought, especially after Mum seemed to have recovered. I saw so little of my parents after I left school. I grinned. 'I used to think of your two extremes as Fattypuff and Thinifer.'

Mum huffed air through her nose in an approximation of a laugh. 'Very appropriate. You used to love that book.'

'And now you're just Middleton,' I said, thinking of Toby with yearning in my throat.

'Yes, thank goodness,' said Mum, putting on the kettle for coffee. 'I'm sorry, dear, for that little outburst. It's just that it's so painful, wondering if one did the right thing or not. I think back to you and those boys, driving around America in a van, unchaperoned, hardly more than children. We let you go with barely a murmur. It seems such a terribly irresponsible thing for us to have permitted. Anything could have happened to you.'

'Yeah, it did; we got rich and famous,' I said, gesturing towards the bank of gold, silver and platinum discs which covered the wall of the utility room — I'd thought it vulgar to have them anywhere more prominent.

'Well, as long as it's brought you happiness, Helena,' Mum said.

Happiness? That was a tough one, I thought. I pondered it for a minute.

'I guess it did, at first. I really felt as if I'd found somewhere I *belonged*, even more so than with the Church.'

I didn't want to upset Mum, but since we were being honest: 'The boys were like a family to me, like brothers. And Mickey was kind of like a dad, not that I wanted him as a replacement for Dad or anything, but you know, just in terms of looking after us on the road, making sure we were fed and paid and all that.

'You guys weren't bad parents, but I was a teenager, and I'd been taken away from my home and my friends, especially Sam. I needed something else to fill the gap. And then, when we got successful, it was so exciting and everyone wanted to know me. I felt like finally I could *be* someone. Yes, that made me happy, even if it meant that I had to go without a normal life.'

'So do you forgive me?' Mum asked uncomfortably.

Everyone's after redemption tonight, I thought. I got up from the table and hugged her, smelling the chemicals in her hairspray and feeling her stiff hair tickle my forehead, crispy, like strands of spun sugar.

'Of course I forgive you,' I said, adding silently, *As long as you will one day forgive me, too.*

Margie and her suitcases departed the next morning, leaving little gifts thoughtfully strewn throughout the house for me to discover over the coming days – an 'I am the Way and the Light' bookmark in the spare room, a poster of Jesus and some small children in the downstairs loo and a little board book called 'Prayers for Toddlers' in the magazine rack.

Mum had been true to her word and explained that this was a difficult time for me, and that as she – Mum – was returning home to Freehold soon, we really wanted to do some quality mother-and-daughter bonding before then.

Neither of us acknowledged, to Margie or to each other, the bonding that had taken place the night before.

'Ghosts'
Japan

July 1983

Hi, music lovers,

Welcome to the first edition of the Official Blue Idea Fanzine.

Blue Idea are the hottest, grooviest new band on the planet, and if you haven't heard us on the radio yet, or checked us out in your local fleapit, then don't worry, you soon will. In fact, catch us while we're still up and coming, so you can tell your friends you saw us on our first ever tour!

I'm Helena, and since I'm the only girl (!), I'll be writing you all a letter every month to tell you a bit about ourselves and what life on the road is like. I'm sure it's *not* going to be as glamorous as we think it is, but we'll soon find out!

First, here are some proper introductions, in our own words:

Blue Idea: the line-up

On lead guitar and vocals we have *Justin Timothy Becker.*
Hi, fans, I'm Justin, but you can call me the Sex God! I'm 18, 5'8½" and 143lbs. I have blond straight hair and brown eyes.
Hobbies: watching the Knicks play, track running, listening to records, talking to cute girls.
Fave bands: I like mostly British music: Elvis Costello and

The Attractions, Ian Dury and the Blockheads – in fact I wanted to call this band Justin Becker and the Blue Ideas, only the others wouldn't let me! – but I also like Dylan, Tom Petty and Talking Heads.

Fave foods: chili dogs, Coke, fries. You know, the usual.

Aspirations: I WANNA BE FAMOUS!!!

On drums we have *David J. Somerstein.*

I'm 18, medium height, medium weight, cool black hair, short-sighted, great dress sense, awesome rhythm sense. Originally from Pittsburgh, PA; moved to Freehold as a senior.

Hobbies: drumming is my life – I guess my folks wish they'd never bought me that kit! When I'm not playing drums, I watch movies. My all-time fave is still *The Empire Strikes Back* – I know, I know. I support the Steelers. Can't think of anything else real important.

Fave bands: Talking Heads – but I was into them before Justin was! – The Ramones, U2 and R.E.M.

Fave food: bananas – I am the ape man.

Aspirations: to play drums on stage for The Ramones some time. Oh, and to be totally rich.

On keyboards we have *Joseph Jennings (Joe).*

I'm 18, 6'1", 140lbs, brown hair, brown eyes, single and lookin' for lurve!

Hobbies: shooting hoops, making out, watching TV.

Fave bands: Blue Idea, of course.

Fave food: you name it, I'll eat it.

Aspirations: to marry any of Charlie's Angels, preferably all of them.

And finally, on bass and backing vocals we have *Helena Jane Nicholls.*

I'm nearly 17 years old, 5'8", I have dark brown hair, greenish eyes and I'm not telling you my weight! I'm British, but have lived in New Jersey for three years. I just graduated, a year ahead for my age.

Hobbies: playing bass, writing songs, singing, writing letters to my best friend Sam in England.

Fave bands: Blondie, The Cure, The Clash.
Fave food: English fish and chips, chocolate digestive biscuits.
Aspirations: I'd like to really make a difference. I want Blue Idea to be really successful so that I can help promote world peace through my songs.

Well, that's us. And now for some history, so pay attention, you guys at the back!

We all met in high school, in Freehold, NJ. Justin, our resident heart-throb – or so he likes to think – got the band together and gave us our name. To be honest, we were pretty rubbish at first – that's an English term for 'lame', in case you didn't know – but like most things in life, if you practise and practise, you eventually get better.

We spent months rehearsing, and yup, a lot of the time it was totally boring and we thought we'd never get anywhere, but finally we got our break. A guy from the record company spotted us at a show at The Stone Pony down in Asbury Park. His name is Willy Watts-Davis – a Brit, like me – and we love him! He hadn't even come to see us, but had driven down from NYC to check out the band we opened for – who shall remain nameless . . . Saul.

The rest, hopefully, will be history. We've now been signed by Ringside Records, they've got an agent to book us on our first tour and we'll be in the studio later this fall to record our first album! So watch this space . . .

The Tour

Day Two

The tour began yesterday, early on a hot July morning. It would've been earlier, only Joe overslept – no doubt starting as he means to go on. Still, as his dad was the one who got us a great deal on our van, we didn't give him too much of a hard time.

We love our van. It's metallic blue and only a little bit used. We paid for it out of our advance, and it's the first vehicle any of us have ever owned, even if it is only part owned. It has comfortable seats and a radio and everything, and a ton of space in the back for all our gear.

Let me tell you what we packed:

1. Instruments and equipment – amps, cables, microphones, etc.
2. Lots of clean socks and underwear.
3. Bedclothes, so we can sleep in the van if we have to – shudder.
4. A box of cassette singles of our best tune, to sell on the road.
5. Publicity photographs – hey, you never know. Someone might want our autographs.
6. Fake I-D for me (only joking, parents).
7. A ton of blank sheets of paper with 'Blue Idea – Mailing List' printed, by yours truly, at the top. For all you future fans to write down your names and addresses so we can send you fun stuff – this 'zine, for starters, hot off the press. You will soon discover that I love writing lists.

It was sooooo embarrassing; my folks actually came outside and waved goodbye to me when we drove off. My mum – that's mum, not mom, by the way – said that she had to pretend I was off to camp for the summer, otherwise she wouldn't be able to let me go. She can't stand the thought of me and a 'bunch of teenage boys' 'gallivanting off unsupervised around the country'. She even called the record company – cringe – to try and get them to send someone with us, but it doesn't work like that. And funnily enough, nobody wanted to come anyway. Can't imagine why . . . Heh, heh, heh . . . freedom! America is great. I'd never have been allowed to do this in England!

Joe had to swear to his folks that we wouldn't be playing in seedy cowboy bars; he says they thought that every night would be like that scene in *The Blues Brothers*, where they have to play behind a wire screen because everyone's throwing bottles at them. Anyway, we can't play in cowboy bars, seedy or otherwise because (a) I'm not old enough and (b) we don't play country and western.

Day Five

I hoped I'd be able to write this diary every day, but no
chance. I'm either too tired or too busy. But I don't care; this
is the most fun we've ever had! Being on the road is
fantastic! It's incredible to see a new place every single
night, especially for a Brit like me, who hasn't been around
the States much at all. We were in Washington DC yesterday, and I really liked it. The neighbourhood where the
venue is was a bit rough, but on the whole it's such a cool
place. I hope we get to play there lots more times.

We even did a tiny bit of sightseeing. David had a cousin
whose name is on the Vietnam Memorial, so we went to see
who could spot it first – only we couldn't find it, so David
wasn't very happy yesterday. But usually there's no time to
stop and look at anything historical or notable. Here's what
we do on a typical day:

1. Check out of our one, very small motel room. You'd
   think I could have my own room, being a girl and all,
   wouldn't you? But no, I have to put up with these three
   snoring – and worse! – all night long. Thankfully, we
   haven't yet had to sleep in the van.
2. Have breakfast and lots of coffee to wake us up after
   another late night.
3. Drive, drive, drive, drive . . . and then drive some more.
4. Find the venue, without the driver killing the navigator,
   or vice versa. We all take it in turns to drive and map-
   read.
5. Call Mickey, our manager – this is my job – from a payphone, to let him know that we're all still alive and
   haven't caught scurvy or fleas yet. In the meantime, he's
   talked to Willie, our product manager at Ringside, and
   passes on any interview requests or names for the guest
   list – so far, three of each, but it's early days yet.
6. Unload the van, soundcheck, go and eat.
7. Come back, watch everyone arrive, play our set, leave
   again. We're first on the bill every night, so it's not really

surprising that people pretty much stay at the bar. Willie told us not to mind about this. Until our single's out, no-one will have heard of us, so we should just be looking at these first few weeks as warm-ups 'for the cohesiveness of the band'.

Anyway, that's all for now, folks! Tune in again for the next thrilling instalment of Blue Idea on the Road!
Bye from all of us,
Helena xxx

Three months later we made our first album. The studio was in Manhattan, so we mostly commuted back and forth by train from Freehold, although occasionally, when we worked late into the night, we got a cab back to Joe's Aunt Sandi's place, where we'd stayed after our historic first meeting with Ringside, and crashed there instead.

The weeks we spent recording were a revelation in every way, from the infinitely superior studio gear we had on loan – my borrowed bass was so easy to play that notes dripped from its neck like honey from a spoon – to the pressure we felt to finish the record on schedule, to the huge amounts of pot smoked continually by everyone, except myself, probably as a result of the pressure.

People from Ringside were always dropping by to see how we were getting on, although I started to realize that they mostly did this as an excuse for an afternoon off work and a share of a large joint. I felt really frustrated and left out when they all spliffed up; they were so *boring* when they were stoned, and it made the chances of our finishing on schedule diminish even further. I just wanted to be getting on with the task in hand, but if I tried to bully the boys when they were high, they brushed me away like an annoying little fly, and settled further down into their exclusive catatonia.

Willy had booked Dean Barnes to produce our

record. He was a well-respected and talented East Coast indie producer, whose mellow manner and quiet good nature belied his absolute perfectionism. My only problem with him was that he was the biggest stoner out of everyone, but Willy one day assured me that being permanently wasted was pretty much endemic amongst producers, and not to worry about it.

It was, however, a miracle that we, as a band, survived the discipline of the studio. Dean would regularly make us repeat a few lines of a song about thirty times in a row, without raising his voice or sounding remotely disappointed in us, until we were all fit to be tied.

'Come on guys, better. And again.'

'Concentrate, David, you're tailing off at the end.'

'Justin, you're too pitchy on those high notes. Breathe.'

'Nearly there. Keep going. One more time . . .'

Once, after Dean had said 'one more time' nine times in succession, and after we'd already been playing the same song for two days, Justin threw down his guitar and stormed out of the studio, punching and kicking the door frame in fury on his way. I sat down in despair, thinking that we'd never get the bloody record made; we'd been working for a week already and had only finished three songs. I'd had no idea it would take so long. I'd believed we would just breeze in there and do the whole lot in a couple of takes, and that would be that.

Joe echoed my thoughts. 'I thought we just recorded, then it was Dean's job to fix it afterwards,' he grumbled.

Dean just looked up from the mixing desk, through the glass that separated him from us, and said over the intercom, 'OK, let's take a break.'

Slowly and painfully, however, the album came together. We argued about everything, from artwork to liner notes to sequencing, but with guidance and a lot of hard work from Willy, Dean and Mickey, somehow the day came when we received a box from Ringside full of pristine, shiny vinyl copies of *Switch On* by Blue Idea. Suddenly the hard work seemed worth it, and we all stood around like new parents, grinning stupidly and proudly at one another.

The tour continued into the Spring of 1984 on a considerably bigger scale. The album was sent to college radio stations in towns all over the country, the plan being that we should play as many of those towns as possible. We played five shows a week, and by the third week we had moved through Florida and Louisiana, into Texas and then across to Albuquerque, New Mexico. Our audiences got marginally bigger – about forty-five people had signed our fanbase sheets – but still regularly comprised the afternoon drinkers too inebriated to get off their bar stools and go home when we came on stage; or worse, the frat boys who thought they were above us.

Some nights they would just stand there, swaying and swigging cross-eyed from their beers and yelling insults at me.

'Hey! It's *Chubby* Checker on bass,' someone shouted when I wore a checked shirt on stage. 'Play some *Fats* Domino!'

'Yeah, anything but this faggy shit,' an answering shout came from across the room. It was occasionally assumed that because Justin was pretty and wore make-up he was gay, although our music was hardly faggy. On that particular day I was suffering from bad PMT, and I'd started to cry then and there. I'd wanted to walk off the stage, but there was nowhere to go except past our tormentors and out into the parking lot, and I was afraid to go and sit in the van on my own.

The comments, and my reaction, had pushed Justin's buttons so far in they were jammed. He shoved his mic stand over, jumped down into the crowd of approximately fourteen people and socked one of the offenders hard in the stomach. The rest of us stopped playing and stared aghast as a big fight broke out. Then Joe and David leaped into the fray, which, after several bloody noses and a big black eye – Justin's – was broken up by the barman and the club's owner. We were instantly banned from ever coming back, and Mickey was furious with us.

Thankfully that only happened once. Both Justin and I eventually learned to ignore any derogatory comments that flew up to us on stage, telling ourselves they were only the result of jealousy.

In the case of the women who insulted me, I think that was true. They had a way, those college girls, of looking me scornfully up and down, then leaning across and saying something in a friend's ear. The friend would look at me with the same expression of disgust, and they would both collapse in peals of sorority laughter. I tried to remember to 'love thine enemy', and to 'turn the other cheek', and a few times I even tried to go and make friends with them afterwards. It was a naive fantasy I had that maybe I could somehow win them over and become a member of their girly clique. But it never worked; they'd look at me as if I were something they'd found on the bottom of their shoe, and then they'd hustle off to the restrooms, giggling, to apply more lipgloss.

I hated them and their smug catalogue outfits and stiff, humourless hair.

You won't be laughing when we're famous and earning even more money than your daddy does, I'd think.

Justin, moody though he was, was usually very loyal. If he spotted any girls being snotty to me, he'd wait until they inevitably approached him after the set, simpering and sidling, then he'd take my arm and say, 'Come on, Helena, let's go. Don't you think the trash stinks around here?' Unless, of course, he fancied them, in which case I was on my own.

David, who was by nature gentlemanly, and Joe, in his own way, looked out for me, too. Despite our

187

incessant bickering, and my occasional yearning for female companionship, I began to feel protected and safe in the company of the three of them. We were in it together. It was like having a new family, and it lessened the sting, if not the guilt, of exchanging my hymn sheet for a fanzine, and my communion wine for an illegal aftershow beer.

March 1984

Hi, music lovers,
I can't believe we're so far into 1984 already, and what a year it's been, even if it's only a quarter done.

Blue Idea are back on the road again, hence the new issue of *Bluezine*. Do you like the change of title? David thought it sounded better than the boring old *Blue Idea Fanzine*. We all agreed, so *Bluezine* it is! We're three weeks into our Spring tour, but, hold onto your hats, there's more: our first album *Switch On* is in a record shop near you!

We had a fantastic time in the studio. Boy, what a learning curve that was. The record was produced by Dean Barnes, who has also worked with The Mai-Tai Micromen, and R.E.M. – he co-produced their first release, 'Chronic Town', with Mitch Easter. So if you haven't already done so, haul your butts down to your nearest music emporium and treat yourselves. You won't be disappointed, we promise!

Also, if you're in a college town, call up your local college radio station. They should have copies of the record by now, so why not request us? Chances are we'll be swinging by there in the near future.

Here are some pictures of us on stage at the Kactus Klub in Albuquerque at the start of our set. Don't we look miserable? Trouble is, these are the only snaps I have so far, since we all forgot to bring our cameras. It's hard enough to try and remember our instruments, let alone anything else. By the way, I HATE that plaid shirt I'm wearing. You won't be seeing that again.

As you'll see from the tour itinerary, it's been a pretty heavy three weeks, with five shows a week. We're working our way around the country in two giant loops, starting out with the south-east and south-western states. Then a break – phew – then back out to do the top half.

Our audiences are getting bigger all the time, and more of you wonderful folk are signing my fanbase lists every night. Keep it up, and tell your friends! We love you all!

*** NEWSFLASH FROM FLAGSTAFF, AZ ***

I just phoned the record company and guess what, our album has shot up to *number three* in the college radio charts! You guys are fantastic, you really have been requesting us. It seems that 'This Is Your Blue Idea' is the track that gets the most requests, and so Ringside are going to release it as a single on commercial radio, too!

We can't tell you how exciting this is. Thank you!

Come the Fall we were still driving. We were on the second stretch of the tour, and had driven up the north-east coast for a brief stint in Canada, and a long jaunt across the northern states of the US to do Oregon, Washington State, California, then across the Rockies, Kansas and Ohio, back into Pennsylvania and home to New Jersey.

Driving through some godforsaken part of Middle America, which having been summarily christened by Justin was henceforward known as Buttfuck Ohio, the alternator on the van suddenly went. We knew we were near a town by its prominent landmark – not a church tower or town hall or even a water tower, but a fifty-foot mast with a large revolving sign on top of it, bearing the words 'Adult Books'. It was lucky, we supposed, that in addition to the adult books, Buttfuck did also offer a garage and a tow truck, but we had to cancel our show that night and stay over while a replacement alternator was installed.

The lugubrious garage owner, whose name was Leland, dropped us off in his pick-up at the town's only motel, after taking what must have been a lengthy detour to a farm where, he said, he had to 'git his baby

189

boy'. A sixteen-stone acne-ridden youth about our age lumbered out in dungarees and a checked shirt, and sat in the back of the truck with us and as much of our gear as we'd been able to carry. He said nothing, but glared suspiciously at each of us as though he'd like to bash in all our heads with a pitchfork handle. We were very relieved to arrive at the motel, where we booked one room and bad-temperedly resigned ourselves to a night in what was possibly the weirdest place on earth.

'There's only one thing for it,' said Justin, 'we have to get drunk. All of us, including you, Miss Goody-Two Shoes.'

I wasn't having any of it, but at that point I thought it best not to argue. 'Whatever,' I said, bagging one of the small twin beds. Both beds had yellow nylon bed-spreads which looked and smelled like old curry. 'Whose turn is it to be on the floor tonight?'

'I'd rather sleep on the floor than share with Joe,' said David, hurling himself onto the damp Z-bed under the window.

Joe made smoochy faces at a glowering Justin, 'It's you and me then, honey.'

'I'm *definitely* getting drunk,' Justin grumbled. 'Let's go. This room stinks.'

After a plate of limp pot roast in a deserted diner, which doubled as the town's pharmacy and general store, we found the local bar. It was as empty as the rest of town, apart from a boot-faced barmaid on the wrong side of thirty with an enormous chest. Justin and Joe cheered up a bit, and I saw money change hands as they very unsubtly placed their bets on her.

'God, they're so juvenile,' said David to me. 'As if either of them stand a chance with her. And why would they want to? She's awful.'

I agreed. On a whim, I also agreed to have a beer from the boys' first pitcher. I'd decided some months ago that I didn't like the taste of beer at all, and I fully intended to have just a few sips before moving on to the Cokes. But to my surprise, this beer tasted delicious, cold and refreshingly moreish. Before I knew it, I was on my third glass.

I talked mostly to David, as the other two were doggedly vying for the waitress's attentions, and we decided to make a list of the top-ten weirdest things about Buttfuck. It got more and more riotous. After a while, Justin and Joe joined in, and someone decreed that each good suggestion merited a shot of tequila. It was an easy game, and we all managed to consume five or six shots. I began to understand exactly why people enjoy getting drunk so much. Tequila, which I hadn't tried before, turned out to be delicious, too.

'Leland's baby boy!' A shot for Justin.

'That "Adult Book" sign!' A shot for David.

'The way that no-one seems to live here!' Another for Justin.

'The vending machine in the motel lobby! Did you see it? It sold driving gloves and jewellery.'

I hadn't been able to get over this, and was very tempted to buy a cheap gold locket to accompany the dubious-looking sandwich in the next compartment, just so I could tell people where I'd got it from.

'That's a great one. A double for Helena!' cried David, clapping me on the back.

'Uh. I saw a licence plate on a truck that said, "I'm so *horny* I get *excited* at the *crack* of *dawn*". Does that count? It was kinda neat, there was a little cartoon guy in the background with his hand down the front of his pants and the sun coming up,' Joe contributed.

I laughed so hard that I didn't notice there were two more tequilas in front of me in place of the two I'd just downed.

Some time later I realized I was *very* drunk. Squinting at my watch, I saw that it was past midnight. 'Don't you think we should get shome shleep?' I suggested hazily. 'We gotta long drive tomorra . . .'

David stood up, swaying. 'Yeah, guess we'd better make a move. I feel kinda wrecked, too. Come on, guys.'

Justin looked at Joe and then at the barmaid, who was bending over, putting mixers on the bottom shelf.

'I think we'll stay here a while longer, yeah Joe?' Joe nodded in assent, his eyes glazed with lust.

David and I staggered out of the bar to the sound of Joe telling a very unimpressed barmaid that we were a famous rock band, and he could get her backstage passes to our next gig.

Back at the motel, our room still smelled like damp cumin. It was extremely chilly, but I was too drunk to notice. Uninhibited for once, I yanked off my clothes, stumbled into my pyjamas and collapsed into bed. A few minutes later I heard a small voice from by the window.

'H, I'm cold.'

'Put some more clothes on, then,' I mumbled groggily.

'I'm already wearing all the ones I have with me. Can't I share with you?'

'No way, David. Go to sleep.'

'Oh purlease, Helena. Pleeeeease. I'm frozen. This mattress is all lumpy, too.'

'So's mine. Get over it.'

'Oh, come on, H. Don't be so mean.'

Being the only girl meant that, even though we had to share rooms, I always got my own bed. And drunk or not, I would never have let Joe or Justin anywhere near me. I didn't fancy David, either, but I was more fond of him than I was of the others. He was much less sex-obsessed than they were, and he changed his underwear more often, too.

'Oh, all right. Just this once.'

David rolled off his mattress and into bed with me in one fluid movement. He was still fully dressed, including his glasses. In a moment of inebriated tenderness I pulled them off his nose and put them down by the side of the bed, folding their arms together over the frames. He looked so sweet and vulnerable without them that I couldn't resist giving him a little kiss on the forehead, and pulling his shivering body towards my chest. I must have fallen asleep like that, for a short time later I was awakened by someone prodding me in the thigh.

'Wassamarrer? Are they back yet?' I opened my eyes and looked into David's face. He was gazing at me intently. We were still alone.

'Helena,' he whispered. 'Have you ever done it before?'

'Done what?' I asked. At that point I realized that David had taken all his clothes off and was lying naked, still in my arms. He was warm now, and smooth. I yelped and scuttled over to the edge of the bed like a sand crab.

'You know what. Have you?' He reached over and stroked my face. I debated jumping out of bed and going to sleep on the floor, but decided I was too drunk and comfortable to move.

'No. Have you?'

'Sure!' he replied indignantly. 'I dated Courtney Norman for ages, you knew that.'

'Well, I didn't know if you two had done it or not.'

'Oh get real, Helena. Of course we did. I can't believe you haven't, though. Is it because of your religion?'

Admitting it wasn't as embarrassing as I'd feared. 'Yeah, I guess so. And, to be honest, well, I've never had a boyfriend.'

David was shocked. 'What, never? I've seen guys checking you out at our shows. They think a chick on bass is just about the coolest thing ever. Surely you did before you were in the band.'

'No. Anyhow, I'm not worried about it,' I said defensively, although I was secretly delighted that boys checked me out. 'I don't want a boyfriend anyway.'

David edged nearer until our noses were touching. 'I don't want a girlfriend, either,' he whispered, kissing my mouth and pushing his tongue inside. It was nice, not as yukky as I'd always imagined. I understood what it meant in books when people's lips were described as velvety.

'So, don't you think it's time to lose your virginity?'

I sat up too fast. 'Certainly not! I'm going to wait until I'm married. And besides, how would we ever face each other afterwards if we did that?'

David laughed and pulled me back down again. 'Relax, H, it wouldn't be a big deal. We would just decide right now that we won't mention it again, and it'll just make us better friends. I swear I wouldn't tell Joe and Jus, or anyone. Oh come on, it's real fun.'

'No way, David. Go to sleep or I'm kicking you out of this bed. Besides, I don't want to get pregnant.' I felt very mature, talking about taking precautions as though I was actually going to have sex like a normal, healthy teenager with a boyfriend. I didn't for a minute think I would, but the idea didn't seem nearly so scary with sweet old David offering. I lay down on my back with my legs firmly crossed and my elbows sticking out, so he couldn't get near me.

'Too bad. Oh well, if you change your mind just holler,' he said amiably. A few minutes later I heard gentle snoring and so I relaxed and fell asleep myself.

Later still I was woken again, this time by an amazing melting sensation coming from between my now loosely crossed legs, and a familiar prodding against my hip.

'You won't get pregnant, I swear. I have condoms,' David said in a low voice. I was surprised at his persistence, but even more surprised at the feeling of mellow heat which I realized was caused by David's forefinger rubbing me through my pyjamas. Actually, it was utterly blissful. At that point I pushed aside the memory of my promise of celibacy to God, and the fact that David wasn't my boyfriend. I didn't even worry about the others bursting in, or David realizing how fat I was. All I could think about was how I felt, and how I wanted more.

I moaned, and David rolled on top of me. He didn't seem to weigh anything at all. He kissed me again and I tasted toothpaste. Not fair! I thought. I haven't cleaned my teeth. The gentle rubbing was replaced by the persistent prodding, but it felt just as good, and even more satisfying. My pyjama bottoms were rolled down over my thighs and I barely noticed until he entered me with one huge, accurate lunge. I waited to feel pain, but there was none. Part of me couldn't believe this was happening, and part of me didn't ever want it to stop.

The next morning I was woken by the splutter and roar of a recalcitrant car engine coming from the motel forecourt. I had a thumping headache and my legs felt very stiff. As I gathered up my clothes and a towel and staggered over to the bathroom, I made out David and Joe's prone figures crashed out on the next bed, top to tail, with only the curry bedspread draped over them. David had his T-shirt on again. As I passed by, an audible fart emanated from his end of the bedspread, and I shuddered, bolting into the bathroom. The previous night seemed to have happened to someone else, and had I not felt an unfamiliar soreness down below, I might have thought I'd dreamed it.

Justin burst into the room just as I emerged, washed and dressed, from the shower. He was on fine form, full of stories about his conquest of the previous night, and insisted we all went, en masse, to the diner for breakfast so he could brag some more and taunt poor Joe. Over hangover fodder of pancakes and maple syrup, David and I exchanged small, sheepish smiles.

I felt wracked with guilt, but I kept that between me and God. Guilt aside, it was a relief to be able to write to Sam and tell her what had happened, and I was grateful to David for making me feel like a normal person, not someone who was too hideous ever to lose her virginity.

195

18 November 1984

Dear Mar Tangs (Clam Digger and Lobster Trapper),

I did it, I did it, I finally did it! And you'll never guess
who with? David! Yup, geeky little David. What a sly dog.
Our van broke down in Buttfuck, Ohio – sorry, Justin's
name for a hick town! – so we had to cancel a show and
spend the night there. I got drunk, too – don't be too dis-
approving; it's only rock and roll (but I like it). Have you
ever had tequila? It's yummy, but it doesn't half give you a
terrible hangover. To be honest, I don't really even remember much about *It*. One minute I was asleep/passed out on
the bed, the next, David's all snuggled up with me; and the
next, he's . . . you know. The others weren't there –
obviously. They were trying to make out with the barmaid.

I think I enjoyed it. It was good, and bad, that I did it
with David and not some strange boy. Good because I trust
him and know him so well, but bad because it's not like
we're gonna be an item or anything. We were both drunk.
Also, bad because it feels a bit incestuous. Still, at least I
am officially *No Longer A Virgin*. I was getting worried,
after you and Martin Trubshaw had that night of passion –
what's up with him these days? Is he still blanking you?
– I am a year older than you, after all.

Love from your experienced friend,

H xx

25 November 1984

Dear Helena,

Oh my God! Congratulations! Send more details – if you
can remember them. Is he, you know, small all over? And
is everything OK now? I mean, isn't it a bit awkward
having a one-night stand with someone you spend all your
time with?

Martin 'Nadger' Trubshaw is still avoiding me. I think he
fancies Mel; she's always telling me she bumped into him,
and I haven't bumped into him for weeks. I don't know if I
should tell you this, but I heard Mel say to the Nadger's

196

friend – whose name is Chris – that *her* friend Helena is a famous popstar in America, and if he liked, she could get your autograph for him! So you see, she hasn't changed a bit. You'll be pleased to know that, while I'm inordinately proud of you, and boast about you as often as possible, I wouldn't dream of prostituting your good name – well, your name, you old tart – in that wanton way.

School is quite good at the moment, I'm really enjoying the A-level courses, especially History and English. I've decided that the only men in my life are going to be Urban VIII, Bishop Frederick Nausea and Oliver Cromwell. Olly's a bit ug, bless him – he really should've had those heinous warts seen to – but we must not forget that he was a Healer of Breaches. Or was that breeches?

'Anthony and Cleo' is great, too. Apart from the death issues, I wish I was Cleopatra. She manages to be a vamp and a romantic heroine at the same time: 'O! my oblivion is a very Anthony, And I am all forgotten'. I wonder what the Nadger would do if I turned around and said that to him one day? 'O! my oblivion is a very Martin Trubshaw . . . etc.' No, doesn't have quite the same ring to it, does it?

And there's another funny thing, why do people 'turn around' and say stuff to each other? Usually they're already facing them. It makes no sense.

French is OK. Here's an insult for you to try out on Joe next time he annoys you: '*Joe, tu es un grouillement continu!*' It means, 'You are a seething mass.' That'll confuse him.

Anyway, I'm rambling now. Write soon, you exciting, nearly-famous person.

Lots of love and kisses,

Sam xxxx

PS. Handy phrases for you to remember if you're ever on tour in Germany:
1. '*Ich habe meinen Totempfahl verloren*'– I have lost my totem pole
2. '*Meine Beutelmaus hat eine Verstopfung*' – My wombat is constipated

Aside from being the most memorable, that Fall leg of the tour was a lot more rewarding, as our reputation slowly began to precede us. The autumn scenery was absolutely stunning, too. To be confronted with majestic sweeps of red, orange and yellow around every corner made the driving infinitely less tedious. I could quite happily stare for hours out of the window at the rich foliage presenting its last colourful stand. The leaves on some of the trees were such a perfect, delicate shade of peach that they made me want to cry. I would search for these particular ones whenever we stopped for gas or lunch, kicking ankle deep through the carpet at the sides of the road, and if I found any I would put them carefully in the glove compartment of the van, meaning to send them to Sam. I didn't recall ever seeing that peachy tint on English autumn leaves. But after a couple of days their colour always faded to a nondescript dull russet, and I ruefully threw them away, along with the myriad McDonald's boxes and Twinkies wrappers which littered the van floor.

We finally made it back to the East Coast. We were driving through Vermont on our way home, engaged in some pointless but vaguely entertaining bickering about whether a girl in my year at high school had suddenly begun to stuff her bra. The mountain vistas were particularly ravishing, but I was driving, and so couldn't allow myself to gaze at the foliage too much.

'She did not! She just discovered those push-up bras. Believe me, women know these things.' I was getting interested, despite myself.

Justin snorted. 'Excuse *me*, but I think us men spend more time staring at girls' hooters than you do.'

'Generally speaking, I wouldn't count on it,' I replied, pulling into the fast lane to overtake an octogenarian couple in an RV, who were rubber-necking at the trees above them.

'Do girls stare at other girls, then?' asked Joe curiously.

'Well, yes, of course. Just out of interest and to

compare. You do the same, don't you? Except that boys have a name for it.'

Justin wasn't so keen on this line of questioning. 'Since when were you such an expert on men, Miss No-Boyfriends Nicholls?'

I blushed.

Joe joined in the inquisition. 'Yeah, Helena, why *don't* you go out with guys? You haven't dated anyone since we've known you.' He stared at me with mock horror. 'You're not ... you're not ... one of those *lesbians*, are you?'

I spluttered with outrage. 'No! Of course I'm not! Jeez. What's the matter with you? When have any of us had time to have dates and stuff in the last two years, anyway?'

The boys exchanged glances, implying that they'd somehow managed to find the time. Thankfully, David kept quiet in the back of the van. I was worried for a minute that he'd be tempted to chime in with the benefit of his first-hand experience. But Justin was like a terrier with a toy between his teeth.

'You don't hang out with anyone from school, girls *or* boys, H. I've never seen you put any names on the guestlist, except your folks once or twice. Why are you such a loner?'

I misheard him. 'I'm not a loser! How dare you call me a loser!'

Justin grinned, making a winding-up motion with his hands.

'For your information, you bunch of mutons, no *way* am I a lesbian. I *do* have friends, Mary-Ellen Randall and ... er ... Margie Westerburg, but they just aren't into our sort of music. And my best friend, Sam, is coming to stay with me soon. She lives in England, otherwise I'd be hanging out with her the whole time. Satisfied?'

'Oooh, Sam! She wears the pants in your relationship, does she?' sang Joe from the back.

'Shut up, Joe. Shut up, Justin. I'm really sick of

199

hearing your voices. Turn the radio on, can't you?'

Justin smirked maliciously, knowing that yet again they'd succeeded in embarrassing me. He did switch it on, though, and after a few minutes of chasing up and down the dial, he stopped twiddling the knob when we heard the final bars of a Jonathan Richman tune. It faded into something else, a song which made us all, in one split second, think, That sounds familiar. What is it? before recognizing it with a scream of joy.

'Turn it up!'

'Oh my God, it's us!'

'Louder!'

'Stop the van!'

Quickly, I pulled over to the side of the road. Cranking the volume up full blast, we opened the windows and let the sound of the first track on our album pour out over the crisp colourful hillside, accompanied by our voices yodelling along in unison. We were bouncing around with so much excitement that the van shook from side to side, and passing motorists stopped looking at the scenery to wonder what on earth was going on. We'd heard Blue Idea tracks on the radio before, but only when we'd actually been at the station, giving interviews. It was indescribable, the sensation of hearing on the radio, unanticipated, a composition that had come from my own head. As the last note approached, we shushed each other and listened attentively, leaning our heads towards the radio to hear better, even though the speakers were in the doors.

'Shh, it's ending.'

'Yeah, we know, Joe, we were there, too.'

'Shh, see if he says anything!'

There was a moment's pause and we held our breath. Then the DJ came on air. I would have known this was a college station even without him playing our song, because of the sound of his voice. Every college DJ in the country seemed to have the same voice, languid but slightly hesitant, as if they were smoking reefer while the records played, which they probably were.

'Yeah . . . um . . . that was a band with a new record out. They're called, uh, Blue Something – wait, I've lost the sleeve – oh, here. Blue Idea, kids, out of Freehold, NJ, and that was "This is Your Blue Idea", the first track from their brand new album *Switch On*, out on Ringside Records. Yeah. Actually, they seem, you know, really cool. Check it out. And next up, here's Japan with "Ghosts".'

Every time I hear 'Ghosts' now, David Sylvian's autumn voice washes over me like falling leaves, and I see layers of things: peach and red, curried bedspreads, the head-spinning of tequila, hazy sexual pleasure, the purity of unplayed vinyl and the first thrill of success.

Sam's Treacherous Blonde

Somebody was lurking around my house. Over the years I had, of course, come across quite a few assorted lurkers, loomers, anoraks and saddos, but fortunately I'd never had my very own stalker. I'd known plenty of other artists who'd had privacy-invasion issues, though. Adam Ant once told me that he had someone living in his roof space for months, spying on him through holes drilled in the loft floor. God, how did he not notice? Ever since I'd heard that, I had examined my bedroom and bathroom ceilings through a magnifying glass. And what about poor Bjork, with the nutter who blew his brains out on home video for her? Nightmare.

So, no peepholes in the plasterwork, but an intermittent, undeniable, lurky sort of presence; enough to make me feel extremely nervous. A shadow past the side of the dining-room window, as if someone was trying to peek through a gap in my muslin curtains. A fresh footprint in the mud next to the garden path, which couldn't belong to the bin men because they'd been two days earlier. A dry bottom-shaped patch on my swinging garden seat when the rest of the garden was wet.

One night, after Mum had returned to New Jersey, I was sitting at my refectory table sorting through boxes and boxes of photographs, fanning them out in cascades around me, wondering how to begin to make sense of them all. It was part of a get-my-affairs-in-order campaign.

I'd sorted through the Hel-Sam Box of Important Stuff as soon as it had arrived from Cynthia, and had pulled out some letters and *Bluezines*, which I intended to copy into the manuscript. The whole correspondence, plus accompanying photographs and press features, etc., was a great source of Blue Idea memorabilia. Might be worth quite a bit after I'm gone, I thought. The rest of the stuff was more personal and pretty much as I'd described to Cynthia: a gruesome collection of baby teeth, Sam's beloved dormouse keyring, the aforementioned four-leafed clover, my second-favourite gonk – the top favourite was still missing in action, last seen at Salisbury Fair in 1977 – oh, and a big Genesis badge, which I'd won at the same fair. I'd worn it on my coat lapel for ages, thinking myself quite hip and unusual to have such a badge. It was only after an older kid at school asked me if I had all their albums, that I discovered Genesis wasn't just a book of the Bible.

But personal as it all was, I found that these things, though important, didn't move me as much as, say, hearing two minutes of a song that reminded me of Sam. That could reduce me to an emotional jelly, as could the sight of her tiny, spidery handwriting, but her keyring was just a keyring, however much she'd prized it.

I looked at all the photographs in front of me. It was odd, looking at a lifetime's worth of little shiny Helenas: teen Helena, tummy pooched out over the top of tight jeans; Helena in a yellow bikini ten years later, the same stomach shrunken and bronzed; Helena scruffy, chewing her cuticles; Helena wealthy and manicured. I wondered if I scanned all these different images into a computer, would it come up with the one definitive Helena? And if it could, what would she be like? Thirty-two years of a digital me, assembled from the sum of my parts and the snaps of my holidays. I was sure she would look better than the real thing, this wrinkly, one-eyed, lonely failure.

The telephone rang. I let the machine pick up. Unless it was Sam, calling to say hi from the Other Side, or Toby, I wasn't interested. But the machine clicked off again without recording a message. I had a sudden hopeful vision of Toby cradling the receiver between his neck and his chin, leaving the scent of his aftershave on the earpiece, a feeling so strong that I got up and dialled 1471. 'The caller's number has been withheld,' said the robot inside the phone, and I was disappointed that I couldn't even smell a trace of Toby.

Sam was in at least 80 per cent of the photographs, always smiling: Sam in shorts, on a bike, with Cynthia, with me. There was one of us at about nine years old, topless, arms round each other's shoulders. Her chest was flat, brown and smooth; mine lard-white and flabby, the whisper of cotton-wool breasts budding. It looked as though Sam was carelessly pinching my pudgy nipple between thumb and forefinger.

The phone rang again. Again the caller declined to speak into the machine. I put the Cocteau Twins' *Heaven Or Las Vegas* on, loud, but it wasn't loud enough to drown out the phone ringing a third time.

I toyed with the idea of hiring a bodyguard. Perhaps that would add another twist to The Plan. The police might think I'd been kidnapped, or assassinated, if I suddenly disappeared after employing security. No, I thought. Keep it as simple as possible, like Richey from the Manic Street Preachers did. No fuss, bye bye. Gone.

But in the meantime, I didn't want to be trussed up and knifed to death by a stalker, not before the manuscript was finished.

I picked up a blurry photo of two people kissing, and peered at it for a while until I realized it was Sam and Justin. God, I wished she were here to show it to! What a pity it was out of focus. If it had been sharper I'd have mailed it to Justin with a note: 'You and Sam. Remember her now?'

There was a picture of me with Sam and Sam's travelling buddy, Andrea. Ondrea, she pronounced it. It was taken in New York, right before the two of them set off on their travels, their gap-year round-the-world trip. Even thinking about it now, jealousy twisted like chicken wire in my guts. Andrea looked so smug in the photo. She was tiny and blonde and brittle, with big, high *Baywatch* breasts, and I remembered how hard it had been for me to donate a smile to the camera when this horrible blonde interloper was about to take Sam off to the other side of the planet.

It was a funny sort of jealousy, one I'd had to get used to since leaving Salisbury; jealousy that Sam was having experiences in which I should be sharing, but wasn't. And the Australian trip had aroused an all-consuming resentment that, now we were old enough to make our own decisions, Sam had decided to go off without me, to have adventures of which I was no part. I'd tried to explain it to her before she left, but she'd laughed.

'But you're on the road all the time! What's that if not an adventure?'

'Well, come on the road with us instead,' I'd replied.

How secretly gleeful I'd felt, when, six weeks later, Sam had called collect from Australia to ask if she could come and spend the rest of her six months with me after all, since she and Andrea had fallen out. Blue Idea were about to set off on tour again, but I instantly arranged for Sam to fly to Seattle and meet us there.

When she arrived at our hotel, I'd listened, tutting and head-shaking, to her tale of woe and false friendship. Apparently the trip had got off to a great start in Sydney: they'd both got waitressing jobs and had rented a flat with a three-month lease. Then one day a beautiful tanned surfer with luminous lime shorts and a washboard belly had sauntered into the café where Sam had worked.

Sam had fallen, instantly and passionately, in love, and nearly passed out with excitement when the Sex God – whose name was something ridiculous like Dwayne – had asked her out that night. She'd raced home after her shift, and tarted herself up like she'd never tarted before, rabbiting incessantly to Andrea about how wonderful he was, how gorgeous, how sexy, and consequently how nervous she was feeling.

'What if he's late? What if he stands me up? What if I'm left sitting there all night like a prat? What will I do?'

Andrea had magnanimously suggested she accompany Sam, just to make sure that Dwayne showed up. Sam could introduce Andrea and Dwayne, and then Andrea would push off, pleading a prior engagement, and leave them to get on with their date.

Only it didn't turn out quite like that. Sam and Andrea arrived at the venue on time, and sat twirling on bar stools, sipping daiquiris. Just as Dwayne walked in, a woman sat down on the stool next to Sam. Before she had the chance to tap the woman on the shoulder and say 'sorry, this seat's taken', Dwayne had sashayed over and, with a glowing smile and a hello to Sam, had perched his two walnut-tight buttocks on the stool next to Andrea.

Sam waited and waited for Andrea to leave, but she didn't. Sam kept looking at her watch and saying, 'Golly, Andrea, you'd better hurry up. You're going to be late for the cinema,' but Andrea just shook her Hollywood hair and said, 'Oh, actually, I don't fancy that film tonight after all.' Then Sam had waited for Andrea to go to the Ladies', so she could casually change seats with her, but Andrea's bladder was evidently extra capacious that night. Instead of including her in the conversation, Andrea gradually and subtly moved her shoulder around so she almost had her back to Sam. Sam had sat miserably sipping her third cloying pink drink and wondering how best to go about cutting off Andrea's breasts.

Eventually Sam had got up and said, 'Well, I'm off then. Anyone coming?'

Dwayne and Andrea had looked at the floor and muttered, 'We'll just stay for one more, I think, don't you?'

The next morning, when Andrea returned to the flat, wearing the same clothes and with a red stubble rash around her mouth, Sam was packed and ready to go.

When she asked Andrea, tearfully, how she could have done such a thing to her, Andrea's only defence was, 'Well, he was just *so* gorgeous, and it's been such a long time since a man paid me that much attention.'

Sam was on the next plane to Seattle, and I had a worm of vindication wiggling guiltily in my heart for months afterwards.

I decided not to use the story of Sam's treacherous blonde in my manuscript. It was tempting, but not really relevant to my own life. Instead I would just record the facts: Andrea would get a mention, but that was all she merited.

I managed to get most of the photos into some kind of order, chucking away all the overexposed and blurry ones – except the one of Sam and Justin – and filing the others under headings like 'Band' and 'Salisbury' and 'Sam'. As an afterthought, I pulled out three of my favourite shots of Sam and put them into the Hel-Sam Box, on top of everything else. I wanted them to be the first thing anyone saw when they opened the box.

When I was getting ready for bed that night, I thought I heard a heavy dull sound, like a stumble, in the back garden. It must have been quite loud for my one ear to pick it up. Creeping into the spare room, I watched for a long time through a gap in the curtains, but I saw nothing but the dusky shapes of trees and the silhouettes of shrubs. There was usually a movement-triggered security light on the patio, but the bulb must have blown, for it remained dark.

I wondered again whether to call the police, but suddenly I felt too tired. Plus, dialling 999 might lead to publicity, and I couldn't risk that. Not yet. I'd just have to take my chances with the stalker.

Nonetheless, I double-checked that all the doors and windows were locked, made sure the alarm system was switched on before I went to bed, and slept with a rape siren and a baseball bat under my pillows.

'To Be Someone'
The Jam

2 March 1985

Dear Ram Gnats (Turkey Plucker and Duck Stuffer),

I hate the boys. I HATE THEM I HATE THEM I HATE THEM!

I can't stand being on the road a minute longer. Why am I doing this? Why? I could be with you in Salisbury, doing A levels, having a laugh with you over all the things you find funny in your English texts, but instead I'm stuck in a van, which STINKS to high heaven, surrounded by hideous mutons.

The books you sent are keeping me sane, though. Oh, I found a quote for you: 'The man opened the door and hurriedly threw his eyes down the street.' What do you think? Good one, eh. It's from D.H. Lawrence.

Writing this has already made me feel less like killing the boys. A little bit less . . .

David's not so bad – as he once proved! – but, man, Joe and Justin are SO JUVENILE. Last night was about the final straw. Bastards. Wait till you hear what they did. We were all stuck in this one tiny dressing room in a venue in Northampton, Massachusetts, running three hours late – we'd got stuck in traffic and arrived to find out the club's curfew was midnight, which left us twenty-five minutes to do our set. It was a college crowd, but they'd been waiting for ages, and were chanting and stamping their feet. Troy, our new tour manager, who doubles as a roadie, and David got the gear set up in record time, and Joe, Jus and I were all scrambling over each other to get changed, do our make-up and hair, and get out there before there was a riot. Usually there's a bathroom where I can get changed; I don't mind sharing a motel room with them – if I have to – but I never get undressed in front of them.

I was nagging them like mad to turn round so I could put my skirt on, and Justin was fed up with me. He goes, 'Just do it, Helena. Like we care. I'm far too busy here to be looking at you naked.'

I begged them, though, and eventually they faced the wall, and I turned around, too, and ripped off my sweat-pants and sneakers – my van-driving clothes.

I didn't notice how quiet they'd both gone until I turned back, half into my tights, wobbling all over the place on one leg, and met their eyes in a mirror on the wall they were facing! I could have died. I burst into tears and they just laughed. Oh, Sam, I was wearing my horrible huge old knickers, and they'd had a perfect view of my massive bum. I hate them.

Anyway, I'm feeling a bit better now. I'm just worried they'll tell David what a massive ass I have, and then he'll feel sick at the thought that he actually went to bed with someone as repulsive as me. Wish I was skinny like you.

Write soon and tell me about Martin. I'm glad he's finally asked you out. Have you 'tweaked his deak' or maybe even 'pronged his dong' yet?

Oodles of love,

H x

PS. Further to your enjoyment of *Around the Aardvark in Eighty Days*, might I suggest a few more titles for your reading pleasure? *80,000 Aardvarks Under the Sea*; *To Kill An Aardvark*; *The Aardvark of Casterbridge*; *The Decline and Fall of the Roman Aardvark*.
PPS. I tried to get Joe to play this game, and the best he could come up with was *101 Aardvarks* – duh . . . xx

19 June 1985

Dear Rusty Harcourt,

That's your porn-star name, in case you ever fancy a change of career. You take the name of your first pet, and the name of the first street you ever lived in.

Thanks for your letter. Your language gets worse every time you write. I must say, you were a better class of girl altogether when you were going to that church all the time!

Only THREE more months till I see you again!

I'm right in the middle of exams. They seem to be going OK so far, although History was a bit of a nightmare. You're so lucky you don't have to do all this studying, you tart, off round America being a rock star. I can't wait to hear you play live. I'm still playing your record like mad, and I make everyone else listen to it, too. It's fabby.

So, my big news is that I am definitely going to take a year off before law school. There's a girl called Andrea Parsons who's started a Saturday job at Russell & Bromley with me – did I tell you I wasn't working at Price Rite any more? – and she's saving up to backpack around Australia. She's asked if I'd like to go with her. I'm so excited. I've always wanted to go to Australia. So what I thought is, I'll still come and stay with you for a month first, then Andrea can fly out and meet me in New York.

Right, this was just a quick one, got to get back to the revision.

Lots of love and kisses,
'Hammy Chestnut'
xxx

PS. You know that Squeeze song about Maid Marian and William Tell – 'Pulling Mussels (From The Shell)'? It was on the radio the other day, and the Nadger said to me, 'You know, I've always wondered what exactly that *means* – "Pulling Muscles off a Shelf". It doesn't make sense.' I couldn't stop laughing.

25 August 1985

Dear Gas Mnart (Monkey Shaver and Sheep Dipper),

First, CONGRATULATIONS! You little brainbox; there's
just no call for anyone to have such a disgusting amount of
grade As. What a creep. I'm not sure I can be friends with
you any more. Don't take a year out; get into that law
school and hurry up and qualify, so you can become Blue
Idea's lawyer. Wouldn't that be great?

Second, sorry I haven't written for so long. I've been
saving it all up for this letter, so make sure you're sitting
comfortably.

I can't wait to see you. I wish you were coming for more
than a month. In fact, I wish you were spending the whole
year with me instead of swanning off to Oz with Andrea
Parsons, whoever she may be, but that's your choice! Just
remember, backpacks are really heavy, Australia is full of
those horrible black-widow spiders, which bite your bum
when you go to the dunny, and there are fifteen-foot
crocodiles who'll rip your foot off as soon as look at you.
Don't say I didn't warn you.

I'm sorry that I probably won't have much time to show
you the sights in NYC – although the interior of our tour
bus is a complete sight after a few days, and so is Joe in
the mornings. Would that do? – but at least once we're on
the road you'll get to see some of the bars and diners of
America.

Can you believe it, Blue Idea's been on the road for two
years! I was so shocked when David told us that yesterday.
I hadn't realized we'd been touring for so long. So much
has changed, and a ton of it has been really gradual; it's
sneaked up on us. We're headlining more and more shows,
in bigger, packed-out venues. I feel so sorry for the poor
bands who are first on our bill; they look so despondent,
hammering away valiantly to an empty room. It seems like
only yesterday that that was us.

We still have a little table at the back of the venue where
people can sign our fanbase sheets; that's worked out
really well. I remember, on the first tour, feeling really

212

stupid when I collected all those blank pieces of paper at the end of a show, thinking that nobody would ever sign them. These days Troy leaves out about eight sheets a night, and by the end they're all full up, with about thirty names and addresses per sheet. He sticks them in the mail to Ringside, and half the time they're all beer-stained and illegible. I really pity the poor minions who get the job of typing them onto our master mailing list. Still, at least we know who to send the fanzine to.

Have I sent you the famous *Bluezine* lately? What an exquisite work of art it is – Joke! I really hate writing it these days; I never have time, and I can never think of anything new to say, apart from droning on about chart positions and new singles, etc. I think I'm too hung up on the idea of trying to make it 'a good read'. Justin teases me about it. 'It's not supposed to be *Catcher in the Rye*,' he said last time, when I wanted to put in a story about that weird fan we had – you know, the one who kept sending David his toenail clippings.

Touring has got easier, though. I'm much less self-conscious on stage these days, since 'This Is Your Blue Idea' was a hit (and I think losing my virginity also helped!). It was a real turning point. Suddenly it was like people were starting to respect us, and not just lust after Justin.

The best thing was when kids in the audience stopped yelling insults at me. In fact, these days they quite often make suggestive remarks, or compliments, even. I love it. Some guy shouted, 'Lovely tits!' from the crowd last week, so I have to assume that he was talking about me! Actually, I've lost quite a lot of weight. I'll never be as slim as you, but I'm down to an American 8 – English 12 – and my hips and cheeks and other assorted bits are much less wobbly. Touring is surprisingly hard work, considering how much sitting around on the bus we have to do.

Did I tell you that the second single, 'Conditions Of Love', is in the Billboard Top Ten? It's currently number four, up from seven last week. We've been on a bunch of regional TV shows in the places we're touring, and girls

213

are recognizing Justin in the street quite a lot. We even made a video for it! I'll try and get you a copy. I had this letter the other day from a thirteen-year-old girl in Michigan who said she wished she could meet me because I'm 'really cool'. Isn't that hilarious? I wish twenty-year-old boys would write to me and tell me that!

God, I wish I had a boyfriend. You're so lucky to have the Nadger, even if he does get song lyrics wrong. At least he didn't think the first line of 'You're The One That I Want' by John T. and Olivia Neutron-Bomb went, 'I got shoes/They're made of plywood,' which Joe claims he thought were the words, although I can't believe even Joe is that dumb.

For a while I wondered if David was going to make another move. I don't fancy him, and I know it's a bad idea, what with us all being on the road the whole time, but I do have some nice, if a bit vague, memories of that night. You'd been telling me for ages how lovely sex is, but I never quite understood. You don't until it happens to you, do you?

Anyway, I'm wasting my time with David. He's got a big crush on the sister of some friend of his. And none of us have time for lurve at the moment. 'Love And A Door' – hopefully not 'that difficult second album' – is coming out in a month's time.

Write soon, and I'll see you NEXT MONTH! CAN'T WAIT!

Oodles of love,

H x

We arrived in Manhattan for our New York show on a chilly late-September afternoon. I was on pins because I'd told Sam I'd meet her at the venue at four, and it was twenty past by the time we got there. The boys were taking bets amongst themselves about who'd cop off with her first; the idea of a woman on tour with us was almost too exciting for them to stand, especially as I'd built Sam up to be an English Charlie's Angel.

'Get lost,' I said to them. 'She's far too good for any of you. She likes *real* men.'

Justin groaned lasciviously. 'And she'll be in the van with us for four whole weeks. She'll give in to the Becker charm eventually, I just know it.'

I snorted with derision. 'In the van? You must be kidding. We're renting a car and we'll be in a different hotel room, so you've got no chance.'

'Oh goody, a choice of two hotel rooms to screw her in,' said Joe, half-heartedly joining in to wind me up. He'd been as quick as Jus and David to place his bet, but we all knew that when Justin decided he wanted something, he usually got it. I was beginning to wish I hadn't raved about Sam's attributes quite so enthusiastically.

When I burst through the door of the club, Sam was sitting alone at the bar, stirring a swizzle stick around a glass of cranberry juice. Her face lit up when she saw me, and she jumped off her bar stool.

'Sourcil! *Ma cherie!* I've been looking at all these posters with you on them, I can't believe you're so famous!'

She waved an arm at the wall of our tour posters next to her, and then hugged me. 'My famous friend. Who'd have thought it? And look at you, you're so glamorous, too! You *have* lost masses of weight.'

'Thanks. Well, you look as cool as ever. I have to warn you, the boys are gagging to meet you. Justin will definitely try to get off with you, and so will Joe, if Justin's not around, so just keep your eyes open and your legs crossed, OK?'

Sam laughed. 'I don't know, Justin looks pretty cute to me.'

'But what about the Nadger?'

'Oh, he's history. He wanted to know if it was all right for him to go out with other girls, seeing as I was going to be away for such a long time. The cheek of him! He's just had an ingrowing toenail operated on, too, and he's got to wear this really horrible sandal thing everywhere. So I thought, Hmm, schoolboy with ingrowing-toenail problems, or up-and-coming gorgeous American popstars? Tough choice, but the Nadger had to go.'

I made a face at her. 'Well, I hope that's not the only reason you're here: to try and seduce my fellow band members!'

Sam hugged me again. 'Of course not, you old tart. God, I've missed you so much.'

With trepidation, I introduced Sam to the rest of the band, none of whom seemed remotely disappointed by meeting her in person. She was very casual with them, shaking hands and saying 'pleased to meet you', without even raising a blush. I envied her insouciance.

After we'd finished loading in and sound-checking, we parked the van in a nearby lot and went out for something to eat. The boys and Mickey steered us towards a noodle bar on Avenue A, so they could ogle the gorgeous Indonesian waitresses, but at the last minute I whisked Sam off to a pizza place a few doors down. I wanted to have her to myself, for a gossip and a leisurely Hawaiian pizza, without having testosterone dripping like stringy cheese over our plates.

By the time we got back it was around 9.30 p.m. The first band, Loud Licks, had finished, and our support band, Kabuo, were setting up. A smattering of people sat at side tables, drinking and chatting, and Loud Licks fans were drifting away from the stage towards the bar. They were a local band with quite a healthy fanbase, but it didn't look like a good turnout for them. I hoped their set had gone OK; the challenge of being first on the bill was still fresh in my mind.

There was no backstage, as such, which was ludicrous in a venue of that size. Instead, Sam and I were directed to a door at the opposite end of the venue to the stage, which led down a narrow flight of stairs and through a passageway, with crates and crates of beer stacked on either side, to a tiny boiler room.

This was, laughably, our dressing room. Its ceiling was less than seven feet high and was covered with ancient hissing and banging pipes. The temperature in there must have been 95 degrees or more. A door off the back of it led to a small bathroom, into which I disappeared with relief to get ready, dragging Sam with me. The others, with the exception of Joe and Mickey, who were doubtless at the bar trying to meet girls, were all sitting round a small table, whose centrepiece was a black plastic basin full of bottles of beer in rapidly melting ice.

Troy, our tour manager/roadie, was there, as was Dean, our producer. Dean lived in New York and always came to our shows when we were in town. He, Justin and David were smoking a joint and discussing Joe's sartorial shortcomings as we emerged from the bathroom and sat down with them.

I glanced at Sam, who was staring open-mouthed at the sight of the enormous joint. I could tell she was shocked, even though she immediately pulled herself together again, not wanting to appear uncool.

'He's gotta lose that hair,' said Dean. 'Does he think he's in a glam-rock band or what? Not that that's an excuse; he just needs to get over it. And as for that hideous black-and-tan suede bomber-jacket thing ... Dave, have a word with him, will you?'

David looked down over his shades at him. 'No way, Dean. That is absolutely not my department. *You* talk to him, you're the producer.'

'Like it has anything to do with me? Ah, here's Helena and Sam. You're the women, you do it.'

'Don't be so sexist,' I said. 'And anyway, I don't think Joe's hair is all that bad.'

'Actually, I think it's quite attractive,' said Sam demurely, fluttering her eyelashes at David and Justin. Justin looked horrified at the thought that Joe might be a rival. I never realized Sam could be such a flirt.

In between puffs on the joint, Justin was chewing the skin around his fingernails, picking at it until bright spots of crimson welled up on three of his fingers.

'Oh for God's sake, Jus,' I said, noticing. 'We're on in half an hour. Stop it.'

Sam handed him a Kleenex, which he wove around his fingers and held clamped in his fist, and they exchanged a smouldering gaze.

I caught the look and began to feel kind of at sea. I didn't know whether I should warn Sam off Justin or not. But my dilemma was temporarily forgotten as I started to get a familiar cramping in my stomach, heralding my pre-show need for the toilet, and I had to focus all my energy into not giving in to it. Once I started I couldn't stop, but I knew if I just held out till I was on stage, then the feeling would pass. Besides, there was no way I was going to disappear back into that not-very-private bathroom with the others sniggering outside.

Joe came back into the room, in a bad mood because Mickey was copping off with Ringside's press assistant. 'Give us a hit,' he said, grabbing the joint from Justin and inhaling deeply.

'You look nice tonight,' Justin remarked to me sweetly, transferring his bloody tissue to the other hand so he could suck his fingers instead. 'That colour suits you.'

I was pleased. I had on a new purple silk shirt, with a long black skirt and a purple-and-black drifty shawl over the top, and I felt hot in more than just temperature terms. It occurred to me, with amusement, how many teenage girls would give their eye teeth to have Justin say that to them. We had a joke amongst ourselves: What's thirty yards long, has no pubes and goes 'Aaaah!'? The answer being, of course, the front row of a Blue Idea concert. Maybe it wouldn't be such a bad thing for him and Sam to have a fling. It would be a great story for her to take home.

Being in that sweltering room became like a Zen thing after the first few minutes. It was unbearable but oddly pleasant at the same time. You just had to rise above it. The pipes occasionally spat out a trickle of steaming hot water, and we nervously estimated their age and contemplated the consequences should one of them actually burst. On the wall by my head were scrawled the words, 'Thanks for everything, to Mary, Michael and Michael, from us in Duran Duran', with the autographs of Simon Le Bon and Nick Rhodes underneath. Sam was impressed.

'Duran Duran! I love that band. I can't imagine them all holed up in this little sweatbox. I bet they weren't too pleased.'

Justin said loftily, 'Oh, well, Duran Duran aren't very big over here. We're way better known.'

Dean and Troy shook their heads in disbelief.

'Music, that's what we need,' Joe announced, pulling a tape out of his sports bag and sticking it into our worn-out portable cassette player.

David, Justin and I groaned. We were sick to the back teeth of all the tapes we'd taken on tour with us, and I didn't think I could stand listening to Billy Idol one more time.

'No, no, guys, listen,' Joe said proudly. 'I've got a new one, specially for the Brits among us!' He pushed the Play button, and the tape clicked on in the middle of a song.

Sam recognized the album first. 'Oh, brilliant! The Jam, *All Mod Cons*. But that's hardly new.'

Joe and Justin exchanged admiring looks. A girl with long legs and big breasts who knew about music? Even better.

'I meant new to us. Listen, darling, they're playing our tune,' Joe hammed to Sam, pursing his lips and pretending to strum along. 'God, I wish we'd had real Mods over here; they're so damn cool.'

'I don't know this song,' I said. 'What is it?'

Justin reached over and cranked up the volume to full, and the harsh chords of 'To Be Someone' filled up the room. It seemed to suck out what little oxygen there was left and made us all sweat even more.

David jumped up out of his chair. 'It's about fame!' he shouted over the music.

Justin leaped up, too. 'And money, and chicks. It's our fucking song!'

Joe joined them, and they all began to play air guitar, stoned and exhilarated. Sam and I watched and laughed as Justin, Joe, David, Troy and Dean bellowed out whichever of the words they could remember.

'No more swimming in a guitar-shaped pool,' yodelled Joe.

'No more reporters at my beck and call,' retorted Dean.

'AND DIDN'T WE HAVE A NICE TIME! AND WASN'T IT SUCH A FIIIII-NE TIME! TO BE SOME-ONE MUST BE A WONDERFUL THI-IN-ING'.

I looked at Sam's face, shiny with sweat and delight. No wonder they all wanted to sleep with her, I thought. She was even more gorgeous in the flesh than I'd made her out to be.

This thought made me wonder, for a split second, if maybe I *was* a lesbian. After all, I loved Sam more than anyone else in the world. But then I imagined myself kissing her, tongues and everything, and felt so queasy that I knew I couldn't be.

The track finished and Sam spoke up. 'Well, I hate to be a killjoy, but are you sure you want to make that your song? It's about has-beens; it's all in the past – "No more taxis, now we have to walk"?'

The boys looked sheepish. They obviously hadn't thought about the lyrics that closely.

Sam and I rolled our eyes at this apparently prevalent male shortcoming. '"Pulling muscles off a shelf,"' we chorused, and fell about laughing.

'What?' said David, looking askance at us.

'Nothing,' I said. 'Don't guys ever listen to the words of a record properly, or are you all too hung up on who engineered it, what studio it was recorded in and what sort of strings they used on their guitars?'

'Sure we do,' said Dean hotly. 'It just depends how

220

much of a fan you are, that's all. The more you like the band, the more attention you pay to the lyrics.'

'Well, then, how come none of you realized what that Jam song is really about?' Sam asked.

'We *kind* of knew,' Justin said defensively. 'We just mean that it can be our song in forty years' time, don't we, guys? When we've spent all our millions on gambling and loose women.'

The others nodded gravely, and Justin went into the bathroom, as if to indicate that the discussion was closed. Dean rolled another joint and lit up, and we continued to listen to the album at a lower volume.

A young black-haired girl in a miniskirt appeared in the doorway, looked us up and down, and disappeared again in disgust, not realizing how unlucky the timing of her Justin-hunt was. She obviously thought the rest of us looked too frumpy and stoned to be worth her attention.

Even though the press were all over us as the latest 'big thing', the teen magazines were still capitalizing on Justin's dreamboat looks, which meant the rest of us hadn't really got a look-in yet – the promo shot for our first album featured Jus in prominent sharp focus, with David, Joe and I lurking blurrily in the background. I was secretly happy with this state of affairs; I was dreading the individual interviews and photo shoots which I knew would be inevitable once the press ran out of ways to describe Justin's eyelashes.

'Want to come upstairs for a bit of fresh air, Sammy?' I asked. She nodded, and we headed out of the room, away from The Jam and the fug of sweat and spliff.

A welcome blast of air-conditioned air struck us when I opened the door back into the now-packed club, so we stood there for a while, flapping the collars of our shirts and turning our hot faces up to catch the artificial breeze.

Once we'd cooled down a bit, we managed to find a tiny space at the bar, where we stood nose-to-nose in the crush, drinking water from plastic cups and trying to catch up on almost three years' worth of news.

Fifteen minutes later, Joe came to find me, carrying my bass. 'Come on, we're up.'

With a nervous swallow of the rest of my icy water, and a quick hug to Sam, I turned and followed Joe through the crowd to the stage. Across the room I noticed that Justin and David were making better progress. Justin was holding his guitar in front of him like a battering ram, separating the ranks like a hot knife through butter. People were cheering and reaching out to touch him as he passed. I had a shiver of recognition that this was just the start of it, and that very soon we wouldn't be able to push through a crowd like this without getting torn to pieces. It was a sobering thought, but once we climbed the steps at the side of the stage and took our places, it didn't matter any more.

The cheering intensified as Justin struck up the intro chords of the first number, and from that point the set flashed past, seemingly in seconds. The four of us were in harmony, literally, emotionally and almost spiritually. I felt a strange, blissful connection with the others, just as I used to get when I went to church: a feeling of true belonging.

When I was on stage, I never focused on my surroundings too closely. Small details caught my attention for a second, and then flitted away again: the way Justin's ears got pink and transparent when backlit by a red stage light; the way the girl in the front row recoiled in pain when her boyfriend shouted too loudly in her ear; and how silly Joe's guitar-playing stance was – he always put his feet in a balletic fourth position.

I tried never to look right into the audience's faces when I was singing. Justin stared hard at them, trying to intimidate them, but I found that very off-putting. Instead I became an expert at the sweeping glance that roved over thousands of eyebrows, foreheads and hairlines, but never directly into the eyes.

I also loved to chart the progress of one individual through the crowd. I would pick someone distinctive – usually a tall man with a punk hairdo or a hat – and glance discreetly over at him every now and again to see if he'd moved or not. He would almost always end up in an entirely different spot from where he'd started. Sometimes he'd push his way to the front, elbowing and ducking and weaving, eliciting scowls from those who'd been waiting patiently for hours to get that close. More often, though, the person was just borne sideways, organically carried across by the ebb and flow of moving bodies packed together. That night, though, I just kept my eyes on Sam, and the Cheshire Cat grin of pride splitting her face told me I'd finally made it.

The show went really well. When we finally left the stage, glowing with triumph, I grabbed Sam's hand and heaved her through the crowd with me to the exit, wanting her to share the moment. I could see Mickey and Willy at the side, grinning maniacally at each other. Then they, too, started shoving towards the back, paralleling our progress, but getting there much faster. They didn't have the congratulatory slaps on the shoulder or attempted kisses and hugs to deal with *en route*.

Unable to bear the sweatbox any longer, we all went out to a nearby bar to celebrate the successful night. Mr Wallberger – or Rob as we now called him – had arrived in time to catch the last few numbers, and obliged us by putting his much-vaunted credit card behind the bar so the drinks could flow freely. Besides us four, Sam, Mickey, Willy, Troy, Rob and Dean, there was a small crowd in attendance, which included several Ringside promotions people, our product manager, Tom, a couple of journalists and radio-programme directors, Aunt Sandi and her latest boyfriend, and a few of the boys' old school friends, who had driven up from Freehold for the show.

Sam, predictably, snogged Justin in a corner, and

223

then crashed out from jet lag and excitement. Mickey carried on what he'd started with the press assistant, and David got off with a young Chinese fan. Only Joe and I failed to score, but I didn't care, since I hadn't been trying. My spirits, like my knickers, remained undampened. It was a great impromptu party, and I felt on top of the world, successful, happy, replete.

I danced over to Joe, standing hopefully by the door of the Ladies' restroom. 'To be someone must be a wonderful thing,' I sang joyfully in his ear.

He grinned and clinked his beer bottle against mine in a triumphant toast. 'It's a *damn* wonderful thing, baby,' he crowed back at me.

Mary-Ellen Applebaum

It was 8.30 a.m., I'd been writing for two days solid,
including since three o'clock that morning, and I was
exhausted. I was starved of fresh air, my limbs felt
numb, my back was stiff from being hunched over my
computer – not only was I writing new stuff, but I'd
also been transcribing the notebooks I'd filled in
hospital – and my eye was red, watery and aching.
Above all, I was *furiously* angry.

Rather irrationally, the object of my rage was my
eighteen-year-old self. I remembered, with crystal
clarity, the elation fizzing up inside me after that New
York show with Sam – Joe and I clinking bottles and
congratulating ourselves. That night, in that sweaty
venue, I'd had it all, and I didn't realize. I was beautiful and I didn't notice, healthy and didn't appreciate
it, talented and took it for granted. I couldn't imagine
ever feeling that happy again.

There was a strange silence in the house. At first I
welcomed it, since it indicated that my stalker had
gone to the garden centre, or on a day trip to Hastings,
or whatever it is stalkers do in their spare time. Then I
realized that it was the prolonged absence of the sound
of my own voice. Since Mum had returned to New
Jersey five days earlier I hadn't spoken once. She had
left several messages, beginning with a sarky, 'Thank
you for checking that I landed safely,' and working up

to a stroppy, 'For heaven's sake, Helena, pick up the telephone,' but I'd ignored them all. I decided to talk to her only when she started sounding actively panicked.

Now I was alone I no longer even had to pretend to be coping. Plus, the more time passed, the harder it got to cope. The adrenalin of mere survival had finally dissipated, dispersing into the air around me like the smell of my mother's hairspray. Only a teeth-gritting determination to finish the manuscript prevented me from giving up completely.

I knew I should try to snap out of it, but I didn't have the energy to do anything more than glance at the psychotherapist's phone number, which my mother had left on a Post-It note, stuck prominently to the top of my computer.

I had refused to see Dr Bedford again after leaving hospital, much to Mum's chagrin. I was all in favour of the concept of therapy; I'd just found it too damn difficult, and in my case irrelevant. After a few bed-side talk sessions, I'd decided it was a waste of time for me to concentrate on any kind of long-term recovery.

I peeled off the Post-It and flicked it into the corner of the room, where it lay, forgotten, behind my dusty bass.

I didn't need therapy, but I did need a rest, so I decamped to my TV room and lay down on the squashy leather sofa. Remote in one hand and can of Coke in the other, I embarked on a marathon of daytime television. I started with the breakfast programmes and post-breakfast chat shows, the tame English versions of Jerry Springer and Ricki Lake. Instead of 'My Son is Having Sex With My Mother', the subjects were, 'Am I Doing Too Much Gardening?' and 'Help! I've Got a Crush on my Dental Hygienist'.

Then I moved onto the children's programmes – *Teletubbies*, *Noddy* and someone called Kipper the Dog and his friend Tiger. Lurid, unlikely representations of humanity in all shapes and sizes. I wondered what toddlers made of those fake beings, those day-glo, padded mutant creatures who talked baby talk and danced. Did it make them believe they might see Dipsy or Laa-Laa strolling down the high street, doing a spot of shopping?

I thought of Ruby, proud little Ruby with her twangy curls and fun-fur coat, her inexhaustible capacity for cuteness and her sad eyes. I wondered how she was, and then realized this probably depended on how her parents were.

Through a lunchtime quiz show, I daydreamed about Toby, and how he had got me through those weeks in hospital simply by treating me like a normal, whole, appealing person. God, that was more than most men had ever done when I *was* whole and relatively appealing. Suddenly I missed him. Why,. with his wife unconscious down the corridor, had he kissed me and flirted with me and then gone cold?

I supposed, over the one o'clock news, that there were a few possible reasons. He could be some kind of groupie, clinging on to an idea of Helena Nicholls from a long time ago. Perhaps he'd collected my records, masturbated to my poster and featured me in his own private porn movie. Then again, maybe he'd just been trying to prove something to his wife. Happily married people whose spouses were in a coma didn't, on balance, start affairs with other patients in the same hospital. Or perhaps he really was in love with me.

I dismissed all of the above. The groupie scenario because Toby was about my age, and unless he'd been a fan in the early days he would have been a bit old for all that adolescent fantasy stuff. Besides, he'd never come across as star-struck, or even particularly as a fan. The proving-something-to-Kate theory was also unlikely, because it was a nasty thing to do, and Toby wasn't a nasty person. Plus, he'd obviously felt guilty about it. Which left the last option: that Toby was in love with me. Well, this was also unlikely, despite him

227

professing that he'd fallen for me at first sight. He'd only kissed me twice, and he hadn't tried to contact me since our argument in the hospital.

Hang on, though, I thought to myself over another can of Coke and the weather forecast, how did I know he hadn't tried to get in touch? I toyed with the idea of calling the hospital to see if he might have asked Grace or Catriona for my telephone number, but then decided against it. I realized that since I'd put the fear of God into the nursing staff about guarding my privacy, they were unlikely to have handed out my home number to the first person who requested it.

In the sudden, vain hope that the postman might just have brought a passionate epistle from Toby, I hauled myself off the sofa, swaddled my head in a huge woolly scarf – despite the temperature being a sunny seventy-two – and ventured outside for the first time in five days to inspect the contents of the mailbox by the front gate.

Seven takeaway menus representing the cuisine of four continents, three free property newspapers, a plethora of leaflets advertising the services of local handymen and gardeners, five assorted envelopes from banks and credit-card companies, and one flimsy blue airmail letter with American stamps on it were jammed into the box. The return address on the airmail letter was smudged and illegible, but it was postmarked Freehold, so I suspected a sugary note from one of my mother's bridge friends. There was nothing at all that might conceivably be from Toby.

Just as well, I thought as I trudged back into the house again, heading towards the TV. It was good that he hadn't got in touch, however much I missed him. I had to look at the big picture, the limited future. The reason I'd picked a fight with Toby in hospital still stood: what was the point of pursuing a new friendship, let alone a relationship, when I wasn't going to be around after the show?

Ensconced on the sofa, in the indentation left by my

morning's viewing, I ripped open the American letter and extracted two tissue-thin wisps of writing paper and a photograph of two strange children – as in, unfamiliar children (although all children looked pretty strange to me, with the exception of Ruby, who was gorgeous).

June 1998

Dear Helena,

I know it's been years and years since we last talked, but I always wished you well and followed your progress as much as I could in the papers. I felt so proud that we were once friends. I had a feeling that great things would happen in your life. You always had that air about you. I remember when you first came to our Bible study meeting, you were kind of heavy, and so shy and nervous, but at the same time you still had this sort of inner confidence. I don't know what it was, but I remember watching it grow and grow, once you joined the choir and started writing songs. You just got more and more beautiful, inside and out. It was a lovely thing to see. I guess it was a kind of power, that you could do anything you wanted.

Margie said you'd been feeling kind of down since your accident, which is understandable. I thought it may perhaps make you feel a little better to know that an old friend is thinking of you. I don't want to preach or anything, but please try not to let this ruin your life. You still have so much to offer in so many ways. Jesus will take care of you, if you let Him.

Mary-Ellen Randall! Well, well. I snorted with derision at the notion that I still had so much to offer. Thanks, hon, I feel *so* much better now.

I couldn't summon up the energy to read on, and instead I turned back to the TV. An old Ealing Studios matinee had just begun on Channel 4, and I watched a violent but very gentlemanly murder take place in a frightfully well-coiffed lady's front parlour, but somehow my attention kept drifting back to Mary-Ellen's loopy writing.

I don't know if it's of any interest to you, but I run a program here in Freehold which organizes missionary trips to Africa. Don't be misled by the name 'missionary'; they aren't colonial dictators trying to brainwash the natives into their way of thinking. These days they are more like volunteers who go to remote villages to live with the locals to help them with basic health and education issues. Some of the people who go out there aren't overly Christian, although obviously it helps if you believe in God. It depends more on the type of person than how religious they are.

Anyways, I just wondered if you were looking for a change, or a break of some kind? It might appeal, and I'm sure you'd be great at it. I'm always looking for good new people who don't have too many ties at home – Margie said you weren't married, but she didn't know if you were in a relationship or not. If you are interested, let me know and I'd be happy to send you some literature. But please don't think that I'm trying to coerce you into anything. What's that expression, A change is as good as a rest? Well, the work sure isn't particularly restful most of the time, but I have known other folk who've gone out there after a big personal tragedy, and they certainly say it helped.

A missionary! Me! If the idea hadn't been so pre-posterous I'd have found it hilarious. Idly, I wondered how the well-coiffed Ealing lady, who by now had been taken hostage by the murderer, managed to go to the toilet, since she'd been held in her parlour for over twelve hours. This reminded me of my own need for a wee, so I peeled myself off the sofa and staggered into the downstairs loo, still clutching the letter. I sat on the loo and read on:

Also enclosed is a snapshot of my family: my husband,

Scott, who's a PT instructor; Scotty Jr, who's six; and Cathey, four. My little angels!

I do hope you don't mind me writing to you. Margie gave me your address. I know I could have gotten it from your mom when she still lived in Freehold, but, truth is, once you got real famous I thought you'd be too busy to want to hear from me, or else that you might think I was only sucking up because you were so big and successful.

It would be real nice to hear back from you, even if you think the missionary idea is dumb. Next time you visit your folks – I hear their new house is beautiful – please take a drive over to Freehold and visit us. I would love to see you again.

Take care and God bless,

Your friend,

Mary-Ellen Applebaum

PS. Oh yes, I nearly forgot: I don't know if you knew this, but I married my neighbor, Scott, after he got back from the Marines. He always brags to folk that he got your career started when you bought his bass guitar! I feel kind of silly telling you. Do you remember we used to think his family were so weird? Well, his mom kind of was, but she died ten years ago. Not an easy woman to get along with, may she rest in peace. Scotty's sister, Janeane, turned out real well, though. Sells real estate in town. x

Even in the depths of my doldrums I couldn't resist a chuckle at the memory of the absent Scott and his Clampett-esque family. Life was certainly full of surprises.

I flushed the toilet and trailed back into the TV room to reinstate myself in front of the box. There were now a lot of 1950s cars driving slowly around Piccadilly Circus, with pedestrians in hats and long overcoats striding past the statue of Eros. One of them looked like Toby, or perhaps Toby's grandfather as a young man. I tried to get back into the plot but, annoyingly, my mind kept wandering back to the letter.

After a couple of years of living in America, I'd ceased to notice the Yankness of the place, but as soon as I left, it jumped out at me like a cowboy from behind a saloon door. My first thought after reading Mary-Ellen's letter was, How *American*. Everything about it: her hoopy American cursive, her name, her phrasing, her Scotty Jr. The photograph gave out the same message: Scotty Jr in a baseball mitt and cap; Cathey in Kmart frills, with real ringlets; Scott in the background, tending to a barbecue on a deck. The fact that it made me cringe slightly indicated to me that America was another country I'd never really belonged in. It was merely a place going past outside the tour-bus windows, or expectant faces in stadiums, or airport concourses and baggage carousels.

I sighed. It was nice to hear from Mary-Ellen nonetheless. I reread the letter, paying more attention to the part about missionaries. 'Some of the people . . . aren't overly Christian . . . I'm sure you'd be great at it'. What did she know? She hadn't seen me since I was sixteen. I wasn't sure if I even still believed in God.

For a few moments I wondered whether it could be an alternative. If I couldn't face going through with The Plan, perhaps I could disappear from public view for a few years and become a missionary instead?

Immediately, however, I foresaw a few logistical problems. One, I hated hot climates; two, I'd been known to throw a wobbly if my hotel suite didn't have a spa bath and chilled champagne waiting for me – the notion of actually living somewhere without flushing toilets, air-conditioning, shopping by phone, or chocolate Hobnobs was too horrific to contemplate. I thought I'd really rather be dead – and three, I had extremely sensitive, and succulent, skin. A mosquito in a room full of 300 people would always make a mozzie-line straight for me, sampling at least twenty-seven different parts of my body before declaring itself sated. Whenever we'd toured in hot, humid climates, I used to walk around practically shrouded in mosquito nets.

I remembered doing an MTV interview in the Dominican Republic during the rainy season. I'd bought a new, natural mosquito repellent made from tea-tree oil and citronella, and had smeared it on every exposed inch of skin I could reach. It hadn't smelled too bad in the tube, but somehow it reacted with the heat of my body and, within minutes of leaving my hotel room, people were behaving as if I had appalling body odour. The interviewer, a beautiful, haughty Cherokee Indian girl, had moved gradually farther and farther away from me, and eventually began to snigger so hard that the interview had to be suspended. I found out later that Justin had whispered to her beforehand that, although I had good fashion sense, I had the most hideous taste in perfume, and insisted on wearing the cheapest, most disgusting brands, which I thought were divine.

And finally there was the fourth reason: I was the most squeamish person in the world. It wouldn't just be mosquitoes, would it? There were all manner of creepy-crawlies: scorpions, hornets, blood-sucking flies and poisonous spiders. Urgh! And as for crapping in holes and having to kill my own food, forget it.

It obviously wasn't such a good idea after all. My squeamishness meant that my suicide was, technically speaking, going to be a bit of a dilemma, too. I knew there was no way I'd be able to blow my brains out, which was a shame really, since that would have the biggest impact, thus creating the maximum of publicity for the manuscript and the best prospects for my future place in rock history.

Slitting my wrists would be too messy, and there were no bathtubs or showers at New World to do it in, so that left pills and booze. The best way to go, I supposed, if not the most dramatic. I'd just have to lock myself in my studio and do it.

God, this was all such hard work. It was tempting just to stay in my house for the rest of my life. The TV could be my friend. I'd be safe, and I could get everything I needed delivered via the phone and Internet.

But then I realized I'd never be remembered. Nobody would hear my story, or Sam's. I felt I owed it to Sam for people to read about our friendship, and how brave she had been.

It would have to be the original Plan, then. I'd treat today as a day off before knuckling back down to the manuscript tomorrow. Settling into the sofa again, I channel-hopped until alighting on *Can't Cook Won't Cook*, and was grateful to Ainsley Harriott for reminding me that life really wasn't worth living.

'Shipbuilding'

Robert Wyatt

Two years later Blue Idea played New York again, this time at The Academy on 47th Street. It was five times the size of the venue Sam had seen us at, and there was no question of us hanging out at the bar before the show, or of having to load our own gear into the van. We had two roadies to do that for us now, and Troy, rather unnecessarily, had a walkie-talkie to coordinate them. There were fans hanging around the stage door after the gig, and a limo to take us to and from the hotel.

I hadn't seen Sam for ages, apart from a long weekend we'd had in Paris together the year before, which I'd organized as a birthday treat for her. She was well into her law degree in London, and worked in the holidays, too, so the days of her being able to accompany us on tour were long gone.

She had returned home after her abortive round-the-world trip, not speaking to Justin because he'd given her crabs, but otherwise having had a fantastic time, she assured me. After four months of her continuous company – except when she was off shagging Justin somewhere; a casual but apparently mutually satisfying relationship – I missed her even more than when we'd first moved to New Jersey, but I was too busy to indulge the hollow ache of her absence. Four days in two years felt unbearably meagre to both of us, but we coped with it by speaking weekly on the phone.

The Academy show went pretty well, although I couldn't really remember it that clearly. With a few exceptions, our gigs had all blurred into one over time. Aunt Sandi had come to the show, and partied with us afterwards. On a drunken whim, and to her delight, we invited ourselves back to her place to crash that night. It was a lot less comfortable than our suites at the Royalton, but we felt quite sentimental about Sandi's apartment, the epicentre of the action when we were first signed. Plus the appeal of hotel accommodation, however smart, wore very thin after a few weeks of a tour.

I remembered waking up, staring at the orange flowery wallpaper of the spare room and feeling rather queasy. It had probably been way past four by the time we'd finished at the party Ringside had thrown for us after the gig, and the limo had driven us over the vast, glittering peaks of the Brooklyn Bridge. In the end Sandi had only had to accommodate Joe, David and me, since Justin had left with a pretty student he'd met at the party; he was such a cliché, on average he went through two groupies a month.

At first I'd kept this fact from Sam, in case it upset her, but she was remarkably nonchalant about their dalliance. 'He's cute; it passed the time. We were never planning to keep in touch or anything,' she said. I was surprised at her attitude; I'd always assumed that she'd take these things much more seriously. It was a part of her life I didn't really know that much about.

I got up and dressed, sandpaper on the insides of my eyelids, feeling like I'd woken with a squid on my face. Stepping over the prone sleeping figures of Joe and David in the living room, on my way to the kitchen, I glanced at the incongruous Superman clock on Aunt Sandi's kitchen wall, and noticed with horror that it was already twelve forty-five.

Simon, Ringside's radio-promotions guy, had impressed upon us that we needed to be at the office

236

by 3 p.m. for a couple of radio phoner interviews in the Ringside conference room. Our third album, *Spin Shiny*, had just come out, and the promotions machine was at full throttle.

I made coffee and took it in to the others to herald the start of their long, drawn-out waking process, which was accompanied, as usual, by much moaning and groaning. Eventually we were all up, showered and in a chauffeur-driven car, arriving at the office only a little after three. I desperately hoped Justin hadn't forgotten the commitment, and to my surprise and relief he was already there when we arrived, lounging on Ringside's visitors' sofa, looking peaky.

He grinned weakly but proudly at me, and shoved his hand in my face as if he expected me to kiss it. 'Look, see, bet you thought I'd forget.' He had 'R'SIDE 3PM' in faint but thick wavering blue letters on the back of his hand.

'Very good, Jus. Well done; we're all impressed,' I told him, not entirely sarcastically.

Tom, the product manager, and Simon ushered us into the conference room, plying us with more coffee and some welcome bagels, as we'd had neither the time nor the stomach for a proper breakfast, let alone lunch. They conferenced Joe and Justin in with the first radio station, and myself and David with the second. After a few minutes we switched round and talked to the other station.

When we were finished, Tom got us to sign some posters and LPs to give away as prizes in competitions, or as incentives for record-store clerks. We were working away at the conference-room table when I had a sudden thought.

'Oh my God. What's the date today?'

Being on tour for so long seemed to have confounded our sense of time. None of us had a clue what city we were in half the time, let alone what day it was.

'It's August twenty-eighth,' said David. 'Why?'

'Shit! It's not, is it?' I wailed as the door opened and Willy came in with a fresh supply of posters.

'Hi, guys. Tom's on the phone, so he asked me to bring you these. What's the matter, Helena?' he asked, looking at my stricken face.

'Oh, nothing. It's just that I've missed someone's birthday, that's all.'

It was Cynthia Grant's birthday, and I always sent her a card. I'd thought about it the week before, but had promptly forgotten again.

Willy put down the posters, and they fanned out in a graceful arc across the shiny surface of the table. 'Do you want to call them?'

'Really? But it's long distance.' I felt faintly cheeky at the thought of running up Ringside's phone bill, until I remembered that they were about to move to new, much more palatial offices, the upgrade funded in no small part by the sales of our albums. They could stand me the price of a phone call to England, and hopefully I'd be able to chat to Sam, too.

'It's no problem, honestly. You can use the phone in my office if you like.' He lowered his voice conspiratorially. 'I'm always on the phone to my mates in London, but don't tell Rob.'

'Well, thanks. I'd love to.'

I stood up, calculating that it would only be nine thirty in Salisbury, and that the Grants should be around on a week night. Cynthia might be working, but would more likely be having a few birthday rum and Cokes in the saloon bar with her girlfriends, and Sam would probably be there, too. I knew she was working in a Salisbury solicitor's office during her summer break. Either way, I didn't think it would be a problem. There was a phone at the bottom of the stairs, where they kept the boxes of crisps, and I knew it could easily be heard from the bar.

Willy led me over to what he had laughingly called his office, but which was in reality a desk in a corner cranny of the open-plan but terribly cramped label workspace. I had to climb over several boxes of Blue Idea T-shirts and a huge and perilously unstable pile of records to get to his chair. A Big Star album was blaring from speakers in the centre of the room, and I wondered how I'd ever be able to hear anything. There was a stack of black-and-white 8 x 10s of us on Willy's desk, and I turned the top one face down so I didn't have to look at my monochrome face looming up while I talked.

With the receiver clamped hard against my ear to try and block out the noise, I dialled the Grants' number. It rang for ages. Eventually an unfamiliar woman's voice answered, and I put my finger into my free ear. 'Prince of Wales, hello?' she said faintly.

'Hello, can I speak to Cynthia Grant please?' I asked.

There was a pause. 'I'm sorry, she's . . . not around at the moment.'

'Well, could I speak to Sam instead, then?'

A longer pause. I heard the sound of a hand being put over the receiver and a muffled question in the background. Then a kind of scuffling noise. The woman, who I assumed must be a new barmaid, came back on the line.

'Who is it?'

'It's Helena,' I said, starting to feel worried. Something didn't seem right.

'Hold on a minute, please.'

The receiver clunked down, and I visualized it resting on top of a box of Worcester Sauce crisps. The Big Star record thankfully came to a sudden, scratching halt, then Mrs Grant came on the line.

'Helena, love, how are you?' She sounded terribly tired, not the festive person I'd expected at all.

'Happy Birthday to you,' I chirped enthusiastically, as usual avoiding having to call her Cynthia. 'How's things? Are you having a nice day? I'm really sorry I forgot to send you a card, but our new album is—'

She cut my apology off abruptly, a terrible catch in her voice. 'Oh, Helena, I . . .'

'What is it? What's the matter? Are you ill? Has something happened to the pub?'

I felt fear begin to swoop down over my head like the corners of a black veil.

'No, worse. Helena, I'm really sorry; it's our Sammy.'

The veil enveloped me completely and I thought I was going to faint. Mrs Grant sounded completely devastated. She's dead, I thought. Oh God, Sam is dead. Then she spoke again, as if from the bottom of a well. 'She's in hospital.'

A sensation, like gravity's pull, assailed me, a strange mixture of relief and terror. Relief that she wasn't dead, terror because this obviously wasn't an inflamed appendix or troublesome tonsils.

'What's happened? Has she been in an accident?' I managed to stammer. I could hear Mrs Grant struggling for breath, or for strength, at the other end of the phone.

'Helena, I don't know how to tell you this. She wasn't feeling well, so she had some tests. They found out that she's got leukaemia. Acute myeloid leukaemia, it's called. She's already started the treatment.'

The wall in front of me rocked violently and I had to grip onto the edge of Willy's desk. My mind went completely blank for a second, and then out of a grey cloud emerged some tiny animated images, like frames of an old home movie: Sam and me as children, cycling home from school on our little kiddie bikes, hers turquoise, mine pale pink.

'Helena, are you all right?' I heard in the distance. 'Don't worry, love. The doctors say she should be OK. There's lots of things they can do these days. We only found out yesterday, and she's started the chemo-therapy right away—' Mrs Grant's voice broke, but she rallied herself. 'It should be fine; she should be fine. Really. Try not to worry. Say something. Are you still there?'

Sam had had a little white plastic basket tied to the

handlebars of her bike. It had pale-blue ribbons, which streamed out behind the fake wicker when she pedalled, and I had coveted it without shame. In the silence I could faintly hear the pub's jukebox playing Robert Wyatt's 'Shipbuilding', and a man's deep, distant laugh. I swallowed hard.

'I'm here. But how is she? Is she in pain? Has she been ill for a long time?'

'Mike and I have just come back from the hospital now. She's feeling dreadfully sick, but she's not in actual pain. They've got her heavily sedated. We have to wait and see how she responds to the treatment.'

I think we may have talked for a little longer, but my mind whirled off somewhere else, into a realm of grief, and I couldn't remember any more of the conversation. For some reason, I couldn't get the image of that little white basket and the doleful lyrics of 'Shipbuilding' out of my head. With every atom in my body I wished I could be where Sam was, and not in that stupid filthy office full of strangers. I sat at Willy's desk for a long time, gazing dry-eyed at the wall, not having any idea what to do next.

A hand touched my shoulder. It was David. 'We're done, Helena. Are you ready to go?'

As I stood up, my stomach suddenly heaved and seemed to flip over. Aware of David, Justin, Joe, Willy and half the Ringside label staff staring at me with incredulity and concern, I careered out of the room, just about managing to grab a nearby office rubbish bin on the way, and was copiously sick.

David came and rescued me from the women's bathroom. Throwing up had also induced a flood of tears, so he tidied me up, clucking and crooning over me, listening to my sobbed-out story while wiping my face with a scratchy paper towel and clumsily stroking my hair. I allowed myself to be led out of the office and into a waiting limo, and was taken back to Aunt Sandi's apartment. I didn't want to go back to the impersonal, empty hotel room.

When Sandi got home from work, she and the boys talked in hushed voices in the next room, then she came in and gave me a sleeping pill and a cup of hot chocolate. Fortunately there was no show that night, and I fell into a deep, exhausted sleep of grief and disbelieving.

Not Such a Coincidence

How did people who lost lifelong spouses handle the pain? Sam had been a friend, not a lover or partner, but I couldn't cope with knowing that I'd never see her again. As I sat at the kitchen table, staring glumly into the middle distance, something inside my stomach snarled at me loudly enough to be heard above the moaning of my depression and the dolorous bass of 'Shipbuilding'. After a moment's consideration I realized, with some surprise, that it was hunger.

Suddenly I knew that I had to get out of the house and get some food. I was absolutely, overwhelmingly ravenous. If I stayed indoors for even one more minute I would start gnawing the kitchen counters.

Mum had stocked up for me before she went home, but now the freezer was empty, except for half a packet of broad beans. I was down to chocolate spread and capers in the cupboard, and my fruitbowl contained four shrivelled grapes and a fossilized lime. I'd been living on noodle soup for the past four days, and I was craving fresh juice, hot bread and colourful salads.

I usually got Sainsbury's to home-deliver my groceries, but such was my frame of mind that I hadn't been able to face the hassle of trying to order over the telephone, let alone exchange small talk with a delivery man. My snap decision to get in the car and go there myself was probably born out of a combination of physical need and mental exhaustion. I needed food, quickly, and I needed to do something to take my mind off my terrible sense of loss.

My daring plan to venture into the outside world filled me with a sudden sense of wild recklessness. Donning shades and a floppy sunhat, I picked up the car keys and left the house, glancing constantly around me as I locked up and got in the car. Still no sign of the stalker, thank God.

I drove to Sainsbury's with the roof open and a fresh summer wind flapping the brim of my sunhat, congratulating myself on my positive decision and beginning to feel a tiny bit less miserable. It was fantastic to be back behind the wheel of my car after so long.

Everything was going much better than expected, until I reached the supermarket. I hadn't realized it was Saturday. The car park was full to capacity, and row upon row of hot metal chassis glinted at me, taunting me with the knowledge that each car equalled one or more people banging up and down the aisles inside. If I went in I'd be face to face with them all. There would be no security men or velvet ropes or limos to keep us apart, not even the soundproofed cocoon of a DJ's studio and the cosiness of my headphones. Just me and the great, ordinary unwashed.

I drove right around the perimeter of the car park and straight out onto the road again, just about managing to avoid a huge wobbly line of pushed-together trolleys being coralled into a pen by two bored employees.

Change of plan. I could go home and phone Home Shopping, but then I'd have to wait for them to deliver, and I was too hungry, so I took a detour past my favourite deli. But in the three months since I'd last been there, the windows had been whitewashed and the door locked. 'Closed down due to death', read a shakily lettered sign in the window. I know how that feels, I thought, and carried on into Richmond.

There was a Tesco Metro in the town centre; it was still a supermarket, but a smaller, less intimidating one. I'd be in and out much more quickly, I reasoned, hunger forcing me to try again. Eventually I found a parking space by the river and made my way back towards Tesco, realizing with rising panic that there were probably even more people jostling around on the sunny town-centre pavements than there had been in Sainsbury's. My legs were already beginning to quiver with the unaccustomed effort of walking, and I was so tense that my jaw and nose were aching. I felt a pang of longing for my mother, wishing she would materialize at my side and proffer a plump elbow for me to hang on to.

I made it, and as soon as I got through the door of Tesco I grabbed a carton of cherry-flavoured milk from the shelf and chugged it straight down. This gave me the energy to continue, and in five minutes flat I was queuing, blissfully unnoticed, at the checkout with a basket full of prepackaged salad, milk, bread, croissants, a bag of individually wrapped cheeses, bananas, oranges and the empty carton. I promised myself that I'd order all other non-essentials by phone when I got home.

The checkout girl barely even glanced at me as I paid. Too preoccupied with trying to hoik her bra strap back onto her skinny shoulder, she short-changed me, but I was too anxious to escape unrecognized to point it out.

Flushed with success, I even dared to sidle into HMV on my way back to the car, where I purchased a copy of The Jam's *All Mod Cons* on CD. I'd only ever owned it on vinyl, and I needed to start thinking about collecting CDs for the show. This was a start.

By now I was beginning to feel really unwell. My legs still felt wobbly, and the hunger and cherry milk had collided in my stomach to form a queasy compromise. I needed a sit-down, and possibly a croissant. I took a right turn, down towards the river and my car, but instead of emerging into a quiet side street, I came out into a large riverside area next to Richmond Bridge. This, too, was crowded with people.

Richmond river front in summer has a definite beach-resort, Club 18–30 feel to it, with sweaty people queuing at ice-cream-van windows, clutching their plastic cups of European lager in one hand and their small change in the other. The bars were packed, there were boats for hire and half-stripped bodies lay sprawled on the grassy terraces above the river. An extremely high tide was just receding and water lapped over the edge of the bank, a wash of dark cooling the hot pavement. A few lads were standing in this puddle, shoes off, trousers rolled up, glugging their pints and looking around self-consciously to see who was watching them. A dog leaped into the river, scaring away a scattering of ducks and making a group of implausibly tanned girls scream as the splash sent drops of murky Thames water into their vodka and limes.

I was about to turn in the direction of my mislaid car when I felt another hot stab of panic. I was in the middle of this huge crowd of strangers, vulnerable, exhausted and sick, and my only protection against recognition was shades and a sunhat. I raised a hand to my head to check that both were still in place. Deep breath, I thought. These people are your listeners, and some of the older ones are your fans. Just sit down and have a rest; no-one will bother you.

Finding a space on the patchy grass by the river, I brushed away a few fag ends and a rusty bottle top, and lowered myself gingerly. It felt nice. The sun was warm on my thighs and scratchy stems tickled the backs of my legs. I rolled up the tops of my shorts, scoffed a croissant and tried to relax.

Not wanting to appear unoccupied, I delved into my bag for my new CD and began to wrestle with the shrink-wrap. As usual, the sticky top spine bearing the band name and album title didn't peel off in one go, but broke away in irritating little slivers, behaving in the way Sellotape does when you're tired. I jabbed at it with my thumbnail and eventually managed to unwrap it.

I opened the jewel case and extracted the booklet, reading snatches of lyrics while trying to recover my energy and courage. A couple near by, in matching Stussy T-shirts and denim shorts, suddenly nudged each other, jerked their eyebrows in my direction and laughed.

I froze with horror as colour flamed across my cheeks. Ramming the CD back into my bag, I stood up, brushing grass off the seat of my shorts, and moved away through the throng to find somewhere else to sit.

'Check her out,' I heard another man say to his companion, and he pointed at me, sniggering.

Why, oh why, hadn't I worn a wig as well? Obviously my hat and shades were not a good enough disguise. I was still recognizable as me, but because I was no longer beautiful all my musical achievements had ebbed muddily away in people's memories. It was a cruel realization to discover how quickly disfigurement could transform me from a respected rockstar into a laughing stock. I had no idea that people could be so mean.

My queasiness had escalated into a full-blown wave of nausea, and I blundered towards the nearest pub to try and find a quiet loo in which to puke. A bottleneck of drinkers were jostling each other in front of the doorway, however, and I couldn't get in. As I stood, jiggling desperately from foot to foot, I realized what the problem was.

A man was holding everyone up, planted firmly in the narrow entrance to the pub and clutching a pint in each hand.

'Come on, mate, get a move on,' someone shouted at him from behind.

'Oh, for God's sake, someone get him out!' yelled a woman next to me, waving her lipstick-printed empty glass. 'I'm dying of thirst here.'

Eventually a large burly person in an unbecoming sports vest and rugby shorts gave the man a shove, and he flew out of the porch, spilling his pints and apologizing profusely to the door frame as his shoulder connected with it *en route.*

Suddenly we were face to face. The man looked exactly like Toby, if Toby's body had been occupied by somebody else, someone loose and miserable. I stared incredulously for a moment longer. It *was* Toby.

Lager dripped off his hands and wrists, dampening down the whorls of blond hair on his arms. I looked down and saw his legs in combat shorts, warm with fuzzy golden hair, and it gave me a tiny thrill, as if I was seeing him naked for the first time. I had a sudden urge to hang on to one of those knees, as if it was the only thing that could anchor me down.

Then I noticed that his legs were swaying, and it sunk in that Toby was absolutely, horrendously and disgustingly drunk.

He looked at me without focusing, looked away and then did a slow-motion double-take. I waited for his face to light up and say hello. Instead, he grinned vaguely, as if something had amused him.

My hand shot out and grabbed his soggy arm. 'Toby? What are you doing here? This is such a coincidence.'

He stared at me as directly as he could and burst out laughing. 'Helena, oh Goditsyou! Youhavenoideahow muchIwannedtoseeyou,' he slurred, handing me one of his half-empty pints and stretching his free hand towards my face. I waited to feel his warm palm cup my cheek, but instead I felt him peel something off each side of my chin.

'Whyveyougotthesestucktoyourface?' he asked, squinting at the two little strips of CD top spine which had somehow adhered to either side of my mouth, like goaty whiskers.

I groaned. For fuck's sake. *That* was why people had been staring at me and tittering.

Without waiting for an answer, Toby gave me an

enthusiastic hug. He smelled of stale beer and sweat, faint aftershave and garlic – a very different smell to the one I remembered as his.

'Listen,' he said. 'Bitpissedatmoment. Reallywanna seeya, though. Missedcha, man, somuch.'

He hugged me again, nearly toppling us both over, sending lager cascading down the front of my favourite dry-clean-only Betsey Johnson top.

I pulled away. 'What's going on, Toby? What are you doing here?' I wanted to add, Drunk, in the middle of the afternoon.

Just then a man appeared at his shoulder. He was thin and balding, but with great big dark eyes and chimney-brush eyelashes, like a little boy's. He didn't seem to be quite as drunk as Toby.

'Where's my pint?' he said to Toby, glancing at me. The lack of interest in his gaze was a refreshing relief.

Toby pointed at the glass in my hand. 'Shesholdingitforyou,' he said.

She? I was beginning to feel a tense, choking sensation in my gut, driving out the previous nausea and filling it with something much more painful: disappointment.

'I'm Helena,' I said pompously, handing him his pint. Since half of it was spilt, it looked as if I'd had several hefty swigs, but I decided it was beneath me to try and justify myself.

'Loveofmylife,' said Toby dreamily, and put his arm around my shoulders.

I shrugged him off crossly.

The man's eyelashes stood to attention. 'I'm Toby's friend Bill,' he said. 'It's a pleasure to meet you. I've heard so much about you.'

Tight-lipped, I shook his hand. 'Listen, I really should get going. I was just passing.'

Bill touched my elbow briefly and bent to whisper in my ear – my good ear, fortunately.

'Ignore him; he's not himself. I expect you know he's never usually like this, drunk and stuff. It's just that—'

Toby caught the word 'drunk' and shoved his head in between ours. 'Noneedtomakeexcuses,' he said. And then, with supreme concentration, he managed to separate his words: 'I'm not as thunk as drinkle peep I am, you know.' He roared with laughter, and then sank into a miserable silence, morosely sucking the beer off each of his arms in turn. 'Sorry, Ellna,' he said eventually, sounding like Ruby in disgrace.

I badly wanted to ask how Ruby was doing, but didn't think I'd get a comprehensible reply.

'I'll call you, OK?' he added, obviously making a colossal effort to hold it all together.

'You don't have my number,' I said.

'C'n I have it?'

I hesitated. I wasn't sure I wanted to see him again. Toby's imploring look suddenly turned to one of horror, and his face went a nasty shade of mustard. 'Aaargh,' he said, putting a hand over his mouth and shoving his pint back into my hand once more. 'Gonnabesick,' and he dashed off unsteadily into the pub.

There was a sound of popping in my head as all my romantic bubbles burst.

'Give him a chance,' muttered Bill again. 'He really needs to talk to you.'

I was about to say, He's married, what is there to talk about, when I had a terrible thought. 'Um, Kate . . . Kate hasn't *died*, has she?'

Bill almost grinned, but not quite. 'No. But Toby's left her. As soon as she came out of hospital she told him that she was having an affair. He and Ruby have gone to stay with his sister Lulu.'

I didn't know what to say. I stared towards the dark interior of the pub, hoping that Toby would be able to feel my shock and sympathy vibes. My first thought was that he must have really loved Kate, for him to get so rip-roaringly inebriated.

'Poor Toby. Poor *Ruby*,' I said.

Bill put a hand on my forearm again, and my skin

crawled with the effort of not shaking it off. I hated it when strangers touched me. 'Helena, listen,' he said. 'It's not as much of a coincidence as you think, bumping into us here. We've been down here for four days, looking for you. Toby's been on this bender, see, and he insisted on coming here because he knew you lived in the area. I told him it wasn't such a good idea, but he wouldn't listen. I mean, you don't want to see him in this state, do you?'

I shook my head. 'Who's looking after Ruby?'

'Lulu and Toby's mum. She's been staying there, too. They've been brilliant, but I think they're starting to draw the line at babysitting just so Toby can go out and get hammered. But at least he's found you.'

I was getting even more irritated. Bill made it sound as if I was a lost puppy or some mislaid car keys. I was tired and unwell and wanted to go home.

'I'm sorry,' I said stiffly. 'I don't give out my phone number. Why don't you give me Toby's address, and if I get the chance I'll contact him?'

Bill produced a biro but couldn't find any paper, so I handed him the receipt for *All Mod Cons* and watched as he scribbled down an address and telephone number.

'Please call him. He'd kill me if he knew I was telling you, but he's really mad about you. He's in shock about Kate, of course, but they both knew it wasn't working out long before her accident.' Bill's eyelashes were practically begging me, and even though my head was pounding I smiled.

'You're a good friend to him, aren't you?'

'Mmm. Speaking of which, better go and check he's OK.' He handed me the receipt, and, with a brief wave, vanished into the throng before I could say anything else.

I was still clutching Toby's drink, so I walked over and left it next to the pub wall. As I set off towards my car, the dog who'd jumped into the water reappeared and stuck his damp nose into the abandoned pint, sucking greedily at the beer. I heard the splintering crack of breaking glass and the dog's whine as his owner smacked him away from the beery shards, but I didn't look back.

Once I was in the car, I glanced at Toby's address. For a split second my heart did a tiny tap-dance, but then I screwed the receipt into a ball, dropped it to the floor by my feet and drove home.

'Deep Blue Dream'
The Big Blue OST

1 October 1987

I don't really have the time to keep a diary, but Cynthia said I should try after I told her on the phone the other day that everything was such a blur. She said, 'Do it so you can remember the tour later on.'

I don't think I want to remember it, though. This tour is a complete nightmare; I can't stand it. I just want to be with Sam. What sort of pathetic friend must she think I am, carrying on like normal while she's lying there so sick? If I could talk to her for more than two minutes at a time then I'd be able to persuade her to let me come over. But she's not too sick for a spot of the old emotional blackmail. She says she'll never speak to me again if I quit the band or leave the tour. I know she's bluffing. Of course she'd still speak to me, but I also know that she'd never forgive herself if I chucked in the band because of her.

I suppose she's right. Wait till the tour's done, and then I can go straight over to Salisbury and stay with the Grants. It'll be easier all round when Sam's first round of chemo is finished. She's too ill even to talk to me on the phone most days, and Cynthia says she can't face any visitors. At least if I wait a while she'll be able to appreciate my company more.

BUT I FEEL SO GUILTY! I think Blue Idea's success makes it worse. *Spin Shiny*'s been number one for four weeks now, but I couldn't care less. It's only success. And money, I guess, although, come to think of it, we haven't seen very much of that. I'd have thought we'd be getting far more royalties than we actually do. Oh, who knows. Who cares.

Boston, NYC, Philly, and D.C. this week.

9 October 1987

We were on *Saturday Night Live*, and *The Tonight Show* last week. It was kind of funny. The whole time we were playing, all I could think of was whether the hospital lights hurt Sam's eyes the way the studio lights hurt mine. Dumb, really. It's this awful dream I keep having: Sam's lying helpless, strapped to a table in a great big empty operating theatre, with one huge white light glaring right in her face, while all that poison gets pumped into her body, killing *all* her cells, not just the leukaemia ones in her bone marrow. I wish there was an easier way to make her better.

Shit, crying again. My eyelids are permanently like two great big puffy waterwings; the make-up lady on *The Tonight Show* nearly had a fit. Cucumber slices just don't do it for me any more.

Still, let's look on the bright side. I've lost tons more weight.

New Orleans, Austin, Dallas. A bunch more places, too, but I can't remember where and I don't have the itinerary to hand.

18 October 1987

I'm crossing off the cities on my tour schedule one by one, after each gig, like a prisoner counting the days to freedom on his cell wall. Half the time I don't even know where the hell we are. Why am I wasting time writing this when I should be finishing writing to Sam?

Well, at least if I try to get some of the terror, pain and guilt out of my system in this diary, then hopefully it'll be easier to find something light-hearted to tell her in my letters. Blathering on to her about the band, even though she always says she wants to hear it, makes me feel awful. Here am I, banging on about our success when she's fighting for her life.

Surprise surprise: crying again. Change the record, Helena.

Success is definitely going to Justin's head. He's started taking cocaine. How predictable! Joe has, too, but thankfully David's got more sense. I have to admit that I tried it – a tiny bit – and yes, it was pretty nice. I felt great. But somewhere, from the depths of my being, however tempting it is to get completely out of it and forget about Sam, I haven't repeated the experience. I only tried a weeny little amount, a line as thin as a piece of cotton, practically. Justin's already on great big thick ones. He can handle it, but I don't dare. The last thing Sam needs is me becoming a drug addict! I remember when she came to New York that time, she was horrified when the boys spliffed up. I have to keep focused on her recovery; it's the least I can do when I'm stuck on a different continent to her.

David and I have had a few whispered conversations about whether or not to confront J&J about the coke – I didn't dare mention to him that I'd tried it, too. But we decided that, unless they seem to be getting out of control, it would cause more trouble than it's worth. David's gone for a spot of damage limitation instead. He figured out who they were buying it off, and apparently it's Trish, our roadie Gavin's girlfriend. He took Trish aside and told her, totally politely, that she was NEVER to tell Jus or Joe that she had more than a gram at a time to sell them; and that if she did, he would personally see to it that she went to jail! I hope he knows what he's doing, Gavin's built like a brick shithouse. But I think David's so brave.

I wish David and I fancied each other. He'll make someone a lovely husband. And he's been so supportive to me in the past few weeks. He didn't even gang up on me with the others when we had that row. OK, so he didn't exactly take my side, either, but it can't have been easy for him. It was after I cried on stage in Chicago last week.

I don't know what happened; I'm usually pretty good at holding it together when we're playing. When my eyes fill up, I just turn round and fiddle with the amp or my bass cable, or something. It's a weird feeling, looking at stage

255

lights through teary eyes. They all swirl together, like gasoline in a puddle. I've never dropped acid, but I think it might be like that. Anyhow, last week we were in the middle of 'Love And A Door' and I got an image of Sam's hair falling out and her face getting all sucked-in and grey. Suddenly I just felt so fucking furious. I wanted to scream at God, How could you let this happen? Sam is a beautiful person and she's never done anything to deserve this! It's not fair! And it wasn't just like my eyes filled up, it was as if my whole body filled up. I couldn't blink it away that time, not a chance. I thought I was going to explode. It was all I could do not to throw my bass into the crowd; I wanted to hurt them for being so trivial as to care about stupid us and our stupid, dumb songs when there were much more important things to care about.

I unplugged my bass and walked off-stage mid-song. I saw David's face from behind the drum kit; his jaw just dropped. I didn't stop to see what Justin and Joe's reactions were, but after the show they had such a go at me. It was awful. I was crying and crying and they just kept shouting about 'professionalism' and 'commitment'. Then Joe even yelled at me for not being pleased about our success. If it hadn't been for Sam, and for David intervening, I would have quit then and there. Even Mickey told me to 'try and pull myself together' on the phone. He said that Justin had complained about me. Well, to hell with the lot of 'em. Those are all my songs they're playing every night, so they can hardly fire me, can they?

9 November 1987

Fantastic news! Sam's come through her first round of chemo, and it's been successful! I knew she could do it! Please God, I know I don't talk to you much these days, apart from to complain, but please carry on making her better. Please. She's fighting so hard. And help her get through the next round, too, if she has to do it again.

Oh, and *Spin Shiny*'s gone platinum. That's pretty cool, too.

I'm completely exhausted.

Atlanta, Athens, Tampa, Miami. I like playing in Athens; I'm glad I had some good news before going on stage there. It was the first show I've enjoyed in ages.

Plus I'm getting on better with the boys now, too. It was pretty shaky there for a while, after the row, but we all went out for margaritas after the Miami show, and it was fun. Although I was pissed off when Joe said, 'Careful, Helena, you just smiled. You don't want to make it a habit, your face might shatter.' He's so juvenile.

God, I'm so tired.

31 March 1988

Having a few problems with the folks at the moment. I don't know why Mum gets so upset when I don't come home in between tours; it's not as if she pays me any attention when I am there. But apparently I'd told them that I might be down in February, when we got back from those dates in Canada, and of course I just flew straight over to England to see Sam. I've tried to make Mum understand that Sam needs me, that it's still one step forward, two steps backwards, and that I can't risk not being there – especially to go and be paraded in front of Mum's friends and their spotty teenage sons gurning at me and asking for autographs.

Last time I went to Freehold I hardly even saw Dad. He was either working or on the golf course. If I wasn't getting so famous I think they'd forget they even have a daughter.

They're a complete mystery to me, those two; a totally self-contained unit of coupledom. I don't know why they bothered to have a child. Maybe they didn't, and I was a mistake. It's so weird being around them: they complain, laugh, cry, cook, shop and live for each other within the exclusive confines of their relationship. Dad's been so protective of Mum since she had that eating disorder, or whatever it was, when I was a kid, but she seems fine now, and he's still just as clucky over her. Well, I guess they always were a couple with a child, not a family. I suppose that was why they encouraged my friendship with Sam so much; it gave them more time for each other.

Still, I don't resent them. Not really. I probably wouldn't

be in the band if it weren't for them. And it's not as if they haven't given me a lot of love and encouragement, too, in their own way. They'd better just understand that Sam always comes first, that's all.

20 June 1988. Salisbury.

Dearest Sam,

I can't believe that I'm here and you don't want to see me. I can't begin to understand how ill you feel, but I know how hard it's been for you to have to go through radiotherapy as well as the chemo.

Your mum says you're too frightened to see anybody. Oh, Sam, if only you knew how heartbroken I am that you're so afraid. Please, please don't be scared; we're all here for you. I hope this doesn't sound too trite, but I really believe that angels are watching over you.

I wish there was something I could do to help you. You know I'd go through this for you if I could.

I'm in the UK for ten days, so I can come down again at any time. We're opening for Simply Red on their tour. No pressure, of course, but I would love to see you while I'm here, even just for a few minutes.

Listen to the enclosed tape. It's the soundtrack from *The Big Blue*, and it's all about struggle and achievement and bliss. I've been learning to meditate, and this is the best music to do it to. Listen to it and imagine yourself well again. If it works for you, visualize yourself floating weightless in a warm, clear sea full of light. Imagine that you're made of light. Please listen to it over and over again. Even if you don't have the energy to meditate, I'm sure it will help you feel more relaxed.

All my love,
Helena xxx

PS. I've written a song for you; hopefully it'll be on the next album. It's called 'Over This'. As soon as we've recorded it in the studio I'll send you a tape. x

258

Hi fans,
What do you think of the impressive new-look, glossy *Bluezine*? Do send in your comments for the band.

At the moment they're still out on the road, but they want to let you all know how much they appreciate you coming out to see them in your hundreds of thousands, and for keeping *Spin Shiny* in the charts for so long.

They were in the UK for ten days in June, opening for Simply Red – see page 3 for a photograph of Justin and Mick Hucknall meeting Princess Diana – and this Fall they're off on another big world tour, The Blue Ceiling Tour. Check out the attached dates, and see page 4 for a fabulous chance to win a pair of tickets to their show in Tokyo, flights, accommodation and backstage passes included.

Blue Idea have hired a new Top of the line tour bus, which you may have spotted outside a venue; it's the size of a barn and therefore pretty hard to miss. It even has its own recording studio inside, so not only are the band travelling in way more comfort, they've also been whiling away those long hours on the road by recording demos for their new album. The title will be *Painting The Ceiling*, and it's scheduled for release in October.

The lucky winners of the competition in the last issue of *Bluezine* were Julie Weatherley and Charlotte-Emma Moore, from Lawrence, Ks., both aged sixteen. Well done, guys! They joined the band on the road for a day, and wrote the following note describing their experiences:

We are Blue Idea's biggest fans in the world, and we couldn't believe it when we won. The band treated us real good, they even sent a black stretch limousine to meet us at Chicago airport and take us to the bus. The bus was so neat; it had everything on there. Ovens and showers and beds and recording gear and everything. We had an awesome time, it was the coolest thing that ever happened to us, ever. Everyone in the band was real nice. Justin is a beautiful person, and David gave us some drumsticks, and Joe gave us the shirt he wore in the video for 'Conditions of Love'! Helena had real bad hay fever, her eyes were streaming the whole time, so we gave her some shades to wear on stage that night, and she wore them! The concert was unbelievable. It was the second time we'd seen the band, but the first time without our folks being there.

Thank you, Blue Idea, WE LOVE YA!

Love from Charlotte-Emma and Julie xxooxx

The band want to thank all of you who've sent them gifts while they've been on the road. They've promised to write a letter to send out to all fan-club members; but please be patient, there's a whole bunch of you fans out there.

Finally, here's a personal note from each of the guys, and what they've all been listening to on the road this summer:

Justin:
Hey, thanks so much for all the soft toys, people, but please stop sending them; I have so many on my bunk in the bus that there's no room for me to sleep! Seriously, we're gonna have to start giving a few away to charity soon. Appreciate it, though. Catch you later.
(*Lovesexy* by Prince)

Joe:
Did you hear the one about the guy who visited his doctor naked except for some Saran Wrap around his waist? He said 'Doctor, doctor, am I going crazy?' and the doctor goes, 'Yes, I can clearly see your nuts.' Geddit?
(*Tougher Than Leather* by Run DMC)

David:
Oh well, at least Joe didn't tell you one of his *drummer* jokes. Thanks for coming out to see us, everyone. We love ya, too.
(*Tracy Chapman* by Tracy Chapman – buy this album; it's awesome)

Helena:
Another summer, another tour. The sands of time slip on by, folks, so take my advice and make the most of *everything* in your life. Tell your family and friends you love 'em as often as you get the chance.
(Soundtrack to the movie *The Big Blue*)

Love from us to you,
Justin, Joe, David and Helena xxxx

REVIEW IN *Q MAGAZINE*, NOVEMBER 1988
Painting the Ceiling
Blue Idea
Ringside RNG 2075

****

Presumably there is something about Freehold, New Jersey that drives the youth of the town to escape. Perhaps the high school forces each pupil to study the social insights of the self-appointed 'Boss' of blue-collar rock. If so, no wonder this quartet left town on tour when the youngest of their number was just sixteen.

They started out as the darlings of the American college scene in 1983, purveyors of bubbly post-post punk, and since then they've gone from strength to strength, learning how to adapt to the times in the way that only those in the highest echelons of the rock world – REM and U2 – have managed.

Despite the rather facile and dated title – Blancmange, circa 1982, anyone? – British born songwriter Helena Nicholls has pulled off the not-inconsiderable feat of creating a complete change of direction without losing the lively intensity that hallmarks Blue Idea's earlier material. Rumour has it that Nicholls is going through some un-specified 'personal difficulties', but if that's the case, they've certainly taken her writing to another level. The songs have a much more wistful air to them than the boisterous energy of the band's three previous albums: the subdued loveliness of 'Over This', for example, forces an unconscious overemotional response which seems at odds with the adrenalin-filled passion of their hallmark sound. 'Take Me Away' manages to be effortlessly breezy and grin-inducing, but with heavy overtones of bleeding-heart vulnerability – 'If you're easily pleased, you'll be happy with me' – and 'Pop Artie', 'National Health' and 'Royal Flush' are all vogueishly attractive pop songs, but with a detached, stylish coolness to them.

Vocalist and lead guitarist Justin Becker is still as engaging as ever – surprisingly, this more mellow delivery seems to suit him – while keyboard player Joe Jennings and drummer David Somerstein are able to turn their hands equally expertly to anything from a polka to a punk anthem. Fine songs, fine musicianship and beautiful artwork by Russell Mills.

There isn't a weak track on this mature, complex album. *Painting the Ceiling* will turn Blue Idea from interesting intercontinental journeymen into heavyweight contenders.

27 November 1988, Auckland

Dear Sam,

Thanks for your letter. That's wonderful news about Dylan being compatible. Would it be churlish of me to suggest that this is about the only time in his life he's ever been compatible with anyone, apart from that fiancée of his!

Will I be able to visit you during the transplant? It looks as if we'll have a few days off after we've toured Japan, and I could fly back for a quickie visit then. I did ask your mum this question on the phone the other day, but she thought you might have to be in isolation, my poor baby. Another six weeks in hospital. God, you must be so fed up with it all. Well, if I'm not allowed to see you this time, I'll be over for Christmas.

Hang on in there. I think it's fantastic that the doctors are saying you're now strong enough to go through with the operation. I have a very positive feeling about this. You can do it. This'll be the end of this whole nightmare, I know it will.

Good old big brother. I was just kidding before, I knew

Dylan would come into his own one day. Will he have to take a lot of time off work to donate the bone marrow, or is it a quick in-and-out-of-hospital job? Does he actually *do* any work in that pub, anyway? I have this vision of him being 'mine host', drinking the profits and only getting up from the bar stool for a couple of leisurely games of darts. Although now that he's giving you his bone marrow, I am his number one biggest fan. I'll even marry him if it all goes horribly wrong with Fiona — as long as he promises not to give me any more Chinese burns, of course.

I'm so happy that you're still playing *The Big Blue* so much. It feels like a kind of spiritual lifeline between us, don't you think? — Pretentious, *moi*?

I realized something profound this morning, Sammy. I woke up in this posh Auckland hotel, and the first thing I saw was a huge half-opened pile of fan mail on the table in my hotel room, as much of it addressed to me as to Justin or Blue Idea. It blew my mind, the idea that all those strangers had taken the time to sit down and write to me, another stranger, to try and make me a part of their lives, or for them to become a part of mine. Seeing that big stack of letters brought something home to me in a way that all our increasingly luxurious hotel rooms, the flights on Concorde and the screaming fans hadn't; in all the horror of you being so ill it seemed to have somehow passed me by, but suddenly it really sank in. I'm twenty-two years old, Sam, our new album is number one on both sides of the Atlantic and I'm really, really famous. But you know what else? I'd give it all up in a heartbeat if it would make you better.

All my love, H xxx

PS. I'm glad you like 'Over This'. Ringside are going to release it as a single next year, in the UK as well as over here.

Fame

Fame hardly ever lasts, though, not unless you really work at it. You have to water it and feed it and pamper it, plumping up its brittle ego in the hope that it rewards you with its continued existence. That was what The Plan was for: so I could stay famous without the hassle. I thought I was still famous as a DJ, but it seemed people forgot quickly.

After all, fame was all I had left. It was my anchor, the thing that reminded me of who I was and what I'd achieved. Perhaps other people had friends whose faces lit up with pleasure to see them, and that was their reminder. But now Sam was gone I could only get that from my fans. There was no-one else, not now that I'd decided Toby was out of the picture. I felt like Blanche Dubois, depending on the kindness of strangers.

For the second time in the month since I'd been home, I was going out. Not publicly, as such – not after the river-front disaster – just into town for a meeting with my agent Ron. I could have insisted he come round to me, but once again I was filled with the desire to feel the thrum of London's streets, to see office girls out in their lunch hour buying their Pret a Manger avocado wraps and their Boots reinforced-gusset tights, to watch faceless motorcycle couriers give taxis the finger and prowling traffic wardens tap into their hand-held ticket machines. As long as I could observe it all from the safety of my car, I'd be fine. I was people-hungry, and I missed my listeners, living their ordinary lives with their secret hearts.

Not that they were my listeners any more.

I'd scheduled our meeting for 10 a.m., to coincide with the late rush-hour traffic. I actually felt well enough to want to pretend that I was a normal person commuting into town for a normal job, plus it afforded me another opportunity to drive my car. I hadn't yet bothered to inform the DVLA about my mislaid eye, as the doctor had told me I was required to, but since I was never, never going to touch cocaine again, driving and drinking – separately, as opposed to drinking and driving – were about my only remaining pleasures.

Taking no chances this time, I put on my smallest eyepatch, my darkest shades and the Abba wig. Then I tied a cotton bandanna around my fake hair – the belt-and-braces approach to anonymity.

With a mixture of trepidation and exhilaration I left the house. As I was opening the garage door I found five cigarette butts, clustered together by the corner of the garage, and my heart sank. There was only one person I knew who smoked Gauloises. I had discovered the identity of my lurker.

I decided not to think about it until after my meeting with Ron.

After a careful lookout for paparazzi loitering in cars on the road outside, I backed my metallic-blue 5-series BMW out of the gate and pulled away towards the A316 and Central London. I felt lucky that the papers didn't seem to have discovered where I lived; I'd been sure I'd be fending them off night and day as they tried to worm out confessions of drug addiction and God knows what else, but it had been surprisingly quiet.

I was thankful that I'd been almost paranoiacally circumspect about my home and possessions, even if the corollary had been to turn me into something of a recluse. I could have afforded a much flashier car, for example, and a mansion in the country, but after the band broke up, and the trial, I had vowed that I'd make every effort to keep my public and private personas completely separate.

Very few people knew where I lived, and most of those who did believed I was someone else. I had no close neighbours – my house looked out over the Thames, and was on a secluded plot with only four other houses in the immediate vicinity – all work-related enquiries went care of Ron, and I'd never thrown parties.

When I first moved in I'd entertained a notion of myself having intimate little soirées, impressing all my yet-to-be-made friends with my skill in the kitchen, but since I never actually got round to making any of those friends, the dinners remained uncooked.

Consequently, the only people who knew where I lived were Mum and Dad, Mrs Grant and Sam, who, of course, had practically been a lodger; Justin, Joe and David, who'd all visited on separate occasions; Vinnie and Ron, although he'd never actually been to the house. I had a sweet Serbian cleaner who couldn't speak English, and everyone else who visited had come to give me some kind of private lesson in something spiritual, esoteric or fitness-related – Pilates, yoga, t'ai chi, etc. – and I told all of them my name was Dora. None of them ever let on if they recognized me. The locals knew me as Dora, too, although since almost all of them were elderly millionaires, I doubted they had ever even heard of Blue Idea anyway.

I drove slowly over Twickenham Bridge, crawling along in a fug of exhaust fumes with hundreds of other anonymous commuters, revelling in my proximity to the outside world. I loved to watch people singing in their cars, their silent yodelling through the wind-screen, and the way they picked their noses or pulled faces in the mirror, as if convinced no-one else could see in.

Feeling extra brave, I switched on the car radio, tuned to New World, naturally. I hadn't listened to my show since that brief snippet in hospital, and to my surprise there was someone different to Ralph Porter on air. Millie Myers, a twenty-five-year-old pneumatic 'It' girl – 'It' in my opinion, being an acronym for Intensely Thick. I wasn't surprised; she'd had her eye on my slot ever since she arrived at New World a year ago to do the afternoon show. Consequently, she'd constituted the hard-core base of the anti-Helena brigade.

I'd never had any time for her and her frothy, silly-girly style of broadcasting; I thought it was too frivolous for words. Why on earth did she think London gave a shit about the tragic fact that her Jimmy Choos gave her blisters, or that she'd lost her sodding pashmina? I wondered if she was doing a request show, too. Bet she'd only play a listener's record if they could verify at least one celebrity shag, or prove they'd spent over £500 on one item of clothing.

News, travel, ads. Millie gushing over some execrable TV programme from the night before. Meatloaf back-to-back with a Steps record. Oh, please. Still, I supposed that Millie had to let the computer pick her records if she wasn't doing a request show. Geoff probably didn't give her as much freedom as I'd had.

Nonetheless, Geoff Hadleigh was a sucker for a cleavage and some spindly legs in a miniskirt. I bet he loved Millie, although it was the listeners whose opinions really counted. I was fully expecting to find several sacks of fan mail at Ron's office, demanding to know when I'd be back on air. He wouldn't have forwarded them, since I'd told him I was away recuperating in the US.

'And that, darlings, was the fab-ulous Steps, who you recently voted seventeenth best band ever in our New World poll, between dinosaurs like Led Zeppelin and Fleetwood Mac. Well-deserved success for a

happening new band! And next up, we've got . . . um
. . . Lucy and Meg from Bounds Green. Hi, are you
there, girls?'

A ripple of crackly tittering filled the airwaves. I
accelerated with irritation through an amber traffic
light at a pedestrian crossing.

'Hiya, Millie,' they chorused eventually.

'So what are you two up to this morning?' Millie
asked unimaginatively. DJing by numbers.

More tittering. 'Oh, you know, just getting ready for
school an' stuff.'

Yawn, I thought. After a couple more tedious
minutes of chat about which school, which teacher,
which subjects, Millie finally got around to asking
them why they were calling.

'Well, like, we just wanted to say, we think your
show is really, really wicked, and the music you play
is deadly. All our mates used to listen to Radio One
before school, right, you know, when that other
one was on New World, Helena Whatserface, but since
you've been doing the show our whole French group
listens to you, and we all think you're totally
happenin'.'

Millie laughed, a tinkly, frosted-pink, Met Bar kind
of laugh.

'Hey, thanks, girls. That's soooo nice of you to say
so. Can I play you both a record this morning?'

'Yeh, Millie, can you play us "Over This" by Kitsch
N'Sync?'

'No problemos, consider it done. This one's for Lucy
and Meg – the fantastic Kitsch N'Sync, hottest band
around, with a really, really amazing new single,
"Over This". I believe it's an old song, but they've
certainly made it a hit this time – number one for the
second week running.'

I turned sharply off the road into a petrol station and
screeched to a halt beside the car vacuum. Surely not.
But instead of my tender bass and the mellow
Hammond Joe had spread like treacle on top of the

intro, I heard the same notes tortured out of a synth, and a naff five-part harmony vocal 'choo-choo chooooo' sound preceded the start of the verse.

It got worse. My lyrics were delivered in a hideous faux R&B style by some teenage pretty boy who probably thought Ronan Keating was a pop legend; he rendered it completely devoid of any real emotion, and was obviously more concerned with how complicated he could make it sound.

Banging the radio's Off button with my fist, I put my head down on the steering wheel and wept with the humiliation of fifteen-year-olds liking Millie Myers better than me, the shock of hearing my precious tribute to Sam's strength and courage reduced to such soulless crap, and the fury of that daft bimbo not even *knowing* that it was my song, Sam's song.

Everything I'd felt when the record was released — all that joy and relief and optimism — was erased, like a chalk masterpiece on a rain-washed pavement.

Tears poured down one side of my face. I sat, lost in memory, until there was a loud 'beep' behind me. Blearily I lifted my head and saw in the wing mirror a man gesticulating at me from his Ford Escort. He was parked right up next to my rear bumper.

'Is yer gonna use the soddin' hoover or wha'?' he demanded, leaning out of his window.

Giving him the finger, I put my car in gear and shot back onto the road, but I could only drive a few hundred yards before I had to stop again. One blurred eye, a deaf ear and a head full of grief did not make for entirely safe driving conditions.

This time I pulled up outside an antique shop, which had a large amount of very unantique anaemic pine piled up on the pavement outside it. My head throbbed as I stared unseeing at spikes of blond chair leg and smooth Swedish table tops, some inverted for ease of stacking.

There were so many bitter, sad thoughts crowding my head that it took me a few minutes to begin to articulate them, even mentally. When I finally stopped crying I managed to think up a small, furious list. I should:

1) call Ringside Publishing to find out who gave permission for Kitsch N'Crap to use my song, then have them fired.
2) Sue Kitsch N'Crap for using my song without clearing it first, if that was what they'd done.
3) Phone Millie right now, to point out that actually Blue Idea's version of 'Over This' had been number one for three weeks in 1989 and raised a million pounds for leukaemia charities – how could she not know that?
4) *Finish the manuscript and do the show.* No more assing about, no missionary trips to Zaire, no question of a cop-out. I had to go through with it; if not actually on air, then in the studio. It was the only way I could be sure that the Millies of this world didn't get remembered when I was forgotten. Life sucked, and now more than ever I wanted out.

'Lovesong'
The Cure

I sat down on a window ledge in the VIP area to watch The Cure's set through the thick plate glass, my knees drawn up to my chin, giddy with the combined bliss of having played a fantastic show *and* being back in England. On a practical level it was also nice to get my feet off the sticky floor – at every step my soles had stuck to the filthy beer-soaked carpet tiles with tiny, uncomfortable squelching sounds. And this was meant to be the 'luxurious' hospitality area! We were in a long, narrow room which faced the stage, directly underneath the balcony. It wasn't enhanced by the dingy lighting – everything around was black: walls, curtains and carpet, presumably in an attempt to render cleaning less necessary.

Justin was loving it. Every time he moved out of the relative safety of his vantage point next to me on the window seat, he would be surrounded by a group of gossip-hungry journalists, competition-winners seeking autographs, or plain old groupies who had somehow inveigled a backstage pass, and he happily chatted away to all and sundry, revelling in the attention. I, on the other hand, had the black curtain practically wrapped around my head to avoid being quizzed, despite the resultant reek of stale cigarette smoke which enveloped me.

Our set had gone extremely well, and I was content;

I just wasn't in the mood to socialize with strangers. Besides, I wanted to watch The Cure's show, even though the sound was muffled from up here. Blue Idea and The Cure were alternating between the middle and headline spot every night on this tour, and it was their turn to go on last. I preferred it that way as there was more of a chance to get a relatively early night. I loved to slip back to the hotel, as soon as I could escape, to the peace of a crisp white pillow, some top-class British television and a usually futile attempt to get through to my new boyfriend, Patrick, on the phone.

Patrick was a film actor. He'd recently played the lead in a medium-sized Hollywood movie called *Time Waits for No Man*, and since then he'd been inundated with offers of different sorts from film directors and nubile young waitresses. We'd met after he'd hosted a charity gig in San Francisco which Blue Idea headlined, and we'd spent a thrilling week together, licking Ghiradelli chocolate off each other's navels in my hotel room, or walking hand in hand over the Golden Gate Bridge at dawn when the paparazzi weren't around to see us.

That had since been followed by the odd night of passion here and there, when we were in the same country, but I sensed, without asking, that Patrick saw it as a casual thing, and I felt somewhat hesitant about calling him my boyfriend. It was quite depressing, really; after the first thrill, it no longer seemed different to any of the other flings I'd had on the road. Patrick was handsome and funny and successful, but I still felt like an accessory, or some kind of trophy.

I wished Sam was there. She'd nearly puked with envy when I'd told her about me and Patrick, and I'd been trying to think of a way to engineer a meeting between them for weeks. But it was hard enough to pin Patrick down at all, let alone get him and Sam both on the same continent at the same time.

Unbelievably, Sam hadn't heard us play live since

that time in New York, almost four years before, and she'd never heard me sing her song to her. But although the bone-marrow transplant had been a success and her life was no longer under threat, she had been suffering from a condition called graft-versus-host disease, where the new bone marrow had begun to reject her body. She'd been trying different treatments to combat it, but they all seemed to have horrific side-effects, and consequently she felt awful most of the time. She was definitely too delicate to endure a hot, smoky venue.

She kept telling me that all she had to do was turn on the radio and her song still seemed to be blasting out. She couldn't get over the fact that a song about her had been at number one, let alone that it was still in the charts a year later.

I told her that next time, hopefully, we'd be playing a huge outdoor gig, and then she'd have no excuse not to come and see us. The UK success of 'Over This' ensured that we were big enough already. In the meantime, while I was in the UK, I had to be content with talking to her for hours on the phone every day, with just one swift trip to Salisbury on our only free weekend.

Sam, although still poorly, looked much better than when I'd last seen her the year before. Then she'd been all chubby from the steroids she was taking, and her hair had grown back in stringy patches, but this year there was a definite improvement. She was back to her old slim self, albeit much thinner than she should have been, and with a wheezy chest. She had an attractive fuzz of really short hair which made her look trendy and boyish. I'd cried with relief to see the improvement in both her spirits and her health. Some of her old verve had returned, and she was full of plans to go back to university as soon as she could, and catch up on all the work she'd missed.

I became aware that I was panting slightly from the heat. Even the air seemed to be sweating. I'd forgotten, until I walked in, that English venues never had air-conditioning. I pressed my cool champagne glass against my hot cheek. Condensation on the black shiny walls had made most of the blu-tacked posters announcing the release of our new record hang disconsolately down at at least one corner, and I could see the harassed-looking junior product manager from the record company running around trying to make them stick up again.

The Cure struck up the opening sequence of their current single, 'Lovesong', and the audience went wild, dancing frenziedly, seeming not to care that it wasn't the most uptempo of numbers. It was all about people expressing their appreciation with the movement of their bodies, an extension of applause. I could see flying drops of sweat caught silver in the spotlight which swept across the crowd's heads as they waved their arms and jumped up and down.

I heard Justin announce, 'Back in a minute, guys,' prompting a synchronicity of heads turning to gaze after his retreating back. Deprived of his company, the groupies drifted instead towards me.

'That was a fabulous show, Helena.'

'Your voice sounded great.'

'Please could you sign this for my little sister?'

The question was from a boy of about fourteen; he was wearing his laminate proudly over his Blue Idea T-shirt, and a big button badge stating 'I Won the Radio 1 Blue Idea Competition!' I smiled at him and took the sticky biro he thrust at me, scribbling my name and three large X kisses on the front of the poster he was holding. The others, I saw, had already signed it. 'Cor, thanks,' he breathed reverentially. 'Now I've got you all.'

The other two people who had spoken to me did not expect an answer. They were trying to be ultra-cool and had already drifted away, probably rehearsing how they would say to their friends, 'Yeah, of course when I was talking to Helena from Blue Idea backstage after their show . . .' Their sort would never deign to ask for an autograph. They usually either worked for the record company in some minor capacity or had a friend who was a crew member who had somehow managed to get them on the guest list. They always adopted an aloof and slightly superior attitude to us, a sort of, 'just because you're famous you needn't think that I'm going to fall all over myself to be nice to you' look. Not that we ever did think that. But they always managed to get a piece of me somehow – a carefully posed snapshot of them, taken by a friend, which just happened to have me looming in the background; a seemingly casual request for a light, or use of a pen, some trivial thing; or just a throwaway comment in my direction.

I really didn't mind when true fans came up and introduced themselves, or plucked up the courage to tell me how much they liked the band, or the record, or my bass playing, or whatever. At the risk of sounding corny, the light and passion in their eyes was what kept me going, what made it all worthwhile. I needed it. It was just those shallow, self-important industry liggers and their hangers-on that I had a hard time dealing with.

The wife of the president of Ringside Records hove into sight, and I leaned forward to try and avoid her by swinging the damp curtains of my hair across my face. Focusing intently on an ugly bar ashtray next to me on the window ledge, I began to push it around in a circle by its heavy glass corners, the fug of old cigarette ash black and condensed in the bottom. Luckily Justin returned at that moment, and we both pressed our noses against the warm glass window, pretending to be engrossed in watching the band. He did not like her, either. He said she once propositioned him in the back of a limo, plying him with Cristal and cocaine, then leaning seductively towards him until her famous breasts were almost completely adrift from their flimsy silk mooring. He told me he wasn't having any of it, but he didn't sound entirely convincing.

275

'Has she gone yet?' he muttered as she teetered by in high heels and the latest Dolce & Gabbana miniskirt.

I looked sideways through my hair, which by now reeked of smoke. 'Yes. You're safe – if you want to be.'

'Phew!' He knocked back the contents of another glass of champagne.

Holly, Ringside UK's cheerful press officer, rushed up to us, puffing and sweaty.

'Hello, Jolly Holly,' said Jus.

'Hello, you two. Gosh, it's hot out there. Are you ready for your interview? David, Joe and Toby the journalist are waiting for you in the dressing room. Hurry up!'

I'd forgotten that we had an interview with *Melody Maker*, and Justin must have done, too, as he normally loved giving interviews, but we'd done so many on this tour that we were all heartily sick of the same old questions. One particularly naff feature was for a glossy women's magazine with the headline, HELENA – SHOOTIN' FROM THE HIP! which had me parading around with a cap gun in cowboy clothes, chaps and fringes. Sam told me she'd laughed like a drain when she saw it.

Holly chivvied us along through the maze of narrow backstage corridors until we reached our dressing room, which was so cool and comfortable in comparison to the dingy mêlée we'd just left that I wondered why I'd ever let Jus persuade me to go up there in the first place. Much as I loved The Cure, it wasn't as if I hadn't seen them a million times already. David and Joe obviously had more sense, and were lounging on an outsized sofa, looking relaxed and refreshed; Joe puffing on a joint and David slugging a beer.

'This is Toby from the *Melody Maker*,' Holly said, introducing us to a sweet-faced youthful guy in jeans and a checked shirt, with curly blond hair and huge red-framed glasses. He had such a gorgeous smile that I was prepared to forego summoning the fashion police to have him arrested for the awful specs – it being a good year after they'd become a must in the wardrobe of every journalist and architect.

Toby shook my hand firmly and, still smiling broadly, looked me steadily in the eyes. I liked him right away. In fact, I *really* liked him. It was as if something zinged between us, a flash of connection acknowledging our mutual attraction. It hit me in the stomach, an unfamiliar hourglass-shaped feeling of quick suction.

He got on with the interview in a very businesslike manner, individually asking us interesting and well-researched questions, and proffering a hand-held cassette player for our replies. After a while it seemed that he was asking me a lot more questions than the others, more even than Justin, who began to fidget restlessly.

I talked about the tour and the new record, and the usual topic of what it was like being the only girl on the bus with the others, as well as the all-male crew, and all the time Toby looked at me with his friendly crinkled-up eyes, and nodded enthusiastically so that his curls boinged around his head like an animated halo. I did have a weakness for men with curly hair.

'So how do you feel about your younger fans emulating your trademark style?' Toby asked seriously.

'What trademark style is that? Singing flat and spending hours in front of the mirror?' asked Justin derisively. I punched his arm hard enough for him to squawk.

'Well, there are several girls outside wearing long coat jackets over straight-legged trousers, with big shawly scarves,' Toby explained.

I was as surprised as Justin, and very flattered.

'Oh that's not emulating a style. That's because they obviously have as little taste as Helena,' said Justin.

I knew Justin was jealous of the attention Toby was giving me, but I was embarrassed by Justin's put-downs nonetheless, and blushed scarlet.

Joe slapped Justin around the head, and David told

him to shut up. Holly looked anxious, worried that a fight was about to break out, but Justin put his arms around me.

'Only joking, honeypie. We all know you're gorgeous and totally fashionable, really.'

Toby acted as if nothing had happened. 'Having done quite a bit of research on Blue Idea for this interview, I noticed that girls who join your fan club can actually send away for a Helena scarf. Didn't you notice how many of them were being waved in the audience when Helena was singing "Over This"? And Helena, if I might say so, you shouldn't look so surprised that young girls are choosing to look like you. You are, after all, a very well-respected songwriter, not to mention an extremely attractive woman.'

'Wa-ay hey!' sniggered Jus lewdly, an English expression he had picked up from our Yorkshire bus driver. I felt my face grow hot again, but this time with pleasure and gratitude. Toby sounded as though he really meant it.

'Thanks,' I said, coyly. Even David and Joe tittered this time.

Toby mercifully took another tack. 'Now, "Over This" is your first chart-topper and obviously a huge success, not to mention the first charity record by a single band ever to get to number one. Did all the proceeds go to help fund research into leukaemia? David?'

David said, 'Well, it's our first number one in England, but the third in America. Our first number one at home, "This Is Your Blue Idea", only got to number twenty here. You'd better ask Helena about the charity thing. I'm not really sure of the details.'

'Yes, yes, of course. *Third* US number one. Yes, I did know that. I meant in the UK.' Toby looked flustered, as if he was afraid we'd despise him for a potential error in research.

'So, Helena, can you tell me the story behind this song? It's about a friend of yours, isn't it? Is that why you sing it instead of Justin?'

'Yes, it's about my best friend Sam. I wrote it when she was really sick with leukaemia, and at first, whenever Justin used to sing it, it made me cry. So we thought if I sang it instead it would give me something to concentrate on, and I wouldn't be able to cry. And it did work, sort of.'

'So, Sam, did she . . . er . . . I mean, is she . . . ?' Toby looked sympathetic and embarrassed at the same time.

'The leukaemia's in remission, thanks, but she still hasn't properly recovered. She had a bone-marrow transplant from her brother about a year ago, although since then she's had all sorts of problems as a result. Anyway, I offered to donate the song to the Leukaemia Trust, and a couple of months back they called and suggested that we released it ourselves and give them the proceeds. I don't think they thought we'd agree to it, but we talked about it for a long time with our manager and Ringside, and decided that it was the least we could do. I'm just really happy that she survived it.'

Toby smiled at me again, as if he was really happy she had, too. I had the sudden thought that Sam would approve of him.

'It turned out pretty well all round, then, didn't it! Well, I think that's about everything I wanted to know. Thanks, all of you, you've been great. Congratulations on the number one and best of luck with the new album. It's absolutely brilliant. It hasn't been off the office turntable since we got it. When will you next be in the UK?'

We all concluded that we didn't know, but hopefully soon, depending on how the record went, and then after we'd all shaken hands with him again, Holly ushered Toby out into the corridor. As she opened the door, a pretty but ditzy-looking red-haired girl grabbed Toby's elbow and whispered something in his ear. He turned reluctantly back into the room, the girl still hanging on to his arm.

'Er, this is Lorraine, my girlfriend. She was really hoping to get to meet you all.'

Lorraine, however, had eyes only for Justin. She rushed up to him, practically elbowing me out of the way, and started gushing about how wonderful he was, and how she was a singer, too, and that she had several songs down on four-track, etc., etc. Justin recovered his lost good humour and, steering her over to the empty side of the room, gave her a beer and settled down to enjoy some good, wholesome ego-bolstering.

Suddenly I felt deflated. For some reason, the words 'Lorraine, my girlfriend' had put a damper on the whole evening. Awkwardly, I turned round to Toby. 'Well, I think I'll go back to the hotel now. I'm kind of tired. It was very nice meeting you. Please come and say hello next time we play in London.'

He looked at me with what I interpreted as the ghost of a resigned expression, his eyebrows raised in an almost apologetic way, and then there was that smile again.

'Yes,' he said. 'I'm sure we'll meet again.'

A couple of weeks later, when the tour had finished and I was temporarily imprisoned *chez* parents back in Freehold, Holly sent me a package via the US press officer, with the *Melody Maker* interview clipped onto the top of a pile of press cuttings and reviews. The headline for the feature was BLUE IDEA . . . AND THEIR GREEN-EYED DEAR, and the whole article glowed with praise for my talent, humility and striking beauty – all Toby's words, not mine. Holly's sardonic note read, 'Hmm, he didn't fancy you much or anything, did he!'

I hadn't had a chance to tell Sam about the interview, so I mailed her a copy of the clipping and the note. She phoned me when she got it, laughing. 'Well? Was he as nice looking as the divine Patrick, then?'

'What do you mean? I just wanted you to see your name in print, that's all.'

'Oh yeah, pull the other one! Come *on*. Like the woman said, he wasn't interested in you just because you've got a record out.'

'Yes, he was, actually. Interested in the record *and* nice looking, in a very cute sort of way. But he has a girlfriend, and I have a boyfriend.'

'Oh well, it's probably not serious; his girlfriend, I mean. I'm sure you can get rid of her.'

'Sam! The man lives three thousand miles away. Get a grip! She was awful, though. And she fancied Justin, so you never know.'

'There you are then,' Sam said triumphantly, and we both laughed. She sounded as though she was talking to me from around the corner. 'How are things with Patrick, anyway? Have you spoken to him since you got back?'

'He hasn't returned my last three calls.'

'Oh no,' said Sam. 'Are you upset?'

I considered. 'Not really. The sex is nice, but it's just so hard to maintain a relationship when we're on the road. He's filming now, and can't jump on a plane every time he wants to see me. I did think I'd get to see him when we got back, but there's no chance now. We're off to Japan on Monday. It was fun at first, but I can't see how it's going to last.'

'Oh, Helena. Poor you. But I hope you're going to settle down some day. I want to be godmother to your kids, remember.'

'Jeez, give us a chance, Sam. I'm only a year older than you, not ten. Twenty-three is far too young to think about babies.'

Sam was silent for a minute. 'Not if you can't have them, it isn't.'

I could have cut my tongue out. Poor Sam had been told that she wouldn't be able to conceive, after all her treatments. It was one more cross that she bore without complaint; in fact, so uncomplainingly that I'd been selfish enough to temporarily forget the fact.

'I'm so sorry, Sammy. I don't know what to say.'

She sighed, a long, weary sound which travelled slowly along the wire connecting us. I imagined that sigh, deep down underneath the ocean, and wished I could make it stay there for ever, trapped, with all the rest of Sam's ailments and worries.

That night I lay uncomfortably on a bed which, although it was in my old bedroom in my parents' house, felt as strange and unwelcoming as a hotel bed. I must buy myself an apartment, I thought. Surely I could afford one by now. Mum and Dad were always pleased to see me, for about fifteen minutes, after which they'd resume whatever leisure activity – golf, canasta, bridge, gardening – they'd been involved in before I'd arrived. Apart from the home-cooked meals, I hated going back to Freehold in between tours.

I thought of Sam's poor shrivelled-up ovaries, her indefatigable courage and her constant small triumphs over adversity. I thought of my own life, how exciting it must seem to everyone else, but how exhausting and pressured it really was. I thought briefly of delicious Patrick, his plucked eyebrows and exfoliated cheeks, manicured nails and colour-coded socks, and of how many thousands of women would kill to sit in bed with him and eat a bag of post-coital Cheez Doodles, as I had. But I felt nothing except a desire to sleep.

I got up, retrieved my Sony Walkman and slotted in a Cure tape. Climbing back into bed and snuggling up into the pillows, I lay there listening to 'Lovesong', a song I wasn't remotely sick of, even after hearing it on tour every night.

But I wasn't thinking about all the arenas and academies, the theatres and ballrooms, the clubs and festivals. As I finally drifted off to sleep, I was dreaming of a journalist called Toby, and the way his eyes had held me, and the nice things he'd written about me.

☆

You Ain't Ms Nicholls

I was in a complete state by the time I finally arrived at the private car park at the back of the building in which Ron's office was housed. Hearing 'Over This' murdered by some spotty adolescents had upset me far more than listening to Millie Myers' listeners diss me. I felt as though I'd been driving drunk, emotions were whirling around inside the car and I missed Sam so badly that I wanted to slam my head down on the steering wheel.

I pulled up at the automatic barrier and collected myself together enough to talk to Cecil, the large, black car-park attendant. If I'd been less distraught I'd have been delighted to see him. We always had a chat whenever I came for a meeting with Ron. Cecil was such a genuine, sweet man, and would tell me about his kids' triumphs and his wife's gallstones.

'Hi, Cecil, long time no see,' I managed through the open window.

Cecil loomed out from the doorway of his dinky little booth. He frowned and scratched his head. 'Who you here to see, ma'am?'

I glared at him. 'Ron, of course! Who else do I come and see? He's expecting me. Do I park in the usual place?'

The barrier remained resolutely down.

'Sign the visitors book first, please, ma'am.'

Cecil passed the book through the window, and the proximity of his huge, creased brown hands made me want to grab them and hold on to them for dear life to protect me from feeling this way. He was still looking at me, trying to place me.

Suddenly it clicked. Of course, he didn't recognize me. I whipped off the bandanna and the wig, and shook out my short brown hair.

'Sorry, Cecil, what was I thinking. No wonder you didn't recognize me. It's me, Helena Nicholls.'

But Cecil's frown merely deepened. I scrawled my name with irritation in the book and handed it back to him.

'You ain't Ms Nicholls,' he said slowly. The buttons on his uniform blinked suspiciously at me in the sunlight.

I didn't think the day could get any worse. 'Of course I'm Ms Frigging Nicholls! Look at me! Listen to my voice! If I wasn't, how would I know that your kids are called Cheryl and Simon, and that you've worked here for eighteen years? Don't you even remember my car, for God's sake? I had an accident, OK? My face looks different. I broke my nose and my jaw. I've lost an eye. I'm scarred. Call Ron right now if you don't believe me.' I burst into tears.

Cecil looked mortified. He reached his big sausagey fingers through the window and stroked my sleeve tentatively. 'Ms Nicholls, I'm really, really sorry, ma'am. I see it's you now. You don't look all that different, honest. It's my eyes, they ain't what they used to be, and it's been a while since you was last in. Please forgive my rudeness. I'm so sorry to hear you had an accident. Ron never told me.'

He retreated into his booth and the barrier shot up at speed. I drove in without another word, and had to sit in the car for a full ten minutes until I'd stopped crying. Whenever I glanced up into the rear-view mirror I could see Cecil staring at me, anguished, from the safety of his Wendy house.

The irony of the situation didn't strike me until later. For the last twelve years I'd been trying to make myself inconspicuous, unidentifiable, but now that people really didn't recognize me I was devastated. So much for the kindness of strangers, I thought. That only worked if the strangers actually remembered who you were. First they had to recognize you.

'Helena, darling! How *are* you? Great to see you again. Feeling all right? Bet you were glad to get out of that hospital, weren't you? What's it like being home again? Coffee? Cindy, can we have two coffees in here, please?'

Ron, ever the PR man, bombarded me with questions so as to avoid commenting on my appearance, which was by now even less appealing due to all the crying I'd done. I'd gone into the Ladies' to try and repair my make-up, but the sight of my reflection threatened to start the tears off again, so I'd left it blotchy.

Still, Ron was no oil-painting himself. He used to work as a director of promotions for a major record label, but I had a theory he'd been sacked for wearing Pringle jumpers and slacks. He was the only gay guy I'd ever met who had absolutely no fashion sense.

'Yeah, yeah, fine thanks.' I moved across Ron's office to the window, so I could stand with my back to him. 'So what's new, then? Any suggestions as to what to do for an out-of-work DJ?'

Ron laughed nervously. 'You aren't out of work, darling. Geoff offered you another job, didn't he?'

I leaned my forehead against the cool glass of the window; only the prospect of more stitches prevented me from headbutting it. I tried to keep my voice measured and calm.

'I don't consider the graveyard shift a proper job, Ron. It's humiliating. Plus I won't be able to do my request show at that time. I just wondered if anything else had come up. Before I . . . the accident . . . didn't you tell me that you had something really hot in the pipeline for me? You were getting more details; you were going to let me know. What about that? Is it still available?'

There was a silence, broken when Cindy, Ron's PA, brought in two mugs of coffee.

'Well?'

Ron swivelled awkwardly on his chair, making it squeak uncomfortably. 'Er, Helena; well, no, that turned out to be a blind alley.'

'What was it, then? An offer from another station? Was it Radio One?'

Another silence. Ron tore a day off his Dilbert desk calendar.

Something about the sound made me turn round, puzzled. I stared at him. 'Do that again for a second?'

'What?'

'Tear a page off that thing.'

Ron gaped up at me as if I'd asked him to take his trousers down. 'I can't. I'm up to date now. I can't tear off today until tomorrow, or at least not until the end of the day. It's Tuesday today.'

I couldn't believe that I'd entrusted my career to such an idiot. But nonetheless, his voice sounded different, too.

'Please, just tear off another one. You can Sellotape it back on again afterwards.'

Ron obviously thought that my concussion was worse than I'd let on. I gave up waiting for him and, reaching over his desk, ripped off Tuesday myself.

The little jagged sound it made was in *stereo*!

'Oh my God, Ron, my right ear's just started working again. I can hear properly. I can't believe it!'

Misery temporarily on hold, I jumped across the room and hugged Ron round his pudgy middle-aged neck. For a second I felt so exhilarated that for the first time I seriously imagined abandoning The Plan.

'This is fantastic! It means I can work again as a DJ.

Maybe Radio One would hire me after all. No problem with driving my own desk now, and—'

Ron interrupted me, disengaging himself from my arms. 'Er, Helena, I thought your hearing returned ages ago. Didn't you already tell Hadleigh that it had? He wouldn't have even given you a night-time slot if it wasn't back to normal.'

Crushed, I realized this was true. 'Oh. Yes. Well, I lied. But now it really is better, so maybe that will help find me something else? You were about to tell me what the other job was.'

Ron looked crossly at his Dilbert calendar. 'Look at that – you've made it Wednesday now when it's still only Tuesday.'

'*Ron!*'

He sighed and took a slurp of coffee. 'Sorry, darling, but it ain't happening now. You were up for a job as presenter on a new celebrity chat show Channel Five are scheduling. Lisa I'Anson got the gig.'

I sat down opposite Ron and let my head sink onto his desk in despair.

TV! I'd been about to start a career in TV, something every prime-time DJ dreams of, but now I was disfigured. Like deaf DJs, you didn't see too many ugly TV presenters.

'And you don't have any other other jobs lined up for me?' I asked in a small, muffled voice, my breath dampening the shiny surface of Ron's mahogany desk.

I didn't have to look up to know that he was shaking his head.

My emotions couldn't stand the pace; they'd been up and down all day. It looked like we were back on course for The Plan again. I stood up.

'Ron, listen. I just wanted to say, in case I don't get the chance again, thanks for everything, you know. You've been a really great agent, and—'

Ron leaped up, too, cupping his hands to his chin in a big queeny gesture of horror. 'You're *firing* me? I don't believe it! After everything I've done—'

'Ron, for God's sake, I'm not firing you. I'm certainly not looking for another agent. I just . . . well, you never know what might happen. It's always good to tell people how you feel. And I want you to have this as a gesture of my appreciation.'

On the spur of the moment I pulled off the plain silver ring I wore on my forefinger. It had been given to me by a fan in Singapore, and I was very fond of it, but suddenly I thought, What do I need it for now?

Ron looked overcome. 'And you're sure you aren't firing me?'

He tried to cram the ring onto his little finger, but it only reached as far as the first joint.

'Sure. It's just a present to say thanks for maintaining my privacy, you know, keeping the press off my back when I was in hospital and stuff.'

'Well, thank you, darling, that's ever so sweet of you. I don't know what to say. I'll put it on a chain round my neck. Mwah, mwah.' He kissed me on both cheeks and I tried not to flinch.

'If there's nothing else on the job front, I'll get going. Got a busy day ahead of me, you know, doing . . . stuff. I really just came in to get my post and catch up.'

'Ah, yes, your post. I'll tell Cindy to fetch it.' Ron rushed to the office door. 'Cindy, could you bring in Helena's mail please.'

I waited for Cindy to arrive with a huge sack, like Father Christmas. She was gone long enough; perhaps there was more than I'd thought, and she'd gone to get a palette to bring it on.

While we were waiting I remembered what else I'd been intending to ask him.

'Hey, Ron, you might know this. A bunch of brats have covered "Over This". Kitsch N'Sync. Apparently it's number one . . .'

'Oh, I *love* that record! Of course it's number one. Congratulations. That'll be a nice little earner for you. I think they've done a really great job, don't you?'

I glowered at him. 'No, I do not. "Over This" is a

very important song to me, and I certainly would never give permission for it to be slaughtered by a posse of pre-pubescent morons. I want you to call Ringside Publishing for me and find out who was responsible for letting them.'

Ron was shaking his head again.

'What?'

'Helena, I can't call the publishers. There's no point. They don't need the publishers' permission to do a cover version of a song, because it's an interpretation. You only have to get permission if you sample it. You ought to be pleased; it's more money for you.'

I thought of Sam's face and wanted to weep again.

Just then Cindy appeared back in the office clutching a faintly paunchy A4 brown envelope. She handed it to me.

'There you go, Helena. Sorry I didn't bring it straight in, but I was desperate for a pee.'

I blinked at her, which in my one-eyed state must have looked like a wink. I hoped furiously that she didn't think I was coming on to her.

'Is that it?' I was genuinely surprised.

Cindy nodded, blushing and not meeting my eye. I took the envelope and peered inside to see about ten unopened letters.

'There must be some mistake. Where's the rest?' The words fell out before I could stop myself.

Cindy and Ron exchanged looks, and Cindy edged tactfully back out of the room. Ron assumed his best long-suffering expression. 'No, sweetie, I'm afraid that really *is* it. Don't take it personally. Being a DJ isn't the same as being in a band, you know. People don't get so attached. I'm sure you got heaps of letters when you were in Blue Idea, but that's because kids really loved your music, wasn't it? They don't bother to write to DJs on the whole. DJs are just part of their life, like their mates, or bus drivers, or whoever. I bet Chris Evans and Zoë Ball don't get that many letters.'

I bet they did, but it wasn't worth arguing about.

289

'You did an awesome job, Helena,' Ron ploughed on. 'You know how far you bumped up New World's ratings, but trends change so fast in radio. That confessional thing is a bit, well, *over* now. We all just have to move on.'

'Oh don't worry, Ron. I'm going to be moving on all right.' I laughed bitterly.

'So you're going to take that night-time slot then?'

I looked at him for a long time, thinking how little I cared about never seeing him again. 'Yeah, I'll give it a whirl. Let's just see what happens, shall we?'

'Kinky Afro'

Happy Mondays

Two years later I was back in London for another show, although it didn't feel that long. We'd been around the world twice, and had number one hits in eighteen different countries. I was older, more tired, much richer and utterly ecstatic because Sam was with me.

'It's going to be *really* hot today, I heard it on the radio this morning. It's boiling already, and it's only eleven thirty,' she said when she came to meet me in my hotel room. She was wearing baggy denim cut-off dungarees and an antique sleeveless lace top which buttoned up the back.

'I love your top,' I said, fixing her a cold drink from the minibar.

'Gee thanks, *hon*,' she said, trying to imitate my American accent. 'I swear, Helena, you sound more like a Yank every time I talk to you. I'm afraid if this continues we will no longer be able to maintain our friendship.' She grinned, and pushed past me into the room to inspect everything.

'This is incredible. This room is bigger than my whole flat. You didn't stay in such a posh hotel last time, did you?'

'Not quite, but almost. Onwards and upwards, you know.'

'That was my school motto. What was yours?' Sam

looked out of the window at the spectacular view over Hyde Park.

'Oh, I dunno. No, wait, I remember; it was "The Fighting Bucks", or, as Justin called it, "The Biting—"'

Sam cut me off. 'I can imagine, thank you, Helena. Moving swiftly on . . .'

I laughed. 'OK. Well, speaking of your flat, how's the decorating coming on?'

The Grants had sold the licence to the pub, and bought a house on the outskirts of Salisbury with a basement granny flat for Sam, so that she could have her independence but be near the family, too. Mr Grant had got a job as a brewery sales rep, but before he started he was decorating Sam's flat from top to bottom.

Sam still wasn't very well – the legacy of the graft-versus-host disease, exhaustion, miserable skin problems and a nasty asthmatic-type wheeze, still persisted – but it hadn't stopped her from continuing to study for her law degree, part-time and by correspondence. I couldn't fathom how she had the strength of character and determination to do it when every ounce of her energy was at a premium.

'Great,' she said, taking the cellophane off my huge complimentary fruit basket to get to the grapes. 'I can't believe I've got the whole place to myself, and I can still take my washing upstairs to Mum! Mum loves not having to work in the bar. She's always off having these really long lunches with her mates, and she's taken up aerobics and done a tie-dying course. She wants to tie-dye my curtains, but I've told her to forget it.'

'I would have thought she knew how to tie-dye already, without needing a course,' I commented, zipping my stage clothes carefully into their plastic carrier and hooking its coat-hanger top over the bathroom door.

'Oh, she did. It was like a refresher course. Actually, I think it was really just an excuse for her to get together with a load of other old hippies-turned-housewives.'

Sam's voice got a bit echoey as she disappeared into the bathroom to riffle through the freebies by the sink. 'Can I have this shampoo? I love Molton Brown. Are you going to steal the bathrobe?'

The phone rang. It was the front desk to tell me that my car had arrived.

'Yes, take it – the *shampoo*, not the bathrobe. And you can have that little shoe-polishing thing, too, if you like. Are you ready? The car's here.'

I ran around collecting everything I needed for the gig: vanity case, a bottle of mineral water from the minibar, my toothbrush and toothpaste. Sam was emptying half the contents of the fruit basket into her backpack.

I thrust the suit carrier into her arms. 'Here, you carry this. I'll take your backpack, it'll be heavy with all that stolen fruit in it.'

She made a face at me, then grinned. 'Wembley, here we come!' she said as we set off down to the marble-and-glass lobby.

I handed in my key and pushed through the heavy revolving doors, Sam being swept along in the next segment behind me. The roasting sunshine hit us as we emerged from the air-conditioning onto the sticky tarmac of the hotel's driveway. It felt more like Arizona in high summer than London.

A huge black stretch limousine was purring in front of us, both the passenger door and the driver door opening simultaneously as we approached. Mickey leaned out and beckoned us into the back seat, and the driver came round and put our things into the boot with a courteous, stiff-faced nod and a muttered 'good morning, ladies' in our direction. A doorman leaped forward and needlessly held the already-open passenger door. At the same time, five Japanese girls rushed up, squealing, with Blue Idea records for me to sign. They snapped a volley of shots of me with their

Nikons, laughing and nodding at each other ecstatically as I scribbled my name for them. Sam's mouth was hanging open at the size of the car and the spectacle of me signing autographs, and I had to prod her in the back to make her get in as I waved goodbye to the fans.

Once inside, I was grateful to feel cool air on my cheeks again. Sam and I sat facing the driver, and Mickey made his way across the carpeted floor to sit opposite us. The car was so long and low that he had to walk with a movement like a hunker in motion, which made him look like a chimp loping through the forest.

'Sam, this is our manager, Mickey. Mickey, this is my friend Sam, who "Over This" is about.'

'Ah, the famous Sam. We meet at last. I'm honoured. I would shake your hand, but you're too far away.' Instead he blew her a smarmy kiss and inclined his head in a little bow.

Sam smiled graciously at him. 'Actually, we have met before. When Blue Idea played New York about six years ago. But I'm not surprised you don't remember me; you were otherwise occupied that night.'

Mickey laughed uneasily as the car glided away from the hotel and swung out into the London traffic. There were many shows to which Sam's comment might have applied.

'We're meeting the boys at seven, aren't we?' I asked Mickey, making sure I had my facts straight. We had been out there the previous day for rehearsal and sound-check, and as we were headlining, technically none of us needed to be at the venue until the evening. But Sam had wanted to watch the entire day-long concert, and Mickey said he had some business to attend to there, hence our early departure. I didn't mind going early. I was looking forward to a day out with Sam.

We stopped at a red light, and laughed at the pedestrians gazing curiously at the car, trying to make out who was behind the black tinted windows.

'It's funny how people always stare at limos, even though they know they can't see anything inside,' Mickey said, making a rude face at a Chinese boy who almost had his nose pressed up against the glass.

'They're just wishing that for once they could be the one inside, being driven around in luxury, and not having to go down the market and get fish for dinner, or deliver the newspapers, or go to their dreary Saturday jobs. I think it's envy as much as curiosity, and who can blame them?' Sam was looking with sympathy at the crowds of harassed shoppers.

We drove on until the shopping streets turned to residential ones and a few scrappy trees began to dot the roads outside dusty rows of semis. Not many had front gardens, and those that did had mostly been paved over to make off-street parking. Everything seemed much smaller than its American counterpart: cars, houses, birds, even the people appeared hunched and melted-looking. The sun had bleached every sparse blade of grass to an almost colourless shade of bile.

'Where are we, anyway?' I asked.

Sam and Mickey both shrugged.

'Don't ask me.' Mickey reached over his shoulder to slide back the glass partition separating us from the driver. 'Where are we, bud?'

'Willesden Green, sir,' came the faint reply from under the driver's peaked cap. 'Shocking roadworks on the A41, so we're much better off going through town.'

There seemed to be shocking roadworks everywhere. The sound of pneumatic drills hung in the air, and orange traffic cones and big yellow diggers were strewn around countless junctions. Sweating road menders toiled away, their upper bodies as bronzed as if they'd been lying on a Caribbean beach for a fortnight.

The white twin towers of Wembley Stadium eventually hove into sight. The driver whisked us through various security gates, following handwritten signs tied to fences which read, 'Artist Entrance This Way'.

Sam squeezed my hand. 'I'm so excited,' she said, her eyes out on stalks as she looked at the other limos lining up in front of and behind us. 'Isn't that Kylie Minogue over there?'

Mickey dug in his bag and produced our laminates in a tangle of black shiny cord strings, which he separated and put over our heads, as though awarding us medals. They had swirly red-and-yellow patterns on their shiny plastic, with thick black letters over the top saying 'RADIO ONE'S BIG DAY OUT: ACCESS ALL AREAS'. Mine also said 'ARTIST' at the bottom.

'Right,' he said. 'Let's go find the dressing rooms so you girls can dump your stuff, then I'll see you back there at seven.'

He consulted a Xeroxed map, and motioned for us to follow him. As we climbed out of the limo, the heat once again filled my eyes, nose and mouth. I dreaded to think how hot the stage would be after baking in the sun all afternoon. Sam and I set off behind Mickey, me carrying Sam's backpack and her with my suit. After a few yards, however, Sam was lagging behind.

'What's the matter?' I asked, anxiously. 'Aren't you feeling well?'

'No, I feel fine,' she said a little crossly. 'It's just this plastic stuff; it keeps wrapping itself around my legs. It's making my shins sweat.'

She was trying to hold the suit protector by its coat-hanger handle, aloft and away from her body, as though it was a lead with a snappy dog on the end. Sure enough, the thin plastic casing was drifting back as she walked and tangling itself around her. I laughed.

'Why don't you just fold it in half and put it over your arm?'

'Well, because then I have to hold all that sweaty plastic, and that's even worse.'

'Shall I take it?'

'No, I can manage. I just need to twist it out of my way, that's all.'

Mickey turned round to see where we'd got to, almost bumping into a huge black man wearing a PVC bib-type garment emblazoned with the words 'SECURITY'. The man glared at him.

'Come on, girls, hurry it along there,' he chivvied, glaring back slightly nervously at the security guard. We trotted after him again.

'I didn't think shins *could* sweat,' I mused aloud to Sam.

'I bet they bloody can in this weather. Let's see, shall we. Shin check,' she barked in a military fashion. We bent down, giggling, and rubbed our respective bare shins. Sure enough, there was a thin film of condensation on our skin.

Grumbling at our childishness, Mickey managed to lead us to my dressing room, whereupon he promptly disappeared in the opposite direction to try and locate the production manager, muttering worriedly about stage plots. Once inside, I relieved Sam of the troublesome suit cover by hanging it on a metal rail between the mirror and the wall. Sam gazed around.

'It's even got a star on the door,' she said in an awed voice.

'Come on,' I said. 'I'll show you the stage.'

We dumped our bags and headed off again, both keen to get back outside. The glaring sunshine and rocketing temperatures were still preferable to the strip lights and dingy corridors of the interior.

I opened a door marked 'TO STAGE', and we followed a passageway round a couple of corners until we saw daylight. Emerging as though from the bowels of the earth, we came out blinking like moles. All we could see was blue sky and what seemed like miles and miles of scaffolding, with heavy black material covering parts of it.

'Blimey, it's *enormous*,' said Sam, sounding faint. 'Just look at all those people.'

The stadium loomed hugely all around us – towering banks of seats as far as the eye could see, and the massive central area, still filling up with bobbing heads. A dull roar from the crowd could be heard over the throb of the music from the towering stacks of speakers on either side of the stage.

The sound desk in the middle looked like a little boat on a big lake. It had all looked very different yesterday when the seats were empty – blank and less intimidating. The expectation from the waiting audience was hanging in the air like a heat haze, mingling with the smell of hot dogs and the slight acrid scent of sweat. I sniffed the air and got an additional inexplicable whiff of fresh raspberries.

We were right at the back of the stage, an area itself about the size of four tennis courts. Technicians, sound and lighting men, stage managers and promoters, all with their laminates flapping as they ran, were milling around frantically. People were marking out lines on the floor with duct tape. There were men swinging from lighting rigs; popping up from trap doors in the stage like rabbits from a magician's hat; tapping microphones and fuzzily intoning, 'Testing, testing, one-two-three;' screwing together drum kits and tuning guitars. One minute thumbs-up signs were being proffered; the next, obscenities were ringing out. Everyone, without exception, was sweating like Nixon. The first band of the six on the day's bill was about to come on stage.

'I feel as if I've just walked into a beehive,' said Sam, staring at all the activity before her. 'I'm certainly sticky enough.' She fanned the neck of her shirt and wiped her forehead. Then she looked more serious. 'How can you stand the thought that there will be seventy *thousand* pairs of eyes looking at you this evening?'

I wished she hadn't asked. It was almost twice the size of any gig we'd ever played before, and up to this point I had chosen not to consider this bowel-loosening statistic. The whole day-long show was also being broadcast live to the nation on Radio One, but I didn't remind Sam of that fact.

'Er, I'll be OK once we start playing,' I said nervously.

Sam suddenly threw her arms around me.

'This is incredible,' she said. 'I am so proud of you! I can't believe I'm here, and you're here, and you're doing this unbelievable thing.' She had tears in her eyes.

'I'm just glad you're here to see me do it,' I said, hugging her back.

We found an out-of-the-way space at the side of the stage, and perched on top of a huge square flight case; Sam nearest the audience and me, trying to be inconspicuous, lurking out of sight behind her, watching the excited crowd prepare for their day's entertainment. I fanned my hot face with a tabloid newspaper I'd found next to me, and thought about how all those people had come to be there. Maybe they'd heard the show announced on the radio, and had been delighted at the thought of three or four of their favourite bands playing at the same gig. Perhaps *all* their favourite bands were playing. They'd have mustered up a group of friends, or told their partner to mark it in his or her diary, and then got their credit cards out to phone the ticket hotline; or maybe they had sent away for tickets in the post.

Either way, their tickets would have arrived a week or so later, plopping onto the doormat in an anonymous envelope, with that compelling, shiny new-paper smell. They'd have put them somewhere safe – a drawer, or stuck to the fridge door with a magnet in the shape of a London bus – and told all their other, unluckier friends that they were going to the big show. Finally the day had arrived, and they had climbed onto trains at dawn, or filled up their cars with petrol and packed lunches, or boarded charter coaches.

And now here they were, many at Wembley for the first time, smelling what I was smelling, staking out their spot on the covered-over football pitch, wondering if it was better to go further back where it was cooler and where they could sit down without being stepped on, or whether to go for it, right up the front, elbowing their way to a prime viewing position close enough to see the little hidden nuances of performance that the huge video screens never picked up. I imagined the real fans who had been queuing outside for hours and hours, bursting through the turnstiles and running across the pitch at Wembley to be the first to the security barrier at the front. They would risk losing their place if they had to go to the loo or get something to eat; perhaps they just didn't go all day, and their enjoyment of the show would be marred by the pressure of a bursting bladder.

'They look so excited, don't they?' said Sam from her perch. 'Look at that girl down there in the front with the Blue Idea baseball cap on. She's jumping up and down already, and nothing's happening yet.'

I looked at my watch. 'Well, it must be about to; it's two o'clock.'

As I spoke, music abruptly ceased thumping from the speakers and a lone figure in a sparkly grey suit ran onto the stage. A massive cheer went up.

'That's Jeremy Jackson, the comedian,' I said. 'He's compering the show.'

'I *know*,' Sam replied. 'Everyone knows who he is.'

Actually, I'd never heard of Jeremy Jackson before that week, but Sam assured me he was very famous in the UK. He welcomed everybody, made a few lame jokes and read off a list the coming attractions for the day. Every time he moved, his suit twinkled and glittered in the sunlight. After each band he announced the crowd cheered, louder and louder until he said, 'And, of course, closing the show tonight, your favourites, the amazing, phenomenal, spectacular – BLUE IDEA!' Everyone went absolutely wild. Their arms were raised, waving and punching the air, and the sound of whistling and screaming was deafening. I felt a cold but excited shiver build in the pit of my stomach, and Sam leaned across and squeezed my knee with both her hands.

We stayed in our spot at the side of the stage for most of the day, as Sam was absolutely riveted by seeing the best bands of the moment from such close quarters, only leaving it between sets to get more water, eat or pee. Occasionally other musicians came up to introduce themselves to me, and I made sure they all shook hands with Sam, too. The guys from the Happy Mondays were surprisingly sweet, and autographed a photo for her to keep.

It was a great day. Over the previous couple of years I'd become so jaded and sick of these self-congratulatory, bombastic events, which I believed served only to boost egos and extract hard-won money from star-struck children. Sam's genuine, whole-hearted excitement put me back in touch with what it *should* be about: the spirit of the occasion. She always seemed to show me the positive in an experience.

The next time I looked at my watch, it was six forty-five, and the stadium was still steaming with heat and excitement. The Happy Mondays, who were the penultimate band, were about to take the stage, but Sam and I were starting to wilt.

'If *we're* this hot, just think what it must be like in the crowd,' she said, feebly puffing air onto her face from the corners of her mouth. 'I'm feeling a bit tired. Is there somewhere I could go and rest for a while? I want to make sure I'm on form for your set.'

She was beginning to look very pale. I felt concerned for her.

'Well, I need to have a shower and get changed, and the guys will be here shortly. Why don't we go down to the dressing room, and you can have a lie-down on the sofa while I get ready?'

Sam nodded, and we climbed off the flight case to make our way backstage. As we got through the door a

301

massive cheer rose from the crowd, and we heard the opening strains of 'Step On' strike up.

Sam looked torn. 'Oh, I *love* this song! I really need to lie down though, but I really want to see them. Especially after they were so nice to me. Oh, what shall I do?'

'Go and lie down,' I said firmly. 'They'll be on for at least an hour. Have a rest, and then we'll go back up and catch the end of their set.'

Sam capitulated, but walked very slowly, with one ear cocked towards the ever-fainter sounds from the stage.

We got back to the dressing rooms, where in the one adjoining mine – an identical harshly lit, un-airconditioned cell – I found Justin, Joe and David smoking and playing poker. I stuck my head around the door while Sam lurked in the hall behind me, partly from shyness, but more to avoid the effects of the cigarette smoke.

'Hi. You're early,' I said to them, impressed.

'Yeah, we've been here ages. What kept you?' asked Joe, flapping the collar of his shirt in the direction of a fan in the corner, which was half-heartedly moving air around.

'Guys, you remember Sam, don't you?' I pointed proudly at her. She waved from the doorway, and blew Justin a provocative kiss. 'I'm not bringing her in because you're smoking out the place. But she'll be around later. We're going next door so I can get ready.'

I caught a momentary flash of shock in Justin's eyes as he clocked the difference in Sam's appearance, how much older and gaunter she'd become, and I found myself willing him to still fancy her. But nonetheless he rushed over and pecked her on the cheek enthusiastically. 'Hi! Fantastic to see you again.'

Totally unprompted by me, he added, 'Hey, you know, we're all real glad that you're better now. Helena was so upset, and we all, like, thought of you and stuff.'

302

Joe and David mumbled agreement. I felt like a proud mother at a nativity play.

'Thanks,' said Sam, uncharacteristically shy all of a sudden. 'See you later.'

'They've gone all kind of designery and smart,' she commented to me as we entered my dressing room.

'Yeah, well, no more jeans and T-shirts for us world-wide superstars,' I said, going to stand in front of my own floor fan, which someone had kindly turned on in advance. Sam flopped down onto a big velveteen couch in the corner, putting her feet up on the cushionless arm.

'I'd never have believed Joe could look so much like a model. Justin looks the same, though. Has he got a girlfriend at the moment?'

'Why do you ask? Fancy another dose of crabs, do you?'

Sam shuddered and giggled. 'Ugh, no thanks. But you know, I like to keep my options open.'

'Well, the answer is, yes he has. She's a model, six foot two, looks like Cindy Crawford and is very possessive. She's arriving any minute from a fashion shoot in Paris, so you'd better not encourage Justin or else the feathers'll be flying.'

Sam closed her eyes. 'Don't worry, I'm far too knack-ered to flirt. She can keep him. Nice to see them all again, though.'

'Yeah, they obviously thought the same about you. Have a bit of a kip – I'm going to risk this dodgy-looking shower in here. See you later.'

'Mmm,' said Sam with one arm thrown over her eyes. She looked out for the count.

She was fast asleep when I emerged from the bath-room fifteen minutes later, having washed and dried my hair and done some energetic singing in the shower to get my voice warmed up. The make-up lady was coming round at seven fifteen, so I didn't touch my face. Normally I preferred to do my own make-up, but given the excessive heat I thought I'd better defer to her professional expertise on this occasion: I didn't want my mascara sliding down my face after the first number.

I zipped my suit out of its plastic sheath, examining it for wrinkles, but it had been hanging all day and was fine. I slid the black nubby raw-silk jacket over my bra; it was too hot to wear a shirt as well. The fabric was shot through with a subtle gold thread, which picked up the light and shone faintly when I moved my arms to do up the big gold buttons. I worked each foot through the tight leg of the pedal-pusher-style trousers until they were liberated and I could straighten to do up the zip. I'd been wearing this style of outfit for two years now; an old Hispanic lady in Manhattan made them individually for me.

The genesis of the idea had come when I'd started wearing big long shirts over tube skirts, back in the early, chubby days. I'd wanted something that would cover up my hips and thighs, but somehow shirts weren't smart enough for the image I wanted to convey, so one night I wore a long jacket with its buttons done up over some thick black leggings. I felt instantly transformed; my trunk was hidden underneath its length, but I could show off the respectable part of my long legs, from mid-thigh down. From there I'd graduated to trouser suits with frock-coat jackets, and even after I got slim enough to wear miniskirts I still loved my suits. I could look chic but not girly, smart but not secretarial.

I made it my mission to find as many funky, unusual fabrics as possible, and whenever we toured in exotic places, like the Far East, I would disappear to the local markets for hours, returning joyously with a bolt of thick bronze satin, or ten yards of sari material – probably a throwback to the days I'd spent happily rummaging around jumble sales. Annie Lennox had said more than once in interviews how much she admired my dress sense.

It was the first time I'd worn this particular suit, and

even I had to admit I looked pretty hot. I had recently had a gold streak put in the front of my short chestnut hair, which I'd dried and gelled back into a kind of high rockabilly quiff, and the outfit was completed by a pair of sparkly gold brothel creepers. It didn't seem to matter that we weren't even remotely a rockabilly band.

There was a soft knock at the door. I opened it to admit the make-up lady, Glenda, with her big zip-up bag of tricks. I pointed at Sam, comatose on the sofa, and put my finger to my lips.

'I don't want to wake her just yet,' I whispered, motioning Glenda over towards the spotlit mirror. She sat me down and got to work in silence, painting and lining with a rock-steady hand, puffing and brushing my face with an assortment of tiny little sponge-tipped sticks and twirly brushes, and applying metallic brown-gold shades of eyeshadow and lipstick to match the rest of my outfit. The only sounds in the room were Glenda's concentrated breathing, the whirr of the fan and Sam snoring softly in the background.

Just as Glenda had finished and was packing up her bag, Sam woke to the sight of me in my finery standing before her. She rubbed her eyes and stared at me with disbelief.

'Ta-daaa!' I said, spreading my arms and grinning. 'Whaddaya think?'

Sam sat up. 'Oh my God,' she said incredulously. 'You look so different. It's absolutely amazing. Helena, you look so beautiful.'

'Oh please,' I said, pretending to be offended. 'Could you try and sound a little less surprised?' But I was glowing with pleasure as I picked an imaginary speck of fluff off the sleeve of my suit.

'Bye now,' said Glenda, who was also looking rather pleased with herself. 'I'm off next door to sort out those boys of yours.'

'Good luck. Tell them I hope they're ready in ten minutes.'

'Good luck to you. Break a leg. I can't wait to see your set. You lot are great. I've got all your records.' She blushed and edged out of the room, closing the door behind her.

'Right,' I said to Sam. 'Are you set? Feeling better? You look a bit less pale.'

'Yes, I feel much better. I'll just have a glass of water and a pee, and then can we go back up to the stage?'

'Sure. I'll tell the guys to meet us up there. Are you hungry?'

'No, I'm much too nervous for you. I'll take some of that fruit up for later, though.'

Sam went into the toilet and I went next door, where Glenda was trying to put eyeliner on Justin while he smoked a cigarette.

'Oh, for God's sake, Justin, can't you stub that out for two minutes?' I said, as Glenda coughed pointedly. 'Poor Glenda doesn't want to breathe in your disgusting smoke. Or better still, give it to me and I'll smoke it.'

I was beginning to feel very nervous by now, and decided that a few puffs would calm me down a bit. I snatched the cigarette from his dangling hand and inhaled deeply, hoping to finish it before Sam returned.

'We're going to catch the end of the Happy Mondays. See you by the monitor desk in ten minutes, OK?'

Justin nodded with his eyes closed, making Glenda paint a black line on his cheek by mistake. As I left the room, she was tutting and scrubbing at his face with a cleanser-covered cotton-wool ball. I stubbed out the cigarette as Sam emerged from my dressing room.

'Let's go,' I said, leading the way back upstairs.

We emerged to a tumult of cheers and shouts of 'More!' Shaun Ryder and the others were running back to their mics and picking up their instruments again, bowing and dancing and grinning wildly at each other. As the introduction to 'Kinky Afro' thudded out around the stadium, the crowd erupted. Everyone, including Sam and me, began to dance on the spot, the infectious rhythm making it impossible not to. I saw colour in Sam's cheeks for the first time in years. She looked ecstatic.

The Happy Mondays sauntered off stage for the last time, waving at the audience and shoving each other with manic delight. They grinned at Sam on their way past, and she turned to me, clapping enthusiastically, thrilled.

A lull followed; the calm before the storm, it seemed to me. Once the crowd's screams for the Happy Mondays had died down, a small tumult brewed amongst them as they realized this was their last chance before the end of the show to buy beer or queue for the loo without missing our set. The music came back on over the speakers, and all the techs scurried onto the stage to do our line check. I wondered whether I had time to go back down to the dressing room for a final pee myself, but decided it would only make me more nervous. Instead I stayed, watching the crowd and chatting to David and Joe with Sam.

The boys had appeared next to us looking very dapper; Joe in a baggy cream suit and Panama hat, David in smart black trousers and an open-neck patterned silk shirt.

'You look great, H,' said David affectionately, squeezing my arm. 'Nervous?'

'So do you two. Yup, nervous,' I replied. We hung out in a state of limbo for the next fifteen minutes or so, gathering our respective strengths. I was beginning to get very anxious about where Justin had got to.

Jeremy Jackson reappeared in front of the audience to a howl of applause. We knew the cheers weren't for him, but rather because his appearance heralded our own imminent arrival, and that made me more nervous. Jeremy made a gesture with his hands for everyone to quieten down.

'Here's a small joke for you, ladies and gentlemen, in honour of the nationality of tonight's headlining

307

artists,' – renewed screams from the crowd – 'If you're an American in the kitchen, what are you in the bathroom?' – various unintelligible and derisive yells from the audience. Jeremy adjusted his tie smugly. 'You're a-peein, ladies and gentlemen!' He gave a low bow. A collective groan arose.

I leaned over to Sam, affronted. 'Who's he calling American, then? I'm not bloody American!'

She replied, 'Maybe he meant that you're the European.'

'Charming,' I sniffed, no more mollified.

Jeremy made a couple more limp quips, and concluded with a very big build-up for us: 'And any minute now, the moment you've all been waiting for. Your favourites and mine, BLOOOOO IDEEEEAA!!' More hysterical screams, and then another groan as the music came back on again.

'Must be a technical hitch somewhere,' I muttered to Sam, feeling pretty hysterical myself.

Justin sauntered up to where we stood, a fresh cigarette between his lips, accompanied by his drop-dead gorgeous Amazonian girlfriend. He looked incredibly sexy in a chocolate-brown pinstriped gangster suit.

'I'm friggin' boiling in here,' he grumbled. 'What are we opening with?'

The rest of us raised our eyes to heaven. ' "Lotus Flower",' we chorused.

'Oh yeah. Sorry, it just went right out of my head.'

I checked nervously that the set lists were all taped to the floor by our mic stands. They were. Mickey rushed up, sweating profusely.

'Everyone all right?' he asked, sounding by far the most nervous of all of us. 'Sorry I didn't see much of you earlier. You know, bit of business to take care of.' He looked very shifty and distracted. I wondered if there was a fresh-faced groupie somewhere downstairs who was at that moment tucking in her shirt and hoping she wasn't pregnant.

Five more endless minutes passed in anxious chit-chat and last-minute activity from the crew, until one by one they left the stage and we got the thumbs up. The crowd's excitement was hitting me in waves; I could feel it running through my veins and into all my nerve endings. All our gear was set up and ready by our mic stands. David pulled a pair of drumsticks out of the back pocket of his trousers and twirled them around in the fingers of his right hand. I went over and hugged Sam hard.

'Good luck,' she whispered in my ear, hugging me back.

Justin stubbed out one cigarette and lit another, wedging it firmly in the corner of his mouth. The music stopped, stage lights came on, despite the still bright evening, and the loudest cheer I'd heard all day rose up all around us. In the split second before we ran on stage, I analysed the sound, thinking how strange it was, how it seemed to have nothing to do with all the thousands of people whose eyes were about to be fixed on us. I wouldn't watch sport on television for the simple reason that I could not bear the constant background baying of the crowds, but this didn't bother me.

Oh well, I thought, taking a last deep breath and tensing all my muscles as we launched ourselves towards the centre of the stage, I suppose it's different when they're screaming for you.

A Familiar Hand

It really was good to have my hearing back to normal
again. As I drove home despondently from Ron's
office, I tried to remind myself to at least be thankful
for small mercies. But it seemed a bit pointless, really,
like everything else in my life. The option of a glass
eye, the ability to hear pins drop, one-off kisses from
sweet guys and lisped songs about stormy weather,
what was any of that to me now? I could bear all of it,
all the bad stuff, if only I still had Sam to help me. But
I didn't, and I couldn't.

The tide was high as I drove down the gravel road to
my house, water lapping over the top of the rushes and
reeds on the bank. It was almost up to the riverside
footpath, washing up detritus from a careless con-
sumer society: cans and plastic and yesterday's news.
I knew that by the next day, when the water had
receded, I'd be left with all those scraps of litter, plus
the faint smell of sewage and lots of mud outside my
front gate. It was the least pleasant part of living near
the river. Oh well, I wouldn't be going out tomorrow,
so I wouldn't have to see it.

I pointed the remote control at my electric gate, and
it heaved slowly open to let me through. As it clanged
behind me, I thought once more how nice it would be
to never leave the house again.

Pulling off my wig and glasses, I felt my body relax

slightly as I climbed out of the car, clutching the meagre brown envelope from Ron. I was looking forward to holing up inside for another long stint of wallowing in solitude.

As I headed for the front porch, a small but familiar sound filtered in through my newly responsive ears. It was emanating from the bushes, a series of crunchy little clicks, ensuring that my terrible day was made even worse. I knew what that noise was, I'd been dreading it for long enough.

Cursing myself for removing my disguise prematurely, I dithered for a split second. Should I run inside or stay and fight? Then all the rage and grief and disappointment from the day boiled up inside me, and there was no contest, whoever was out there wasn't going to get away with it this time.

With a huge, painful bellow, I charged towards the bushes. There was an alarmed rustle and the glint of a camera lens being hastily retracted. As I crashed through the scratchy greenery, I saw a skinny back spin around and try to head for the gate, but his camera strap had become entangled with a branch and he lost valuable seconds trying to extract it. The delay enabled me to get close enough to grab the strap, and to see the hand of the photographer pull at the camera itself. He was wearing a black balaclava, but once I'd seen his hand my suspicions were confirmed; I didn't need to see his face.

The bitten nails, the shape of the ovals of wrinkles at his thumb joint, the nicotine stain on his middle finger from so many Gauloises; this was the hand that had given me a thousand orgasms, belonging to the person who'd given me a thousand more sleepless nights.

'COME HERE, VINNIE, YOU EVIL LITTLE SHIT!' I roared at the top of my voice as we engaged in an unseemly tug-of-war in the shrubbery. 'I'M GOING TO KILL YOU!'

With one last terrified wrench, Vinnie hauled the

camera strap out of my grasp, legged it across the lawn and over the gate in one smooth leap, and away down the riverside path.

I ran after him, still screaming like a fishwife. 'HOW DARE YOU! YOU WON'T GET AWAY WITH THIS, YOU BASTARD!'

But he was out of sight by the time I got to the end of my drive.

For the fourth or fifth time it occurred to me that the day really couldn't get any worse. Turning back to the house, I stooped like an old lady to pick up the letters and cards which had spilled out of the A4 envelope I had dropped after giving chase. They made a pathetic little bundle; scribbled messages of . . . what? Most likely they were from people whose records I had played, making them feel important for two minutes of their life.

Suddenly I didn't care what they had to say. I walked round to the dustbin next to the garage, lifted the heavy metal lid and dumped the whole lot in, unopened, with the smell of rotting vegetables and stale takeaways. Slamming the lid down on the only feedback from my career as a DJ was a symbolic gesture, I knew.

It didn't make me feel any better though.

'I'll Be Home'

Randy Newman

That Wembley show was the last time Blue Idea ever played in England. A year later it was all over; two years later I was still recovering.

It was a letter from Sam that finally spurred me into making a decision. I had my whole life ahead of me and an exceptionally large bank balance at my disposal, but all I'd done for sixteen months was mope around rural New Jersey as though in extended shock.

I had been required to stay in the area for the duration of Mickey's trial, because the prosecution needed me to give evidence, so I'd holed up at my parents' new place, an architect-designed house in the countryside, ten miles out of Freehold. I'd paid for most of it myself, so I figured that justified my extended residency there. My name was on the lease of a blandly luxurious apartment in Manhattan, but I never stayed in it because the paparazzi knew the address.

I hadn't even seen Sam since the band had broken up. I was happy that she had a life of her own again, but I hated the fact that I currently wasn't part of it. She had eventually finished her law degree, and was back in London starting her one-year postgraduate LSF course at Store Street, still frail, but well enough to move into a hall of residence.

We wrote to each other regularly – it was too

problematical to try and get through to her on the payphone in her digs – and she always asked me when I was coming over, preferably to live. But then she'd launch off into a description of her latest boyfriend, or what dinner party she'd been to, or what all her college friends were up to, and I would be assailed by such a feeling of alienation from this life which could have been mine. A normal life. It felt as foreign to me now as a Martian existence. The only place I felt safe was within the whitewashed walls of my parents' dream home.

Then I'd got this letter. I had noticed that Sam's handwriting was getting worse, but I had put it down to the probable hurry with which she scrawled my letters, anxious to get out and about with her new friends. With difficulty I deciphered:

'I'm writing this with my nose about an inch away from the paper. It gives me hideous backache, but the only alternative is to pile textbooks up to eye-level in front of me and rest the letter on top of them. That method is fine for reading, but it gives me cramps in my arms when I try and write that way. Even with Coke-bottle glasses my sight has got so bad; that bloody radiotherapy just completely screwed it up. Lectures are a nightmare. I'm having operations for cataracts in the next few weeks, and although I'm nervous, that should fix it. I don't think it'll be too bad; they just zap them with lasers, one at a time. I can't wait to "see" you again. I miss you. Come and live in London. It would be so great. We can go to Salisbury in the holidays; it'll be like the old days. I've been listening to Randy Newman's *Little Criminals* a lot recently, and the track 'I'll Be Home' really makes me think of you. It's so sad, and it makes me miss you so much. I just want you to be home, too . . .'

I put the letter down, my mouth agape with shock. I thought only old people got cataracts. Sam was still by far the most important person in my life, and if something as serious as that was going on without me being aware of it, then something was very wrong with me. Why hadn't she told me before?

I asked my mother that question when I found her in the kitchen taking a bubbling roast out of the oven. I got myself a glass of wine from the fridge.

'Would you like one, Mum?'

She was bending over the cooker with her oven gloves and apron on, her hair disarrayed from the steam.

'No thanks, Helena. Is that your second glass already? We haven't even sat down to dinner yet.'

I ignored her. 'Sam's having an operation for cataracts.'

'Cataracts? Oh, dear, that's terrible. I didn't know young people got cataracts.'

'Nor did I. It was those leukaemia treatments she had.'

Mum tutted in a shocked manner, and stuck a long roasting fork into the centre of the meat to see if it was done, sending a thin plume of steam up towards the ceiling.

'Why do you think she didn't tell me? She's having the operation next week and I didn't even know she had problems with her eyes. She normally tells me everything.'

Mum turned the oven down to a warm setting and put the joint back in while she strained the vegetables.

'She probably thought you had enough problems of your own, dear.'

'None as big as practical blindness, though,' I'd replied vehemently. But now I thought about it, it was possible that I'd been moaning rather excessively in my letters about how miserable life had been recently. In a flash I made a decision. I downed the rest of my glass of wine in one gulp. 'I'm moving to London,' I announced.

My mother looked relieved. She'd done a lot of laundry for me in the past year. I'd bought her a brand-new washer-dryer, but still, laundry was laundry. She

315

untied her apron and sat down next to me at the kitchen table, putting her hand over mine.

'I think that's a great idea, Helena. You're only twenty-seven; you should be out having a social life and making new friends, not cooped up here all day like a hermit. You miss Sam, and besides, I think it's time for you to move on. I wish London wasn't so far away, but I truly think you'd be happier back in England, near Sam.'

I smiled at her. Whether she was trying to get me out from under her feet or not, I appreciated the good intentions behind her words.

Dad came home and I told him my plan over dinner. He too agreed that it was probably for the best.

'When will you leave?' he asked, spearing a forkful of meat and roast potato and trying not to sound too enthusiastic.

'As soon as possible. I'm going to start sorting through my stuff after dinner,' I announced firmly, placing my knife and fork together on my empty plate.

The lethargy which had plagued me for months suddenly dispersed, and I felt adrenalin course back through my veins for the first time in ages.

When we all finished eating, my parents retired to the living room, Mum to call one of her bridge friends, and Dad to smoke his pipe and read the *New York Times*. I went down to the basement where I had shoved all my boxes of band-related memorabilia. I hadn't been in there for a year, as I had been trying to forget the band had ever existed. Leaning against the wall, in between Dad's golf clubs and the brand-new mountain bikes which I'd bought us all but we'd never ridden, was the battered guitar case containing my old, cheap second-hand bass, the one on which I'd learned to play.

I laid it down on the dusty carpeted floor and, with difficulty, popped open the rusty clasps. I remembered how wonderful I'd thought it was the first time I'd set eyes on it at the Applebaums' yard sale, and how desperately I had wanted to have it. I hadn't even known it was a bass guitar then. All I'd known was that it had been, literally, the answer to my prayers.

I still felt guilty at the memory of the pure desire which had fuelled my original acquisition of the instrument: to serve the Lord, if I was not mistaken, I thought ruefully, remembering my teenage fervour. In the grand scheme of things that guitar and I had done very little serving of the Lord, and a great deal of serving myself, the band, the record company and Mickey's bank balance. The Lord certainly gave me more than I bargained for. Perhaps this was His way of punishing me for transforming my religious ambitions into secular ones.

I lifted the guitar out of the cheap velvet-lined case by its neck. It came out stiffly, like a corpse from a coffin. The pearly scratch plate I'd thought so pretty looked warped and yellowed with age, and the enamel of the guitar's body was scraped and battered-looking. Everything about it was cheap and shoddy. I recalled how difficult learning to play it had been, and how I'd only been able to persevere because I really believed it had been a gift from God. I put it back in the case and moved it to a space on the far wall of the garage, which was the start of my trash pile.

Before getting stuck in, I ran upstairs and got my CD of *Little Criminals* and my Discman. Putting the headphones in my ears, I came back down to the basement and played track nine over and over again as I attacked the big sealed boxes, ripping off the brown tape holding the top flaps closed. It gave me strength to think of Sam all those miles away, listening to the same music for the same reason. 'I'll Be Home' was such a simple, moving song. I wished I'd written it instead of Randy Newman. Blue Idea should at least have done it as a cover; we could have done a great version of it.

When I'd moved out of the New York apartment I'd stuffed everything in these boxes, and a lot of the posters and album sleeves were creased or torn. I toyed with the idea of chucking everything out, but I couldn't quite bring myself to do it, so instead I selected one of every item in the box: a copy of each of our records, a press shot from each album, one copy of each *Bluezine* and programmes from a couple of the bigger gigs we'd played. I picked up the programme from the Radio 1 show we'd done at Wembley, and something fell out. It was a photograph of Sam and myself on stage, taken during Blue Idea's set that day and sent to me afterwards as a kind gesture by Holly, Ringside's press officer. I was very pleased to see it. At the time I'd intended to make a copy of it for Sam, but I forgot that I'd put it in the programme to keep it flat, and later assumed it to be lost.

Everyone said that Wembley show was the best we'd ever played. It certainly felt that way. To me it represented what I perceived to be the very highest pinnacle of our success and my own personal sense of achievement, despite the fact that Blue Idea were just as hot for most of the following year.

The proudest part of all was when I sang 'Over This', turning away from the audience and beaming at Sam in the wings throughout the entire song. Out of the corner of my eye I noticed the front rows of the audience trying to follow my gaze to see who or what I was looking at. When the final note from Joe's Hammond hung in the charged summer air there was a moment of pure silence, and then an overwhelming storm of cheering and applause which felt as if it would knock me off my feet with its warmth.

I ran forward to where Sam stood clapping, grabbed her wrist and pulled her back onto the stage with me. 'Sam Grant,' I'd said to the audience. 'My best friend.' We'd hugged in front of all those thousands of people, and, strangers though they were, it had felt as though they supported and understood us, too. Sam told me afterwards that it was the best moment of her whole life, bar none.

I put the photo aside to send to Sam that very day. I

could make a copy of it later, I thought, and borrow it back from her. Continuing to sort through the three big boxes, I found several gold and platinum discs, more photos, laminates, press interview schedules, masses of copies of *Bluezine* and newspapers which had run features on us. I systematically junked most of it.

At the top of the third box was a copy of *Rolling Stone* magazine, not the one with us on the cover, but an issue from a few months afterwards. I looked at the date: May 1992. I flipped it open, and found the huge feature with the headline screaming out at me, BLUE IDEA BREAK UP! They'd printed a photo which I absolutely hated, of us leaning over a freeway bridge somewhere, shot from below, all concrete and steely grey skies. We looked incredibly pissed off, I appeared to have an enormous double chin and even Justin looked moronic. There were lengthy quotes from the four of us. I picked out a random paragraph and read:

> It really just seems the right time to move on. I've been writing a lot more songs lately, and making a solo record is a new and exciting direction for me. Blue Idea have come to the end of their natural lives. We've been getting stagnant. I wish the others all the best of luck, and strongly encourage them to continue without me, if that's what they want to do. I hope we will stay friends.

Justin's smug words brought back some of the anger I'd felt at the time. Writing songs, my ass! He had churned out a few trite little numbers which we some- times did live, or used for B-sides, but none of which Ringside or the rest of us wanted on any of the albums. His fans were in for a bit of a shock, in my opinion. Justin's ego had been inflated to the point that he really thought he was the key factor in Blue Idea, and that was what I couldn't stand. He might have been the good-looking one, but my songs and David and Joe's excellent musicianship had been equally important.

319

The truth was, I had secretly been quite relieved when Justin had dropped his bombshell. I was furious with him for making the decision for us, but we were all so tired. We had been on tour, whether in the US or around the world, for the best part of ten years on and off, and when we weren't on the road we were in the studio. I couldn't remember when I'd last had more than two straight months off. It had got to the point where I simply didn't have the energy or the inspiration to write any new songs. I felt completely drained. We had no private lives; we couldn't even walk down the street without getting mobbed. Everyone knew who I was, but I had no real friends, except Sam and the band. I'd had no time to make any.

To carry on without Justin hadn't been an issue; David, Joe and I hadn't even given it a serious thought. We didn't want to become one of those sad, once-huge bands who struggle on with the old name but without the frontman who helped make that name.

'Let's quit while we're ahead,' David had said, and I'd agreed heartily. 'We're rich enough,' Joe added.

But it turned out that we weren't nearly as rich as we'd thought. As soon as Mickey heard the news about us disbanding, he became impossible to contact. After trying to get hold of him in every way we knew, including sneaking down to his office in disguise – to no avail, it was locked and empty – I eventually phoned our accountant directly to find out what state our finances were in. I had never spoken to him before, as Mickey had handled our money from the start. He, too, had sounded shifty.

'I just operated on Mickey's instructions,' he'd said. 'I paid you what he told me to pay you.'

We had got artist royalty cheques quarterly through Mickey, usually for a lot less than we'd expected, but he told us that a lot of the money needed to be funnelled back into Ringside's coffers to front tours, or to pay off producers' percentages, or a variety of other plausible-sounding reasons. We saw no reason to doubt him, as heeding his advice from the outset never seemed to have done us any harm.

But there was something I found very suspicious in the accountant's defensive tone of voice. With the agreement of the boys, I ordered an audit of our accounts by an independent accountancy firm, and it became apparent that both he and Mickey had been stitching us up like kippers for years. We instantly informed the IRS, who contacted the police, and a warrant was issued for their arrests.

They found Mickey in Key West, clad in a pineapple-patterned shirt, sipping lurid cocktails with umbrellas in them and flashing wads of cash around, like the cliché he'd always been. He was brought back to New York for trial and, after a long drawn-out court case, both he and the accountant were put behind bars for two years.

The trial had been a media circus, and during the days I was required to give evidence I'd been practically blinded by the flashbulbs in my face as soon as I set foot outside the court room. The whole experience had been a trauma of epic proportions, with daily reports on the local news, gossip plastered over the worldwide press, tons of really unflattering shots of me trying to put my hands over my face or scowling at reporters. Once it was all over I just wanted to be somewhere safe and completely out of the public eye, where I could lick my wounds in peace. I really started to understand what Princess Diana went through.

I pulled out a photograph of us with Mickey and one of his bimbos from the box, and ripped it up in disgust. Financially I was extremely well-off, because of my publishing royalties, but I felt really sorry for Joe and David who had hardly any money to show for their hard work and dedication. Justin hadn't come out of it any better, but he'd got a massive advance for his solo album, so he wouldn't struggle to get by. But the worst thing was that we had really trusted Mickey, and the sting of betrayal hurt more than the feeling of being made fools of before the world's media.

I finished my sorting, having compressed the contents of the three boxes into one half-filled one. My hands were black with dirt, but I felt a cathartic satisfaction from my efforts. I carried the box upstairs to my bedroom, washed my hands and face and got on the phone to my travel agent. If I booked a flight to England in a week's time, I could be around for Sam's operations and convalescence.

Then I took the photo of Sam and me at Wembley, clipped it to a piece of writing paper and wrote, 'Dear Sam, "I'll Be Home" next week!' put it in an envelope and sent it to Sam's address by courier service.

It didn't take me long to find a place in London. I had no need of a mortgage, as I was paying outright for it, so it was really just a question of knowing where and what.

'How about Richmond?' said Sam when she'd recovered from the shock of my arrival. 'Handy for Salisbury. Close enough to town, really beautiful and not full of posers like Notting Hill. I'm going to move there when I finish my LSF.'

She'd had one eye lasered and was waiting till that healed to get the other one done. She said it hadn't been painful, more uncomfortable really, and she felt like a wally with an eyepatch. It made her look a bit like a cocker spaniel.

'People will think I was faking it when they see me next month with the patch on the opposite eye,' she grumbled.

So the Richmond area it was. I went to an estate agent, told him how much I wanted to pay, and that I wanted somewhere as anonymous as possible which wasn't too built-up. The agent's name was Adrian and he was chubby and sandy-haired, all clumsy and panting and overenthusiastic, like a Labrador puppy in a cheap suit. I hated the way all his colleagues nudged each other and stopped talking when I walked into the office, but Adrian did sell me the perfect house, albeit reluctantly. I'd spotted it in the property paper and pointed it out to him, but he hadn't wanted to even show it to me at first.

'You won't like it, Ms Nicholls,' he'd said. 'I'm sure you need something much more ... upmarket. We have some lovely modern houses on Richmond Hill which are in your price bracket.'

'I want to see this one.'

'It's not in Richmond, more Twickenham way, really.'

'It's by the river, isn't it? That's even better.'

'It needs an awful lot of work done to it. There was an old lady living there for forty years and she didn't even have central heating.'

'That's OK. I told you I don't mind spending money on a place, especially one this cheap. Is it big?'

'Oh, indeed it is. Six very spacious bedrooms, an extremely sizable kitchen, three huge reception rooms, two bathrooms and a big garden.'

'Do you know what the neighbours are like?'

'The nearest neighbours are a fairly elderly couple, I believe. There are four other similar houses in the road, but they're all quite far apart. All the others have been extensively renovated; it's a very affluent and secluded little road, directly opposite the Thames.'

'Perfect. Can we go and see it?'

The mention of the elderly couple next door made me even more convinced, as they were unlikely to phone up their friends and say, 'You'll *never* guess who just moved in!' Or, as my neighbours in Manhattan had done, invite people round to hang out in the hallways in the hope of catching a glimpse of me coming back from a jog.

So Adrian and I went to see it. We had to drive there in his car, a low-slung Capri-type affair, out of which I had to haul myself inelegantly when we arrived. To my complete embarrassment there was a Blue Idea CD case visible on the floor by my feet. I discreetly kicked it out of sight underneath the passenger seat and felt thankful that at least he hadn't tried to play it in my presence.

Adrian drove down a little gravel road, more a lane really, running alongside the river, before pulling into a driveway. We surveyed the property gloomily. It was a great Victorian pile, with curlicues of paint peeling away from every window sill and a scruffy front door with a cracked pane of frosted glass at eye level. Weeds sprouted enthusiastically from the gravel drive, and the house had a blank, unloved look of despair.

Adrian let us into the damp, chilly hall with keys which he fished from the depths of his satchel-type briefcase, chatting inanely the whole time about what a great investment a house in that area was. I followed him into the malodorous but enormous living room, and gazed around at the swirly walls, blotchy, balding carpet and dead house plants.

Adrian had slung his satchel over his shoulder, and with every step he took the strap made a loud, insistent squeaking noise, as though there were a small furry animal held prisoner within. I was beginning to wish I'd listened to him when he'd told me I wouldn't like the place.

Then we walked down the hall to a 25 × 20 foot sunny kitchen, and my doubts began to subside. Despite the terrible sagging wallpaper, the dripping taps and the dark cracked linoleum, I could see that the place had immense potential.

All the rooms were huge and high-ceilinged, with original cornices and skirting boards which I hoped weren't rotten. Both bathrooms sported titanic free-standing, claw-footed baths, and there was a plethora of wonderful original fireplaces, tiled in rich colours with marble surrounds.

We returned to my favourite room, the kitchen.

'It's worse than I remembered,' Adrian commented sheepishly, looking with disdain at the black-encrusted gas oven in the corner. 'Of course you'd have to get a new kitchen fitted. A new everything fitted, really. Although the extremely low asking price does, naturally, reflect that fact.'

'It's a great space,' I said enthusiastically. 'I love all the original features, too. In fact, I think I could really like it.'

Adrian cheered up. I went off and explored all the rooms again, trying hard to look at the space itself and not the damp musty carpets and dark walls. My biggest concern was that there might be something structurally wrong with it. My father's advice on surveys, dodgy roofs and dry rot was still ringing in my ears. I looked out of the window and was relieved to see that there were no huge trees close enough to cause any obvious subsidence, and decided that, pending the results of a full structural survey, I wanted it.

I informed Adrian, and he nodded vigorously in assent, causing the little creature in his bag to agree hysterically.

The survey duly showed that the property was basically sound, if rather damp, and I was overjoyed. I wrote Adrian a massive cheque, then engaged builders and decorators to install central heating, do damp courses, fit a new kitchen, lay new carpets and generally transform the place from attic to cellar. It took four months, during which time I commuted between a small hotel in Chiswick, the Grants' house in Salisbury and Sam's hall of residence.

Sam recovered well from both her eyes being zapped and said she felt a million times better now that she was able to see properly again. She took me to Habitat to pick out my new wallpaper and to look at furniture and curtain material, but we soon realized that, as I needed *everything*, from beds to bottle openers, it would probably be best to stick with one big department store.

So early one morning, about a week before the

workmen finished, I donned dark glasses, opened an account at Selfridges, and Sam and I did a total blitz on the place.

'It's like those game shows where you win two hours to go round a shop and fill up your trolley with as much as you can,' said Sam, looking overwhelmed at the task ahead of us. 'Where do we start?'

'Bathrooms – that's easiest,' I said firmly. 'Let's break ourselves in gently.'

I had told the store how much I intended to purchase, so they gave me carte-blanche to go round with a clipboard, marking down item numbers and prices for them to deliver to me later. I had a feeling they suspected Sam and me of choosing items for a wedding list for our lesbian marriage, and when I told her this she kissed me extravagantly on the cheek and declaimed, '*Please* say we can have Hers and Hers bathrobes. Oh please!'

After buying a shower rail – circular – a clear shower curtain with gold stars on it, a wrought-iron-effect toilet-roll holder and towel rack, four matching sets of honey-coloured towels, screw-in iron hooks with dolphin noses, bath mats and toilet-rug things – neither of us knew what the little horseshoe-shaped carpets were called – two toilet brushes, soap dishes and a toothbrush holder, we were both exhausted and had to go and have a cup of tea.

I felt like an ant in a giant's doll's house, scurrying around the massively ornate halls and high-ceilinged rooms, and wondering if at any moment the whole shop front would open on its hinges and a gigantic hand would reach in and move the fittings around on a whim.

After choosing four different double beds and a single, five wardrobes, three chests-of-drawers, bed-side tables, curtains, eight rugs and a magnificent walnut sideboard from Selfridges' antiques department, our heads were reeling. Sam had to go back to the bedding department and take a small nap on one of the mattresses.

'It's all right,' she said haughtily to the blue-rinsed sales assistant who kept coming over to check on her, obviously thinking she had been testing the bed for longer than was acceptable to store policy, 'We're buying it.' Her head plopped back onto the crackly plastic-covered pillow and she closed her eyes.

'Are you OK, Sam?' I asked, beginning to worry that I'd tired her out completely. 'Do you want to go home?'

'Home?' She opened one eye and squinted at me. 'No way. We still have the kitchen, dining room and living room to do. Tell you what, though. I can live without the fridge and washing-machine department. Can you buy that stuff over the phone instead?'

So we battled on, amazed at how many things were needed to furnish a home from scratch. For the first time ever I enjoyed the fact that I was able to spend money in such a carefree fashion. I had bought presents for my parents and the Grants before, but having been on tour so much, I'd never really needed anything other than the essentials for myself. It was fun.

A week later I stood in my newly refurbished house, revelling in its transformation. The smell of fresh paint and new carpets filled my nostrils, a welcome change from the previous musty odour. I walked slowly down the hallway, marvelling at the slickness and dazzling white of the freshly glossed skirting boards and door frames, trailing my fingers across the rich yellow wallpaper. I felt very grown-up and proud of myself. The air around me was very still and somehow charged, as though a small indoor thunderstorm could blow up at any moment, and it occurred to me that this might just be my own excitement.

The place was still empty, apart from the few possessions I'd brought with me from Freehold – two cases of clothes, my bass, some pedals, a practice amp, a few CDs, my boom box, and the stuff I'd cleared out of the garage – plus a little television set Mrs Grant had insisted on giving me. The Selfridges delivery vans were due any moment, but for now I was enjoying being completely alone in this wonderful new space.

Carrying my boom box and *Little Criminals*, I went upstairs to the master bedroom. I put on the CD, programmed track nine, cranked up the volume loud and lay down, stretching my arms and legs out on the bare chestnut floorboards, a big smile on my face.

'I'll Be Home' flowed over and through me and around my house, cleansing us, clearing out the old energies like burning sage, creating a fresh start.

I *was* home. I wanted to fill this huge empty shell with my new life, with what I would soon see as the essence of me. I would make new friends who would come over and say, 'Oh, this place is really *you*,' and I would be relieved and thankful, because from that starting point maybe I would be able to figure out who *I* really was.

I was twenty-seven and, despite all my wealth, I'd never owned a car, lived permanently away from my parents – the Manhattan apartment was just a temporary change of scenery – or spent any of my money. I'd never even had a serious long-term boyfriend.

I felt as if my life was just beginning, and I was convinced that everything would be plain sailing from then on.

My new brass door-knocker banged resoundingly, and I clattered down the stripped wooden staircase to open the front door. It heralded the start of a long procession of large square yellow boxes and pieces of furniture coming into the house, carried by four bulky, sweat-stained delivery men. They would curse when trying to get something cumbersome around the corner leading to the second floor, and then they'd remember that they worked for Selfridges and weren't allowed to swear on the job, so they'd bite their lips and exhale sharply instead. One of the mattress bases and two of the bigger wardrobes proved particularly onerous, but they struggled manfully on. I hadn't expected quite so many boxes, and I wondered how on earth I was going to get rid of them once I'd emptied them. The place would be full to the ceiling with packaging.

I wished Sam were there, not only for a bit of assistance with the unpacking, but so we could have had a reminisce about my last major house-moving experience with the Shipleys-Ships-Safely guys thirteen years ago. Wow. What a lot could happen in thirteen years, I thought idly, watching two beautiful Chinese vases being carried into the dining room. Those vases alone were probably worth more than the entire houseful of furniture which had been shipped off to Freehold that day, even allowing for inflation.

But Sam had her exams coming up, and pleaded infirmity and overwork.

'I'll help you with the fun part, spending the money, but count me out of the boring unpacking bit,' she'd said airily when we'd last met. I couldn't blame her, but I wished she could have been there just for moral support.

Several hours later the men had eventually cleared the huge Selfridges lorry. They puffed up the garden path for the last time carrying, respectively, a standard lamp, an ironing board, a very large pot plant and a boxed microwave oven. I signed the delivery note, and was so excited at the thought of unwrapping all my new possessions that I didn't even mind when the youngest of the men asked if I would sign an autograph for his twelve-year-old daughter.

Once they'd left, I tied a silk scarf determinedly around my head, in the style of a 1940s munitions worker, and attacked the boxes. Sure enough, within minutes I was wading through a sea of white paper and crinkly cellophane wrapping, big boxes and the smaller boxes in which the household items were packaged – saucepans, an iron, light bulbs, some silk flowers, a laundry drying rack, four telephones and an answering machine. I tried to be more organized about the procedure, breaking each big box down flat after unpacking it, and leaning the sheets of folded cardboard against the kitchen fireplace.

Everything was so ... *new*. I felt as though I was furnishing a model house, and that I would never be able to sully these beautiful shining implements by doing anything so base as actually using them.

I braced my back to lift a heavy canteen of silver-plated cutlery out of a box. Furniture aside, this had been one of the more expensive purchases. Sam had nearly fainted when she'd seen the price tag. 'Are you *planning* to have ten people round to dinner?' she'd asked sarcastically.

'I might. You never know,' I had replied. I felt as though anything was possible. I made sure I bought a long enough oak refectory table to seat my eight other – so far imaginary – friends. I really liked the image of me entertaining: cooking in my own kitchen, bunches of dried herbs hanging from the ceiling, pots of pasta and sauce bubbling fragrantly on the stove, everyone lolling around the table chatting, windows steamed up from the warmth of the room's mutual companionship.

Yes.

I lifted the wooden lid of the canteen and admired the chunky reflective knives, forks and spoons within. The box was lined with soft green baize, and each piece of cutlery was neatly trapped between a deep ridge at the bottom and a little green flap at the top.

I had forgotten nothing, from food processors and cafetières to teapots and egg-timers. Each found its own natural place in my pristine Smallbone kitchen, and gradually all the cupboards and surfaces began to chatter with the noise of tin rubbing shoulders with copper, china rattling next to glass. I felt as though my soul was filling up at the same pace as the kitchen cabinets. I trashed rectangular bits of card with holes or pieces of nylon string top and bottom, which had backed slatted spoons or chopsticks or skewers, and ripped-open sanitary plastic casings which had served the dual purpose of hanging the implement on the display rack, whilst also preventing the germ-laden breath of the customer from miring its virgin purity. I thought that I, too, had been hanging like this for years, behind a plastic sheath, pawed and gaped at, untouchable on my own display stand. But now I'd torn the plastic bubble from my existence. I was no longer on display, or for sale.

After a few weeks the square shop-creases on all my sheets fell out, I figured out how to programme my video, I stopped making fresh orange juice every day just as an excuse to use my new juicer and I burned through the first set of candles I'd bought. I remembered not only everything I'd purchased, but also where I kept it all. The curtains were hung, the rugs laid, pictures and photographs arranged on walls and over fireplaces. By Spring, flowers had bloomed in the garden. Music filled the rooms of the house; I always had a CD in the stereo, or the radio on.

Sam passed her exams and moved in temporarily. We danced and sang together, clowning around, laughing, tipsy and sober, night or morning. My house became a home.

Cynthia

After the Vinnie incident, I didn't even bother to lick my wounds. I just let them bleed freely all over the house. There were framed photographs of Sam in every room, and I trailed in and out looking at each one in turn, cursing myself for never videoing any of our time together. I'd have given anything to see her dance and sing again, even just on a TV monitor.

Sam became the personification of my grief, a symbol of everything I'd lost. When I thought about it, it made me feel guilty. Sorry, Sam, I told her repeatedly. Forgive me. I'm sure you've got enough of your own stuff to think about up there, but please just help me out this one last time.

I began to wonder if I was losing my grip on reality; I didn't eat properly, sleep, or bathe. I just roamed the house, stared at Sam's image or, when I was completely worn out, lay on the sofa and stared at the television. I didn't play music any more; it either irritated or upset me. The silence inside my home whenever the television was off was deep, dark and endless, a kind of oblivion. It was how I wanted the inside of my head to feel.

The only concrete action I managed was to phone up my local newsagent and arrange to have every tabloid delivered daily to my door. I didn't want to see Vinnie's photos of me splashed over the front page, but equally I couldn't bear not knowing. Plus I wouldn't be able to sue anybody if I didn't see the evidence. I wasn't sure whether I felt up to being litigious, but I wanted to have the option.

When the papers arrived each morning in a big bundle, which the paperboy flung resentfully over the gate, I got my only fresh air and exercise for the day. Heavily disguised, I trotted out to meet them, and then lugged them back to my front porch, where I sat down on the mosaic tiled floor and cut the string holding them together with a pair of scissors I kept by the door-mat. I didn't even bother to take them inside the house.

I flicked rapidly through each paper, from cover to sports pages, only looking at the images, before chucking it aside. I saw inky breasts in all shapes, sizes and colours, but no photos of me. Within five days my porch was almost full of newspaper, but I didn't have the energy to take it all outside and throw it away.

After a week of doing this and nothing else, the monotony was broken by a message on my answer-phone:

Hello, Helena, sweetheart. It's me, Cynthia. I just wanted to know how you're getting on. Actually, I'm coming up to London tomorrow to do some shop-ping, and thought I might call in on my way home, if that's all right? It's been a while. I hope you got the hat box all right. I'd love to see you. I'll be there at about five o'clock, OK? See you then. Bye.

I noticed that she hadn't even considered that I might be out or away.

Ugh, a visitor. Of course I adored Cynthia, but I didn't want to see anybody at all. Plus I'd fired my cleaner in a fit of pique three weeks earlier, and the house was a tip. Oh, who cared. Cynthia could come over and cluck over my face, we'd sit and have tea and not talk about Sam. If it made her happy, fine.

*　*　*

I came out to meet Cynthia when she arrived the next day, teetering up the drive, getting mud stuck to her kitten heels. She hugged me, and chatted on about whether the car would be all right by the river, the tide didn't rise that fast did it? She'd locked her shopping in the boot because you never could tell, someone might put a brick through the window when they saw lots of Liberty bags on the seat . . .

I wondered how she could act so normal. The last thing *I* felt like doing was shopping for clothes in Liberty. She even had a fresh perm.

Cynthia held me at arm's length and scrutinized me. 'You're in a bit of a state, aren't you, love?'

'Well, losing an eye after colliding face first with broken glass tends to have that effect.' It seemed tactless to bring up the loss of my best friend, too.

We climbed into the house together, over all the piles of newspaper.

'I didn't mean your appearance. Actually, your face isn't nearly as bad as I'd imagined. I thought you'd look completely different, but you're almost the same old lovely Helena. Bit pale, but still you.'

'What are you talking about? I'm hideous!'

I led her sulkily down the hall, our footsteps chasing dust balls out of their hiding places by the skirting board.

'Good grief, Helena; don't be so ridiculous, love. Of course you aren't hideous. You can hardly see the scars on your cheek, you've just got that tiny patch covering your eye and you'd never know anything had happened to your jaw. OK, your nose is a little bit bumpy, but unless you really look hard you wouldn't notice. Honestly, I'd say you've recovered brilliantly.'

I felt like saying, Don't fob me off, I'm not a kid any more, but out of respect for her I refrained.

'Tea?' I offered, putting the kettle on.

Cynthia glanced around my scummy kitchen. 'Yes, please. Tell you what, while you make it I'll have a little clean-up, OK? And you can fill me in on what's been going on.'

'Nothing's been going on.'

Cynthia took off her coat and began squirting washing-up liquid into the sink.

'Well, for a start, what's with all the newspapers in the porch?'

I sighed. 'My ex, Vinnie. Do you remember him?'

'We never met, but I remember Sam telling me about him. She wasn't his biggest fan. Have you got any rubber gloves?'

Cynthia had already mentioned Sam's name! I felt an odd little thrill, as if she'd just passed me a joint to smoke. I unearthed some unopened gloves from the utility room and handed them to her.

'Yeah, I know. She couldn't stand him. When we were dating I didn't think he was *all* bad. A bit of a sponger, maybe, but he did come to the hospital with me when Sam . . . But now, of course, he's proved me completely wrong.'

'What happened?' Cynthia attacked the dishes with gusto.

I blew air in an exhausted puff out of my mouth, suddenly finding it hard to talk. 'Hardly anyone knows I live here. Not the press, anyhow. There was someone prowling around here for days, but I didn't know it was Vinnie until about a week ago. I came home from a meeting and he was hiding in the bushes taking photographs of me. I know he's going to sell them to the papers because he's always skint – even more so now that we've split up and he hasn't got me paying for everything any more. Plus the press haven't managed to get hold of me yet, not since the accident. He's bound to make a fortune out of me.'

I unhooked two mugs from the Welsh dresser, and found some tea bags in the battered tin near the kettle.

Cynthia seemed appalled. 'My God, Helena, the man's a monster. How could anyone do something like that? Especially since he must know what you're going through. Treacherous bastard. If I could get my hands on him, I'd . . .' She waved her soapy yellow gauntlets in the air, causing bubbles to fly across the room, and I couldn't help a small grin. I'd never heard her swear before.

'Can't you stop him? Get an injunction or something? It's not that I think the photos would be terrible – like I said, your face doesn't look bad – it's just the idea of him profiting from your misery. It's awful.'

She sounded exactly like Sam, leaping to my defence. I didn't know whether this made me happy, sad, or just even more confused.

'There's nothing I can do. If someone prints a picture, then maybe I'll be able to sue for invasion of privacy. It's just really depressing. We parted on bad terms and he probably wants to get back at me. And you know what the worst thing is? Even his damn camera was paid for with my money.'

Cynthia came over from the sink and put a wet forearm around my shoulder. 'Poor old you,' she said, with so much warmth that I began to crumble.

I shook her off. 'No, please, don't be nice to me or I'll cry. I'm fine, really. How are you? It must be just as hard for you.'

Cynthia snapped off the gloves and sat down at the table. 'Let's have that tea.'

I managed to make two cups of tea without sloshing too much over the side, and carried Cynthia's over to her, remembering to touch the table with my free hand first so I could see where to put the cup. Having one eye meant that my depth perception was all shot to hell, and several mugs had already gone for a burton because I hadn't checked first. Then I went back for my own tea.

'In answer to your question, I'm OK. As OK as you could ever be a few months after losing your only daughter.'

Now she was openly talking about Sam. I envied her; she had obviously turned a corner in her acceptance of Sam's death. The tremble in her voice was still there, though.

'It's terribly hard, Helena, you know. We all loved her so much. I miss her every minute of the day. I'm sure you do, too. And Mike's taken it dreadfully hard. He just mooches around the house all day; won't do anything. Doesn't even want to play golf.'

I couldn't speak at all by then. I wondered if I'd actually preferred it when Sam's name never came up.

'But let me tell you something amazing, Helena. You read that book Sam once lent me; you know, *Testimony of Light*? So do you believe in life after death and reincarnation and so on?'

Cynthia took a few sips of her tea. She had an odd expression on her face: grief, sheepishness and a look that willed me to agree with her.

I nodded warily, not sure that I'd be able to handle whatever was coming.

Even though Sam hadn't known she was going to die, in the months leading up to her death we had talked quite a lot about the concept of the afterlife. At first she wasn't at all sure about it; and the nebulous belief system I'd built from my teenage dabblings with Christianity was fine with Heaven, but pretty much precluded such esoteric ideas as reincarnation. But then we'd both read *Testimony of Light*, and it had changed our way of thinking.

It was written in the Sixties, allegedly by the spirit of a deceased ex-nun, communicating via automatic writing through her lifelong friend, who 'physically' wrote the book. It was a completely plausible and wonderfully reassuring description of the afterlife. In Heaven there were beds and gardens and artist's pallettes and canvases. There was beautiful music, rolling hills, clothing and telepathic conversation. You were reborn into this place with a spiritual body, which was like a perfect, ethereal version of your last human body, to review your life's lessons and bide your time until you either incarnated into a new body, if you needed to learn more earthly lessons, or moved on up through the spheres of light towards God and perfection. I was so glad Sam had read it.

I wondered if Cynthia was going to tell me that Sam had been in touch in a similar way, and already I felt myself getting jealous. If Sam got in touch with anyone, there'd be trouble if it wasn't me.

'Well, you see, the reason I mention it is this: you know my friend Amanda, who runs the Three Feathers?'

I nodded.

'Well, she's into these, you know, spiritualist meetings. After Sam died she kept asking me to come along and try it out, but for the first few months I couldn't face it. I thought it would be far too upsetting. Mike was against the idea, too.'

'But you went to one?'

Cynthia nodded, twisting her wedding ring around her finger. 'A few days ago.'

I leaned forward. 'What happened?'

'It was incredible, Helena. I couldn't believe it. There was this enormous woman on a stage, sort of swaying around, and then suddenly she says, in a great, big deep voice, "I have a message from someone who left us recently after a long illness."'

I was sceptical. 'Why didn't she know Sam's name, then?'

'I don't know. It wasn't her speaking, anyway, apparently. Someone from the Other Side was communicating through her, and that was why her voice was all gruff. Although, if you ask me, it sounded a lot like her real voice.'

'What did she say next?'

'She says, "She wants to talk to her mother." I look around at everyone, but nobody else moves. Amanda nudges me, but I can't say anything. So Amanda says, "Is it Sam?" and points at me.'

My eye opened wide and goose bumps rattled down my back. 'And it was?'

Cynthia nodded, tears already beginning to leach out over her cheeks. She got up, tore herself a square of kitchen roll and sat back down again. Involuntarily, I reached out and gripped her hand, as if we were watching a horror movie together. I waited for her to continue.

'The medium says, "Sam wants you to know she's very happy here."'

That was more than enough to start me off, too. Cynthia squeezed my hand back.

'Wait, that's not all. Then she says, "But she's telling me she's worried about . . . Oh, I can't catch the name. Someone beginning with the letter H. Do you know who that could be?"

'I said, "Helena?" and the woman nods. "Tell Helena I love her," she says.'

I was sobbing by now, all restraint gone, in Cynthia's arms. I still felt almost furious that Sam hadn't come and talked to me. It was like a tantalizing glimpse of something denied me. I was delighted that she was happy after all her suffering, and that she still existed somewhere else, but until I wound things up here and did the show, somewhere else was simply too far away.

Cynthia stroked my hair and kissed the top of my head, her arms wrapped tightly around me, holding me in the fierce protective way she used to hold Sam; the same way I always witnessed with such jealousy when I was a little girl.

'You let it all out, sweetheart; it'll do you good.'

'But I miss her so much,' I howled into her chest, barely able to form the words.

'I know you do, darling. I know. So do I. It's OK to say that; it's OK.'

I cried so much, tears pouring out of my right eye, that I had an image of my body shrivelling up from dehydration on the right side only, like a bath pillow with a hole in it.

Eventually Cynthia prised me away from the

temporary security of her cleavage, and gently wiped the tears off my face with her thumb. She got up and handed me a new sheet of kitchen towel so I could blow my nose.

'Helena, love, you shouldn't have to go through this on your own. Promise me something?'

I looked at her mutely. I wasn't in a position to start making promises to anyone.

'Promise me that you'll talk to me in future, whenever you feel like this. You're like another daughter to me, you always have been, and I want you to know that I'm there for you if you need me, OK? I'm so sorry if I've upset you by telling you all this, sweetheart, about the medium and everything. I just wanted you to know that Sam's happy now; that's helped me so much. I hoped it would help you, too.'

Our mugs of tea had turned cold and treacly on the table in front of us. Refilling the kettle and making a fresh brew provided me with a moment to try and reknit my unravelled edges together. I couldn't promise Cynthia anything, but I did manage to thank her. After we'd drunk the fresh tea, and the teary blotches on both our faces had subsided, she hugged me again and picked her coat off the back of her chair.

'Best be off now. Hopefully the rush hour will have died down a bit. Remember what I said, won't you? You're a very special person, Helena. Look after yourself, please, for Sam's sake as well as yours. It will get easier.'

I walked with her to the front door and, resting one knee on a slippery stack of *Suns* and *Daily Mirrors* in the porch, watched her pick her way back down the drive again. She turned at the gate and waved, and I waved back, catching a glimpse of Sam's expression in her profile.

In a way, what she'd said about Sam had helped, but it had also strengthened my resolve. I'd nearly finished the manuscript. I was ready to do the show. I wanted to be happy, too. I wanted to be in the same place as Sam, as soon as possible.

I double bolted the front door and stood in my silent hallway, alone.

'Safe From Harm'
Massive Attack

Life in Twickenham moved smoothly along, counted
off from month to month by the flow of rugby traffic to
the stadium and the highs and lows of the tide along
the river opposite my front gate. Whenever I wasn't in
Salisbury with Sam I tended to stay inside on
Saturdays and Sundays, as there were more people
around to spot me and snigger behind their hands at
the novelty of sighting someone famous.

Sam lived in my house with me for the first year,
before moving out to rent her own flat in Mortlake,
nearer the legal firm where she was doing her Articles.
She also acquired a new, flash boyfriend – Timothy –
who I believed prompted her defection. Mortlake was
quite near by, and she did still come and stay, but it
was obvious she preferred the carnal pleasures
Timothy had to offer over another night watching TV
round at mine. I was hurt that she hadn't stayed with
me permanently, but she claimed it would have been
too easy. I did understand, I supposed. After all the
time she'd spent living in her parents' basement, she
was ready to taste complete independence.

Occasionally I went out with them and their old
college friends, but I always felt uncomfortable. Her
friends never said anything directly, of course, but
they made such an effort to be normal around me that
the evenings were invariably terribly strained and

342

awkward in their forced jollity. Sam told me that I was paranoid and imagining things, but I'd had a lot of experience of that type of situation. I knew they couldn't get out of their minds the fact that they were having a drink with someone who was as widely recognized as a member of the royal family.

I couldn't understand why, but it seemed to bug Sam that I was happy just staying home, tinkering around with my bass.

'Why don't you get out more, meet more people? You could get a job,' she asked me several times, until I snapped at her.

'I had a job I liked, and I made enough money to not work any more. I've just taken early retirement, OK?'

'But aren't you bored?' she'd say incredulously.

The truth was that yes, I was beginning to get a little bored. I had undoubtedly needed a really long break after the stress of years on the road, and then the trauma of the break-up and the publicity of the trial, but enough was enough. I needed to do something with my time.

I thought about setting up a music publishing company for my newer songs, but somehow I never got round to it. Besides, all my existing songs were in the firm grasp of Ringside Publishing, who were understandably unwilling to relinquish their 10 per cent, and there wasn't much point in having my own company without my old material. Then I thought about music management, but decided it would be too much like hard work. I even toyed with the idea of becoming a kind of up-market chef. Since buying my ten-piece dinner service and cutlery canteen, I'd whiled away many a day teaching myself to cook exotic dishes in preparation for the big dinner parties I had planned to have, but that one got nixed on the grounds that I was far too famous to go into catering – this was all before the cult of the celebrity chef had invaded our TV screens.

After that I was stuck for ideas. But then Vinnie

came into my life, and suddenly I was no longer bored.

I met him on a winter Saturday in my small but exclusive local deli, the only place I deigned to visit personally to do my shopping. I never went to the goldfish-bowl supermarket, preferring the privacy of ordering my groceries by phone and having them delivered. But the deli was lovely, and I couldn't resist the occasional browse. I'd never been recognized in there, and it felt safe.

So when Vinnie came up and earnestly quizzed me in a strange but sexy accent on how to cook fennel, having, he said, spotted it in my basket, I thought he had a sweet ingenuous smile, and explained at length my favourite fennel recipe.

All the time we were talking, Vinnie showed no signs of knowing who I was, which endeared me to him still further. We chatted for about ten minutes near the sun-dried tomatoes and porcini mushrooms, and then amicably moved towards the till together. I was flushed with exhilaration when, once we had both paid and packed our stuff in brown bags, he invited me to come for a drink with him.

Sitting in a nearby pub, drinking pints of dry cider, our respective bags propped up on the velveteen-covered benches next to us, I couldn't believe myself. A pub and pints of cider! It was an old fellas' pub, full of gnarled hands cradling creamy Guinnesses, and nobody asked for my autograph or even looked askance at me. I got such a huge buzz out of the normality of the whole situation that I even deigned to remove my shades.

After establishing the origins of each other's strange accents – mine mid-Atlantic, his half-Zimbabwean – I discovered that he had lived briefly in Florida, and we got embroiled in a slightly bizarre discussion about the cultural differences between Britain and the USA. This turned into a debate on the comparative merits of English and American supermarkets, although I had to pretend that I knew more about Sainsbury's than was strictly true.

'Don't you just *love* Sainsbury's! There are some good supermarkets in the US, too, but they're pretty few and far between. The towns around where I grew up in New Jersey had these terrible poxy places where you had to check the sell-by dates on everything, and the cashiers were so dumb that tomatoes were about the only produce they could identify.'

Vinnie giggled, a weird high-pitched girly giggle, obviously thinking I was exaggerating.

'No, really, I'm serious. They were so ignorant that they'd hold up a mango and ask what it was, and I'd say, "Oh, those big peaches. Ten for a dollar," and they'd just ring it up at ten cents when actually they were a dollar seventy-five each. Once my mother was buying broccoli and the girl picked it up and said, no joke, "Is this cabbage?"'

Vinnie had laughed and laughed, rather excessively, I realized in retrospect, and I'd felt witty and entertaining, a girl who could make strangers laugh without them knowing I was worth millions.

After the second pint Vinnie said, 'What are you doing tonight? Can I see you again?'

I was thrilled. 'What do you want to do?' I asked with genuine innocence.

Vinnie looked seductively into my eyes and my spine suddenly seemed to dissolve.

'I mean, where do you want to go?'

Vinnie just kept gazing at me, until he leaned forward and gently brushed my lips with his. 'How about your place?' he said casually. I hesitated. I never let strangers come to my house, but Vinnie wasn't a stranger, and I had a feeling he was going to become something much more important. Besides, here was someone besides Sam who I could try out my cooking skills on.

'Shall I cook you dinner then?'

Vinnie grinned triumphantly and thrust a sticky beer mat and a biro at me.

'Great. I'll be there at seven. Write down your address for me, would you?'

When I got home half an hour later, slightly drunk from too much Dry Blackthorn, I dumped my up-market groceries on the kitchen table and immediately tried phoning Sam. Timothy picked up the telephone.

'Hi, it's Helena. Is Sam home, please?'

Timothy answered in the guarded, slightly dis-approving tone he always adopted with me. 'Sorry, Helena, she's having a nap at the moment.'

'Is she OK?' I'd thought Sam had stopped having afternoon naps months ago.

'Yeah, I think so. She's just feeling a bit under the weather at the moment.'

'Oh. Right. Could you just let her know I rang, and that I'll give her a buzz tomorrow.'

'OK. Bye then.'

I hung up, concerned for two minutes until thoughts of Vinnie swarmed back into my head. It was three-thirty; he'd be here at seven. Three and a half hours to prepare.

First, what was I going to cook? I had a quick flip through a couple of cookery books, and decided on Penne with Ricotta, Basil and Rocket – quick, hearty and quite posh. We could have that, with some fennel in orange sauce as a starter. Bit of an odd choice, but with some hot bread it would be OK, and after all, it was the fennel that had got us talking. The whole thing would only take fifteen minutes, and I had all the ingredients.

Next I ran myself a hot bath with lavender bubble bath, and put Massive Attack's *Blue Lines* on the stereo. The bath was my favourite place to listen to music since I'd had extra speakers wired through and wall-mounted in there. After drawing the blinds and lighting a couple of candles in the bathroom, I climbed slowly into the steaming bathtub, one toe at a time because the water felt as though it was scalding my chilled feet. As I gradually immersed myself and my body acclimatized to the temperature change, I relaxed and listened to

Blue Lines in a tipsy, euphoric state. I lay motionless as the bubbles died around me, with only my face, breasts and knees breaking the surface of the fizzy water like icebergs.

When I raised my hand, steam flew from my outstretched fingers in the flickering candlelight, and I felt like a witch. I wondered if I'd put a spell on Vinnie, if he was as excited as I was about the forthcoming evening. Already I couldn't quite remember his face, other than his sly sexy smile and his crinkly green eyes. He was whippet-thin, medium height and sinewy. A little tremor of lust juddered through me as I visualized him naked, disturbing the tiny uniform bubbles outlining my body.

I couldn't quite recall the last time I'd had sex. It must have been at least three years before, because Blue Idea had still been together. I had a vague memory of an unsatisfactory liaison with a marketing director from Ringside's Mexican company, after a promotions dinner and too much tequila – best forgotten about, like most of my dalliances.

All being well, I estimated that Vinnie would become about the seventh notch on my bedpost. I made a brief tally in my head to check. First had been my one-night stand with David. Then there'd been a particularly persistent French fan called Claude, who had followed us across the Alps in his 2CV when we were on tour in France and Switzerland. After one show, drunk, I had conceded to let him into my hotel room. He'd smelled of pesto sauce and body odour, but that was all I could remember about that night, or any of the other nights of that particular tour.

Next there was a highly public but very short-lived relationship with the lead singer of a West Coast grunge band, who ceremoniously dumped me for a soap star after only four weeks. I'd been totally humiliated, having made the cardinal mistake of believing myself to be in love, and telling the papers so.

Then there was the lovely Patrick, who, much to her

chagrin, Sam never got to meet. He never did return my calls, and eventually I just gave up trying, writing him off as another disaster.

The others I couldn't even identify, apart from the Mexican marketing director. I was ashamed of myself, but they were just groupie shags, one way or another, and they always left me with the belief that men only wanted me for *what* I was, rather than *who* I was. I think a few of them probably had wanted to see me again, but when I'd sobered up I invariably gave them the kiss-off, in no uncertain terms.

After Grunge Boy and Patrick, I decided I couldn't risk having a relationship, and anyway, it would never have lasted with the amount of touring we did.

But I wasn't on the road any more . . .

I decided that it was of paramount importance for me not to repeat the mistakes I'd made in the past if I wanted this one to last. No drunken sex, certainly no sex on the first date, and *definitely* no being sweet-talked into bed. If Vinnie wanted me, he could have me on a grown-up, mature relationship level, taking things one step at a time.

Of course I wasn't saying that I wanted to get married and have kids – not yet, anyhow – but I was ready to make more of a commitment to somebody now. I had the time, the energy and the inclination. Mmm, regular sex, I thought, as my fingers slipped quietly beneath the surface of the now-lukewarm water in search of submerged pleasures.

Ten minutes later, I roused myself and washed my hair thoroughly, sluicing off my shampoo and conditioner in alternate hot and cold rinses, which made my scalp tingle and my hair feel soft, like wet silk. I shaved my legs and armpits – well, you never knew. Even if sex was off the agenda, I might let him fondle my calves, if he was lucky – and climbed out of the tepid bath. I dried myself, then slathered Issey Miyake body lotion over every inch of my skin. I wrapped my head in a neat hand-towel turban, baby-powdered everywhere that didn't require body lotion, and donned the towelling bathrobe which hung on the dolphin peg behind the door.

Planning to start my make-up, I wiped the steam off the bathroom mirror with my sleeve, but the warm moist air immediately put another, thinner layer of fog on the cleared surface, so instead I went into the bedroom and blow-dried my hair until it sat in a sleek, smooth chestnut bob around my face.

So far so good. I decided to get dressed before doing my face, so I could match my make-up with my outfit, so I slipped out of my dressing gown and deliberated for a long time in front of my open wardrobe.

The phone rang, and my heart leaped at the thought that it might be Vinnie, ringing to cancel, but when I picked it up, it was only Sam.

'Hi, what's up?' she asked.

I walked with the cordless phone over to the full-length free-standing mirror in my bedroom, and stood naked in front of it. 'I've got a date, that's what's up,' I said proudly.

There was a screech from the other end. 'Who with?'

I surveyed my body, trying to see it through someone else's eyes. Large but perky breasts, tight stomach, hips and thighs a tiny bit bigger than I'd have liked, but still a safe size twelve. I thanked God that I hadn't stayed chubby. It was so difficult to be in the world's spotlight if you were carrying even a few extra pounds.

'He's called Vinnie. I met him in a shop, and he's originally from Rhodesia, Zimbabwe, whatever. He's coming round for dinner.'

There was a slight pause.

'You met him in a shop? What shop? What does he do?'

'The deli. He doesn't work there or anything. We just got talking and then went for a drink to the pub. He's a mature student, does art and design. Oh, Sam, he's so hot. All thin and trendy, with a really sexy way of talking. Confident. I like that in a man.'

'And does he – I mean, did he – know who you are?'

'That's the best bit, I really don't think he did. He didn't say anything, anyway. Isn't that neat? He just fancied me for my own sake.'

Sam sounded thoughtful. 'Yeah, that's great. Just be careful, OK, Helena? Don't get carried away. I'm not sure how I feel about him coming to your house, though. He could be anyone. Do you want me and Timothy to come over for moral support? We're not doing anything tonight.'

I laughed. 'No way! I don't want you gatecrashing my romantic dinner, thanks very much! But I appreciate your concern. I'll call you first thing in the morning and tell you how it goes.'

'You'd better.'

'Anyway, gotta go, Sam. I have to start cooking. Thanks for ringing. Lots of love.'

'Good luck. Lots of love to you, too, Helena. Let's meet up tomorrow, OK? You can give me all the gory details over lunch.'

'OK. Deal. Bye.'

'Bye.'

It was only after we'd hung up that I realized I'd forgotten to ask how she was feeling.

I got dressed, finally deciding on my Agent Provocateur underwear underneath a low-key but very sexy Ghost dress. The steam had dissipated from the bathroom mirror when I returned, so I leaned against the sink and got to work on my face. Foundation, blusher, golden-brown eyeshadow, black eyeliner and mascara, and finally a tawny-gold-coloured lipstick. Then a generous squirt of Issey Miyake completed the transformation.

I flung my wet towel over the shower-curtain rail, and picked the sodden bathmat up off the floor, feeling new, polished and as ready as I'd ever be. It was six twenty.

* * *

350

By six thirty I was in the kitchen quartering fennel and mashing garlic. There was a bang at the door at around six forty, just as I'd put the fennel into boiling water and weighed out 100g of pine kernels.

'It's Vinnie,' he said through the stained-glass panel in the front door.

'Oh, hello,' I replied from the hall, completely overcome with panic. Thank God I'd put my make-up on before beginning to cook.

'Well, are you going to let me in then?' he called, mock-impatient, through the letter box.

I opened the door.

'You're early,' I said nervously.

Vinnie looked me up and down appraisingly. 'You look totally *gorgeous*,' he said. 'Great house, too. Do you live here alone?'

I nodded, blushing at the compliment. He looked exactly the same as he had earlier, right down to the large brown paper bag he held in his arms. A five o'clock shadow gave away the fact that he probably hadn't spent hours in the bath, and the same clothes indicated the unlikelihood of him agonizing in front of an open wardrobe. Still, that was guys for you.

Vinnie stomped down the hall into the kitchen as if he'd been there a hundred times before, plonked the bag down on the table and unpacked it. It turned out to contain not his groceries from earlier, but a medium-sized bottle of gin, a large plastic bottle of tonic, two lemons, a packet of Gauloises and a family-sized bag of tortilla chips.

'Thought we could get started with a few G&Ts,' he said airily. 'Where do you keep your glasses?'

Somewhat surprised, I took two tumblers out of the cupboard. 'How do you know I like gin?' I asked.

'Oh, most people like gin. You do, don't you?'

'Well, yes, but . . .'

'There you are then.'

He sloshed a large measure into each glass, topped it up with tonic and helped himself to ice from the freezer. I stood and watched, mouth agape, as he deftly chopped up lemons, found a bowl to pour the tortilla chips into, opened his packet of cigarettes and, without asking my permission, lit one from the gas ring on the hob.

'Make yourself at home,' I said sarcastically.

'Cheers,' he replied through a cloud of evil-smelling smoke, handing me a glass. 'Your good health. Now, shall we adjourn to somewhere more comfortable before dinner? That looks done,' he added, turning off the gas underneath the boiling fennel. 'Why don't you just strain it, and then you can finish the cooking later?'

'I'm surprised you don't want to strain it. You've done everything else,' I said, fetching a colander. Again the sarcasm seemed lost on Vinnie.

'Oh, no, you're in charge.'

Somehow I found his assertiveness attractive. He was so different to any other man I'd ever met, and I wondered if it could be because he wasn't in the slightest bit in awe of me. I showed him back down the hall, into the sitting room, and offered him a choice of sofas. But he leaped at the stereo, and pounced on the Massive Attack CD case I'd left out from earlier.

'Hey, I love this. It's amazing. Is it in the machine? Great, let's listen to it.'

He pressed Play, and the opening bars of 'Safe From Harm' chugged out around the room again. 'Fantastic album, this. Much better than the follow-up. Although that was pretty great, too.'

'Bit of an expert, then, are you?' I enquired. If he was that knowledgeable about music, surely he'd have known who I was.

'Well, I know a lot about most things,' he replied shamelessly, grinning at me.

The first G&T slid down very easily, and Vinnie insisted on dashing off to the kitchen to replenish our glasses himself.

'I just love this house,' he kept saying to me.

During the second drink, I learned that Vinnie shared a place in Richmond with an Oriental girl from his course, that he was twenty-seven, that he used to be a graphic designer but had gone back to college because he wanted to be an artist instead, and that, like me, he was an only child. He didn't ask me anything about myself, not even what I did for a living, for which I was grateful.

By the time he'd rushed off to fix us a third gin, I was feeling very drunk. On the verge of being too pissed to either cook or want to eat, I decided that I'd better get back to my pasta and the orange sauce. Unsteadily, I followed him back into the kitchen.

Vinnie had his back to me. He was hunched over the little portable TV which lived on the end of the kitchen work surface, concentrating on something hidden by his shoulder. I wondered what he was doing; at first I thought he was writing, using the top of the television to lean on.

I studied the part of his profile visible to me: pale skin, one or two not-unattractive pockmarks and lovely cheekbones. Light from a halogen spotlight above him glinted off the lenses of his round tortoiseshell-rimmed glasses and filtered through his stubble. He was actually not as good-looking as I remembered him from the pub; his appeal came more from his sexual confidence than his physical attributes. He had wiry hair, which defied gravity and stood straight up, like Kramer's in *Seinfeld*, and I could smell his aftershave from where I was leaning against the door frame. At least he'd bothered to put aftershave on, even if he had skipped the actual shaving part.

I stood watching his thin back curved over in its black-and-white stripy T-shirt, and for a second I felt an overwhelming attraction to him.

Then I realized exactly what he was doing, and attraction turned to fury. He was chopping out two neat lines of cocaine, with *my* credit card, on top of *my*

TV. I couldn't believe it. All Sam's words of warning came flooding back.

'What the hell do you think you're playing at?' I said, outraged at his lack of manners and presumption.

Cynthia Grant gave me that TV, I thought. She'd be horrified. It was a nasty old little twelve-inch, encased in grimy white plastic, with a bunny-eared aerial that sat shakily on its top. She'd wanted me to have it when I first bought the house; it had been her kitchen telly, but, she said, she'd nearly sliced the tips of her fingers off by trying to watch soap operas and prepare meals at the same time, so please would I take it away? I'd laughed and said, 'So I can slice my own fingers off?' but it had been in my kitchen ever since.

Vinnie had moved the aerial down onto the worktop so as to have more room to manoeuvre. The cocaine he was expertly chopping out hardly showed up at all on the white surface, but this didn't make it any more acceptable.

'How dare you do that in my house,' I spluttered. 'Get out, now!'

Vinnie looked a picture of contrition. 'Oh, God, I'm so, so sorry. I had no idea you'd object. You just seem like such a cool person, I was sure you'd be into a little livener now and again. You know, special occasion and all that. I'm bang out of order, I know. If it upsets you, I'll leave now.'

He immediately swept the cocaine back into its white paper package, folded it safely into the corners and put it back in his jeans pocket, before standing up to face me. He hitched up his baggy jeans by the belt loops and shuffled from foot to foot like a guilty schoolboy, and I suddenly had the urge to put my arms around his hard waist. In my heels I was about two inches taller than him, so he had to look up into my face.

'You don't have to go. But I warn you, I won't sleep with you,' I blurted, feeling foolish.

'Who said anything about sex?' he asked innocently, touching my breast lightly.

'Get off. And don't even think about getting that stuff out again, do you hear me? I don't do drugs, not even spliff, and I won't have them in my house.'

'Aw, you're such a spoilsport. You'll have another G&T, though, won't you, eh?' he said hopefully, turning back to his more legal supplies.

I couldn't believe his nerve. It was extraordinary, but it just made me fancy him even more. I watched him clumping around in his heavy Dr Martens, whistling, opening and closing cupboards, crashing ice cubes from a tray, chopping more lemons, the hiss and fizz of the tonic bottle being unscrewed again.

I felt as if suddenly there had been a tilt, and it was I who had come to visit him in *his* house. It left me standing aimlessly, like an uncomfortable stranger amid my own familiarity, waiting for an invitation to be seated.

Vinnie flourished two more huge gin and tonics and a bowl of chips, and ushered me out of the kitchen back into the living room.

'I really think I should start dinner now,' I said weakly, wondering if perhaps this was all a bizarre dream.

'I don't know about you,' Vinnie said, 'but I'm actually not all that hungry now. We're having such a laugh. What do you say we just keep drinking for a bit?'

As if under some spell – to think that I'd believed I could put a spell on *him*! – I found myself saying, 'OK, well, if you don't want to eat, I'm not very hungry now, either.'

'Cheers,' he said, handing me my drink. We clinked glasses, and he smiled slowly, almost sheepishly. Once I got to know him better, I found out that it was the smile that meant, Come on, play the game, I know you know what this is about.

We gazed at each other for a long time, too long for there to be any doubt about what we both wanted. I must not sleep with him, not yet, I thought. But I was

355

transfixed by the sexy curve of his lips and the way his eyes held mine in a blatantly flirtatious way. I found myself wondering what his kisses would be like.

Vinnie got up to rifle through my record collection, running a commentary on its contents as he did so. 'How can you admit to having a Bruce Springsteen CD? American jingoistic crap! Incredible! You're the only person I know who has the Unknown Cases record.'

He put on a CD, listened to one track, took it off again and put on another. In between tracks he moved from the sofa to the armchair to the floor by my feet, where he briefly pleated the fringes of the rug before hopping back up to the sofa, talking, talking, talking all the time, and chain-smoking.

'Get your shoes off the sofa,' I said, when I could get a word in edgeways. 'Why are you so bloody hyperactive?'

His familiarity with me was causing me to behave in an equally familiar way towards him. I didn't recognize myself.

'Can't help it. Must be my natural high spirits. Speaking of which,' he said, bouncing up from the sofa like Tigger in monochrome, 'another drink?'

If he hadn't sworn he wasn't, I'd have said he was definitely high.

Once more he disappeared into the kitchen, grinning, without waiting for my answer.

Somehow the drinks got topped up more and more often without me noticing, and the chips were reduced to a few greasy crumbs at the bottom of the bowl. It was only 8.30, and all ideas of dinner had gone out of the window.

Vinnie finally put *Blue Lines* on again – the third time I'd heard it that day. He turned up the volume full blast, and pulled me out of my chair to dance, still talking non-stop: politics, music, architecture. Irrespective of his knowledge, or lack of knowledge, of a subject, it transpired that he always had to be right.

He was goading me as we danced, trying to woo me into one of the interminable debates that came to characterize our relationship – besides the sex, that is.

'I can't dance, talk and drink at the same time,' I said. His smell and his weird accent pulled at me like a magnet. I will not sleep with him, I told myself. We were getting closer and closer together, laughing as we danced drunkenly around. I wanted him.

Whoops, I thought, or maybe I said it aloud. 'You'd better go and get me another drink.'

I was drunk enough by then that I kept on dancing even when he was out of the room. All my familiar possessions – pictures, books, chairs – took on a different, jiggly appearance, as though they were my new dance partners. Vinnie came back with two half-filled glasses. 'That's the end of the gin,' he said, laughing.

'You're joking!'

I stopped dancing and suddenly felt exhausted. 'We've drunk the whole bottle?'

'Yup. Come on, let's send it out in style. Down in one.' We clinked glasses again, swigging the remainder of the gin. The room started to spin and I had to hold on to Vinnie's arm to keep steady. Massive Attack ended, but we still swayed together, closer and closer until our heads touched. A hair from one of his wiry curls detached itself and found its way scratchily under my eyelid. I felt his erection press hard up against my thigh and I shivered with excitement. As I blinked the hair out of my eye, I ran my fingers lightly over his bare arm, feeling the contours of his little moles and goose bumps, squeezing a rough elephant's trunk of loose skin at his elbow, my other hand tracing the knobbles of his spine.

He told me that he broke his back parachuting during a youthful stint in the army. 'I was lucky,' he said. 'The person who jumped out of the plane after me was killed; *his* parachute didn't open at all.'

I couldn't imagine him being in the army; I bet he'd

357

been useless, a sort of opinionated, bossy, male equivalent of Private Benjamin. I laughed at the thought and Vinnie kissed me. His tongue felt nice, firm and insistent, not skinny like the rest of him.

'Whoops,' I whispered again, as we went blurrily upstairs to my bedroom, shedding garments *en route*.

I sobered up briefly in the middle of the sex, our limbs a flailing tangle on the bed. The undersheet had twisted itself sweatily off, exposing the little stitched peaks and valleys of mattress beneath it. My body was loving it while my mind yelled furiously at me to stop, but by that time stopping was out of the question.

Afterwards we both had to go and throw up in the toilet to rid ourselves of the lingering alcohol, and I felt as if I was vomiting out more than just the gin. I was puking caution, good sense and discretion. I cleaned my teeth and stared at my face in the mirror; there were two bright red spots on my cheeks which could have been from sex or gin, but which might also have been from shame.

When I got back to the bedroom, Vinnie rolled contentedly onto his back, as at home in my bed as he was in the rest of my house. He grinned at me.

'Do you realize we've just had an entire night's events crammed into about three hours?' he said. 'We've talked, danced, drunk a whole bottle of gin, shagged, puked and slept, and it's only ten o'clock?'

He gave me a triumphant peck on the cheek, and curled up to dream a victor's dreams.

I looked at him, small and vulnerable without his glasses or clothes, astonished at the evening's events. It couldn't have been me who'd just done that, surely: got drunk and had sex with a stranger. Thankfully it had been wonderful, but I had a nagging feeling that I'd had absolutely no choice in the matter. I wondered whether I should kick him out, or perhaps go and sleep in one of the spare rooms, but he looked all warm and soft and inviting, so I climbed back into bed with him instead.

He turned over with his back to me, so I was spooning him, and muttered sleepily, 'You know, I'm a huge fan of yours.'

But by then it was too late.

The Delectable Sandie

After days and days of being unable to do any writing at all, Cynthia's visit spurred me back into it. Suddenly I found that I was actually getting close to finishing the manuscript. I estimated two more weeks of working several hours daily, and I'd be ready to do the show. Not, of course, that I'd actually be reading the magnum opus on air – how could I in a two hour show – but it had to be complete, for me to leave behind as the explanation for my choice of music.

It was time to start thinking seriously about collecting the records. I wanted to be sure that I brought every single CD with me into the studio, just in case New World's library couldn't produce a copy. I wanted to leave nothing to chance.

As I conducted a detailed rummage through my CD collection, I wondered who the producer for the 2 a.m. show would be. I supposed it was too much to hope that it would still be Chrissie, my last breakfast-show producer. She was very professional, and, I'd thought, a lovely person, too; she'd been the only one to visit me more than once in hospital, although she hadn't rung me since. She had probably gone on to much better things by now.

It would probably be better if I had someone awful, anyway. Some thick-skinned, dim novice, who wouldn't get upset when the press asked, 'How could you not have known what state Helena was in?' and, 'Didn't you think she was acting strangely?' Someone who could bask in their fifteen minutes of fame as the last person to see me alive.

I made a tidy tower of CDs next to the fireplace, containing the majority of tracks I'd planned for the show. I'd already bought *All Mod Cons*, which I realized must still be in my car somewhere, a painful reminder of that sunny, hungry, sick day when I'd bumped into Toby. I couldn't help wondering how he was, and if I would be able to find his sister's address, which was also on the floor of the car. I decided I'd look for it when I went out to retrieve the Jam CD.

A few of the other CDs I'd need were also missing: my copy of *Colossal Youth*, the Young Marble Giants record, was nowhere to be found – I suspected Vinnie had half-inched it – and I realized that I'd never owned *The Sandie Shaw Supplement*, 'Wichita Lineman', or any Happy Mondays records.

I rang round all the Richmond record shops to see what they had in stock, and managed to reserve copies of *Thrills, Spills and Bellyaches*, *Colossal Youth* – which was on import only and would cost me a fortune – and *20 Greatest Hits of Country Music*.

Only the Sandie Shaw was missing now. But after ten minutes on the Internet it was ordered, to be delivered in one or two weeks' time. Better not take any longer, I thought.

Even though I needed the album on CD, the original vinyl version – the source of so much friction between Mum and Dad – would have done if all else failed. I decided to phone Dad to see if he still had it, as a backup in case the CD didn't arrive in time. The record somehow felt like a bond between us.

Dad nearly fainted with surprise at hearing my voice when he picked up the telephone.

'Hi, Dad, it's me.'

'Helena, my honeypie. How the heck are you?'

I gritted my teeth with annoyance at his southern

twang. God knew where he'd picked it up from; my mother had managed to cling on to her Home Counties vowels as if her life depended on them. An American accent was fair enough, after more than twenty years' living in the country, but did he really need to sound as if he was just about to go out roping steer?

I was very fond of my father, but in an abstract way; the way one feels about having nicely manicured fingernails. He was a bit of a non-person to me, really, a pipe-smoking appendage to my mother. In fact, the only time I could actually remember seeing him without her was in the early days of the band, when he had reluctantly come to one of our gigs. Mum had refused point-blank to come with him, as she was sure that she would hate it, although she did grace us with her presence once or twice after we'd begun to get successful. Dad had stood at the side, flattened against the wall, away from all the moshing high-school kids, sucking on his pipe and looking so uncomfortable that anyone would think I'd been performing a striptease on stage. Justin and Joe had spotted him and, mid-set, began a lugubrious rendition of a *Sesame Street* song about one of us not being like the other ones. I'd been mortified.

'I'm fine, Dad. In fact I'm going back to work soon.'

'Aw, that's just fan-tastic! I'm real happy to hear that, honey. Me and your mom have been so darn worried.'

I shuddered.

'We wish you'd just come on out here and visit awhile, Helena. Why, it must be over two years since I last saw you!'

This was how all our conversations went.

'But, Dad, you're always off on your cruises at Christmas, and you know how busy I . . . used to be with the radio show. I had to be there every day. I couldn't just go on vacation whenever I fancied it, you know that. I wasn't really well enough to come over before, and now I'm starting a new show. There's nothing stopping *you* visiting *me*, is there?'

Dad hemmed and hawed. 'Well, honey, it's kind of hard this side, too, what with work and me being chairman of the Country Club Society Committee. Anyways, to what do we owe the honour of your call? Want to talk to your mother?'

'No, actually, Dad, I wanted to ask you something. I'm, er, getting some records together for my first show back on air, and I really want to play a Sandie Shaw track. You used to have it on vinyl; I remember it from when I was a kid. The album was called *The Sandie Shaw Supplement*.'

Dad laughed. 'Oh my, I *loved* that record! As I recall, it featured the delectable Sandie spray-painted gold, with lots of hair and a teeny chain bikini. Your mother disapproved.'

'Yeah, that's the one. I've ordered it off the Net but I'm worried it won't arrive in time for my show. Do you still have it?'

There was a pause while he considered.

'You know what? I believe I might do. I sure haven't seen it for donkey's years, though. I'll have a scout around for you. I remember Eve tried to throw it away, but I'm sure I rescued it and hid it in my study.'

Dad's study in New Jersey was exactly the same as his study in Salisbury had been: whole mountain ranges of paperwork, yellowing newspapers, golf books and an assortment of pipes, jumbled together in one huge fire hazard. It was hard enough to spot Dad when he was in there, let alone one thin vinyl record. I didn't hold out much hope of getting a copy any time this decade.

'Oh well, don't worry, Dad. If it turns up, let me know. Is Mum there?'

'No, honey, she's out playing canasta. I'll tell her you called.'

'OK. Well, that's all, then. Thanks anyway.'

'Good to talk to you, sweetheart. We don't do it enough. You take care of yourself, mind.'

I was going to have to hang up pronto, because a

marble seeemed to have got stuck in my throat. 'Yeah, thanks. Bye, Dad. I love you.'

'Excuse me?' Dad must have thought he'd misheard.

'I love you, Dad. Bye.'

'Love you too, angel,' he said in a bemused voice.

I put down the phone and cried for ten minutes.

☆

'Don't Wanna Know Bout Evil'
Spill

'Are you really a fan of Blue Idea?' I asked Vinnie after our first night together.

'Oh, man, yeah. *Painting the Ceiling* is one of my favourite ever records. I can sing all the words to it.'

'Go on, then,' I challenged him.

For a split second, when he thought I was serious, the look on his face was priceless. He later told me that was the moment he fell in love with me, although it was another ten months before he actually said it, in so many words.

The already-subdued lights in the restaurant dimmed further, and a beaming young waiter emerged, bearing a beautifully decorated cake in the shape of a champagne bottle with five tiny flickering candles atop it.

Sam leaned over to me as everyone began to sing.

'Vinnie organized the cake for you,' she said, squeezing my hand.

I threw my arms around Vinnie's neck and kissed his cheek repeatedly, breathing in his distinctive Vinnie scent of aftershave and Gauloises.

'Oh, Vin, baby. It's wonderful. Thank you so, so much.'

'You're welcome, angel,' he replied, a faintly puzzled expression on his face.

As the final 'Hap-py Birth-day to yooouuuuuu!'

faded away, the other diners in the restaurant applauded politely, and Sam, her boyfriend Timothy, David, David's wife, Joe, Vinnie and I all clinked glasses in a noisy and protracted toast to celebrate my thirtieth birthday.

I stood up, fingering the beautiful bracelet Sam had given me earlier, and smiling from ear to ear.

'This is so fantastic,' I said. 'It's the best birthday I've ever had. I've got my wonderful best friend here, my gorgeous and considerate boyfriend, old friends David and Joe, and, er, new friends, too. I just feel totally . . . *great*!'

They all cheered. Vinnie delved into his backpack under the table and brought out a thin flat tinfoil package – from my kitchen; I'd caught him replacing the Bacofoil in the kitchen drawer earlier. He handed it to me, and it was so light that at first I thought there was nothing inside.

'Careful how you unwrap it,' he said. 'It's fragile.'

I gingerly undid the foil corners, and opened the present to reveal a piece of wire twisted painstakingly into the wavy fingers, trouser creases and joint bends of a realistic little wiggly man.

'Oh, Vinnie,' I said. 'It's lovely. Thank you so much.'

I showed it around the table, and everybody duly admired it. Only Sam had a slight frown furrowing her forehead. But Vinnie constantly gave me home-made presents, etchings and sculptures he'd done at college – a cute clay dinosaur with a rose in its snout, a hand-enamelled mirror – and I loved them. After years of receiving vacuously expensive corporate gifts as tokens of gratitude for making Ringside rich – cashmere dressing gowns, vintage wines, state-of-the-art audio equipment and so on – Vinnie's little trinkets touched me deeply.

Vinnie clicked his fingers to order another bottle of champagne. After further toasts to the future happiness of David and his new wife Cherry, Peter Gabriel for kindly coinciding his world tour with my birthday

– the reason Joe and David were in town as they were now employed as members of Gabriel's touring band – absent friends – Justin was making his second solo album in a studio in the Bahamas – and Vinnie for generally being wonderful, we ordered a third bottle and I cut the cake.

As we tucked in and Joe regaled us with tales of how sick-makingly in love David and Cherry were, Sam noticed that a table of older diners across the restaurant were looking askance at us.

'Do you think we're being too loud?' she asked worriedly when she could get a word in edgeways.

'Nah,' said Joe, who was in mid-flow, telling us a story about what the newly-weds had been discovered doing underneath the stage at Earls Court, much to Cherry's embarrassment. 'They probably just recognize us.'

At that moment one of their group, a middle-aged woman with overplucked eyebrows and a tight Jaeger banana-coloured suit, came up to our table and tapped me on the shoulder.

'Hi,' I said brightly to her. 'Would you like an autograph?'

She looked at me for a minute, as if I was being facetious. 'No,' she said. 'Thank you. The thing is, you see, it's my husband's birthday today, too, his fiftieth, and *that*', she pointed at the crumbs and slabs of icing, which was all that remained of the champagne cake, 'was his cake.'

'What do you mean?' I asked indignantly. 'My boyfriend brought it. Maybe yours was the same. Why don't you ask the waiter?'

The head waiter materialized immediately beside the woman. I felt, rather than saw, Vinnie squirming in his seat beside me.

'No, madame,' the waiter intoned sonorously. 'We were only in possession of one birthday cake. Unfortunately my junior waiter was not aware that there were *two* birthday parties taking place, and so when the signal was given for the cake to be brought out, he brought the cake to your table, when, in fact, it was intended for the other party.'

Everybody fell about laughing, and then looked at Vinnie.

'Hey, this isn't my fault,' he protested.

'Well, where's the cake you brought, then?' Sam demanded.

Vinnie lit a Gauloise and managed to blow smoke into the faces of both the head waiter and the cakeless woman.

'Thing is,' he said, 'when I said I'd organized it, what I meant was that I'd asked matey boy over there' – pointing at the greeter by the door, who suddenly became very engrossed in his reservations book – 'if he could sort us out with a piece of apple pie or something with a candle in it. You know, something to bring out for Helena so we could all sing. I was well chuffed when the other waiter appeared with this great cake. I thought, Wow! What a cool restaurant.'

We all slapped our hands against our foreheads, Homer Simpson-style, and a chorus of 'Doh's arose.

'Well, how was I to know that someone else was having a birthday?' Vinnie said to the head waiter. 'You should have been better organized, mate. It's not our fault if you bring out a cake to the wrong people. Here, let's see what we can do.'

He leaped up and went round all our plates, collecting the chunks of discarded icing, which had originally formed the label of the champagne bottle. Piecing them together on a side plate like a sugary jigsaw, he stuck a candle on top, lit it with his cigarette lighter, and, with a flourish, bounded across the room to present the cakeless candle to the birthday boy.

By this time the entire restaurant had ground to a standstill. Vinnie spread his arms wide, Gauloise still in mouth. 'Come on, everybody,' he shouted, and led all the diners in another round of 'Happy Birthday', sung lustily by himself, ourselves and the fiftieth-birthday party, grudgingly by everybody else, who were beginning to look at each other with we're-not-coming-here-again expressions, and not at all by the birthday boy's wife, who was furious.

I put my head in my hands and groaned, although I couldn't help laughing.

David leaned over the table. 'Quite a guy you got there, H,' he said affectionately. 'I'm glad you've met someone you like so much. He sure seems crazy about you, too. I hope it works out. You never were that lucky in love before, were you?'

'No. It's about time, isn't it? I'm pleased you've found your soulmate, too.'

I grinned at him and Cherry, clasping hands with each other across the debris of scrunched-up napkins and misappropriated cake crumbs.

'Thanks, Helena. I'm sorry we didn't invite you to our wedding, but like I said, we just slipped away to Barbados on the quiet. You should try it. Married life is awesome.'

'Maybe we will, some day,' I said. 'You guys are certainly a good advertisement for it.'

Eventually the fuss was smoothed over. The head waiter, a muscle twitching violently in his cheek, was forced to offer the fiftieth-birthday-party desserts on the house, and several free bottles of champagne, and I thought it was probably time to ask for our table's bill.

'It's my birthday, I'm treating everybody,' I said when Sam and David began to protest.

I paid up, and Vinnie courteously helped me into my coat.

'There you go, old lady,' he said, kissing my cheek. 'Have you had a good time, despite the, er, unfortunate incident?'

I nodded. 'Fantastic, thanks. And even if you didn't get it together to actually *bring* a cake, thanks for organizing someone else's for me. It'll be a great story to tell our grandchildren, don't you think?'

'Mmm,' said Vinnie, tilting my head back for a huge, passionate birthday kiss, and wrapping his arms tightly around my waist.

'I love you, Vin,' I said when I came up for air.

'Love you, too, Helena,' he replied for the first time ever.

I grinned and hugged him triumphantly. 'You staying over tonight?'

Vinnie looked at his watch, a Rolex I'd given him for his birthday two months earlier. 'Can't, angel. I really have to get back and work on that project I'm in the middle of.'

'But it's my birthday!'

Vinnie kissed me again. 'Sorry. See you tomorrow, OK, baby?'

Sam looked hard at me. 'He doesn't stay round at your place much, does he?'

Two weeks later we found out why.

Sam and I had gone to Richmond Park on a warm September day, for a picnic. I'd thought of asking Vinnie to join us, but then I remembered him telling me that he'd been enlisted to help his friend Ivan lay a patio that afternoon, but would see me that night at seven to accompany me to a rare function: a dinner party I'd been invited to at Ron's house.

I'd secretly been relieved that Vinnie was busy. Even though I was looking forward to the dinner party, I was feeling quite stressed about the prospect of meeting lots of strangers, and I just wanted a chilled-out afternoon in the sun. Sam and Vinnie would only have sniped at each other; they'd never got on all that well, and it was getting worse. Sam made snide comments about his new Paul Smith suit, his penchant for meals at tiny, very exclusive restaurants and his sudden urgent need for expensive equipment for his art course: computers, scanners, cameras, videos and the like. All paid for by me.

'It's my money,' I'd say defensively to Sam. 'I like spending it on Vinnie.'

I could tell she didn't want to make too much of an issue out of it, in case I thought she was jealous that I wasn't spending it on *her*. I didn't think that at all. In fact, I was touched by her concern; I just thought it was entirely misguided.

So that day it was a joy, as well as a relief, to have Sam all to myself. Since my birthday she'd been feeling a bit low and unwell, and I was terrified that her ill-health might presage the return of her leukaemia.

'It's definitely not that,' she insisted as she unpacked the picnic hamper. 'I promise you, Helena, it isn't. I've been working too hard, that's all, and my lungs are playing up from the graft-versus-host. Plus it's so depressing being dumped for "not being enough fun".'

Timothy had recently decided that he didn't require a girlfriend who went to bed exhausted at nine o'clock practically every night, and Sam had taken it badly.

'Timothy's just a shallow loser, if that's all he cares about,' I said, as I put a compilation tape into the boom box I'd brought with us. My feelings for Timothy were on a par with Sam's feelings for Vinnie. I'd only tolerated him at my birthday party because Sam had wanted him there.

I spread out an Indian throw under a tree in a secluded part of the park, away from all the families biking down the yellow gravel paths and the hesitant children on horseback. Our nearest neighbours were a couple snogging near the next cluster of trees, about fifty feet away, and a father flying a kite with his young son on our other side.

'I'm sorry, though, Sam, I know how much he meant to you. I'll throttle him, if I ever see him again, for putting you through all this. Here, have a sarnie – I made your favourites, look, peanut butter and pickle.'

Sam reclined on a cushion, half-heartedly toying with her sandwich, as we spent an intense hour analysing in excruciating detail every single word and gesture of Timothy's, trying to deconstruct the whys and wherefores of rejection.

'Do you know,' Sam said afterwards, 'I really feel like going away for a bit, somewhere really relaxing. I'm owed some holiday. Fancy coming to Greece with me for a week? Santorini's meant to be amazing. We could get one of those last-minute deals.'

I was delighted, until I thought of the prospect of being without Vinnie for that long. 'Hmm, maybe once Vinnie's term starts again,' I said, pouring us each another glass of wine.

Sam tutted irritably. She wasn't used to me not jumping at the chance of having her company. With a start, I realized that I wasn't used to it, either.

'Oh, come on, Helena. Please. It wouldn't be the same without you, and we haven't been on holiday for ages. Hey, this is good,' she added, turning up the volume on the tape. 'What is it?'

'Just a compilation I made. This track's quite old, from 1992, a band called Spill, who are William Orbit and Beth Orton. Brilliant, isn't it? I'll let you know about Santorini. I must say, I've always fancied going there, too.'

I lay down on my back beside Sam, and we watched the clouds float across the sky as the music drifted over us.

'This sky reminds me of a little poem I wrote once, when I started writing song lyrics. You know, when I was going through that religious phase.'

'Can you remember it?'

'Um, hang on, let me think . . .'

I paused for a while, trying to recall the words. Sam sniggered and pointed over to the lovers by the trees.

'Look at them; talk about hot 'n' heavy. They'll have completely ripped off each other's clothes in a minute.'

The couple were indeed horizontal, him on top of her, bumping and grinding and rolling around. I was temporarily distracted from my poem, remembering the similar behaviour Vinnie and I had indulged in the previous night.

Sam sighed. 'I'll probably never have sex again. Life sucks. So, quick, tell me your poem before I get consumed with depression.'

I cleared my throat dramatically. 'OK, here goes: "Christians kiss with their eyes closed, he said with a sigh/Rolling over to watch heavy clouds drag by./I smiled, and opened one eye."'

Sam grinned. 'I prefer your later stuff,' she said.

She sat up and helped herself to some broccoli quiche. Suddenly she froze, napkin in hand, and her triangle of quiche fell into her lap.

'Bloody hell, I don't believe it,' she said, staring into the middle distance.

'What?'

'Oh,' she said, collecting herself and picking up crumbs of pastry. 'Nothing. I just thought of something I forgot to do.'

I sat up, too. Her tone didn't fool me for a minute.

'*What?*'

Sam shook her head. 'I'm sure it's nothing, but, for a minute I thought that was Vinnie over there.'

I laughed, and looked over at the almost-copulating couple. They were sitting up now, rearranging their clothes and still kissing. The girl looked Oriental, with beautiful long silky black hair. The guy had his back to us.

'No, of course it's not,' I said. 'He's about the same build, though. I can see how you thought it was.'

Then they stood up, folded their travel rug and began to walk, hand in hand, towards us, presumably on their way to the car park.

Within ten paces I saw that it was indeed Vinnie.

My peanut-butter sandwich stuck to the roof of my mouth, and my head whirled with disbelief and panic.

'It can't be,' I whispered thickly. 'There must be some mistake. Perhaps he has an evil twin.'

'Has he?' asked Sam hopefully, her hand grasping my arm.

'No.'

They were getting closer and closer, their heads leaning together, laughing and tickling each other in a nauseatingly lovey-dovey manner. I felt sick. I picked up our quarter-full wine bottle.

'What are you going to do?' Sam looked alarmed.

At that moment, Vinnie glanced over and spotted me. Without breaking his stride, he wheeled round at a ninety-degree angle and steered the Oriental girl away from us, towards the opposite end of the distant car park. He didn't look back, although I sensed a definite tenseness in the way he held the hairy travel rug under his arm.

I took a deep swig of the Pinot Grigio.

'Oh, Helena. I'm so sorry. Are you all right? You've gone really white.'

Sam hugged me hard, partly, I thought, to prevent me leaping up and bottling Vinnie from behind.

'Men, eh?' she continued, with feeling. 'Can't live with 'em, can't shoot 'em.' She looked anxiously at me. I was still silent. 'He's a bastard. Better you found out now than later. Is that the girl he shares a house with?'

I said nothing, but tears welled in my eyes.

'Speak to me, Helena, please.' Sam shook me gently.

I looked at her and took a long, deep breath. 'When can we go to Santorini, then?'

'As soon as we book somewhere to stay?'

'Fine.'

I'd been sure that was the last I'd see of Vinnie, and I was heartbroken. I intended to phone Ron and pull out of the dinner party that night, but Sam nagged me until I agreed to go anyway. She said, rightly, that Ron was new in my life – I'd recently hired him with a vague idea of getting some of my old songs remixed by hot new producers, although nothing had come of it thus far – so it wouldn't do to let him know how antisocial I really was.

Plus, I might meet a new man there – not that I wanted one. Plus, I so rarely went to those sorts of functions. Plus, I was a professional. Plus, it would be good to have something to take my mind off Vinnie, etc., etc. I eventually caved in. I'd bought a new dress to wear, the cab was booked, I'd even been looking forward to it, albeit with trepidation.

Sam declined the offer to come with me, pleading fatigue, but she stayed long enough to zip up my dress and do my hair, before she drove back to her flat for another night in watching *Casualty* and wondering who Timothy was out having fun with. She'd been gone about five minutes, and I was just putting on my lip liner, when there was a hammering at the front door.

Assuming she'd changed her mind, I ran down the stairs and flung open the door, lip pencil in hand.

Of course it was Vinnie, standing there all spruced up and clean-shaven, clutching a bottle of wine.

I was flabbergasted. I stood there, open-mouthed, as he grinned jauntily at me. 'Don't forget to colour in the rest,' he said, gesturing towards my outlined lips. 'Right, what time are we off?'

I hung on to the door frame, blinking in disbelief and fury. 'You have got to be fucking joking.'

Vinnie had the gall to look surprised.

'Is it cancelled? What are you all dressed up for, then?'

I was approaching meltdown. 'How *dare* you!' I spoke through gritted teeth. 'I can't believe your nerve, I really can't. You were all over some whore in Richmond Park this afternoon. How could you think I'd ever want to clap eyes on you again after seeing that? Just get lost, and don't bother coming back.'

Vinnie slapped the side of his head, as if he'd forgotten that he'd snogged someone else in front of me only hours earlier.

'Oh, you mean Miyuki. Man, we weren't all over each other. We're just house mates. You know, old friends.' He paused. 'You saw us walking through the park together, didn't you? Hey, you should have called out; I'd have introduced you.'

Miraculously, I stayed relatively calm, i.e., I didn't actually kill him. 'No, Vinnie, I didn't *just* see you walking through the park. I saw you lying on top of her, dry-humping like a terrier on heat. I saw you suck the face off her. I saw you whisper sweet nothings in her ear. And now I learn that you live with her, too! Please don't insult me by telling me you're just friends. God, it's so obvious now. No wonder you never liked to be seen out with me; no wonder you said you were "embarrassed" by what a mess your house is.'

Vinnie grinned. 'Listen, it's fine. She doesn't mind if I see other women, honestly. She's cool.'

That really was the final straw. To my utter disgust and humiliation, I burst into tears. 'I MIND!' I bawled.

I was about to slam the door in his face and retire to bed with a bottle of vodka when a black cab bumped along the path outside the front gate, tooting at me. There was no way I was going to let Vinnie see he'd ruined my evening as well as my life.

Mustering what vestiges of dignity I could, I snuffled, 'Excuse me, I have a dinner party to attend,' and shot back in the house to grab my make-up and handbag. Ron lived in Highgate, so I had a good long cab ride ahead of me in which to apply enough slap to disguise the fact that I'd been crying.

I locked the front door behind me, ignoring the fact that Vinnie was still standing outside the porch.

'Have a nice life, asshole.' I hiccuped, as I barged past him, grabbing the bottle of wine from his arms on the way.

It was only once I was barrelling safely around the North Circular, having just about managed to repair the damage to my face, that I looked at the bottle I'd purloined from Vinnie. It was Blue Nun.

I left it in the taxi.

*   *   *

It must have been a remnant of the discipline I'd learned in Blue Idea, the same consummate professionalism that had got me through a gruelling national tour knowing that Sam was lying in a hospital bed, but I was *great* that night. Vinnie's betrayal had at least one positive effect: it swept aside all my qualms about meeting new people.

From the moment I sat down at the snowy linen and sparkling crystal-set table in Ron's house – which was ultra-modern, architect-designed and overlooked the cemetery; it had a very public-toiletesque exterior, but was beautiful inside – I was on top form, caring about nothing, allowing my wineglass to be filled repeatedly. I didn't even feel ashamed for not bringing a bottle myself; I told Ron I'd left it in the taxi. He waved away my apology with a flourish of his napkin.

I knew I was a hit, and I loved it. Suddenly I wondered why on earth I didn't get out more, and why I'd wasted yet another year waiting for Vinnie's infrequent attentions.

The other guests were Clint, Ron's young boyfriend, who wrote screenplays and was an absolute sweetheart, and a couple called Maggie and Gus – she worked for Reuters and he was deputy programme director for a London radio station called New World, which I never listened to. I apologized profusely for Vinnie's absence, and told them he'd caught a nasty stomach bug from eating some dodgy shellfish and hadn't been off the toilet for the past five hours. Wishful thinking.

Gus and Ron had been at university together. 'Isn't she fabulous? Didn't I tell you she was awesome?' Ron kept saying to Gus about me, and Gus kept nodding until Maggie looked quite annoyed and stabbed her fork into her *champignons farcies* with enough force to make Gus desist.

Over the course of the evening, in answer to their

377

questions, I told them all about Blue Idea: what it had been like, how we'd got our first deal, how it felt to be in front of a crowd of thousands, what I missed about it, what I'd loathed about it. How I managed to remember it all so well.

I told them that most of the key events of my life had been remembered through the songs that had been in the background, the 'soundtrack to my life'; not Blue Idea songs, because so much work and sweat and tedium went into perfecting each of those, but other people's songs, the ones that struck me deep down, in a way I knew I'd never forget.

'I have a theory, right?' I said, elbows on the table, on my second glass of Beaume de Venise. 'If I were a DJ, I would only play the records that had done that for other people, because, if you think about it, it's rarely the completely crappy songs which people remember and weep over for years to come. My theory is, say something totally momentous happens to you when you're listening to the radio, for example, you open a letter saying you've won a million pounds. If the particular record being played at that moment is, say, 'Agadoo', then you just forget that you even had the radio switched on. But if it's something brilliant, like, 'Life On Mars', then for ever afterwards you associate that song with winning the money, and get all nostalgic when you hear it.'

Ron joined in with Gus on the enthusiastic nods, and handed round the After Eights.

I was on a roll. 'So I reckon if you got people to ring in with the songs that mean something to them, then you'd have a fair chance of getting a decent show. Of course you'd have a few morons saying they'd lost their virginity to 'The Birdie Song' or whatever, but anyone who has that as their favourite song probably isn't articulate enough to ring into a radio station and request it. Because that's the other thing' – I quickly checked that everyone's eyes weren't completely glazed over, but they were all still agog – 'it wouldn't

378

be enough to just make a request; I'd make them explain why the record meant so much to them. In detail. Right down to what colour underwear they were wearing that night. And if they couldn't remember exactly what was going on, then I wouldn't believe the record could be that important to them.'

'Take today,' I plunged on recklessly. 'I was in the park, having a picnic with my best friend Sam, when we saw', at the last minute my sense of circumspection thankfully returned, 'her boyfriend kissing another woman.'

Tuts and sighs rippled around the table.

'We were playing a tape at the time, a song Sam hadn't heard before, but which she'd just told me she really liked.'

'Which one?' interrupted Clint curiously.

'Spill, "Don't Wanna Know Bout Evil",' I said impatiently, wanting to get on with the story.

Clint swooned theatrically. 'Oh, I just love that record. The old John Martyn song, isn't it?'

I hadn't known that, but I didn't want to admit my ignorance.

'Yeah, yeah. So, anyway, I reckon that if Sam hadn't liked the song, she wouldn't even have known we'd been listening to music at the time. But since she did, I'd put money on the fact that for ever more, when . . . Sam thinks of her lousy, two-timing *dickhead* of a boyfriend' – I may have thumped the table at that point – 'she'll think of that song and watching clouds and eating quiche and how prickly the grass felt, and she'll feel really, really sad and hurt and betrayed.'

I was about to have to leave the room to go and splash cold water on my face when Gus spoke. 'How would you fancy a job on New World, as a DJ on the evening session?'

The salty tension which had been building inside the bridge of my nose suddenly disappeared.

'Pardon?' I asked, clutching the tablecloth. Now

they were all nodding, like it was catching, and beaming moronically at me.

'We've got a slot opening up soon. I think you'd be perfect for it.'

'But I don't know how to DJ,' I burbled.

'Don't worry, you'll learn. We'll train you up before you start. The main thing is, your music knowledge is great, your name is already well-known and you've got a great new idea for a show.'

I was astounded. 'I have?'

'Yes, definitely. A kind of confessional request show? I think it would be terrific. What do you say?'

After three seconds thinking about it, I finally joined in with the nodding. 'OK. Why not?'

Thinking About God and Toby

I lay in bed late one humid night, uncomfortable on a creased-up, fusty sheet which I hadn't bothered to change for weeks, and drowsy from the pill I'd had to take to make me sleep. I had taken off my eye patch, and was tracing the stitched-up socket where my eye had been. The skin had healed, but it was twisted and velvety, like a stick-on scar, and the absence of my eyeball made the space feel concave and hollow. I marvelled at how even I had kind of managed to become accustomed to being one-eyed; like anything else, it was a process of adjustment. A bit like having contact lenses really, you eventually just get used to fiddling about with sterilizing fluids and screw-top containers, intermittently blurred vision and the ever-present fear of a lens popping out at an inopportune moment. Not that anything could pop out of my sealed-up eye socket now, but the rigmarole of adjusting eye patches and being vigilant about not bumping into lamp-posts was vaguely comparable. Having to pay attention to one's vision instead of taking it for granted.

Although I was getting used to it, it didn't prevent me loathing and detesting the fact that my eye was gone. I wished fancifully that it would just come back, the way my mislaid hearing had, but it never would, and nor would Sam. Or Toby. It surprised me that I was still thinking about him after the beery débâcle, but I was, albeit with a lot more reservations and a lot less expectations.

It was 2 a.m. and, despite the pill, I still couldn't get to sleep. I wondered if I ought to say a prayer and ask for some sort of spiritual guidance and healing, what with my hour of need being at hand and all. But I couldn't do it. Somehow it didn't seem to work any more. It wasn't that I ever stopped believing in God; He just didn't seem to be around very much.

Perhaps I'd got too confused over the years. I'd briefly dabbled in so many different esoteric and spiritual practices that the easy faith I'd gobbled up in high school had been usurped by something more, well, *cool*. It wasn't cool to think of God as a white-bearded man peering anxiously down at us from his cloud. God was a spark of pure light. God was an essence. God was all around us. God was inside me. God was an energy. I'd had so many different people tell me what God was, or wasn't, that I no longer knew what to think.

I wanted to ask Him to help me, only I didn't know to whom to address my enquiry. Angels didn't seem senior enough somehow, and Jesus seemed too busy. It was a dilemma. But, apropos The Plan, I didn't think God would kick me out if I suddenly turned up on the Other Side prematurely. Whether He was big or small, cloudy or solid, I was sure He would understand. That idea about suicides being eternally damned was a medieval concept; I'd read that somewhere. Besides, Blue Idea had given tons of cash to charity, surely that would stand me in good stead. I might have a bit of extra karma to work off, like calories after Christmas, but it would be a small price to pay to see Sam again, and to not feel this emptiness any more.

It was quite funny, really. I could still recite all twenty-six lines of the Creed, faultlessly. I knew how to chant Nam-Myoho-Renge-Kyo until my voice turned into white noise. I could do the Yang Style T'ai Chi long form and the yogic sun salutation. I'd wrapped myself in white robes and meditated in silence for hours, and been put in touch with my angels – right before they took early retirement, apparently.

The only thing I still didn't know how to do was to get anybody, or anything, to help me cope with what I was currently going through. When I thought about religion, I felt like a tourist trying to buy a 50p pencil sharpener in the Harrods sale while being shoved to the back of the queue by diplomats' wives waving Platinum Amex cards: overlooked and invisible. I was in the right shop, but all the shop assistants were busy swiping credit cards, or standing about examining their fingernails and ignoring me.

I supposed I should have gone back to that therapist, the one who visited me in hospital, but therapy wasn't what I wanted. It was too rational, somehow, and I was afraid I'd end up getting talked out of The Plan. End up calm, but forgotten. No, no, that would be no good.

After I finally got to sleep, I dreamed about Salisbury Cathedral, and Toby and Ruby. They were adjudicating a Great Continental Quilt Bobsleigh Race between two teams: me and Sam versus Vinnie and Sam's ex, Timothy. The event was being held in the Cathedral Close, on the long stretch of smooth grey path outside the West Front.

Toby sat on a big throne in the cathedral doorway, wearing a bishop's mitre, and Ruby sat on his right-hand side in a fetching sparkly crown. As we raced past them, I relived the feeling of thrilled fear I'd always got when Sam and I used to play there as kids: that all the stone saints and gargoyles looking down from their ledges, drains and corners would actually come tumbling off on top of me, and that the whole towering stone façade would topple down and crush me at will. It was as much a sensation of respect as fear; the power of the building pouring into and through me.

Sam and I beat Vinnie and Timothy to the finish line.

'Well done, you're the winners!' Ruby said graciously to us. 'Here's your prizes. You' – pointing a magic wand at Sam – 'get six mini packets of Smarties, and you' – pointing at me – 'get a lifetime supply of being my mummy.'

I was delighted.

I woke up freezing cold, with my duvet on the floor and a fresh pack of memories of the cathedral shuffling around inside my head, sharp as knives, summoned by the dream. As I wrapped myself up in the chilly quilt, I turned the cards over in my head before me, one by one. I was surprised at how many there were. Even at eight or nine years old, Sam and I used to love going on guided tours up the cathedral tower, retracing the steps the drunken shepherd must have taken before he made his maiden flight.

Memories of walking outside along the cathedral roof's base, knowing that its waterproof lead coverings heated up in summer and became soft to the touch of our small fingers, as though the roofs were all lagged with giant slabs of grey toffee.

Memories of looking up the tower, from the inside now, and seeing the criss-crossing scaffolding of thick oak rafters jumbled together, the veins and supporting arteries of the spire getting closer and tighter as you neared the top, a giant pyramidal bird's nest of twigs the thickness of a man's torso.

Memories of climbing from ground level, up and up the tiny winding steps carved into the thickness of the walls, round and round until we felt dizzy with vertigo and the joys of a secret hidden place.

Memories of daylight filtering into the narrow stair-wells from arrow-slit windows, throwing weak dusty stripes of light on our faces.

That's odd, I thought. All those memories and no accompanying song anywhere, not even the vague low chants of the cathedral choir singing matins. It felt like watching television with the sound turned down.

* * *

The other effect of my dream was that I couldn't stop thinking about Toby. If Bill had been telling the truth, that Toby really was mad about me, then I owed it to him to see him just once more. I'd retrieved from my car the receipt with his sister's address scrawled on it, and had put it into the Hel-Sam Box for safe keeping. The receipt was still scrunched into a ball about the size of a hazelnut, and I was putting off unwrapping it until every other part of The Plan was ready.

Although I didn't know them very well, Toby and Ruby were going to be the hardest people to leave behind, because they represented the only part of my life that might possibly look to the future.

'I Can't Stand The Rain'
Ann Peebles

Our trip to Santorini ended up being postponed until the following Spring, not only because of my new career as a DJ, but also because Sam started feeling iller and iller. Within five months she'd had to leave her job and move back to the basement flat in her parents' home in Salisbury again. She got a part-time position at a local solicitors' office, but even that was a strain. Every time I talked to her she sounded more wheezy and exhausted. She qualified for a disabled parking sticker, started popping an array of day-glo tablets and had to embark on a programme of physiotherapy to try and clear her malfunctioning lungs.

I was worried sick. If it hadn't been for the job, I would have moved to Wiltshire to be with her, but by that time I'd been promoted to the breakfast show, and had to get up at five o'clock every morning as it was. Commuting, even in my new 5-series BMW, would have been a nightmare. Instead I sped down to Salisbury as often as I could at weekends, taking her tapes of my best shows from the previous week and entertaining her with stories of who I'd met, how the New World ratings were going up, what songs I had played and for whom.

I did believe that I'd dumped Vinnie for good, but somehow, when he turned up on my doorstep again a few weeks later, wheedling me with stolen roses and come-to-bed eyes, telling me that I was the only one he'd ever really loved – well, I just couldn't resist him. I made it clear that I'd never trust him again, but strangely that didn't seem to worry him in the slightest.

He had moved out of the house with Miyuki – 'Been thrown out, more likely,' Sam said – and was staying with another 'friend' until he 'found his feet' – 'Tell him that they're on the ends of his legs,' suggested Sam wheezily. I immediately realized that he was angling to move in with me, but to my boundless relief I stayed strong enough to refuse him. If it hadn't been for the memory of him and Miyuki rolling around in the park, Vinnie would have had his misplaced feet planted firmly underneath my table; at least that was something for which to be thankful. We contented ourselves with frequent sex and no questions asked. When I thought too deeply about it, it broke my heart, but I was too busy with New World and Sam to allow myself to take it too seriously.

By Spring of the following year I felt established enough at New World to risk taking a week off. I had spotted nine 'Helena Let Me Tell London My Song' bumper stickers on my way home from the show that morning, plus I'd just had a very complimentary review in the media section of the *Independent*. Sam wasn't getting better, but she was no worse, either, and we both really needed some sun and a change of scenery.

'Come on then,' I said to her on the phone. 'Pack your bikini, we're off on vacation. I'll drive down and collect you on Wednesday morning. Be ready by ten.'

At ten thirty the following Wednesday, Sam and I were heading back up to Heathrow to catch an afternoon flight to Athens, from where we'd fly on to Santorini. My car was full of things to maximize Sam's comfort: cushions to support her bony ass on the plane, a borrowed hospital wheelchair to help conserve her limited energy, enough medication to start a small pharmacy and her own feather pillows. I wondered how she had suddenly managed to turn into an invalid, and it made my throat swell with sorrow.

It was a beautiful April day, and we decided to take the scenic route to the airport. Being on tour, with all those years of bleak American highways, had always made me thirsty for the English countryside, so I drank in every bright yellow acre of rape, the green of the patchwork fields and the arches of tree branches overhanging the smooth, arrow-straight roads.

Sam was uncharacteristically quiet for most of the drive. At one point she switched on the radio, tuning it to Radio 1 just as the DJ announced, 'Next up, that classic song which stormed the charts six years ago – seems like only yesterday – the fabulous Blue Idea, with "Take Me Away" . . .' I laughed and cringed a little as the synth intro started up, joined by my bass and then Justin's high-pitched voice, as familiar as my own skin.

'Turn it off, turn it off!' I cried. 'Radio One is banned from this car.'

Sam refused. 'Don't be a spoilsport. You know New World doesn't reach out to the sticks.' She cracked a smile for the first time that day. 'It's funny, but I still get such a thrill when I hear you on the radio or see you on TV; even after all these years I still want to yell out to everyone, "Hey, that's my best friend!"'

And even after all those years I was still pleased.

After a couple of miles speeding along a deserted Roman road, littered with the tiny corpses of squirrels, pheasants and rabbits, the Blue Idea song finished, and was replaced by a dreary interview with a techno band. I clicked off the radio again, and slid my Ann Peebles CD into the stereo to listen to the title track, 'I Can't Stand The Rain'. I was humbled by how far superior that song was to ours; her creamy vocals, the pounding rhythm and the passion of the incredible

Memphis Horns. It made 'Take Me Away' sound like a weedy little preprogrammed tune on a cheap Bontempi organ. Sex versus impotence. Scotch on the rocks versus orange squash through a straw.

I sang along, but Sam was silent again. I sensed something brewing in her, and waited for her to tell me about it.

We barrelled through yet another tiny picturesque village, this one with a quirky little square church tower peeping over the rooftops, with pinnacles on only three of its four top corners.

Sam finally spoke. 'There's something I need to tell you.' She turned down the volume on the CD.

'I thought so. What is it?'

There was a brief pause over the top of the muted Memphis Horns.

'I didn't say anything to you before, but I saw my specialist at the hospital yesterday. My lungs aren't ever going to get better on their own. In fact, they're packing up. He says I'm going to need a lung transplant.'

I got a funny swimmy feeling in my head, and had to grip the steering wheel hard. All I could think of to say was, 'When?'

'Whenever I decide to go on the waiting list, and then as soon as they find a donor. That could be three days or three years.'

The swimmy feeling turned into a sick feeling. 'One lung or two?' I asked, as if I was at some surreal organ-donors' tea party.

Sam laughed, catching my thought, but she had tears in her eyes. 'Just one should do the trick.'

I didn't want to ask, but I couldn't *not* ask. 'What's the success rate for this . . . kind of thing?'

'If you mean what are my chances, the survival rate is about forty per cent in the first year.'

This figure whirled around my brain for a while in a useless way, not sticking anywhere, like the algebraic formulas we had to do at school. I didn't understand what it meant, and this time I didn't ask. It didn't sound at all promising to me.

'But do you *have* to do it?' I was almost pleading.

'No, not immediately. But I should do it before I get too weak to cope with the operation. If I don't have it done eventually I'll probably die.'

She sounded so calm, but also slightly numb, as if it hadn't yet sunk in. Her last statement shocked me even more. I knew it wasn't good, but I hadn't realized her health had got *that* bad. I suppose I hadn't wanted to realize.

We were out of the village, but suddenly the countryside looked drab and uninteresting. I pulled the car into a lay-by, buried my face in my hands and burst into tears.

'Oh, don't, please,' Sam said. 'You'll start me off.'

But she didn't cry. She stroked my shoulder as if it was my life under threat, and then pulled out a packet of fruit Polos, offering me one. 'Go on, it's red, your favourite.'

I took the Polo, but I couldn't look at her. It was too painful to think that something might go wrong and I'd never see her again. The sharp sweetness of the Polo hit the back of my tongue, and I clung to the taste like someone had thrown it to me, a mini red lifebelt.

I tried hard to think of what I'd learned over the years, in my various flirtations with different sorts of spirituality: Christianity, Buddhism, Transcendental Meditation. They all said the same thing, that the soul was eternal, and death of the body meant nothing, not in the grand scheme of things. But not Sam's body! Sam's body had *Sam* inside it.

Cars whizzed past us intermittently in a whining crescendo of painted metal and engine noise, the wake of their momentum making my BMW rock slightly.

Sam leaned her head on my shoulder. 'Listen, Helena, I'm not going to go on the list just yet. I'm going to think about it for a while and then decide. In the meantime I really want to enjoy this holiday, OK?'

'OK.' I blew my nose, and after a minute we drove off again. I still felt stunned, but I tried to be optimistic, to look at it as a piece of good news.

'Just think what you'll be able to do with a new lung – run, swim, *shop*. It'll change your life totally. I'll make you get up early with me and help me with the show. In fact, why don't you come and live in my house with me?'

'I hate getting up early. And thanks for the offer, but there's no way I'm moving in with you if Vinnie's still on the scene,' said Sam grumpily, taking advantage of my vulnerability.

'Then he's history, *definitely* this time. I would happily never see him again, for you to be better and close by. Oh God, Sam, it would be so wonderful to have you back to your old self.'

Sam sighed. 'What is my old self? I really can't remember.'

It was late that evening when we finally got settled in our apartment in Santorini, which was basically a luxuriously furnished cave, carved out of the side of the cliff. Even in the dusk we could tell it was utterly beautiful, but it was also probably the world's most unwheelchair-friendly place. There was a short but very windy walk up steps and round corners from the road to the apartment, so I left Sam and her wheelchair waiting by the car while I puffed up and down the path with all our stuff. When I'd finished I was sweating like a cart horse, and worried that it might finish me off altogether to have to give Sam a piggy back, but thankfully she was able to walk unassisted. She collapsed peakily on one of the beds as soon as we made it through the door.

'Why didn't you rent an apartment that we needed to abseil down to? At least that might have been less tiring to reach.'

She wasn't cross, just being sarky, but I still felt stricken.

'I'm sorry, Sam, really. The brochure made out that it was just by the road. I had no idea.'

'Oh, don't worry. It's just nice to be here. Let's sleep on it, so I've got the energy to face some retsina and sunshine tomorrow.'

We did very little that holiday, except lie on our begonia-bright terrace, gawping at the stunning view around the dramatic horseshoe-shaped cliffs and over the black volcanic island. Sunset was our favourite time. We sat companionably in our deckchairs in the charged silence as the massive sky before us changed into every outlandish shade of red we could imagine. The volcano got blacker, the clouds pinker, and finally the sun slunk down in a blaze of orange into the dark Aegean waters of the caldera. It was so far away from everything: perfidious boyfriends, the sound of my voice echoing out of cafés, cabs and offices all across London, scarred lungs. To both of our delight, Sam felt better that week than she'd been for a long time.

'It's all the negative ions in the air from the volcano,' I informed her one evening when we were out for a 'walk' – I was pushing Sam in her wheelchair. 'Apparently the health benefits are well documented. It says so in the guidebook.'

'Wish we could stay for longer,' she said wistfully as I propelled her chair, with difficulty, up the steep and ill-kept road, struggling womanfully until we got to the brow of the hill.

'Me, too. But I tell you what, healthy, it might be; flat, it ain't,' I puffed, before deciding that perhaps we shouldn't go down the other side as I might not be able to control the speed of our descent.

I laughed out loud as something occurred to me. 'Hey, Sam, this reminds me of The Great Continental Quilt Bobsleigh Race. You know, heaving like mad to get into position, then losing all control on the corners and down the stairs. We nearly killed ourselves!'

'Oh God, yes. I used to be so terrified when you were

dragging the quilt, but I couldn't get enough of it. Hey, how about a quick turn down the hill now? I'll sit on your lap in the chair!'

I started protesting, horrified at the thought, until I saw she was laughing. I gave her a friendly slap on the shoulder, and we looked out at the beautiful view of the sun shimmering across the flat turquoise sea instead; an act much more befitting our age and status.

Later that evening, with both of us glowing pink from the day's sunshine, we polished off a bottle of retsina and were flicking olive stones off the balcony wall in the hopes of starting our own cliffside olive grove.

'We need more wine and some music.' I jumped up and ran to fetch a CD and a fresh bottle. 'I want to hear Ann Peebles again.'

I came back out with my Discman, setting it on the wall next to us and inserting the CD. The introduction to 'I Can't Stand The Rain' quivered, somewhat more tinnily than from my deluxe car stereo, out of the tiny little Discman speakers, filling the ionized air around us.

'John Lennon thought this was one of the greatest songs ever,' I started to say, but about halfway through the sentence my voice stuck and unexpected tears flooded my eyes.

'What's the matter?' Sam asked with alarm.

I shook my head and gesticulated at the Discman. I found that I had just proved my own theory of music and memory. 'I forgot we were listening to this song when you told me about your lung transplant.'

I knew at that point that whenever I heard Willie Mitchell's orchestrated drum 'raindrops' at the start of that song, I would always relive the feeling of driving through a Hampshire village with the trees in bud, and Sam telling me that she had to have a life-threatening operation.

We sat listening to the track in silence, holding hands, me dripping tears all over the begonias. It was such an instinctive reaction: 'I Can't Stand The Rain' equalled tears.

Eventually Sam opened the new bottle of retsina. 'Come on, get some more of this down you. Let's enjoy life while we can, eh? Nobody else can do it for us. It's too short to waste.'

I nodded, held out my glass and swiped my hand over my face.

'I tell you what, Helena,' she added. 'You don't half cry a lot, for an international pop star.' She grinned at me.

I gulped down half the contents of my glass. I wasn't sure whether I was quite ready to be teased or not, but the strong bite of the retsina reassured me that perhaps I was.

'Hey, you know me.' I managed to grin back. 'Some people have weak bladders, I have weak tear ducts. It's a quirk of nature, that's all. Top me up again, would you?'

Sam obliged, and this time we clinked glasses in a toast.

'To enjoying life.'

My other enduring memory from Santorini came on a day when Sam had been feeling a little tired and had decided not to venture away from our terrace. I had set off alone, to find a swimming spot I'd heard about right at the bottom of the cliffs, at the highest point of the island.

I wound my way down 300-odd shallow and uneven steps, overtaken constantly by knock-kneed donkeys bowing under the weight of lazy tourists, to sea-level, past a neat little sea-front bar and round a corner. Here the path petered out, and I had to clamber over heaps of jagged rocks to a small secluded place where a group of locals and a few tourists in the know were sunbathing and diving off a selection of bigger, flatter rocks.

About twenty feet out to sea was a tiny island; less

an island, really, than one huge stone jutting out of the water. Perched on the side of it, facing the volcano, was a stone shrine, simple but beautiful, in the way that rural Greek architecture always is, merely an arch with a bell, a small altar and steps leading from a crude stone mooring place. I thought it was a shrine to the Virgin Mary, but I couldn't clearly remember.

What I did recall, though, was swimming out alone round the island to where the sea suddenly became deeper than I could possibly have imagined. This was where the volcano had blown out the centre of the main island some time during the second millennium BC. When I dived down even a few feet the water became much colder and darker, and it frightened me. I suddenly experienced a sensation of unutterable loneliness. It was as though I could feel the sadness of Santorini's bronze-age inhabitants as what they must surely have dreaded came to pass; in a vast, evil plume of molten lava their beautiful civilization was buried, frozen for ever in time. What was not blown up or covered in feet of pumice was flooded out by the sea, which rushed in to fill up the vacuum left by the collapse of the volcano's magma chamber.

In the silence of the water's depth I felt the grief of a lost people, perhaps even the mighty Atlantean race; this could conceivably have been the farthest western tip of Atlantis. The air was so vibrant there that anything seemed possible.

But being under the water was too frightening, too much like death, and I shot back up to the surface, to where I could once more hear my breath and feel the hot sun warm my chilled face. Seagulls wheeled reassuringly around my head, and I demisted and replaced my goggles before turning to swim back to the shore, unable to shake the feeling that something might grab at my legs from the ineffable depths. As I'd struck out for the rocks at a brisk crawl, my face alternately in the water and to the side for air, something caught my attention and I stopped. Just ahead of me a sharp ray of sun had pierced the water's surface and was shooting down through the blackness, lighting it like a laser beam. I put my face back down in the sea and stared at it underwater.

It was unspeakably beautiful. For the first fifteen feet or so, where the water was still light, it made an effervescing cauldron of blue-green with sparkling white speckles; intense, but the subtlest thing I'd ever seen. Then, as the water got darker, it ceased to have that transformative effect, but the ray itself kept penetrating as strongly as ever. I followed it with my eyes as far as I could, which appeared to be to the very centre of the earth. Its pull on me was so pure, so forceful that I could almost feel myself being sucked down, compelled to go with it. I *wanted* to go with it. At that moment I believed that never in my life had I felt so much joy, or so much peace. The black water was no longer threatening; it was a part of me.

It's OK to trust life, it seemed to tell me. Take it, it's yours. Don't waste it.

Sam was right, I thought, coming back up for air. It was all up to us as individuals. I was the only one who could make my life truly worthwhile, to find the value in what I had been given. I supposed I'd spent so many years being dependent on others for my success and happiness: our fans, Sam, Vinnie, even Ringside and Mickey, and now New World. It was time to be more self-sufficient. It was time to be myself.

'I Like Stings'

Seeing crystal lasers in the sea and believing everything would be all right was all well and good, but nothing was all right, was it? Sam was dead. Vinnie had betrayed me; I'd lost my eye and my job and the only person I felt remotely like seeing, apart from Sam, was Toby, but there hadn't been a peep out of him since the riverside débâcle.

Admittedly he didn't have my address or phone number, and he *had* been hanging around Richmond on the off-chance of seeing me, but that was pretty lame, as far as I was concerned. He could have found out that Ron was my agent easily enough, and contacted me that way. I concluded that, in the cold light of day, he'd probably decided he wasn't interested after all. But I still wanted to see him once more, even if just to say goodbye.

The manuscript was nearly finished, with just a couple more chapters to go, and I felt ready to tie up a few loose ends.

I was going to give Ruby the Hel-Sam Box.

I drove slowly through Fulham, peering at the street names until I found Larchfield Road. For some reason I had expected number twenty-seven to be a sizeable period house, not this narrow-shouldered anaemic cottage, sandwiched apologetically between two similar ones.

I parked badly a little way up the street, behind a large white van into whose bumper I reversed. Since losing my eye, my previously pristine BMW was acquiring more knocks and scratches than a toddler's knees. Still, who cared? I wasn't going to get sentimental about the bloody car.

I gathered up the Hel-Sam Box, locked the car and headed for the pale cottage, trying very hard to swallow down a bubble of excitement at seeing Toby again, despite the inauspicious circumstances of our last encounter. I'd have telephoned first, but there'd been so many creases in the balled-up receipt, when I'd finally picked it up from the floor of the car and straightened it out, that the scribbled phone number was illegible. I'd only just managed to decipher the address.

It was a strange feeling, being excited and suicidal. I hated using the word suicidal, but decided that it was about time I started to. It was a step towards making The Plan more than just typed words on a page and a playlist.

Another step was this meeting. I banged the door knocker twice, with a briskness I didn't feel inside, and waited to see Toby's familiar smile.

The door opened. A woman stood there; she was about my age, with Toby's eyes but a more angular face. She had a pierced eyebrow and the Middleton curls, only hers were dark brown.

'Are you Lulu?' I stuck out my hand to be shaken. 'I'm a friend of Toby's. Is he still living here? I'd have called, but you're ex-directory.' Nerves made me sound aggressive.

Lulu shook my hand, more of a twitch really, and stared at me. 'You're Helena Nicholls.' I couldn't tell if this was a good or a bad thing.

'Yeah.'

Lulu blushed suddenly, and I realized that she wasn't being unfriendly, but was phased by my sudden and unannounced appearance at her house.

'I'm sorry. Toby is still staying here, but he's away on business tonight. He had to go and meet a client in Dublin.'

'Oh.' I'd timed the visit for early evening with the assumption that Toby would have finished work, but I'd never considered that he might be away. I was such an idiot. 'Sorry to bother you, Lulu. I shouldn't have just turned up. Actually, I brought something for Toby to give Ruby. Can I leave it with you?'

We both looked down at the battered old hat box in my arms. Lulu's expression read, 'And you want to give *that* to Ruby?' I resisted the temptation to tell her that this was my last true link with Sam. My last true link with life.

'Ruby's here, though,' Lulu continued. 'She's just getting ready for bed. Why don't you come in and give it to her yourself?'

I tried and failed to smile, allowing Lulu to usher me into an open-plan living room. I was clutching the Hel-Sam Box tightly against my abdomen, its curves comforting me. When I released it there were speckles of glitter on my hands and down the front of my sweater. Grief made my head spin.

'Cool house,' I managed eventually, looking around. It was much more spacious inside than its exterior suggested, and beautifully decorated in muted, earthy shades. There was nothing extraneous, no clutter. Sting's voice drifted out of two state-of-the-art, hanging egg-shaped speakers. A staircase rose from the middle of the room, covered in a nubbly cream sisal carpet. 'It's hard to believe you have a small child staying with you.'

Lulu grinned. 'I've just tidied up.' She indicated a closed cupboard door with a jerk of her head. 'She's going home tomorrow, and I'll miss her, but I'm looking forward to having my social life back again. Would you like a drink? I was about to open a bottle of wine.'

'Thanks, I'd love one.'

Lulu headed towards the kitchen, stopping *en route*

at the foot of the stairs. 'Ruuuu-by! Can you come downstairs, please? You've got a visitor.' She turned back to me. 'Make yourself at home. I'll just go and get Ruby's milk, and the wine. Back in a second.'

'I cleaned my teeth,' said a small voice from the top of the stairs.

I walked over to the staircase and looked up. Ruby was sitting on the top step, a white tidemark of diluted toothpaste crusting around her mouth. Her hair had corkscrewed into a whole new layer of curls, and even her feet looked bigger. I was overjoyed to see her. 'I can see that you did. Aren't you clever? Will you come down and talk to me?'

Ruby bumped slowly down, step by step, on her bottom, until she was sitting at my feet. She was wearing red Teletubby slippers, and a yellow hooded dressing gown over powder-blue flowery pyjamas – a small riot of colour against the pale carpet. I wanted to hug her, but thought it might scare her. Instead I crouched down and sat on the step next to her.

'Do you remember me, Ruby? From the hospital?'

'Mmm, you're the pirate,' she said, gazing at my eye patch. 'Where's your eyebrow gone?'

I usually shaded in the few sparse hairs remaining with a brown eyebrow pencil, but I'd forgotten that day, what with all the tension of planning the visit. 'Um, it sort of got lost in my accident.' I glanced towards the kitchen in the hope that Lulu wasn't following the exchange. I didn't like to draw attention to my missing body parts.

'Never mind, I get my daddy to buy you a new one.' Ruby patted my shoulder in consolation. 'A black one,' she added firmly.

Lulu, laughing, came back into the room with two glasses of wine and a beaker of milk, which she handed to Ruby. She had obviously overheard the conversation. 'It doesn't work like that, Rubes. Helena isn't Mr Potato Head, you know.'

Lulu mistook my frown for incomprehension. 'He's

a character from *Toy Story*. Ruby's got the toy, and all his bits come off, you know, ears and eyebrows and stuff.' Wisely, she tailed off before she dug herself any deeper, but it was too late.

'I know who Mr Potato Head is,' I said frostily, and Lulu blushed.

She changed the subject, wiping the chalky ring from around Ruby's mouth with a spit-dampened thumb. 'Why did you clean your teeth already, Rubes? You'll only have to do it again after your milk.'

Ruby sucked at the spout of the beaker. 'Because I cleaned my teeth,' she said. Then she cocked an ear towards the nearest eggy speaker. 'What's this music?'

'It's Sting,' said Lulu.

'I *like* Stings,' Ruby announced mournfully, shaking her head.

Lulu laughed again. 'That means she *doesn't* like Sting. It's all in the intonation.'

I smiled, deciding after all that it would be churlish to hold the potato-head comment against anyone. Life was too short. 'Her language has improved so much, I can't believe it. She doesn't even lisp any more. It's like she's a whole new person in just a few months. How old is she now?'

Ruby drew herself haughtily up to her full height of almost three foot. 'I not a new person. I Ruby Tabitha Middleton. I'm twoanaharf.'

'Going on fifteen. Helena's brought you something, Ruby Tabitha. Why don't we all go and sit down, so she can show it to you?' Lulu passed me a glass of wine and steered us both over to an immense cream sofa, Ruby jumping up and down on the way.

'Present! Present! It's my birthday!'

'No, it isn't your birthday. Now calm down, please. It's bedtime in a minute, and I don't want you getting overexcited.'

'Sorry,' I said to Lulu. 'I shouldn't have come at such a bad time. Actually, I didn't think she'd go to bed so early. Not having kids, I don't really know how these things work.'

Lulu grimaced. 'Don't worry. It's fine. No, CALM DOWN, Ruby. You'll knock over someone's glass in a minute.'

I lifted Ruby onto my knee. For a second she looked as though she wanted to squirm off, until she remembered that a gift was soon to be forthcoming, and stayed put, drinking her milk and leaning expectantly against me. She was heavy, a great plump bundle of yellow terrycloth and smooth pink skin, more like an oversized baby than a little girl. Her hair smelled delicious, of poppies and warm towels and baby soap, and for a second I couldn't speak. I had an overwhelming urge to touch her soft skin. The baby I'd never have. I gently squeezed one of her bare, chubby calves, feeling it give and mould squashily to my hand. Why was it the beautiful minutiae of life that made it so hard to leave: the downy blond hairs on Ruby's shin, a dog-eared collection of teenage sentiment in a box?

'Ruby.' I turned her gently around so we were face to face again. 'This present is something very special. In fact, it's my favourite thing in the world because it reminds me of a very old friend, and, you know, the best presents are the things that we love most ourselves.'

Ruby nodded, dropping the now-empty beaker onto the sofa, and Lulu sipped her wine, looking embarrassed. I saw her gaze longingly at a magazine lying on the coffee table. Fortuitously for her, a telephone rang at the far end of the room, and she leaped up to answer it, slopping a little white wine on the table in her haste to escape this strange display of sentiment.

'That's probably Toby, ringing to say good night to Ruby.'

'My daddy,' said Ruby to me, lifting up her head. I tried to eavesdrop on the conversation, but Ruby continued to chat to me and I couldn't. 'Daddy come back 'morrow, and we go to live with Mummy again.'

I started, and a small, strange noise came from the back of my throat.

'Got hiccups?' asked Ruby blithely.

'With Daddy? You're all going to live together again?'

Ruby nodded vigorously. 'Yeah, my daddy and my mummy and me. I got all my toys there too, an' . . .'

'Ruby, Daddy wants to say good night,' Lulu called, holding out the receiver. Ruby slid off my lap and ran to the telephone. 'Toby wants to talk to you, too,' she added.

I stood up miserably and trailed over to join the queue for the telephone. After Ruby's revelation, Toby was the last person on earth I wanted to speak to, but I could hardly refuse.

'Na-night, Daddy. Any fireworks? Any scaries?' Reassured, Ruby made kissing noises. 'I shout you in the morning, yeah?'

Lulu prised the receiver out of Ruby's hand and passed it to me. 'I'll just take Ruby up to clean her teeth again, and then we'll come and say good night,' she whispered to me.

I nodded. 'Hi,' I said blankly into the phone.

'Helena. God, I'm so gutted I'm not there. I mean, I'm so glad you're there. I've been going mad trying to track you down. You will leave your number with Lulu, won't you?'

There was an embarrassed pause, which I felt physically, a small, dropping sensation in the pit of my stomach. This was all a mess. I was tired of every-thing, too tired to challenge Toby on his hypocrisy at wanting my number if he was about to get back with Kate, too miserable that once again my timing was up the spout . . . But hold on, I told myself: it was entirely academic whether or not he got back with Kate. It made no difference to me, nor was it the reason why I was there, in Lulu's front room, surrounded by bronze buddhas and artfully arranged piles of smooth stones.

My sense of perspective was, as usual, twisting away from me. I should be happy that at least one of us had a future.

'You were a good friend to me in the hospital,' I blurted, unable to think of anything else to say.

'Not more than that?' Toby asked, hopefully.

Another pause. 'Under the circumstances, I think not,' I said, not elaborating on which specific circumstances: Toby's marriage, my bereavement, our joint vulnerability.

'Oh.' His disappointment swelled into my head, as palpable as the crackling from his mobile phone. 'Is everything OK, Helena? You sound a bit . . . strange.'

I tried to close the lid on my disappointment and frustration, imagining it as an overstuffed suitcase which needed to be sat on before being zipped up. Toby had been a good friend and a good listener. I didn't want his final impression of me to be as an obstreperous old harridan, yet again giving him a hard time. What we both did with our lives was entirely our own business.

'I'm fine. I'm sorry if I sound a bit off. I guess I'm just disappointed not to see you.' I rushed on before he could suggest another meeting. 'Actually, I came over to give something to Ruby. I've been thinking a lot about . . . her and, you know, now that I've recovered and am about to start work again, I figured that it might be a nice gesture to pass something of mine on to her. It might seem a little weird to you, but I really want her to have the box of letters and bits and pieces that Sam and I first started keeping as kids. There are quite a lot of mementoes of the band in there, old fanzines and photos, that kind of thing, as well as the letters.'

Another pause, but this time a reverential one. 'Are you sure, Helena? That's . . . that's just an incredible gift. Why do you want to get rid of it? I mean, those are memories of Sam. Surely you want to keep them?'

'No,' I said firmly. 'Actually, I really don't. I've spent

404

far too long dwelling on them. I need to move on and stop living in the past. I would be honoured if you'd accept it, on Ruby's behalf. If you could just keep it for her until she's old enough to decide what she wants to do with it. Maybe people can come to her when they need to do research on the early days of Blue Idea, or whatever. I don't know.'

'Why wouldn't people come to *you* if they needed to do research on Blue Idea?'

I hesitated, feeling caught out. 'Yeah, of course they would, and do. I'm talking ten, twenty years down the line here. You never know, maybe there'll be a huge Blue Idea revival in 2020, and who knows where I'll be then? I just thought it might be something Ruby would like to have one day.'

Toby still seemed overcome. 'What can I say? Thanks, Helena. This is the most amazing present Ruby will ever receive. I promise we'll take care of it for you.'

Ruby and Lulu came back downstairs, and Lulu hid the Hel-Sam Box behind a large cushion before Ruby saw it.

'Just one more thing, Toby. Can I trust you not to look in it yourself? I mean, of course you can one day, but . . . not just yet, eh?'

'I promise that, too. Ruby should be the one to open it, when she's old enough.'

'Thanks. Listen, I'd better go. Ruby's off to bed now. We'll be in touch, OK?'

Toby started gabbling. 'I'll be back tomorrow. Leave your number; I'll ring you then. Why don't we go out next week, just as friends, of course, but I'd love to see you—'

'Bye, Toby.' I put the phone down. Have a nice life.

Ruby was sitting on the floor by the sofa, one of Lulu's feet in her lap. When I came back over to join them, I heard her say, 'I'm the lady, you be the man. I wash your feet, yeah?'

'Bit young for a Mary Magdalene complex, isn't

she?' I said to Lulu, relying on flippancy to push down my anguish.

'Yeah. I keep telling her that she should stop reading that Bible so much,' Lulu agreed, and I managed a laugh. For a second we exchanged a look which said, loud and clear, we could be friends.

Ruby stopped pretending to anoint Lulu's foot with tears, and dumped it unceremoniously back on the floor. 'Where's my present?'

'Oh, yes. We got interrupted by your daddy on the phone. Oh, Ruby, I hope you won't be too disappointed. It's only an old box full of letters and stuff, but one day I hope that you'll enjoy looking through it and owning it.' I retrieved the Hel-Sam Box from behind the sofa cushion and put it on the floor in front of her.

Lulu squinted at the faded label and smiled, reading it out loud, '"THE HEL-SAM BOX OF IMPORTANT STUFF! KEEP OUT! UNLESS YOU ARE HELENA JANE NICHOLLS OR SAMANTHA GRANT! In the event of the untiemally death of either of us, this box is to go immidiatally to the other one's house and stay there. No-one else is ever, ever, allowed to look inside. It's all completely Top Secret." So how come it's not at Samantha Grant's house then?' As soon as she'd said it, she bit her lip, and I realized that Toby must have told her about me and Sam.

I grinned faintly and painfully, through gritted teeth.

'I'm sorry,' said Lulu.

'It's OK. Don't worry. I hope you don't think it's weird, but I want Ruby to have it.'

Ruby was tugging at the lid of the box. 'Are there sweeties inside?'

'No, darling,' said Lulu.

'How 'bout *Toy Story* video then?'

We shook our heads sadly.

'What then?'

Lulu put an arm around her. 'Sweetheart, it's just a special box for you to keep for when you're older. It's a bit hard to explain now, but it's really a very special present. Say thank you to Helena.'

Ruby stuck out her bottom lip and rubbed her eyes. 'I *like* special box,' she whined.

I wished I'd had the foresight to bring her some chocolate buttons as well.

Lulu picked her up. 'OK, tired girl, now it really is bedtime. Say good night and thank you to Helena.' She leaned towards me so Ruby could give me a kiss, and for a brief, intoxicating moment Ruby nuzzled in the side of my neck, her hair tickling my cheek.

'Tanks, 'Ellna. Any fireworks? Any scaries?'

I glanced at Lulu for the answer, and she shook her head. 'No, Ruby. No fireworks, no scaries. Sleep well, sweet dreams.'

Ruby waved at me as she was carried up the stairs, finger in mouth, her head already drooping on Lulu's shoulder.

By the time Lulu returned several minutes later I had regained my composure. She offered me another glass of wine, some supper, a coffee, but I declined. We chatted for a while longer, and again I marvelled at what easy company she was, but it felt like a snare, the Middleton way of drawing me into their family so I wouldn't want to leave. God, they all did it! If I stayed any longer I'd be tempted to ask about Toby and Kate and whether it was true that they were getting back together, but I was desperate not to. It would be so demeaning, and the truth was that I simply didn't need to know.

'I've taken up enough of your time already.' I stood up. 'I really have to go now. I've got tons of things to do.'

This was true. I had to start thinking about getting my affairs in order: cancelling my next outpatient check-up at the hospital, the smear test I had booked in for October, all my standing orders. At least Toby and Ruby had been dealt with, anyhow. I expected to feel less guilty now that I'd closed the book on that episode, but to my horror the guilt merely transferred itself to thoughts of my parents instead, which was far worse. I felt like the biggest, yellowest coward that had ever lived.

But as I said goodbye to Lulu and left the house, I changed my mind. I wasn't a coward. It was surely more courageous to end a worthless life than to live in misery. Anyone who truly loved me would have to understand that.

'This Is A Low'
Blur

Within six months of our return from Santorini Sam's health had deteriorated even more dramatically. She couldn't walk more than a few steps without getting exhausted and breathless, and had to have constant recourse to an oxygen mask and cylinder. Her need for a new lung finally became extremely pressing; it was no longer a matter of choice. She agreed to go on the waiting list, so the hospital gave her a pager, and she was on twenty-four-hour standby for a call to say that a donor lung had been located.

I still went down to Salisbury every weekend, and spoke to her on the phone every day. I'd have stayed down there permanently were it not for the fact that I had to do my show. My heart was torn to see her getting thinner and weaker every week.

On my last visit, she had just been sitting hunched on her sofa, grey-faced and skeletal, with the oxygen tube now permanently fixed to her nostrils, a slave to the heavy metal tank next to her. She looked so sad and ill that all I could do was sit next to her and hold her in my arms, like a child, rocking her gently against my shoulder. I couldn't stop tears from rolling down my face, and she frowned at me faintly.

'Cry baby,' she whispered. Then she wrapped her arms around my waist, sighing heavily. She was so thin that I could feel all the bones in her shoulders and back as I rubbed them gently with my hand.

Everything in her little flat was as bright and cheerful as ever: the crisp blue and white stripes of the sofa, the pictures on the wall, the thick, colourful rug on the floor. I always used to think how well she fitted this little basement. Like dogs who resembled their owners, Sam's flat was the essence of herself, full of light and colour and energy. Now she looked incongruous in her own place, almost inappropriate, like a grey vase full of wilting flowers in the middle of a florist's shop, surrounded by a riot of fresh, coloured blooms. I couldn't bear it.

I tried to push the image away, and talked to her in a low voice about how wonderful things would be once she'd had the operation, reminding her again of all the things she would be able to do and see once more. How she'd have to lose the 'cripple sticker' on her windscreen and take her chances with the city's traffic wardens, like the rest of us. How she could come to gigs with me, and we could stay out till four in the morning, if we wanted. We'd live together, and cook, and try finally to bag ourselves a couple of decent blokes.

Sam just leaned against me and listened until I ran out of steam. Then we sat, in an undeniably depressed silence, broken only by the soft hissing of oxygen from the cylinder into her poor useless lungs.

Finally she fell asleep, and I manoeuvred her into a horizontal position on the sofa, lifting up her feet and swinging them gently around and up onto the cushions. I covered her with a quilt, kissed her forehead and crept upstairs to tell Cynthia that I was leaving.

When I climbed into my car, inhaling its faint plastic and air-freshener smell, I was overcome with a feeling – empathic, perhaps – of utter exhaustion and desolation. I leaned back and closed my eyes, trying to fight away the emotions of frustration and grief at seeing Sam that way and not being able to help her. I would willingly have donated one of my lungs to her

410

then and there – both, if I could. For the first time ever I really thought that she might die, and the sensation overwhelmed me with pain.

Then suddenly, out of nowhere, the fog in my head lifted and all my senses sharpened up. Everything around me felt hyper-real, and I experienced a huge rush of adrenalin. The leaves on the tall trees across the road became a green so deep they took my breath away. I sat bolt upright, surprised and stunned by this emotional transformation. Into the empty palette of my focused mind sprang five distinct words: 'She's going to be fine.' They stayed there, so clear that I could almost read them in bold black letters, for several seconds, until my grief was replaced by euphoria. I almost rushed back into the house to tell Sam and Cynthia, but changed my mind when I realized that I didn't want either of them to think I'd ever doubted it. Instead, I drove back to London feeling a deep sense of calm and a cautious joy.

On a freezing November day a couple of weeks later, for want of anything better to do, I was cleaning the outside of my bathroom window with balled-up newspapers. The cleaner, who didn't speak English, had indicated via a sketched window with a big X through it that this was a task she declined to incorporate into her routine. I'd felt that it was time to do something about it, since there were ribbons of bird crap festooning the panes, courtesy of the family of pigeons who lived in the bathroom gutter.

I was sitting almost in the sink, with one arm hooked around the closed side of the window, when the phone rang. Cursing, I extricated myself and went to the top of the stairs so I could hear the machine pick up the call. I didn't want to talk to anyone except Sam or Vinnie. With a click and a crackle I heard Cynthia Grant's voice come onto the line, so I bounded downstairs two at a time and lunged for the receiver, my fingers numb with cold and terror.

411

In one sick moment I had a flashback to the time I'd called her from Ringside's offices ten years before.

'Cynthia! What's the matter? Is Sam OK?' I picked up the phone with my free hand and started pacing around the room with it, leaving black newsprint fingermarks all over its cream trunk.

'Now listen to me, Helena, don't panic. She's all right, but she was having so much trouble breathing that they've taken her into hospital, to put her on a ventilator until the donor lung comes through. She needs to get her strength up for the operation; she was using too much of it trying to catch her breath the whole time. This is the best thing for her; she needs the rest. But she's fine and in good spirits.'

'Can I have a phone number for her? When can I see her?'

I was horrified and relieved at the same time. I sat down heavily on my pale armchair, and before I noticed left more sooty fingerprints on the arm and seat.

'Well, there's no point in phoning her; she can't talk. She's got a tube in her throat from the ventilator.'

'Oh my God, poor Sam,' I said, appalled.

'She shouldn't really have visitors, either, but I've spoken to the nursing staff and told them that you should be allowed to come and see her regularly. Only once or twice a week, Helena, mind, and just for a few minutes. She won't be able to cope with more than that.'

This felt terrible; final and deadly serious. I knew then that if Sam didn't leave that hospital with a new lung, she wouldn't leave at all. It was, I supposed, what people called make-or-break time. After I hung up, I sat in the chair taking long deep breaths and wishing I could do the same for Sam. Then I remembered what I'd heard the day I last saw her, and repeated it out loud softly, over and over again, until my fears were calmed. 'She's going to be fine. She's going to be fine.'

Eventually I decided that the only thing I could do was go and visit her immediately. As I left the sitting room to conduct my habitual pocket-rummaging for keys in the coat cupboard and wardrobe, I happened to glance back over my shoulder, the black marks on the chair and phone finally catching my eye. I ignored them.

Sam was on the ventilator for four weeks, every moment of which felt measured by the rise and fall of her machine-manufactured breaths. I carried on doing my show, on autopilot, crying quietly off-mic every time someone requested a song for a sick friend – a sick anyone, really. Someone mourning their dead hamster would've set me off just as easily. I could have claimed any number of other people's records for myself: 'The Bitterest Pill', 'Bridge Over Troubled Water', 'Us And Them'. The requests all seemed to feed my grief and worry, plumping them up like raisins in milk, the pain of others mingling secretly with my own.

I commuted to Sam's hospital in Oxfordshire as often as the staff permitted, even if I could see her only for a few minutes at a time, and I monitored every little change in her condition, for better or worse. After a week I decided that I was going to talk to Geoff and Gus as soon as I could, and ask for some compassionate leave to be with her until she had the operation. I didn't care how long she had to wait for it; they could fire me if they didn't like it.

Of course, as soon as I announced this to Sam, she wouldn't hear of it. Her thin fingers picked up the felt-tip pen beside her right hand and wrote on her notepad in surprisingly firm letters, 'It might be months before they find me a new lung.' I had argued with her, but she retaliated by scribbling, 'If you don't stay at work, I won't tell you when I have my op!'

'Blackmail!' I said, but felt much better about it. She placated me further by adding, 'You know I'm much stronger now.'

It was true. Although she still had an ethereal, almost ghostly quality about her, she had put on a little weight and her eyes were regaining some of their old spark. The doctors were very pleased with her progress, and had told us that, should a donor lung become available, she would be strong enough to have the operation immediately.

'You just don't want me around because I'm better at crosswords than you are,' I whinged. She rolled her eyes and grinned at me.

The message from Cynthia came through in the fourth week, just as I was finishing the show one December morning. A donor lung had turned up for Sam; it was from a young biker killed on a patch of black ice the day before. She'd had the operation immediately, and was in Intensive Care – very ill, but alive.

I must have wondered whether it was the last time I'd ever see her, but my brain wouldn't allow the thought to articulate itself. I created a huge roadblock in my head, complete with armed soldiers barring entry to the enemy territory. It was four days after the operation, and I'd been at the hospital as much as the nurses allowed me to be, catching a few hours' sleep whenever I was forced to at a nearby hotel.

I'd made two phone calls: one was to leave a message for Geoff, to say that I was taking compassionate leave and that I'd keep him posted; and one was to Vinnie, to ask if he would come and be with me at the hospital. I was desperate for his solid reassurance; a real human body to ground me when it seemed like Sam's might be slipping away. I'd given him the address and phone number of the hotel, but two days later there was no word from him. I wasn't surprised.

Initially, Sam's new – or nearly new – lung had taken, and the operation was tentatively declared successful. But then it all started to go wrong.

Within four days an infection had crept into her vulnerable body, tearing at it, trying to oust the unfamiliar interloper crammed inside her ribcage. She was fighting hard, but her body was so weakened from the surgery that drugs and oxygen were having to do what her poor, struggling immune system could not.

That hospital room became my universe, a small, horrible, painful cosmos, with bland textures and tension in the air. There were no flowers in the room; their superficial fussiness would have seemed too trivial amid the far more important business of preserving an existence. All around were pale colours; unadorned walls were framed by plain curtains and colourless lino floor. Even though Sam was barely conscious and hooked up to all kinds of breathing apparatus, there was a full jug of water, an inverted glass and a box of Kleenex on the locker next to her bed.

It was a totally functional room, and despite all the expensive life-saving equipment and awful scent of hospital detergent, it smelled of sickness and despair, heartbroken love and rage. Inexorably, it smelled like a room in which to die, not to get well.

Sam was the room's focus, lying still under a thin, nubbly yellow hospital blanket, her legs and feet defined like a skeleton under a sheet. She was hanging onto her poor cut-up body by the merest of threads, and even as I watched she seemed to drift away and back again. The room was silent except for the mechanical huff and thunk of the ventilator. I wondered if she was alarmed by our appearance, as we were all masked and gowned up to prevent our germs from tipping her precarious balance. I felt as if my mask had an additional purpose: to hold my own pain deep inside my body and to prevent it spilling out of my mouth in a huge, jagged scream of frustration and fear.

Nurses bustled in and out, their rubber-soled shoes squeaking on the linoleum. They adjusted the equipment, took readings, gently plumped the pillows under Sam's blue face and flipped the pages of her chart up and down before replacing it in its holder at the end of her bed. The writing on the pages didn't appear to be in any language I'd ever seen before.

Sam's eyes were closed, and she looked like a very old woman or a wizened, sick child. Cynthia and Mike hovered around, too, talking gently to her and to each other, and Dylan and his wife were outside drinking vending-machine coffee from Styrofoam cups. I walked past them all on my way back from the Ladies'; Dylan's mouth was twisted up and trembling so much that he could hardly swallow his coffee.

There was a sign on a door across the corridor which read, 'Elective Services Directorate. Mattresses and Pillows Stored in Here'. I did not understand what that meant any more than I understood the squiggles on Sam's chart.

Every now and again Mike absently patted my shoulder, but he couldn't look at me. He seemed fixated by the various items of hospital paraphernalia pushed or carried past by the nurses: yellow-wheeled trolleys, stainless-steel kidney trays, boxes of non-sterile latex gloves.

Later, back in Sam's room, her jovial uncle, who I'd heard of but never met, came up to her bedside. His joviality was supposedly his strongest characteristic, but he was really fighting to find it at that moment.

'Hello, Sam love,' he said to her quietly, passing a weary hand over his eyes. 'Your Christmas roses are blooming a treat. You've got to hurry back and chase that damned neighbour's cat out, mind; it's trying its best to dig 'em up.'

Last summer Sam had started cultivating a section of her parents' large garden, and it was her pride and joy. Until it turned too cold, it had become nigh on impossible to reach her on the phone; she was always out in her wheelchair on the lawn, surrounded by hoes and secateurs, either fiddling with her sweet peas and marigolds, or giving orders to her sweating father to carry out the more back-breaking tasks. But she didn't give a flicker of acknowledgement now.

Her uncle stroked her still hand. 'Well, I just wanted to come and see you, you know. Get well soon. Auntie Pauline sends her love – she'd have come, too, but her hip's been playing her up again. Goodbye, love.'

He got up abruptly and lumbered out of the room. Sam stirred and moaned. She seemed frightened and disturbed. Her parents and I leaned forward, as though our proximity could chase away her fears. Tears spilled from Cynthia's eyes.

'It's all right, Sam darling, we're here. Shhh now.' She held three of Sam's fingers, gently, but as though she would never let them go.

The doctor came in and asked us to leave for a minute. As I walked numbly out of the room, he took me aside. He had thick tufts of bristly reddish hair coming from his ears and nostrils, which moved gently when he spoke, like sea anemones in a rock pool.

'Listen,' he said kindly. 'I think it's important that she gets some rest now. Really, the less people around her the better. And I'm sure you could do with a break, too. You've been here all day. Why don't you get a good night's sleep and come back in the morning? She's had a lot of visitors today. I really think it would be best for her.'

I didn't want to leave, but I did want to do what was best. 'Can I say goodbye?'

'Yes, go in now. Be as brief as you can, though.'

Cynthia and Mike stood aside to let me re-enter the room. They looked the way they had all week, blank and stunned, as I'm sure I did, like shipwreck or inferno survivors.

I walked over to Sam's bed, alone with her for the first time all day. I held her hand and stroked her hair; she was so familiar, even in these unnatural surroundings. I thought about that new, strange lung inside her, which hadn't yet proved if it was friend or foe.

417

The walls felt as though they were pressing in on me, and I had a fleeting desire to see something bright and colourful – a Matisse print, or a child's building blocks – something happy. The bed sheets looked like hard, white plywood. I gazed into her face, but couldn't see any peace there.

'I've got to go now, Sam, but I'll be back tomorrow. Hang in there, OK?'

I paused, but there was no reply. I stood up and started to turn away. As I did so I felt, rather than heard, a tiny movement. I turned slowly back around to see Sam's eyes flicker open, and with all her strength she lifted her arms a tiny way up towards me, as though for a hug. I rushed back to her and embraced her gingerly around the tubes, feeling as though my head and heart would simultaneously burst with pain and grief.

I stumbled out of the room, and walked in a daze back to the hotel up the road. It seemed to have been built for people like me; the guests all wandered around the corridors looking anxious and haunted. I sat numbly in an overstuffed armchair in the hotel's big lobby, surrounded by a litter of low coffee tables and the hulks of marooned sofas, while a small, washed-out waitress brought me coffee. I couldn't really think what else to do. I didn't want to go to my room because I didn't want to be alone.

Just then the revolving doors spun around and deposited Vinnie right in front of me. Unshaven, a bit whiffy, and smoking, but Vinnie nonetheless.

'Hi, baby,' he said as I stood up to meet him. 'It's OK. I'm here.'

He wrapped his arms tightly around me, and I thought, Whatever else he's done to me, I'll always love him for this.

'Thanks for coming, Vin.'

He ordered a beer from the peaky waitress and, after I'd filled him in on the details of Sam's condition, we sat in silence together.

'Strange old hotel, this, isn't it?' Vinnie commented, looking around him.

I nodded. He was right; it was a very odd place. Presumably the effect was meant to be that of a large, friendly living room, but it felt, to me, like a plush dream-version of the ICU's waiting room. Perhaps the proximity of the hospital's grim suspense had rubbed off on the designers, I thought with antiseptic-drenched imagination. I still couldn't speak, but Vinnie didn't seem to mind. He swigged his beer, as I grimly concentrated on the pale china of my coffee cup.

I was aware of what was going on around me, but I just kept seeing Sam's face, looking hollow and betrayed. The hotel seemed very busy; perhaps a lot of people were dying at this time of year, winter's inevitable victims.

A mother walked by, crying, two small boys trailing behind her. The boys were making cawing sounds, like wheeling seagulls. They weren't sounds born out of grief, more from the boredom of their mother being so distracted. I wondered who she'd lost, or was losing, and saw Sam's face again.

The two receptionists were chatting loudly and vacuously behind their impressive mahogany counter about a party one of them was planning.

'Spiffy-*cahj*,' she kept saying, shortening the word 'casual' in an affected way. 'I told him, it's going to be spiffy-*cahj*; spiffy-*cahj*, I said. If he's not going to come spiffy-*cahj* like the rest of us, he needn't bother coming at all.'

Vinnie leaned over to me from his end of the sofa. 'That's one party I *really* hope I'm not invited to,' he whispered, and even I managed to smile for a split second.

'I wish I still felt so sure that she'll be OK,' I said.

He took my half-full coffee cup from me and put it down on the glass-topped table. 'Come on, sweetheart,' he said. 'I think you need to go and have a lie-down; you look wrecked.'

419

I stretched my hand out towards him, and let him lead me up to my room and steer me over to the bed. As soon as we were through the door, Vinnie was peeling off his clothes.

'I'll just grab a shower, if you don't mind,' he said. 'Haven't had the chance to have one yet today. Back in a minute.'

He vanished into the bathroom, and I lay staring at the ceiling. I was thinking how unfair it was that I could just jump up off the bed any time I wanted to and Sam couldn't. I was so tired that I began to think I was hallucinating; the slippery brown bedspread underneath me seemed like a vast card table on which my mind was turning over personalized tarot cards: Sam holding up scales; the Grim Reaper; Sam, Sam, Sam; Vinnie holding out his hands. I felt cold, chilled to the bone, and all I wanted to do was get warm again.

Before I even realized it I had slid off the bed and into the bathroom, the hot splash of Vinnie's shower calling me. I stripped off and stumbled in to join him, falling into his wet arms, crying more than I had thought it possible to cry.

Vinnie hugged me so hard my bones cracked, and I buried my face in the space between his neck and shoulder until the pounding water nearly suffocated me. I kissed him then, all salty and sobbing, like he was a lifeboat on a stormy sea.

He was so warm against my iced-over soul that I just wanted to get closer to him. After the shower we crawled beneath the chilly bedcovers and he held me, pressing his body against mine, heavy and warm and curved, almost indistinguishable from my own; the only thing in the world that might possibly stop my pain.

We lay in silence, my grief occupying every ion of the air around us. Vinnie was obviously not finding it easy to be naked in bed with me, but for once in his life he had the sensitivity to realize that what I needed from him at that moment went much deeper than sex. To his credit, he didn't even try to instigate it.

Eventually I fell into a dreamless black hole of sleep, as suddenly and violently as falling off a cliff. The last thing I remembered was the feel of Vinnie's chest against my cheek, and of being lulled by the gentle rhythm of his breathing.

I was woken a few hours later by the sound of a match sparking as Vinnie lit a cigarette. He was sitting up in bed, drinking a beer from the minibar and watching television. It was dark outside, but he hadn't drawn the curtains.

'Hello, gorgeous,' he said, kissing my nose. 'I've got to make a move soon, you know. Things to do.'

I sat up groggily. 'Really? I thought you were going to stay.'

'Sorry, baby, I can't. I've got this big project to finish. I just wanted to make sure you were OK.'

'Thanks again, Vin, I really appreciate it. How did you get here, anyway?'

'Borrowed a mate's car. That's another reason I have to get back. He'll be wondering where I've got to. I didn't actually tell him I was coming this far.'

He put out his cigarette by dropping it in the dregs of his beer, and then got out of bed, picking up and putting on the clothes he'd discarded earlier. I felt bereft that he was going, but didn't have the energy to stop him – my deep sleep had left me with a woozy kind of hangover, as if I'd taken a sleeping pill. Once dressed, he came and lay back down on the bed next to me.

'Oh, by the way, Helena,' he said, matter-of-factly. 'The machine swallowed my card and I'm completely strapped for cash. You couldn't do me a huge favour and lend me a few quid, could you? Say, two hundred?'

I stared at him open-mouthed. I felt as if nothing else had the power to hurt me, but it didn't stop me feeling angry.

'So that's why you came up here?'

Vinnie looked predictably offended. 'No way. You're my baby. You keep kicking me out, but I'm always there for you when you need me. I was just hoping you could do the same for me, that's all.'

'Me and my chequebook, you mean.'

'Is that OK? I mean, I know this is a really bad time for you, and I wouldn't ask unless I was really stuck. Honest . . . I'm sorry, H.'

I wearily hauled myself out of bed and extracted said chequebook from the depths of my handbag. Two hundred pounds was nothing to me; Vinnie was nothing to me. Sam was all that mattered.

'No, it's not OK, Vinnie.' But I gave him the cheque anyway.

I lay motionless on my bed for the rest of the evening, not watching the flickering, muted television, not listening to the mutterings of the radio, which I'd switched on for company.

It was 8.30 p.m. when the call came from Cynthia at the hospital to tell me Sam had died. Before I even picked up the receiver I was already wondering how my positive thought could have been so wrong; how 'she's going to be fine' could have dissolved into these final, terrible words down a phone line.

When the brief call was finished, some impulse made me turn up the volume on the stereo system by my bed, willing there to be a song on which I could hang my grief. Something fitting, something dignified, something for Sam.

It was a gift. Blur, 'This Is A Low'; the opening trippy acoustic chord sequence climbing up my emotions as I began to listen. The most emotive song about shipping forecasts ever written. It was like a tornado whipping all its power round and round into a tiny, deadly funnel. I poured everything into that song. Volume up and up and up until the little speakers of the stereo quivered and shook. I let it lift me up, too, and take me away from there. Away from

422

the feeling of utter and complete loneliness and desolation, the feeling that nothing would ever be right again.

Damon Albarn almost howled the chorus out: 'This is a low, but it won't hurt you/When you're alone, it will be there with you/Finding ways to stay solo . . .'

It did hurt me, though. God, it hurt me so much. But for the next five minutes – at least for that long – I could survive by letting the song take on my pain.

I couldn't feel the light of Sam's soul rising up towards a different world, but I imagined that this song was escorting her there – the chords and words, sentiment and volume – and my own feelings for her along with it.

As the song's final bars faded out, it made it easier for me to understand that 'she's going to be fine' held much truer when it wasn't limited to a broken shell of a body.

£50.00

By coincidence, or perhaps through some strange synergy, Gus from New World phoned and left an urgent message for me to ring him back on the day I was writing the final chapter of the manuscript. Urgent or not, however, I was utterly incapable of returning his call until the next day. By the time I'd completed the last words, about Sam's poor broken body, I was absolutely hammered on vodka and in no fit state to speak to anybody.

The only reason I even heard the phone's distant ring was because I'd just spilled an entire glass of vodka and pulpy orange juice all over my desk, and had had to take a break from my frenzied, weepy typing to wipe it up.

Drunkenness was essential to the operation. It was the only way I could bear to relive those memories without having 'This Is A Low' to act as a dock leaf on the sting, and I couldn't play the record before the show. I'd set myself a strict embargo on all the tracks accompanying the manuscript until the actual broadcast. When I listened to them all together for that one last time, I wanted them to have the maximum impact on me, in case I needed an extra spur to assist me in carrying out The Plan. They weren't just little iridescent plastic CDs; they were computer disks with my memories stored on them, and I wanted them to remain as new and shiny as was possible under the circumstances.

Nonetheless, writing about Sam's operation nearly finished me off. The vodka acted as an anaesthetic, but not a particularly effective one. I had to keep drinking and drinking it, trying to remember the details objectively, and failing miserably.

On reflection, alcohol and sorrow never did go awfully well together. My brain-drilling headache informed me of that fact the next day, when the room had finally stopped spinning enough for me to locate the telephone and dial the number Gus had left on my machine.

'Gus? It's Helena Nicholls. How are you?'

'Helena! I'm great, thanks, but more to the point, how are you? Why are you whispering?'

'Hideous hangover, that's why. But otherwise fine, thanks. I got your message. What did you want to talk to me about?'

'Right, well, I understand you sent Geoff a letter a couple of months ago, registering your interest in the two to four a.m. slot. He wrote back, care of your agent, asking you to confirm a date, but we haven't heard from you. Have you changed your mind? Or didn't you get the letter?'

I guiltily remembered the letters I'd dumped unread in the bin that day when Vinnie was lurking in the undergrowth.

'Um, no, I haven't changed my mind. Yes, I got the letter. I just, er, forgot to ring him with the date.'

'Not to worry. We've been having a reshuffle here, and if there's any chance of you starting next week, Monday the twenty-eighth, that would be terrific. It would get us out of a hole, and it would give us enough time to get your name in the listings.'

'I said I didn't want any publicity!'

Raising my voice, even just to a faint, indignant squeak, caused the pressure in my head to build up still further until I thought steam would come out of my ears. I vowed not to drink another drop of booze until the day I died. Ho ho.

'No, no, honestly, we won't make a song and dance out of it. It's just that we need a name to stick in the *Time Outs*, and so on. Can't leave a blank space, can we? Besides, no-one'll notice. Hardly anyone listens at that time of night anyw—Well, what I mean is . . .'

'Oh, never mind, Gus. I know exactly what you mean.'

I could just see the headline: DISGRACED DJ DEMOTED TO GRAVEYARD SHIFT. Still, maybe a little bit of advance publicity for The Plan wouldn't hurt.

My feet suddenly turned into two immobile blocks of ice at the realization that the end game now had a date: Monday 28th. The day I was scheduled to disappear off the face of the earth.

'All right, I'll do it. Do I need to come in for a debriefing or anything?'

'No, you know the score. You've done it enough times. It'll be just like the morning, only night-time and without requests.'

What a wag.

Gus continued, 'The security code at the moment is eight one five seven. Don't forget it, because no-one else will be around at that time, unless you bump into Pete Harness and his producer on the way out. He's taking over the eleven to two a.m. slot.'

'So who's my producer then?'

An important question, since he or she would be the last person to see me before I left. I found I'd stripped off a jagged piece of cuticle with my teeth, leaving a long white gash of flesh which instantly filled up with red spots of blood that dripped mercilessly onto the leg of my favourite combat trousers. Oh, well, I thought, won't need to wash them again.

There was an embarrassed silence at the end of the line.

'I thought Geoff told you in his letter, Helena. You won't have a producer at that time. Nobody does. Pete only has one that late because he does phone-in quizzes and things on his show.'

I wasn't quite sure how I felt about this. If I'd planned to do the show long-term, I'd have been hideously affronted. It was like expecting Elizabeth I to get dressed up for a state banquet on her own, with no-one to lace her stays or hang jewels in her hair. It also meant that nobody would be manning the phones. It was just as well I wasn't intending to do a request show.

Gus must have picked up on my disgruntled train of thought. 'No point in having anyone taking calls at that time of night. We'd get all the axe-murderers and child-molesters ringing in if we did.'

'Oh great,' I said, trying to sound like someone who cared who'd be listening. 'My target audience.'

Maybe not having a producer was a good thing, if I could get over the humiliation. Practically, it meant I'd have the studio to myself.

I tried to be brisk. 'Right then, I think I'm set. Monday the twenty-eighth it is. I'll give you a shout if I think of any other questions.'

'Good girl. Are you excited?'

How incredibly patronizing, I fumed. Were it not for the fact that Gus had given me my first DJ job, I'd have seriously gone off him at this point.

'No, Gus. To be honest I can't say that I'm wildly excited about having to do the graveyard shift. But it's a job, I suppose, and I'll guarantee you this: it'll be a show to remember!'

Gus laughed uncertainly. 'You bet, Helena. Well, best of luck then. I'll check in with you after the first show, all right?'

On Saturday 26th I donned my sunglasses, even though it was raining, and set off to Richmond for a very specific shopping mission. Sainsbury's home shopping would probably have baulked at delivering the items I wanted, so a personal expedition was required. I parked on a meter on the edge of the green, and strolled cautiously into the town centre, noticing how much less paranoid I felt about being out in public – probably because I knew it was the last time it would happen. Oddbins was my first port of call, where I purchased a large bottle of gin. I didn't care for gin, but the hangover was still too fresh in my memory to even think about vodka without retching.

Next I went into Boots and bought a jar of paracetamol and a Bart Simpson hot-water-bottle cover – to try and make the pills look less suspicious. I'd planned to repeat the exercise in every chemist in Richmond – minus the novelty hot-water-bottle covers, of course – but after an hour of walking around I'd failed to locate any other pharmacies. Bugger. I'd have to drive around instead, looking for those big green crosses that signify chemists' shops.

It struck me that buying booze and headache pills, and gathering together my favourite CDs, felt more as if I was planning a hen party with a bunch of girl-friends. Not that I'd ever gone anywhere with a bunch of girlfriends. My girlfriends hadn't come in bunches, like grapes, but as one perfect piece of fruit. Sam the starfruit.

My meter was about to run out, so I headed back towards the green, going via WHSmith to buy a purple folder for my manuscript. The girl at the till got annoyed with me when I flung the money at her without waiting for my change, but I was paranoid about getting a parking ticket. It was funny how I could still be worried about such trivialities, I thought.

It began to rain again, just as I was circumnavigating the bald, muddy patches of grass on Richmond Green, wondering once more why I bothered. I was planning to kill myself, but it was of paramount importance not to get mud on my Patrick Coxes or a parking fine before I did?

Head down, thinking aspirin, I muttered to myself, 'Only one bottle. Well, that won't get me very far, will it? Where else have I seen those big green crosses? Oh yeah, there's that one in Twickenham, the Maple Leaf, and I'm sure there are a couple in St Margarets, too.'

'A couple of what?' said a familiar voice from behind my car.

I stood on a loose paving slab and water squirted up my trouser leg. There appeared to be no escape from Vinnie.

'What are you doing here?' I glared at him as jaws of cold water sank into my left calf.

'Waiting for you, of course. Good thing you got back when you did; only a minute left on your meter, and a soggy, cross-looking traffic warden heading towards us as we speak. I'd hate to see you get a ticket now.'

Vinnie tutted with mock-concern, and leaned on my bonnet. As usual my shock turned to fury: 'You're happy to make a few hundred grand by selling pictures of me to the Press, but you'd hate to see me get a parking ticket? Just go away, Vinnie. You make me sick.'

'Ah, but that's where you're wrong. I'm not happy to make money out of you, Helena,' he said, brushing a stray leaf off my windscreen. 'That's why I'm waiting for you. I've got something to tell you.'

'Well, I don't want to hear it,' I said shortly, pressing the button on my keyring to unlock the BMW. The little 'pip' it made sounded as grumpy as I did.

'Oh, but you do,' said Vinnie, dancing round to the driver's side and putting his hand over mine as I tried to open the door.

I snatched it away. 'Piss off, Vinnie. I'm not in the mood.'

Vinnie delved into a damp backpack and pulled out a hardback brown envelope. He thrust it at me. 'There you go.'

'What's that?' I asked wearily.

'Prints and negatives. All there, none missing, I promise you.'

I stared at him. 'None missing except the one you

429

sold to the tabloids, right? When's it coming out then? I've been checking the papers, but I haven't seen it yet.'

Vinnie laughed. 'No, straight up. They're all in there. I haven't sold any of them. I'm giving them back to you.'

He dropped suddenly to his knees on the wet road and wrapped his arms around my thighs. 'I've been a complete arse, Helena. I'm so, so sorry. You have to forgive me. For everything: Miyuki, Natalie, the photos, everything.'

Who's Natalie? I thought.

'I miss you so much. Please take me back. I swear I'll never let you down again. Marry me, Helena, please? I love you.'

My jaw dropped so far that, even with the limited movement I'd had since it had been broken, it was close to clunking Vinnie on the top of his head as he grovelled beseechingly before me. I didn't know what to say. No-one had ever proposed to me before. Marry him?

It was lashing with rain now. I disengaged his arms and collapsed speechless into the car. Vinnie rushed back around and climbed into the passenger seat. We both sat there, dripping, until he turned and threw the envelope, frisbee-style, onto the back seat.

'What's the matter with the photos? Were they all blurred or something?'

Vinnie looked hurt; more, I thought, because I was doubting his technical prowess as a photographer. He liked to excel in all things.

'Of course they weren't blurred. They're great, as it happens, crystal clear. I'm telling you, I just feel like a heel for doing something so horrible to you. I was desperate, man. I got into a spot of bother with a dealer friend of mine. You know, I owe him some cash, and he's not happy with me. That's why I did it. If I'd been thinking straight I'd never have done anything to hurt you.'

430

'But you didn't sell them?'

'No. Look, I realized I was out of order.'

'So do you still owe him money?'

Vinnie lit up a Gauloise, but I reached over, extracted it from between his lips and threw it out of the window. We watched it roll away across the tarmac, sparking red, to lie disconsolately in the gutter.

'I can't stand you smoking in my car,' I said.

'Sorry,' Vinnie replied humbly.

I decided to make a generous gesture as he was obviously in trouble. 'Listen. I don't mind if you want to flog all that equipment I bought you – the computer and stuff – to pay off your debts.'

Vinnie looked away, and I realized that he'd sold them long ago.

'Oh, right. I see. Cheers, then,' I said.

I hadn't realized he had such a bad drug problem. Or perhaps he owed money because he was dealing? I wouldn't have put it past him. Either way, I didn't really want to know.

'I was desperate, H. Please forgive me. You were the only good thing in my life, and I let you down.'

I leaned back against the headrest and watched a little boy of about three or four heading our way, followed by his mother. The boy was dressed in yellow galoshes and one of those really cute yellow duck raincoats, where the peak of the hood was the duck's beak. He was carrying a small translucent umbrella decorated with a frieze of tropical fish, which he held down low over his head. I could see his baby breath misting up the inside of the plastic. His mother was carrying car keys and looked harassed.

'Come on, Timmy, hurry up. The car's parked just across the road,' I heard her say.

Timmy broke away, ran a couple of steps and jumped with both feet into a deep puddle by the kerb, soaking himself and his mother. I waited for her to yell and drag him off to the car, and for a second she looked cross. Then, suddenly and unexpectedly, she skipped forward two steps, too, and jumped into the same puddle. They stood there laughing with glee and, even in the midst of Vinnie's machinations, I couldn't help smiling as well.

Suddenly I wished, with a fierce, fearful yearning, that it was Ruby splashing under a duck's beak hood in front of me, and Toby clowning around with her. I could have got out and joined them and forgotten all about Vinnie.

'You've always let me down, Vinnie,' I said. I'd always thought it was a cliché, when people's voices sounded very faraway, but mine did. Probably because it was off somewhere with the rest of me, jumping in puddles with Toby.

'Whenever I needed you, you let me down. You've cheated on me, taken advantage of me, sponged off me. When Sam was dying, I thought for once you'd be there for me, but you weren't. When I had the accident, you didn't even visit me in hospital; you didn't come near me until you decided you could make some money out of me. Why on earth would I want to marry *you*?'

Vinnie made one last-ditch effort. 'I only didn't visit you in hospital because you said you never wanted to see me again.'

'But I'm always saying that. It's never stopped you before.'

I grinned very slightly, and Vinnie sensed that I was weakening. I couldn't help it. I began to remember all the good things about him: his sense of humour and adventure, his amazing prowess in the sack, how he kept me company, how he made art for me.

'Please, Helena, let's give it one more try. I really want you. I'm so sorry about everything.'

Then I remembered The Plan and snapped back to reality. 'Sorry, Vin, no can do,' I said briskly, putting the key into the ignition. 'We can't get back together because I'm leaving in a couple of days. I'm going away, and I'm not coming back.'

'Where? Let me come, too!'

I laughed shortly. 'You can't. Now, if you don't mind, I've got preparations to make.'

His expression turned from peachy wheedle into purple tantrum. So much for contrition, I thought.

I started the car and put it into gear. If I looked straight ahead I couldn't see Vinnie at all, since he was sitting on my blind side. 'Bye then, Vinnie. This time I can promise you that you won't be seeing me again.'

Vinnie opened the door, narrowly missing getting it torn off its hinges by a passing car. 'Aren't you even going to thank me for not selling the photos?'

I cackled again. It felt quite liberating. 'Er, let me think. No. Do you really expect me to be grateful for that? Now please go. I'm not even going to wish you a nice life this time, because your karma's probably so rotten that it's unlikely too many more good things will happen to you.'

I twisted my head so that I could see Vinnie get out of the car, dragging his rucksack like a petulant child. Before closing the door, he stuck his head back inside. There was an extremely nasty expression on his face, worse than any I'd seen before.

'I've got news for you, Miss "I'm a Pop Star",' he said. 'You think you're so fucking famous that you don't like to go out in case you're mobbed? Well, that's just a joke, because I know for a fact that nobody gives a shit any more. No-one cares that you had an accident; no-one cares that you lost your job; no-one cares if you never work again. Blue Idea are naff Eighties has-beens.'

He continued, talking almost to himself. 'Of course, I should've realized that it was all in your head long ago, but you had me fooled, too. All this talk about paparazzi and stalkers and people hassling you. I went out with you for a year, and I *never* saw you get hassled for being famous. I never even saw you sign an autograph.'

'You always made us stay in because you were

afraid of Miyuki seeing us together,' I protested, half afraid and half amused by Vinnie's lame attempt to get back at me.

'It's all in your head, Helena,' he hissed, tapping the side of his forehead with a nicotine-stained finger. 'God, I feel sorry for you. You're living in a fantasy world. I only came near you because you're rich. Why else would I bother? You're a loser.'

I noticed that the car parked across the road contained a uniformed child propped up asleep on the back seat, alone, her face compressed and melted in sleep against the window, her school hat slipping off the side of her head like a little clown's. The front window had been left open for her, just a crack, as if she were a dog on a hot day.

'If you say so, Vinnie. But I think you're the one who's imagining things.' I tried to sound bored, but his voice was so scathing and venomous.

'Ah, but that's where you're wrong, Miss Barking Mad. I've got proof. When I rang up the *Daily Mirror* to say I had exclusive photos of you after your accident, d'you know what they said? They laughed in my face. "Give you fifty quid for them, mate", they said. "No-one's interested in her these days. We only ran the shot of her accident because her mate Justin Becker was involved". So now do you see? It's ALL IN YOUR MIND. You aren't famous at all any more.'

He slammed the door and walked away from me for the last time, whistling a vindictive little tune which sounded a lot like a Blue Idea song. The sleeping child stirred and stretched out on the back seat of her car, disappearing from my view.

☆

'Here's Where The Story Ends'
The Sundays

12.30 a.m. on Monday 28th. I went around caressing all the walls of my beloved house, thanking it for its indefatigable support and hospitality over the years. I turned the radiators down low, just in case an unseasonal frost should happen to nip at the gutters before anyone got back to check on it. I emptied the larder of perishable foods, put the rubbish out, switched off the water and made sure all the windows and doors were locked. It was like going on holiday; that silent, dark creeping-around time before the start of a long journey to a nice, warm, relaxing destination. Yes, that was a good way to look at it.

My carefully assembled props consisted of the following:

1. Three bottles of paracetamol, a half-full bottle of Valium, an unopened litre of gin and a picnic tumbler in my Kate Spade giraffe-print shoulder bag.
2. Box of CDs.
3. Manuscript, with letters and *Bluezines* and diary entries glued carefully in, sitting proudly in its purple folder on the dining-room table.
4. Letter to Ron in my coat pocket, addressed and stamped and ready to drop in a postbox on the way to the studio:

Dear Ron, By the time you read this . . . Keys to house under mat . . . Please come to house and collect purple folder . . . Any advance you receive on publication of manuscript, feel free to keep 15 per cent for yourself. The rest is for my parents, at this address . . . Please also forward the enclosed letter for them. Have informed lawyers, all should be in order. Thanks for everything, Helena. PS, by the way, I'd really like it if you could suggest to the publishers that a CD of the songs from the show accompanies the book. Kind of a new idea, but why not . . .?

5. Difficult tear-stained letter apologizing to parents, enclosed inside Ron's envelope.

I was ready. I went to put the CDs into the car, but when I picked up my giraffe-print handbag the bottle and jars all clinked and rattled together so excessively that I felt compelled to do something about it. I went back into the kitchen, pulled a Ziplock bag from the drawer, unscrewed the tops of the pill bottles, and emptied their contents into the bag.

Small as it was, this unforeseen hitch threw me, and my hands started to shake. I'd have had a swig of the gin, only I couldn't risk being stopped by the police driving to the studio – being thwarted by a breathalyser test at this late stage was too terrible to contemplate. So I remained sober and did some yogic breathing instead. This involved pinching one nostril shut, breathing slowly through the other side to the count of four, holding your breath for the same count, exhaling for eight, then repeating with the other nostril, ad infinitum. I'd always suspected that the reason this actually worked was because you felt such a prat doing it that it took your mind off why you were stressed in the first place.

After several breaths I did feel better. Everything had begun to feel super-real, like my 'revelation' in the car outside Sam's flat that time, when I was convinced she was going to be fine. Now I was convinced that I was going to be fine, too. I was going to be free of my one-eyed, less-than-perfect body. It was an ending and a new start, simultaneously.

I arrived at New World, and parked the car on a yellow line right outside the building. Climbing out, I retrieved the box of CDs and the giraffe-print bag from the boot, locked the car and headed slowly towards the studios. It was 1.45 a.m.

I pressed the number pad outside the front door, 8-1-5-7, and the door buzzed, inviting me to push it open. It sounded so welcoming and businesslike, I felt like kicking it. *If I come in now, I'm never going to leave. Don't you know that?* I thought. The door didn't care. I barged my way in, all elbows and sharp cardboard corners, and it shut behind me with a heavy, ominous click.

A security guard I didn't recognize sat at the front desk. 'Name please?' he said unsmilingly.

'Helena Nicholls.'

'Two o'clock show, right? Studio One.'

I wasn't going to thank him, not if he didn't know who I was. I walked over to the wall of pigeonholes, and looked up to see if there was any post in mine. It was stuffed full of letters, but when I reached up and took them down, the security man said, 'That ain't your box. That's Millie Myers' box.'

I peered at the letters – pink, brown, blue and white envelopes of all shapes and sizes, decorated with stick-on hearts and curly schoolgirl writing, or the scruffy, hormonal scrawl of the adolescent male, addressed to Millie, Gorgeous Millie, Miss M. Myers, I Love You, Mills.

None for me. The label on the pigeonhole bearing my name had been peeled off unceremoniously and a smart new Millie Myers sticker slapped over the top of it.

Crushed, I shoved the fan mail back into the box. Perhaps what Vinnie had said had been right. Perhaps I wasn't half as famous as I thought.

'Where's mine, then?'

The security guard shrugged. 'Try the bottom right. That's usually where they put stuff for new DJs.'

'I'm not a new DJ.'

'Oh wait, I remember. Mr Hadleigh left something for you behind the desk here. This is it.'

He handed me some sheets of printed paper, with a memo from Geoff clipped in the top right-hand corner: 'Dear Helena, Here's your show. As per my letter to you, please stick to the format. Speak soon, all the best, Geoff.'

It was a printout from Selector, the computer which programmed all the music, ad breaks and timings of live links for the station. I scanned it frantically, random lines jumping out at me here and there:

2.04: 00	Bon Jovi: 'Living on a Prayer'
2.18: 00	*Ad: Persil*
2.18: 40	*Ad: Kingsmill*
3.10:10	Live link
3.11.00	Spice Girls: 'Mama'

No. No way. There was no way, after all this, I was playing the fucking Spice Girls and Bon Jovi! None of my records were here, not one. Geoff had completely ignored my playlist. How dare he! My teeth were clenched and I was having trouble swallowing. Don't lose it; don't lose it, I kept telling myself. This is too important.

I sank down on a sofa in reception, causing the neck of the gin bottle to peep out from between the handles of my handbag. The security guard noticed and looked at me with an expression of casual disdain, but I didn't care.

I'd been stitched up! I bet Geoff had never even sent that letter; he must have known I wouldn't do the show if I couldn't play my own records. Oh, God, what was I going to do?

'Five minutes till you're on air. Shouldn't you be in your studio by now?' the guard asked boorishly.

'Mind your own damn business.' I was still reeling from Geoff's bombshell and this awful, pre-programmed, bolloxsy, brain-dead excuse for a show that they seriously expected me to do.

I jumped up, grabbed my things and headed down the corridor, punching in the security code again as I passed through another door, and again as I finally entered the studio. It was my old breakfast-show studio, looking exactly the same as it had the morning of the UKMAs, when I'd done my last request show.

I sank down into the swivel chair behind the desk and, out of habit, slid off my shoes. Putting my hand-bag on the carpeted floor by my feet, I let the bag of tablets flop out slightly so I could feel its soft bulk with my toes.

Three minutes to go. Through the thick window – the glass fuggy and brown as if all the DJs chain-smoked – I could see Pete Harness and his producer finishing up in Studio Two. Surreptitiously, I unscrewed the gin bottle, poured half a glassful into the tumbler and downed it in one, my throat constricting with the effort of not gagging.

Next door they were letting Pete's final record, 'Walking On Sunshine' by Katrina and the Waves – one of my least favourite tunes – play out while they put on their coats and gathered their things. Pete waved tentatively at me through the window and gave me a thumbs-up signal. I could tell that the producer, a pretty young black girl, was scrutinizing me slyly, probably trying to see how different I was from the photos she'd seen of me before the accident. I hoped she hadn't seen me swig the gin.

Two minutes. I hesitated over the Selector printout for a moment, and then swivelled round and lobbed it into the bin by the door. What was the worst thing Geoff could do? Fire me? I was only planning the one show, anyway, and besides, probably no-one would even notice. Feeling giddy with rebellion and adrenalin, I unpacked my box of CDs and lined them up carefully in order, cueing up 'The Ballad Of Tom Jones' first. I watched as the CD slid into the machine with a metallic skid, thinking, Here goes. I was going to completely override Selector.

One minute. It felt so strange, flying solo. Strange, but liberating. Pete and the producer disappeared, waving foolishly at me again. I got the impression they'd wanted to come in and say hi, but my closed-down expression had put them off.

The Selector screen to my left was showing the supposed running order of my show, the same as the printout, but because it was to my blind side it was easy to ignore.

I found a minidisc with the New World jingle on it, and shoved it in the machine, followed by one of my old breakfast show IDs. Why not? I thought.

Thirty seconds. I reached beneath the desk for the bag of pills, selected ten paracetamol to be going on with, and arranged them in a daisy-petal pattern around the base of the tumbler. Taking them throughout the show would mean less to swallow all at once at the end. The pills looked inviting, and I imagined them soft and sugary, like sweeties on my tongue. I decided on two per record, and none of the Valiums until the final track. I wanted to be awake to finish the show.

The clock hand swept gracefully north, towards two o'clock, and I took a deep breath, clamped the cans on my ears, adjusted the microphone and hit the On-air button to take control. No turning back now.

'Good morning, London – those of you who are unlucky enough to be awake at this time, anyhow. Helena Nicholls here. Yes, it's me. Remember me from a few months back? Well, as I expect you heard, I had a rather nasty accident, and they had to get some-one else to cover for my breakfast show. Millie's doing a great job, isn't she? And to be honest, I'm more of a night owl myself, so I thought I'd give this a try. I've got some fantastic music lined up for you tonight; twenty songs in all. It's kind of going to be a request show, but not in the way that you remember my show from before. Sorry, folks, but you can't ring in. Tonight is going to be my songs from my life. Don't worry, I do have quite good taste, so don't touch that dial. I've got some Elvis Costello, Blondie, Dexys and Jimmy Cliff, so stick around. Ten songs in a row coming up after these messages.'

I bunged in a trail and ran an ad break; better make at least a minimal effort to do the right thing, I thought. There was a tap on the window, and I looked up to see Pete's producer standing there, waving a white envelope at me.

I swiftly moved the tumbler, leaned my elbow on the pills so they were hidden, made sure the gin bottle was out of sight, and reluctantly waved her in.

'Hi, Helena, I'm Vicky. Are you really playing ten songs in a row? Won't you get in trouble? That's not the running order, you know.'

She sounded concerned, but her eyes were secretly scanning my face in the hope of a close-up scar. I had a sudden urge to rip off my eye-patch and loom ogrishly up at her, shouting, 'Grrrrrr!' just to see if she'd scream and run away.

'I know. Thanks. I'll deal with it.'

She handed me the envelope. 'Sorry, but this was stuck between the pages of Pete's show. I think it's been floating around for a few days, but you didn't seem to have a pigeonhole.'

'Thanks,' I said again. 'Better crack on now.' I gestured back to the desk.

'Good luck, then.' Vicky edged backwards out of the studio, as if she was worried I might take a bite out of her ass on the way out. I faded up the mic, planning to talk up to the vocals.

'Right, first up we've got the only recent song on this show. It's the song that was playing when I had the accident. Macabre, you might think, but I couldn't leave it out. I think music's like everything else in life. Even the tough things have to be faced up to. They never go away on their own. Here it is, then, the lovely Cerys Matthews with Space, and—'

Damn! Tommy started singing, catching me out. I'd crashed the intro, a cardinal sin for a DJ. Off to a great start, then.

' "The Ballad of Tom Jones",' I added hastily.

It was the first time I'd heard the song since the UKMAs, and it was even harder than I'd imagined. I instantly felt high again, foolish, the metallic taste of coke numbing my teeth and the rush of the bright lights spinning in my head. I thought of poor Justin, having to heave me up and down on his back, and . . . no, I couldn't bear it. Despite what I'd just said on air, I still couldn't face up to that particular song. I lowered the pre-fade to a non-intrusive hum, poured myself some more gin, popped two paracetamol in my mouth and downed them, retching almost immediately. This wasn't going to work. I'd have to take the tablets with water instead – one more mouthful of gin and everything would be coming straight back up again. I should have stuck to vodka.

Dashing out to the water cooler in the hallway, I rinsed out my tumbler and filled it to the brim with icy water, gulping it down gratefully to wash the bitter juniper taste out of my mouth. Not to worry, I had heaps of pills, and after the show I could just hold my nose and pour the gin down my throat like medicine. Filling up the cup with water again, I returned to my desk and glanced at the envelope Vicky had brought in.

It was addressed to me, care of New World, in a strange, plump handwriting. I slit it open and flipped the four sides of paper over to see who it was from. I suspected a nutter, from the amount that was written. Fan letters these days were usually just brief requests for signed photos.

At the very end, I saw, 'All my love, Toby, xxx' and for a split second everything in me turned to water, from knees to nose and all the bits in between. I thought I might just dissolve right there onto my desk, fusing all the electrics in the studio and bringing my show to a premature climax. But I forced myself to remember our last meeting: Toby swaying and running off to puke, calling me 'she' and sucking lager off his arms. Then I remembered Ruby telling me how they were all going to live together as a family again.

I was so distracted that I nearly forgot to cue Jackie Wilson. With no link at all, I segued into 'Sweetest Feeling', knocked back two more pills and devoured the letter, skimming at first through its contents:

Dear Helena . . . fantastic to talk to you when you were at Lulu's . . . can't believe you didn't leave your number. I'd been trying to get hold you ever since you left hospital, via your agent, but you didn't reply, so I suppose you never got the letter . . .

Damn, I must have thrown it away along with Geoff's letter.

. . . Forgot to mention it when we spoke on the phone, and when you saw me drunk that day. So, so, sorry about that; I'm mortified. I made Bill come with me to Richmond in the hope of bumping into you. What a twat, eh? As you noticed, I was hardly at my best. I gather that Bill told you why . . . miss you very much . . . think about you all the time.

Omigod! I read the final page more slowly:

It might seem to you like I'm running after you because I'm on the rebound, but I'm not, I promise. Things hadn't been right between Kate and me for ages, but because I'd already been walked all over by one woman – Lorraine, the one you met – I just wouldn't allow myself to see that it was happening again. It's been a nightmare, but Kate and I will stay in touch; we have to, for Ruby's sake. Ruby doesn't understand what's going on, although I think she'll be fine. She was happy staying at Lulu's, even when I was away on business. Kate did most of her recovering at her lover's flat, where there apparently wasn't room for Rubes. Kate and Giacomo – prat! – have now bought a house together, and Ruby went to live there a few weeks ago. In fact, the day after you went to Lulu's.

So Ruby was mistaken when she thought Toby was coming back to live with Kate too. Jeez! That would teach me to take the word of a two-year-old as gospel. I couldn't believe my idiocy.

The Italian prat is actually a fairly reasonable guy, and Kate's keen to be 'mature' about access (so I should bloody well hope!), so I'm sure I'll still see lots of Ruby.

Anyway, listen, I'm worried about you, Helena. It's fine if you've decided that you don't want to pursue a relationship with me – well, actually, it's not fine at all, but I'll live with it – but you seemed upset when we spoke on the phone. Even though she hadn't met you before, Lulu thought you were acting a bit strangely, too. I still can't believe that you really wanted to give away something as precious as your memories of Sam. You aren't planning anything stupid, are you?

Whatever you think of me now, please do me one last favour and call me to let me know that you're OK. It's 020 7386 9162. It's Lulu's number. I'm staying there until I find a place of my own. We're selling the house in the country.

I've been scouring *Time Out* ever since the girl in your agent's office told me that you were going back to New World, and I was delighted to see your night-time show listed. I'll be tuning in, you can count on it. It will be great just to hear your voice again.

All my love, Toby. xxx

When I looked up from the letter, I saw that there

were only two seconds left of Jackie Wilson. I'd been intending to talk a little bit about Sam, and how we first met before I played 'Route 66', but I was too flabbergasted. Leaving three unprofessional seconds of dead air, I hastily pulled down the fader to start Sandie Shaw and flopped back into my chair.

This truly was radio at its worst. I hoped nobody was listening. And this was the show that was supposed to be going down in history. I'd have to pull myself together and concentrate harder.

It also occurred to me that I hadn't once thought about Sam while the record was playing. Perhaps my theory about music and memory wasn't so infallible after all.

Still, there was a long way to go. Three down, seventeen left. I touched my Ziplocked stash of tablets with my toe, rubbing them affectionately against my sock. I'd never felt so confused. I took two more tablets, then another two, quickly, to prove that Toby's revelations weren't going to change my mind.

Damn you, Toby, I thought through the jolly brass of 'Route 66'. It's too late. I can't go back now. This show sucks so badly that even if I hadn't ditched the format, I'd probably get fired for it.

I replaced the cans and listened to the end of Sandie Shaw, before opening the fader on my mic again.

'That was a little-known but fantastic track from the great Sandie Shaw; her version of the classic song "(Get Your Kicks On) Route Sixty-six." I know I said these were my songs, but that one's for my dad, over in New Jersey.

'Hey, it's a good thing this isn't my old show, isn't it? For those of you who remember it, I never used to play a song unless the person requesting it could practically write a thesis on the reason they wanted it played. And I have to tell you, right now I wouldn't play any of these records if I was the punter ringing in for them. But I do have an excuse. I knew there wouldn't be enough time to talk much on air about why these tracks are important to me, so I wrote it all down instead. And if any of you care enough, perhaps one day it'll be made into a book, and you can read it. It's a thesis about my life, I guess.'

I paused. 'Who thinks that maybe I ought to be just a little less self-obsessed?'

I faded up 'Wichita Lineman', determined to talk up to the vocals without crashing them. 'And here's a song which reminds me of being a kid, hanging out with my best friend, fighting with my mother – the way you do when you're nine years old. I thought that it was about a linesman, you know, like they have in tennis matches.'

Bingo. Got it right that time. Suddenly love-struck linesmen and my own self-obsession seemed terribly funny, and I began to laugh. The show wasn't going a bit like I'd imagined it would. All those months, writing and planning and being serious and grief-stricken, and now these songs were making me laugh? Perhaps I was losing it. Or maybe it was the medicinal cocktail starting to take effect.

Well, since Toby had had the decency to write and declare himself worried about me, the least I could do was ring him. I liked the idea that he would be the last person I directly spoke to.

I dialled Lulu's number, feeling a ridiculous heady sensation which I couldn't quite identify.

The phone rang and rang, but there was no answer. Just my luck. Eventually an answerphone picked up and curtly instructed me to leave a message. I spoke quietly, guiltily, in case I woke up Lulu.

'This is a message for Toby. I'm really sorry to call so late. Anyway, I got your second letter, but not the first one. Oh, by the way, it's Helena here. Call me back at the studio, if you like. I need to tell you something. I hope you get this message, but it's two fifteen and you're probably in bed asleep. But if you aren't, then ring me on' – I peered at the number of the XD line written on the studio phone – '0171 935 6906. That's a direct line into the studio. Bye, Toby. It was really great to hear from you.'

Not speaking to Toby had pulled me back down to earth again, and I felt like I was getting down to business as I played 'Sunday Girl', 'Sitting In Limbo', and 'N.I.T.A.'. I concluded that it was probably the pills making me feel weird, so I decided to ease off them for a while in order to stay alert.

I talked a lot in between each record – more than I'd intended – but I kept it to generalities: when, why, what. Inside, I waited to be overwhelmed by memories of Sam and me on magic carpets, of the visitor's pink ribbon and the preacher with the bouffant hair, of my first bedroom sessions on the rickety bass, but it didn't happen. Yes, I remembered Sam and saw her face, and relived the feeling of the love which bounced off the high tapestried walls of the Freehold Baptist church, and heard the flat thud of my bass strings before I knew how to play it properly, but the odd thing was that I felt it all quite *fondly*.

It was like watching a much-loved movie, the way you go, 'Ooh, I love this bit,' but you aren't particularly glued to it because it's too familiar; you've seen it too many times before. The revelation I was half-expecting never occurred.

By revelation, I mean a defining moment; some sort of *It's a Wonderful Life* type catharsis. As if seeing my life unfold before me through those songs might make me appreciate its value and want to live again. This was not happening, but something else was.

Slowly, slowly, as each song shook out and laid before me its patchwork memories, I realized that, yes, these were indeed my memories, for better or worse, but frankly, I'd spent so much time dwelling on them in the past few months that they were no longer quite as interesting to me. The funny bits still made me laugh, but not out loud, and the sad bits brought tears to my eyes, but didn't destroy me. I had become an observer instead of a participator.

I'd thought that playing the music would tip the balance, but it didn't. My memories had, in the writing of them, become downgraded from top priority to day file. By osmosis and obsession they'd become part of me. Suddenly I didn't even *want* to share them with the rest of the world. I didn't want a bumper sticker announcing to anyone that I'd 'Told London My Song'. I wanted to keep my songs. Now that I'd given away the Hel-Sam Box, they were all I had left of Blue Idea, of Sam, of the past. They were mine.

I galloped seamlessly through 'Oliver's Army', 'There There My Dear' and 'Ghosts', and before I knew it I'd done my first ten in a row. I switched over to the news desk for a bulletin, and then decided to run an ad break to help use up some more time.

During 'To Be Someone', the XD line on my phone started flashing, indicating a call. I just happened to glance down and see the little green light blinking at me, and I lunged for the receiver, my heart in my throat.

'Toby?' I said loudly and breathlessly over The Jam.

'No, this is Geoff,' came a cross, crackly voice from a mobile phone. 'I'm in a car in Crouch End, coming back from a party, and this is what I hear? What the hell do you think you're playing at, Helena? I gave you express instructions that you were to stick to the format, and you're totally pirating it.'

'I've played the ads, and had the news,' I said lamely.

'So I should bloody well hope. Get back to Selector, now!'

I swallowed. 'Geoff, listen, I haven't been straight with you. I only ever planned to do the one show. I'm really sorry I've messed you around, but either you let me continue with my own records or I walk out of this studio now. It's going to take you a while to get down here from North London, so unless you want thirty minutes of dead air, you'd better let me keep going.'

I waited for the staticky spluttering to commence,

448

but there was just a brief pause. 'I don't respond well to blackmail, Helena. We'll speak about this in the morning.'

I segued into 'Shipbuilding' without missing a beat, headphones pressed against one ear, an irate passenger in a car in Crouch End connected to the other ear. It was still such a marvel being able to do two different things with two different ears.

'If you like, Geoff. But before you bother to fire me, consider this my resignation. I'll put it in writing and get it to you by ten a.m. I've decided that I don't want to be a DJ any more.'

Or a rock star, or a pushover, or a recluse. I realized then, with complete certainty, that I would still be around at ten a.m. to type up a letter of resignation. I knew that I would leave the building as hale and hearty as when I'd entered it. I knew that Vinnie was right, that no-one really cared any more. And instead of that fact making me shrivel up like a salted slug, I saw that it was all the more reason why *I* had to care, in a positive way. A looking-forward, new-life kind of way, not a wallowing-in-the-past way.

I just wanted to be me, Helena Nicholls, making a new start, hopefully with a new boyfriend and maybe even a few new friends. Sam wouldn't mind. In fact, she'd be cheering me on. Vinnie had done me a favour. Who'd have thought?

I kept the tracks coming, wash after wash of music and faith and recollection flowing over and through me, but then out the other side again. Not sticking around, clogging me up, but rinsing me. And then, as if my body was echoing the sentiments in my head, a great wave of nausea rose up from my stomach. I only just made it to the Ladies' in time to vomit out the gin and eight paracetamols I'd consumed.

Back in the studio in time to cue the next track, I felt cleansed inside and out. It didn't prevent me from feeling sad during 'Deep Blue Dream', though, remembering how Sam had seemed to shrink just a little more each time I crossed the Atlantic to her bedside, but at the same time I was thinking about the future. How I didn't have to run away or plan my death. Who cared? Nobody. Instead of panic and depression at the idea that I might be forgotten, I felt liberated. I could do whatever I liked.

My XD line flashed again, just after I'd cued up 'Lovesong'. I answered, more cautiously this time.

'Hi, Helena, it's Toby.'

I couldn't speak. I was so surprised at how amazing it was to hear his voice again that it took my breath away.

'Helena? Are you there?'

I gulped. 'Yes. Hello. Thanks for ringing me back.'

'I've been listening since the start, only I was in the loo when you rang, and I didn't notice there was a message until just now. Are you OK? You sound fine on air, but . . . Oh, look, tell me I'm being daft, but I really am worried about you.'

I lowered the pre-fade volume on The Cure, realizing, as I did so, that I'd picked 'Lovesong' because it celebrated the first time Toby and I ever met.

'You're being daft. Honestly, I never felt better. Hey, this is the track that reminds me of you, you know. They were on stage at Brixton that time when you were interviewing us downstairs.'

'I know. I'd hoped that was why you were playing it. Does that mean I'm in the book you've written?'

I grinned sheepishly. 'It sure does. So, are *you* OK? I know I didn't mention it when we were on the phone last time, but I couldn't believe it when you said that Kate was cheating on you.'

Toby sighed. 'Yes, I'm fine now. Four days of being roaring drunk in Richmond helped get it out of my system. Except that once I recovered from the hangover I thought I'd blown it completely with you. I was gutted when you didn't call. And then, when I talked to you at Lulu's, you sounded so . . . *off* with me.'

'That was because Ruby had just informed me, with

total conviction, that you and she were moving back in with Kate the next day to play happy families again.'

Toby laughed. 'Haven't you ever heard of wish-fulfilment? You really don't know much about kids, do you?'

I wasn't even offended at the criticism. 'I could learn.'

I could hear the grin in Toby's voice. 'I know a great little teacher. A bit of a bossy one, though.' He paused, and I was convinced we were both sharing a mental image of Ruby wagging her finger sternly at me.

'So, you said in your message that you needed to tell me something. What is it?'

'Um . . .' The word dropped into an ever-deepening chasm of revelation somewhere down the phone line, like a pebble into a loch. I swivelled my chair around to face the wall, picked up the Ziplock bag of pills with my toes and kicked it as hard as I could across the studio. I'd wanted to say goodbye to him. What had I been thinking? Toby's voice brought my complete idiocy even further home to me, right up the garden path, in fact, and into the attic. There were still people who loved me: Mum, Dad, Cynthia, Mary-Ellen, Jus, David and Joe. And now it looked like Toby did, too.

'Oh, it was nothing really. I just wanted to say that . . . I'm really, really sorry about the way we left things at the hospital, and then not ringing you after that day in Richmond. I've been sorting a lot of things out in my head.'

Toby laughed in a relieved kind of way.

'I'm surprised you ever wanted to clap eyes on me again after that day in Richmond. Anyway, stop apologizing. It's all been my fault; I behaved really badly. I felt so guilty, leading you on. So can we meet up soon?'

I looked at the crumpled sack of tablets, destined for the same U-bend as the contents of my stomach.

'Yes, please.'

'How about tomorrow?'

'Yes, please. Hang on a second.' I faded up 'Kinky Afro' and cued 'I'll Be Home'. 'Sorry, I'm back. Hey, guess what? I've already quit this job. That was quick, wasn't it?'

'Why?'

'It's a long story. Suffice it to say that I don't want to be a DJ any more, especially not at this godforsaken hour.'

'Excellent!' Toby said. 'Perhaps that means that you and I could go away somewhere together, for a little holiday. What do you think?'

I wrapped the spiral lead of the telephone around my finger, feeling my excitement coil up inside me in the same way. 'That would be lovely. Can Ruby come, too?'

'I hoped you'd say that, but I think we need some time on our own, don't you? Perhaps we could have a weekend in a hotel in the UK first, and then take her away somewhere warm afterwards. We could all do with a break. Oh, and one last thing before I leave you in peace to get on with your show; can you play me a request, please?'

I laughed. 'Didn't I already say this isn't a request show? Besides, I'm not sure I can get access to the record library at this time of night. What is it?'

'Don't worry if you can't. I just had an urge to hear "Here's Where The Story Ends" by The Sundays, because it reminds me of you.'

I was surprised. I couldn't remember that song figuring in any of our previous exchanges. 'Why?'

'It was after our first kiss – you know, outside the lifts that time. I was driving back to Fulham, and the day before I'd bought a load of albums which I'd never owned but always thought I ought to. The Sundays was one of them, so I bunged it on in the car and went straight for that track, track two, and cranked it right up. All through the song I couldn't get you out of my head. I'd never felt so many different emotions: attraction, love, guilt, worry, euphoria, stress, grief. It was terrible, but wonderful at the same time. And that song just seemed so perfect, even if I wasn't listening to the words. It sounds daft, but I knew right then that whenever I heard it in the future I'd think of your smile, and the smell of the hospital, and me rubbing your poor nose, and your arms around me, and I'd remember driving home, wondering how it was all going to turn out. Are you still there? I'll stop now.'

I was beaming so widely that I dislodged my eye patch. 'Sure, stop,' I said, readjusting it. 'As long as you carry on again later.'

The next track was 'Safe From Harm', and now that I no longer wanted to kill myself, memories of Vinnie were the last thing I needed. I used the five minutes to rush down the corridor to the record library, discovering that I only needed to key in the code once more to open the door. To my joy, New World did own a copy of *Reading Writing and Arithmetic*, and I seized it and ran back upstairs to the studio just in time to fade up 'Don't Wanna Know Bout Evil'.

Another Vinnie song, but to my surprise I had no trouble whatsoever not thinking of him. I was too busy daydreaming about splashing around in azure shallows somewhere with Ruby in a frilly swimsuit and armbands, and Toby snoozing on the beach behind us, worn out by our weekend of passion.

The last two records were my difficult ones, my Starfruit Sam ones: 'I Can't Stand The Rain' and 'This Is A Low'. It was impossible not to sob through those, as impossible as sneezing without blinking, or eating doughnuts without licking one's lips. An involuntary, inevitable reaction. But it felt different, better. Not agony, just a dull, sad ache.

I realized that the real catharsis throughout this whole exercise lay not in the songs, as I'd thought, but in the contents of a shiny purple folder on my dining-room table. All those months of writing it down had begun to heal me, and I was ready to start again, to add

453

some new songs and memories to my well-played collection.

Somewhat snotty and hiccuping from crying, I opened the mic for the last time as the final bars of 'This Is A Low' faded out.

'So, my time's nearly up, folks. I hope you've enjoyed the show. I haven't said as much as I intended to, but I wanted the music to speak for itself. Perhaps something momentous happened to you tonight, and you can claim one of these songs as your own. Be my guest. Just because they belong to my memories doesn't mean they can't belong to yours, too. That's the great thing about music, isn't it? It's for all of us. Anyway, this is probably the last time you'll hear me on the radio, so, it's been a pleasure. Have a great night, what's left of it. I'm going to play you out with one final request: it's The Sundays, "Here's Where The Story Ends", for Toby Middleton. Good night, London.'

I packed up my CDs, Toby's letter, the bag of pills, the cup and the bottle, and left the studio to the sound of jingly guitars and Harriet Wheeler's sweet voice telling me that I had a future after all.

Just as I got to the end of the corridor I heard the early breakfast-show DJ come into the lobby, and I nipped into the Ladies' to avoid him. My face was all puffy and tear-stained, and I felt too wrung out to make small talk with a stranger. One step at a time on the sociability front, I thought.

The gin bottle nudged me in the side, reminding me of its existence. I took it out of my handbag and deposited it in the waste bin underneath the sink. Then I went into a cubicle, removed the Ziplock bag, unzipped it and dumped its contents into the toilet bowl. Booze and pills; it had been a ridiculous idea anyway. If I'd had the courage to blow my brains out all over the desk, then yes, that would have made headlines. But swallowing tablets was such an untidy ending, like a sheet of wrapping paper someone had tried to tear instead of cut, ripping a slash across it whose jaggedness defeated its original, decorative purpose.

Besides, now that I thought about it, I'd always hated making the headlines.

I had to flush the toilet three times to sluice away the tablets from the bottom of the porcelain.

I finally left the building, surprising the dour security guard with a half-friendly wave goodbye, and turned up my collar against the chill of the shut-down city. As I stepped towards my car, a figure wearing a walkman and a big red puffa jacket startled me by walking out of the shadows towards me. The figure removed his earphones, held out his arms to me and hugged me hard. 'Thanks for playing my record.'

I dropped my box of CDs, and they all spilled out on the pavement, jewel cases cracking like ice breaking as I hugged Toby back.

'You look beautiful,' he said, prising my face away from his neck and cupping it with his two cold hands. 'You've been crying. No wonder. That can't have been easy.'

I broke away from him and started picking up the bits of scattered CDs. 'Sam was always telling me I was a great big cry baby,' I said. 'You'd better get used to it.'

Toby crouched down and helped me collect the pieces. 'Fancy walking over to Soho for a coffee at Bar Italia?'

I nodded, grinning. 'Let me lock this lot in the boot first, then we can go.'

Ten minutes later the sound of our footsteps echoed down a sleeping Charlotte Street, drizzle giving the streetlights hazy golden halos. Our arms were wrapped around one another and our feet easily in step.

I put my free hand in my coat pocket and pulled out the envelope containing the letters to Ron and my parents. I'd forgotten to post it.

THE END

Acknowledgements

Huge thanks to the fantastic Jo Frank, top agent, for making it all happen.

Thank you to everyone at Transworld, especially my lovely editor Selina Walker, Larry Finlay, Henry Steadman (for the beautiful cover design), Shauna Bartlett and Zeb Dare.

For endless amounts of support, encouragement, advice and friendship thanks to: Errol Kolosine, Veena Dookoo, Sandie Shaw, Barry Brooks, Richard Jackson, Mark Tyler Edwards, Linda Buckley-Archer, Kevin R. and Regina McBride (whose writing class got me started). For all the above, plus taking time to read and give invaluable feedback on the book as it came along, an extra-special thank-you to Marian Keyes and Sharon Mulrooney.

Thank you to my mother, Veronika Jackson, for always telling me she's proud of me.

For being a welcome distraction, thanks to Gracie Voss xx.

For helping me with various different pieces of research and giving me advice, thanks to: Andy Friedlander from Virgin Radio, Phill J. and Gavin Lawrence (for advice on radio jargon), Caroline Records in NYC, and Don Fleming (New York band stuff), Mimi Wort, Tony Baines, Conor McCabe, and Dominic from the Collectors Record Centre in Kingston.

Thanks for sorting the CD to: Jules Bain, the coolest chick in the business, Teresa Harte, Jenny Fisher and Virgin Records.

For school/childhood stuff, thanks to: Andrea Tucker, Alanda Becker and 'Toeclarth Heartweely'.

Biggest thanks of all to Matt Voss, for everything, but particularly for making me so happy. I could never have done this without his support: emotional, practical, financial, culinary – the lot. Best husband in the world!

Want to hear the songs from To Be Someone?

Listen to the accompanying CD

Out now at all good record stores

CD: CDV2933

SPACE WITH CERYS OF CATATONIA – THE BALLAD OF TOM JONES
JACKIE WILSON – I GET THE SWEETEST FEELING
SANDIE SHAW – (GET YOUR KICKS ON) ROUTE 66
GLEN CAMPBELL – WICHITA LINEMAN
BLONDIE – SUNDAY GIRL
JIMMY CLIFF – SITTING IN LIMBO
YOUNG MARBLE GIANTS – N. I. T. A.
ELVIS COSTELLO & THE ATTRACTIONS – OLIVER'S ARMY
DEXY'S MIDNIGHT RUNNERS – THERE, THERE MY DEAR
JAPAN – GHOSTS
THE JAM – TO BE SOMEONE (DIDN'T WE HAVE A NICE TIME)
ROBERT WYATT – SHIPBUILDING
THE CURE – LOVE SONG
HAPPY MONDAYS – KINKY AFRO
RANDY NEWMAN – I'LL BE HOME
MASSIVE ATTACK – SAFE FROM HARM
ANN PEEBLES – I CAN'T STAND THE RAIN
BLUR – THIS IS A LOW
THE SUNDAYS – HERE'S WHERE THE STORY ENDS

INCONCEIVABLE
Ben Elton

'EXTREMELY FUNNY, CLEVER, WELL-WRITTEN, SHARP
AND UNEXPECTEDLY MOVING . . . THIS BRILLIANT,
CHAOTIC SATIRE MERITS REREADING SEVERAL TIMES'
Nicholas Coleridge, *Mail on Sunday*

Lucy desperately wants a baby. Sam wants to write a hit
movie. The problem is that both efforts seem to be
unfruitful. And given that the average IVF cycle has about
a one in five chance of going into full production, Lucy's
chances of getting what she wants are considerably better
than Sam's.

What Sam and Lucy are about to go through is absolutely
inconceivable. The question is, can their love survive?

Inconceivable confirms Ben Elton as one of Britain's most
significant, entertaining and provocative writers.

'THIS IS ELTON AT HIS BEST – MATURE, HUMANE, AND
STILL A LAUGH A MINUTE. AT LEAST'
Daily Telegraph

'A VERY FUNNY BOOK ABOUT A SENSITIVE SUBJECT
. . . BEN ELTON THE WRITER MIGHT BE EVEN FUNNIER
THAN BEN ELTON THE COMIC'
Daily Mail

'A TENDER, BEAUTIFULLY BALANCED
ROMANTIC COMEDY'
Spectator

'MOVING AND THOROUGHLY ENTERTAINING'
Daily Express

Now filmed as *Maybe Baby*.

0 552 14698 6

BLACK SWAN

IDIOGLOSSIA
Eleanor Bailey

For four generations of women from the same family, madness is
a potent legacy. It tempts, it persuades and it destroys. But it can
also bring a strange kind of freedom. . .

Aggressive, demanding, eccentric, Great Edie curses the
psychological weakness that runs through the family like a fault.
No one would suspect that her psychic powers were anything
more than a business, security for her old age.

Her daughter, Grace, has languished in a mental institution for long
spells of her adult life, after a tragedy years ago. Grace's only child,
Maggie, grew up, working with her father on a fading cruise liner.
But the golden age of ocean travel is over, and a relationship with
the mysterious comedian, Rudi, leaves her pregnant and alone.

Now Maggie's daughter, Sarah, is truly dispossessed and, through
gratuitous sex, seeks revenge on her loveless childhood. She
rejects the world of overused clichés and overpriced coffee but
can see no alternative – except to let go. . .

0 552 99860 5

BLACK SWAN

WHAT WE DID ON OUR HOLIDAY
John Harding

'A WONDERFUL NOVEL . . . WRITTEN WITH GREAT HUMOUR
AND RARE GENEROSITY OF SPIRIT. TRULY ORIGINAL'
Deborah Moggach

**How old do you have to be before you stop going on holiday wth
your parents? Nick's 36 and married and he hasn't cracked it
yet. . .**

Nick could have a great time on Malta if it weren't for one thing.
His family. His wife Laura, biological alarm clock ringing, is
desperate for children which means a nightly test of Nick's
ingenuity to resist her amorous advances. There's Dad, afflicted
with Parkinson's Disease, scarcely able to walk or talk, unsure
which country or decade he's in and obsessed by sex and
lavatories. And there's Mum, weighing in at a formidable 18 stone
(although she's convinced she's a size 10) with a personality to
match. Then there's the ghost from Dad's wartime past, come back
to haunt them all. . .

Tackling a taboo subject with sensitivity, compassion and a total
lack of sentimentality, *What We Did On Our Holiday* recalls that
time in your life when roles are reversed and you find yourself
looking after the very people you'd always assumed would be
there to look after you. And it is also almost certainly the first
novel in English literature to begin with the word 'toilet'.

'A WONDERFULLY FUNNY, ORIGINAL AND MOVING NOVEL
. . . HARDING HAS A KNIFE-SHARP OBSERVATION,
IMMACULATE TIMING, AND THE GUTS TO TAKE HIS STORY
AS FAR AS IT WILL GO'
Helen Dunmore

'POIGNANT, HILARIOUS AND ULTIMATELY DEEPLY MOVING
. . . A REAL PAGE TURNER . . . A WONDERFUL NOVEL'
Marika Cobbold

'A BEAUTIFULLY CRAFTED NOVEL: THE PERFECT MARRIAGE
OF HUMOUR AND HEART"
Glenn Patterson

0 552 99847 8

BLACK SWAN

PERFECT DAY
Imogen Parker

Can one day change your life?

If we were a song, what song do you think we would be?

On a perfect spring morning, Alexander catches an early train into London, but he never reaches work. Instead, he spends the day with Kate, a waitress he has met the previous evening, a woman so unlike anyone he has ever known, she makes the world shimmer with possibility.

Such a perfect day, Nell takes her child Lucy to the seaside, hoping that the sea air will blow away the doubts she has about her life.

As Nell ponders why falling in love is so different from loving someone, Alexander allows himself to imagine leaving his old life behind and starting afresh. And by a strange turn of fate, there's an opportunity to do just that — if he chooses to take it.

0 552 99938 5

BLACK SWAN

A SELECTED LIST OF FINE WRITING
AVAILABLE FROM BLACK SWAN

14721 4	TOM, DICK AND DEBBIE HARRY	*Jessica Adams*	£6.99
99313 1	OF LOVE AND SHADOWS	*Isabel Allende*	£7.99
99619 X	HUMAN CROQUET	*Kate Atkinson*	£7.99
99860 5	IDIOGLOSSIA	*Eleanor Bailey*	£6.99
99824 9	THE DANDELION CLOCK	*Guy Burt*	£6.99
99854 0	LESSONS FOR A SUNDAY FATHER	*Claire Calman*	£5.99
99686 6	BEACH MUSIC	*Pat Conroy*	£7.99
99836 2	A HEART OF STONE	*Renate Dorrestein*	£6.99
14698 6	INCONCEIVABLE	*Ben Elton*	£6.99
99587 8	LIKE WATER FOR CHOCOLATE	*Laura Esquivel*	£6.99
99910 5	TELLING LIDDY	*Anne Fine*	£6.99
99851 6	REMEMBERING BLUE	*Connie May Fowler*	£6.99
99760 9	THE DRESS CIRCLE	*Laurie Graham*	£6.99
99681 5	A MAP OF THE WORLD	*Jane Hamilton*	£7.99
99847 8	WHAT WE DID ON OUR HOLIDAY	*John Harding*	£6.99
99800 1	BLACKBERRY WINE	*Joanne Harris*	£6.99
99867 2	LIKE WATER IN WILD PLACES	*Pamela Jooste*	£6.99
99737 4	GOLDEN LADS AND GIRLS	*Angela Lambert*	£6.99
99959 8	BACK ROADS	*Tawni O'Dell*	£6.99
99938 5	PERFECT DAY	*Imogen Parker*	£6.99
99862 1	A REVOLUTION OF THE SUN	*Tim Pears*	£6.99
99909 1	LA CUCINA	*Lily Prior*	£6.99
99810 9	THE JUKEBOX QUEEN OF MALTA	*Nicholas Rinaldi*	£6.99
99645 9	THE WRONG BOY	*Willy Russell*	£6.99
99872 9	MARRYING THE MISTRESS	*Joanna Trollope*	£6.99
99864 8	A DESERT IN BOHEMIA	*Jill Paton Walsh*	£6.99